DEVIL
IN
THE
DEVICE

ALSO BY LORA BETH JOHNSON

Goddess in the Machine

DEVIL IN THE DEVICE

LORA BETH JOHNSON

RAZORBILL

RAZORBILL

An imprint of Penguin Random House LLC, New York

First published in the United States of America by Razorbill,
an imprint of Penguin Random House LLC, 2021

Visit us online at penguinrandomhouse.com.

LIBRARY OF CONGRESS CATALOGING-IN-PUBLICATION DATA
Names: Johnson, Lora Beth, author.
Title: Devil in the device / Lora Beth Johnson.
Description: New York : Razorbill, 2021. | Series: Goddess in the machine ; book 2
Audience: Ages 12 and up | Summary: Battling the dangerous forces buried within their
minds, Andra and Zhade will have to find a way to work together before two power-hungry
leaders and a deadly swarm of rogue technology destroy humanity for good.
Identifiers: LCCN 2021017008 | ISBN 9781984835956 (hardcover)
ISBN 9781984835970 (trade paperback) | ISBN 9781984835963 (ebook)
Subjects: CYAC: Science fiction. | Artificial intelligence—Fiction. | Space colonies—Fiction.
Classification: LCC PZ7.1.J6287 De 2021 | DDC [Fic]—dc23
LC record available at https://lccn.loc.gov/2021017008

Printed in the United States of America

1 3 5 7 9 10 8 6 4 2

LSCH

Design by Rebecca Aidlin
Text set in Iowan Old Style

For Emily Suvada—

You are The Best™

PART ONE

THE FALL

We've put all these procedures in place—the colonist program, the Ark—but are we truly saving humanity?

I consider human identity as a collection of memories. As long as those memories stay intact, the central identity remains. The problem is that memories are ever shifting and changing. So, then, does human identity.

—Sim recording of Dr. Alberta Griffin,
date and location unknown

ONE

THE GUV

ZHADE WOKE TO a knife at his throat.

Darkness shrouded the figure above him, its weight pressing down on Zhade's chest. Metal bit into his skin, warm and slick. His covers were twisted round him, and there was no way to fight, nowhere to run. There was nothing sole to lie there and accept his fate.

Stardust swirled thickish in the air, waiting for a command from the Crown, but he didn't call to it. Couldn't.

Instead, he sighed.

"You again?" he asked his would-be assassin.

The blade fell away. The weight scuttled off him.

"You need better guards," a high voice said.

The first rays of light peeked through the seams in Maret's dark curtains, illuminating Doon's face, pink from the sun, her clothes coated in sand. Her dark eyes—the exact shade of brown as her brother's—glinted fierceish as she sat crouched on the edge of the bed, blade still ahand, a single eyebrow raised.

Zhade threw his arm over his eyes. "I have Gryfud. You can't find a better guard."

Doon huffed. "Gryfud's at home with his fam. You have Meta standing guard this moren."

Zhade wrinkled his nose and ruffled his hair. The blond strands

3

tickled the back of his neck, longer than he'd ever worn it. Longer than he liked. "Rare form. I do need better guards."

His guards *were* loyal to Tsurina, full true. And if it was Meta at the door, she probablish held a sign that said "Assassins welcome."

He gentlish pushed Doon off the bed. "You're getting sand in my sheets, little warrior."

She landed on the carpeted floor with a soft thud. "If I *had* been an assassin, sand would be the least of your worries." She sheathed her knife and looked round the Guv's room, taking in the heavy curtains, dark furniture, and haze of stardust. "It looks like you haven't cleaned since you became Maret." She sniffed. "And that Maret didn't clean since he became guv."

"Then I can't full well start cleaning now if I want people to reck I'm Maret." Zhade groaned as he climbed out of bed, which, for all its luxury, still felt uncomfortistic and cold to Zhade. But he was here, and his brother was sleeping frozen agrave. *So there*, as Andra would say.

He stretched his aching muscles, twisting from side to side.

"Turn round," he said through a yawn. "Can't I have some privacy?"

He started riffling through the discarded clothes next to the bed for a clean shirt.

Doon turned her back to him. "Maybe you should sleep in armor soon and now, if it's this easy for someone to sneak past your guards."

Zhade sniffed one of Maret's dark purple tunics and was assaulted by the smell of sour sweat and something coppery. He could have sworn this pile was the laundered one.

He shrugged the tunic on and froze when he saw himself in the wardrobe's mirrored doors. There were dark hollows neath his eyes, and his hair hung in greasy clumps. Everything bout him looked thin—his nose, his pointed chin, his body. His presence. It had been over a moon since he'd used the graftling wand, but his stomach still tightened when he saw his brother's face reflecting back at him.

"I have to convo you something," Doon said. She was slumped in a chair, face drawn in an imagineful expression.

"Is it where you've been?" Zhade asked, searching through the wardrobe for one of Maret's capes. "You have to stop disappearing. You can't mereish wander off whenever you feel amood. You should convo Skilla where you're peacing to. Or Dzeni. Or take Xana with you."

"For certz, *Guv*." She said the word the same as she used to say his name. Something more than irritation but not quite disdain.

"I'm not saying this as your guv—" he started. But what was he saying this as? Not her brother, for certz. Not her guardian. He'd convinced her brother and guardian to abandon her. Then gotten him killed.

"Good, because you're not for true the guv." Doon gave him a hard smile. "You reck that, marah? It's still Maret on the throne."

Zhade rolled his eyes. It was true that he still wore Maret's face, but he was ruling by his own values. The dungeons had been emptied, the executions had stopped. He'd found housing for those displaced by the pocket and found workings for those without. Maret would have done none of that. He would have given in to Tsurina's demands to punish those who looted during the panic after the dome had been destroyed. He'd have left the homeless and workless to fend for themselves. Then he'd have thrown a party to distract everyone from the state of the city.

The Eerensedians may imagine Maret sat on the throne, but it was Zhade who led them. Things were . . . good. His plan was working. He'd taken the throne, the gods' dome was fixed, and now he was focusing on chipping away at Tsurina's power. Slower than he would have liked, but Tsurina's influence was more embedded into the government than he'd realized. There were a few pebbles in his shoe, but after a moon as Maret, Zhade was more certz than ever that his plan would succeed and Eerensed would finalish be free.

Zhade gave Doon a playful shove. "Mereish because I took his face—"

Doon pursed her lips. "Mereish his face?"

"Evens," Zhade conceded, winking. "His face and Silver Crown."

Not that the Crown had been of any use to Zhade yet. No meteor what he tried, he couldn't harness its powers. Through it, he could feel the stardust round him, sense the angels and magical conduits, but they wouldn't answer his commands. The Crown was now mereish a decoration, part of the trappings of his deceit. At luck, Zhade hadn't had need of it. If the Eerensedians realized the Guv could no longer wield his greatest weapon, his power would start to dissolve.

Zhade collapsed into a velvet chair and rested his forehead gentlish against his hand. The skin next to the Crown was tender, the muscles sore.

Doon plopped down on a nearish sofa and started twirling a knife on the tip of her finger. "Dzeni got a job akitchens. She begins tomoren."

Zhade sat up straightish, the stardust round him swirling in agitation. "What?"

Doon nodded, eyebrows raised in mutual comping. "I reck, marah?"

Zhade shook his head. Dzeni wasn't safe apalace. If Tsurina recked the promised of Zhade's best friend—the man Maret had killed—worked akitchens . . . He closed his eyes, pinching the bridge of his nose. "She should have gone to stay with the Schism."

Zhade would visit her, convince her to go belowground. If she didn't want to stay with the Schism, maybe he could convince her to live in the Vaults with the goddesses. He'd bring her some flowers. Maybe get a toy for Dehgo. What did kidduns play with, anyway? Charms? Knives? He'd ask Gryfud—the soldier who had let him into Eerensed all those moons ago and was anow the captain of Zhade's guard. He and his husband had recentish adopted a kiddun. For certz they'd figured what it played with soon and now.

6

Gryf was always willing to help. Without Kiv as part of his guard, Zhade needed someone he could trust to infiltrate Tsurina's ranks. He'd chosen Gryfud not sole because he had let Zhade and Andra acity, but he'd also been friendish with him as kidduns. It was still a risk, but one Zhade had to take.

Gryfud had sole shook his head when Zhade had revealed who he for true was.

"You're a fool boyo," he'd said, in a way that purposed he was agreeing to help, if sole because he recked the plan wouldn't work without him.

"Be at care what you say to your guv," Zhade had teased.

"For certz," Gryfud had replied. "If I see him, I will."

Doon stretched out on the sofa, throwing her hands behind her head. "Convoing the Schism. You do reck that you missed your last meeting with Skilla, marah? She's for true full angry."

Zhade waved a hand. "She'll make it peacish." He grinned, gesturing to himself. "Who can stay angry at this face?"

Doon scowled.

There was a knock at the door, and both Zhade and Doon froze.

No one should have been able to enter his suite—the outer door was sealed with blood magic. Somehow, while he and Doon had been convoing, someone had entered through his receiving room, walked down the hall, and stood outside his bedroom for who recked how long.

"Did you leave the door open?" Zhade hissed.

Doon shook her head. "I didn't come in that march."

His eyes darted toward the balcony, and she nodded. He slowish made his march to the door, making certz Doon was hidden before opening it. A guard stood on the other side, plated in gold armor, her sharp face frozen in a stern expression.

Meta.

How had she gotten in? The sole person—other than him—with

access to the suite was Tsurina. Had Tsurina messed with the blood magic so the guards could enter too?

Zhade groaned inwardish.

Meta was bout Zhade's age. A refugee from the Wastes who, after sole three years in the guard, had been promoted to second-in-command, poised to take the captain's place. Sfin, the priorish captain, had died during the battle against the Schism, the night Zhade had morphed his features to match his brother's and slid into his place as guv. To the people of Eerensed, it was the day the palace had nearish been destroyed, the Third caught and executed, and the gods' dome restored.

With Sfin dead, Meta was spozed to become captain, but Zhade had promoted Gryfud instead. Gryfud, who had been mereish a border guard, and a lower-level one at that. Meta had been less than pleased. She made it recked as oft as possible.

"Guv," she said through gritted teeth, jaw clenched, a strand of brown spiked hair falling over one eye. The westhand side of her head was shaved like a Waster; the other side was long and slicked into pointed strands. It wasn't reg, that was for certz.

"Firm?" Zhade asked.

"Do you have memory you have a guv-asking in half abell?"

"For certz," Zhade lied. "Be there soonish."

Meta turned to go.

"And Meta?"

She halted.

"How did you get in the suite?"

Meta blinked slowish. "The door was open. I imagined you left it that way apurpose."

Zhade swallowed. He for certz hadn't left the door open. Which purposed that either Tsurina had let her in, or the guards now had some way to pass by the blood magic. He couldn't ask bout it though, not without seeming suss. Instead, he gave Meta a tight smile. "For certz. I'm still half sleepy. I'll be out in a tick."

Meta didn't smile back.

THE DAY PASSED in a sandcloud, each activity sifting into the next. It was always the same: meetings and appearances and half-walking the thin string between maintaining his ruse as Maret and making decisions that would improve Eerensed's fate. Each day he held himself busy from moren to even, but this day he convoed his guards he needed a bell in the aftermoren to himself. They didn't question him. He was guv, after all.

After his last meeting of the day, he retreated to his room, donning some of his old clothes and a glamour mask sorcered to a generic Eerensedian face and marched out acity.

Once he was free of the shadow of the Rock, he sighed and let himself enjoy Eerensed. The bustle of citians, the hum of tiny flying angels, the flashing of scrys. The bright sun shining down on all of it. He saw no askers, though they'd always been scarce in Southwarden. There were flowers in windowboxes and in the midway. Zhade picked a handful of starflowers to give to Dzeni.

The sole thing that marred his mood was the pocket looming out-side the city to his westhand side. It was quiet—as much as pockets were quiet—and it didn't seem to be growing or moving. But it was a fulltime memory of the events of last moon, when the gods' dome had failed and a full district of the city had been destroyed in an eyebeat. At the least, it was full early in the day the pocket didn't yet block the setting sun. Each even, night came a full bell earlier than it used to.

It was a short trip to the bakery that had once belonged to Wead's uncle, who'd left it to Wead when he'd sunk into sand. Zhade imag-ined it belonged to Dzeni now. Or maybe Doon. It was a small place, hidden in the tangle of alleys in the resto district in Southwarden. The bell rang as Zhade pushed open the door.

The bakery was empty, except for a few picked-over baykuds in the case. Zhade cleared his throat and leaned against the counter. A face popped out from the back room. Flame hair, grizzled beard. Cheska.

"What happens?" he asked, dusting flour off his hands. His voice was a basstring played in a cave. His hair was bright as a goldenlilly, his pale complexion ruddy. He was a big man, could probablish hold his own in a fight with Gryfud, maybe even Kiv.

"I'm—" Zhade tried to deepen his voice. "I'm looking for Dzeni."

Cheska narrowed his pale eyes. "How you happen to reck Dzeni?"

Zhade leaned across the counter, looking up at Cheska til he was full close the bigger man could see through the glamour mask to Zhade's face neath it. Maret's face.

Cheska immediatish scowled. He was one of the few people who recked Zhade was wearing the Guv's features. Dzeni had insisted on telling him. "What do you want?"

Zhade rocked back. "Many things. Butterjam tarts, a new silk cape, fishes and wishes. But anow, I'd like to convo Dzeni."

Cheska stared him down a moment, before shaking his head and disappearing behind the curtain in the back. Zhade swiped up a near-ish crumb. It was burnt. He stuck his tongue out and let the crumb fall to the counter.

The curtain opened, and Cheska motioned for Zhade to follow. Behind was a storeroom. A door to the left led to another room, windowless and dark, but homeish. Dzeni stood draped in a thick cloak, Dehgo clinging to his mother's hand. She'd lost weight, her cheeks hollow and bags neath her eyes. Her dark hair was pulled back from her heart-shaped face into a rattish bun.

"Dzeni!" Zhade stepped forward, opening his arms for a hug, but he was met mereish with an icy stare. He dropped his arms and took a step back. For certz, he was wearing a glamour mask. "It's Zhade."

Dzeni cocked an eyebrow. "I reck. That's the worst disguise."

Zhade didn't bother to convo the face neath his glamour wasn't even his own, so it was actualish a full brill disguise.

Cheska moved to stand next to Dzeni, placing a protective hand on her shoulder. Dehgo pulled on his mam's arm, eyeing the toy angel in Zhade's hand.

"Heya, boyo," Zhade said, trying to sound like himself and not Maret. Rust was growing on his own voice with disuse.

Dehgo slipped out of his mam's grasp and ran to Zhade. "I like your toy sir may I see it?" The sentence came out in a rush.

"This?" Zhade asked, lifting the small angel. He'd sorcered it to do nothing more than walk in circles and say a few brief phrases, but kidduns were easyish amused, marah? Gryfud had said so. "This toy?"

"Firm!" Dehgo reached for it, big brown eyes alight.

"Evens, this toy isn't mine." Zhade held the toy just out of his reach.

Dehgo stuck out his bottom lip. "'Snot?"

"Neg, you'll have to ask the owner if you can play with it."

"Whose is it?"

Zhade knelt and held out the angel. "It's yours."

Dehgo squinted and puffed out his lips, and Zhade realized he didn't comp the joke. But he must have decided it didn't meteor because he snatched the toy from Zhade's hands and ran back to his mother.

Dzeni placed a hand on her son's curlish head. "What convo, Dehgo?"

"Thank you," he mumbled, placing the angel on the ground and watching its small silver body stumble over the uneven stone floor.

Zhade stood. Dzeni was watching him with a measured stare.

He scratched behind his ear with a single finger. "You don't belong akitchens."

"Zhade," she said in a soft reprimand.

"What I purpose is . . ." How to convo this? Zhade should have prepped something, but he'd never had trouble making words before. "You and Dehgo. I can give you a place to live."

Wasn't that the least he owed them? Owed Wead?

Dzeni canted her head. "We have a place to live."

"A *better* place."

A growl came from Cheska's direction.

Zhade lifted his hands in placation. "I'm certz Cheska's place is charred but probablish crowded. You could move belowground. You wouldn't need to work. The Third would give you somewhere to stay. Things to do. She'd protect you."

"Like she protected Wead?" Fire burned in Dzeni's eyes, and Zhade flinched. This was not the Dzeni he recked. She seemed to realize the anger had taken over because her face softened. "Sorries and worries. I didn't purpose to convo . . ."

"That wasn't her fault," Zhade muttered, his stomach souring. He didn't want to convo this. Wead's death. Zhade's part in it.

Andra.

Dzeni laughed, saddish. "She's a goddess, Zhade."

"Neg, Dzeni. It's complicated. I don't full comp half of it, but if you would mereish convo her, she could explain. Please. If you blame anyone, you should blame me."

Dzeni looked away. The corners of her mouth tugged down, and her eyes were vagueish wet. Zhade would have given anything to see her smile again, but he wasn't certz if he wanted it for her, or to assuage his own guilt. For a moment, they both watched Dehgo play with the angel on the stone floor.

Zhade sighed. "I mereish imagined . . . hear, I reck this is my fault. And I want to do something to . . . make things right."

Dzeni's eyes met his. "I reck, Zhade. It's mereish . . . this is not the way to do it."

"If you want to make things right," Cheska cut in, "then you should pass more of your time out of the palace."

Zhade bit the inside of his cheek. "What happens, Cheska?"

Cheska started pacing the cramped room, running a hand through his red hair. "How are you for true helping our people, *Guv*? The Lost District held many businesses. They're gone now. The harvests will be short this year. When the gods' dome failed, it took most of our water supply. The people—*your* people—are hurting, dying. What are you going to do bout it?"

"Cheska," Dzeni said, placing a hand on his shoulder. For the first time since Wead's death, she sounded like herself. Gentle but firm. Holding the peace.

Cheska shook off her touch. "Neg, Dzeni, he should hear this."

"I'm doing everything I can," Zhade said, slipping into Maret's whine. "It's diff to make real change while Tsurina is still round, but I've found housing for everyone, all my people have workings who want them. The water is sole a meteor of time, and the harvest isn't for several moons."

Cheska paused his pacing and started counting off on his fingers. "The housing is overcrowded. The workings you've provided are demeaning. And we need water soon and now."

Zhade clenched his jaw. "I can't make water from wine. Magic has its limits." It was a well-recked axiom of magic that it could sole mimic the natural, not create it.

"And I'm certz," Cheska said, crossing his arms over his chest, "it full imports to have water in that big showy fountain afront of the palace, marah?"

Zhade winced. Cheska was right. It had been a stupid mistake not to order the fountain turned off while water was scarce.

Zhade sighed. "Evens, you're right. I can turn off the fountain. And I'll . . . consider what I can do bout the other stuff," he muttered.

"*Consider what you can do?*" Cheska mocked. "Now you sound like a goddess. Are you full certz the city is better with you as guv instead of Maret?"

Zhade opened his mouth to reply, but Cheska turned and stormed back to the bakery, the door slamming shut behind him.

Dzeni gave Zhade a sorries look.

"Seeya. That was awkward." Zhade smiled, but his stomach plummeted. For certz, things weren't perfect. But they were getting better each day. And unlike his brother, Zhade actualish *cared* bout his people.

It was evens.

Everything was evens.

"That was awkward," Dehgo said to his toy angel, mimicking Zhade's cadence.

They stood in silence, Dzeni shifting from foot to foot, Zhade ruffling the back of his head, watching his feet.

He cleared his throat. "I brought something for you too." He pulled a disc out of his pocket and handed it to Dzeni. "It's a small gods' dome."

Dzeni blinked, staring down at the shiny metal disc in her hand. "For what?"

Zhade shrugged. "I mereish imagined . . . you should have it. Just in case."

Andra had given Zhade a few small domes that would protect anyone inside from pockets. Evens. She'd given some to Kiv to give to him. She'd called them backup in case the gods' dome failed. Kiv had said she'd said it pointedish. It was now Zhade's job to maintain the dome, but tween holding the secret of his identity and ruling Eerensed, he'd had little time to focus on it.

"I did blame you," Dzeni said, her voice wavering, and it took Zhade a tick to realize she was talking bout Wead's death. "I blamed you. And her. And Maret. And Wead." Her eyes met his, and they shimmered with tears. "I'm so angry, all the time, and it hurts. I don't reck what I've become."

Zhade reached for Dzeni, but she moved away.

"Sorries, Zhade," she mumbled. "Maybe I will go belowground. It's best for Dehgo, marah?" She knelt and pushed her son's curls from his face. He looked so much like his father.

Zhade tried to smile. "He wouldn't want for anything. And you have to reck how much the Third cared for Wead, and how much she regrets his death. She . . . Maret gave her a choice. He was either going to kill me or Wead. And she chose me to die and Wead to live. Sole Maret didn't listen and killed Wead instead."

Dzeni was quiet for a moment. "She chose you to die?"

Zhade nodded, swallowed. He didn't want to convo this. Not that he blamed Andra. But it hurt and probablish always would. He didn't fool himself how much it would have tortured her if he *had* died from her decision, but the answer had come so quickish. So detached from what her feelings for him had been. Those feelings were for certz gone anow he wore the face of the boy who had killed Wead afront of her.

"I—" Dzeni started, but whatever she was bout to say was cut off by a scream.

Both she and Zhade turned toward the noise. It had come from the street, and it sounded like a kiddun.

"Stay here," Dzeni told Dehgo, at the same time Zhade said it to her.

She gave him an exasperated look and followed him through the bakery into the street.

A crowd had gathered. There was another scream coming from the center of the square, but it was cut short.

"Out of the march," Zhade demanded, and the citians parted.

In the mid of the crowd, a kiddun was held aloft by the neck.

By an angel.

Zhade didn't have time to reck how impossible it was. The kiddun's face was going slack, her attempts to fight growing weaker, her dark hair spilling over an angelic hand.

On instinct, Zhade reached out with his mind. From the few times he'd tried to use the Crown, he recked what angels "felt" like through the magic connection, and this was not it. The angel felt . . . wrong. Dark. Some deep abyss.

"Do something!" Dzeni shouted.

"I'm trying." Zhade gritted his teeth, focusing harder.

Release her, he commanded in his mind. Wasn't this how Maret had done it? Speaking through the magical connection? This was High Magic. No conduit, mereish thought. The angel should heed his command soon and sooner.

But it didn't. It continued choking the kiddun, her pathetic kicks now nothing more than muscle spasms. Her mam was reaching for her. Her da was crumpled on the ground below, crying.

Release her, Zhade thought harder, but nothing happened.

Dzeni shot forward, arms stretching toward the kiddun, but couldn't reach her. She started banging on the angel's chest, her fists hitting with empty thuds. The angel's other hand clamped round Dzeni's throat. The crowd gasped, as the angel stretched out its arms, offering both Dzeni and the kiddun to the sky.

"Mam!" Dehgo cried, appearing behind Zhade. Could no one stay put where they were told?

He tried to catch Dehgo, but the kiddun slipped through his grasp. He was almost to the angel when a pair of arms wrapped round him. He screamed as he was lifted off his feet by a woman with dark skin and a shaved head.

She turned, and Zhade was met with Xana's cool glare, her magic eye narrowing in on him.

"Do something," she commanded. The words were lost in the screaming of the crowd, but Zhade felt them in his bones.

He tried again to command the angel.

RELEASE THEM.

He felt something ooze down his cheek, a dull pain thumping in time with his pulse. His body began to shake.

Cheska burst through the crowd, red hair blazing, pushing people out of his march with his enormous arms. He punched the angel as hard as he could in the chest. There was a dull thud, nothing else, but Cheska kept punching. And punching. Punching as though something had possessed him. The angel's chest cracked. Cheska's hand was bleeding, but he kept attacking.

The kiddun was released first. A villager shot forward to catch her before she hit the ground. They called for a meddoc, and immediatish started giving her seepar, a technique of blowing one's own air into the afflicted's lungs.

Cheska was still punching. The angel's insides were spilling out. People were screaming. The angel finalish released Dzeni, but he didn't stop.

The angel fell, and Cheska climbed on top of it, hitting it til there was a hole the size and shape of his fist in its chest. He reached in, the angel's metal skin shredding his fist into a bloody mess, and pulled out the heart of the angel. It was a dull black box, but everyone in the crowd comped that Cheska had removed the thing that held the angel alive. A flurry of stardust rose from the dead angel—its soul escaping—and disappeared into the air.

Some citians applauded Cheska with awkward relief, while others crowded round the girl, who was now sitting up and coughing. He tossed aside the angel heart and went to Dzeni. Xana had helped her to her knees, fingers now running cross the bruise on her neck. In the other arm, she held Dehgo. It was the most tender Zhade had ever seen her.

Then she turned toward the noisy crowd, her fierce gaze searching past them to narrow in on him, her expression murderful.

Zhade mereish stood there.

Powerless.

An angel had attacked a little girl. In his city.

An *angel*.

Angels didn't attack people, except in one circumstance: at Maret's command during executions. What Zhade had mereish seen—it was impossible without the Crown.

The Crown Zhade was wearing. And if Zhade hadn't done it, then . . .

Someone else in the city had the magic that should sole be Zhade's.

He was bout to move forward, kneel next to the angel and start examining it, when he caught the sight of a familiar half-shaved head in the crowd.

Meta.

As Andra would say:

Fuck.

She would almost for certz see through his glamour.

He gave Dzeni one last look. Cheska was helping her to her feet. Xana still held Dehgo. Zhade slipped out of the crowd, holding to the shadows as he made his march back to the palace.

TWO

OOIIOOIO

ANDROMEDA OPENED HER eyes, gasping for breath.

A dizzying array of numbers swirled from her thoughts, disappearing as the room around her came into focus. The same room that had encompassed her entire world for the past three months. One half was covered with personal items—her cot, her clothes, blankets Lilibet had stitched for her, a vase of daisy-like flowers that kept showing up though Andra didn't know how. The other half was a lab/conference room, the work'station and holo'table used for meetings like today's.

Her fingers dug into the armrests of her ergo'chair as three faces watched her expectantly.

"Anything?" she asked.

Lilibet grimaced but quickly turned it into an awkward smile. "They moved . . . a bit . . . I reck."

Rashmi shook her head. "Your human eyes are deceived in ways my neural perception cannot be. They are unmoved." She sighed, leaning back in her chair. "As am I."

"Why are we here again?" Skilla asked.

The four of them sat around the 'table in the corner of a former Vaults display room. The Vaults had been Riverside's tech museum, and due to its air'locks and superior environmental controls, it had

19

remained perfectly preserved beneath Eerensed's palace. Andra's bedroom had been the EMP exhibit—a display of various devices throughout history that could interrupt any technological function within range. Including a cylinder the size of an oil drum specifically designed to neutralize AI—which Andra was. She'd had it cleared out immediately. She'd spent the last month up to her neurons in Vaults tech, inventorying and repurposing it for the rocket, and if an EMP went off, it would destroy all her hard work. And knock her out for several minutes. So, they were now safely stored in the Vaults' Faraday cage, and Andra was left with the shell of a display room, its once-windowed walls now turned opaque, a new DNA scan at the door.

She had started out using it solely for her meetings with the Schism and lab experiments, but she'd spent so much time here, she'd simply moved in, gathering a few personal items and lots of discarded tech, and building her own work'station. It was a mess of holos and sim components. Most were on sleep mode, and a blinking red light reminded her of the 'display that held a manifest of all one million colonists.

Colonists that still lay under the earth, in the huge warehouse Andra called the Icebox. Frozen. Waiting.

Because she wasn't sure what she should do with them. Wake them up to the nightmare of what the earth had become? Wait until she had a rocket that was nearly impossible to rebuild? Griffin hadn't left her any instructions, besides the memory in the holocket that had told Andra where to find the frozen colonists and that she'd know what to do.

Except Andra didn't know what to do. She had to get everyone to Holymyth, but she had no idea how.

She sighed, staring down at the two mini'domes on the table, connected by a thin vacuum tube. Inside the left mini'dome was a pocket.

It was a tiny pocket. Andra had managed to trap a clump of nanos the size of a hand from the pocket hovering outside the city. It had been delicate work, like scraping moss from a tree without damaging the bark. It had taken all her concentration, and though she'd controlled the pocket so easily that day in the throne room against Maret, she'd had trouble accessing any of her newfound powers and programming since. Something had taken over her that day, some innate sense of power. She referred to it as her AI state, and she'd yet to achieve it again.

She'd spent the last few weeks trying to move the pocket from one mini'dome to the next, but so far she'd just seemed to make it angry.

"If the Third One can move the small pocket," Rashmi said, answering Skilla's question, "she might be able to move the large pocket."

Her voice was still high and wispy, but there was more intention to it. She no longer sounded like she would give up halfway through a sentence. Most days. Her white hair hung in wisps around her face, instead of tangled and matted. After weeks free from captivity, her skin glowed in a way that made her look more . . . human. Which was more than Andra could say for herself at the moment. She couldn't remember the last time she'd brushed her hair or taken a shower. At least she'd eaten something today. Maybe. Or was that yesterday?

"And then she'll save the city!" Lilibet added, her dark hair swaying, as she bounced in her chair.

Skilla raised a thin eyebrow. "I didn't realize the city needed saving."

"But the 'dome—" Andra started.

"Is evens anow," Skilla finished. She sat back, arms crossed.

The door slid open and Xana walked in. She was covered in weapons, and Andra thought she saw a smudge of blood on her cheek. She shared a brief look with Skilla, the pupil in her modded eye expanding, before taking her seat at the other end of the 'table.

"Sorries I'm late," she muttered.

If Andra concentrated, she could feel the vibrations of hearts, the intakes of breaths, through interfacing with the nanos in the room.

Listening to where they bumped up against life. Skilla's heart only beat faster, her breath only taken away, by the thought of rebuilding the Schism. But Xana's heart fluttered every time she looked at Skilla. The same flutter Andra felt whenever Zhade was around.

They were both fools.

"The gods' dome is new," Skilla continued, as though they hadn't been interrupted, "and Zhade has that . . . control room you built him. If something goes wrong, he can fix it without you."

Andra's eye twitched. Though she'd built a new 'dome, it required constant maintenance. She could do it herself, but it had been wearing her thin. Without the AI state, she wasn't meant to interact with such vast tech without some kind of barrier. The energy the 'dome used often overwhelmed Andra's nanos. And each time she sent them out to keep the 'dome working, fewer and fewer returned. It hurt her about as much as scratching off dead skin cells, but over time, scratch too much and you'll bleed.

So she'd set up a control room in the cathedzal—a way for Zhade to perform maintenance on the 'dome. It kept Andra from having to replenish her own nanos so often and let her focus on finding a way to get humanity to Holymyth.

In theory.

She didn't know if Zhade was actually using the control room. They'd barely spoken since Andra had realized Zhade's mother was Dr. Alberta Griffin, since he'd learned Andra was a robot. An AI. Whatever. Maybe he was scared. Or maybe he was glad to have an excuse to cut ties with her. She'd done what he'd needed her to do: remove the Crown from his brother's head, fix the 'dome, save Eerensed. She'd been a tool to help him retake his throne. And now he was finished with her.

No. That hadn't been all she was to Zhade. But now it didn't matter. That was over.

"The 'dome won't last long with a pocket so close to it," Andra argued. "And Zhade—" Andra swallowed. "The Guv is new to this technology. He doesn't know it as well as I do. The best way to keep Eerensed safe is to move the pocket."

Skilla tossed her raven ponytail over her shoulder. "Maybe if he deigned to show up to one of these meetings, he could speak for himself." She leaned back in her chair and nodded at the mini'pocket. "So is this what you've been focusing on? I thought you were working on collecting material to rebuild the rocket?"

Andra wanted to slap the smirk off Skilla's face. The "general" had made it clear what she thought of rebuilding the rocket. No matter how much material and tech Andra had mined from the Vaults, Skilla didn't seem at all interested in continuing the project. Andra wanted to point out that it had been the entire reason the Schism existed. That they had been formed after whatever disaster had released the pockets onto the earth to create a way to get humanity off the planet. That they had been loyal to Griffin once she'd woken.

But Andra knew that Skilla had lost faith in the First and everything she'd stood for. The rocket, saving a few hundred people, escaping Earth for some distant planet: these were all abstract ideas, and Skilla was more interested in rebuilding the Schism's militia, which Andra thought was a complete waste of time. There was no Schism anymore. Most had died either in Maret's raid or in the pocket, and what was left was nothing more than a few soldiers and some refugees.

Besides, Zhade was guv now. And though Tsurina was in the way, he had a plan to loosen her grip on the guards and Eerensedian troops. But when Andra asked Skilla why she needed an army, Skilla replied that if you wait until you need an army to build one, it's already too late.

"I'm still working on sourcing materials for the rocket," Andra said. "I just feel that this"—she gestured to the small pocket in the mini'dome—"is more important right now."

Actually, it was a distraction. Andra had spent weeks trying to piece together what Griffin had intended for her to do, but she kept coming up empty. Though there was plenty of technology in the Vaults, they were missing one vital material.

Cryo'chamber plating.

The same metallic glass that protected the frozen colonists also prevented the rocket from being destroyed by pockets. Or fire—like the last one had been. The problem was there was very little cryo'plating in the Vaults. There was, however, quite a bit in the Icebox. But it was currently being used.

The irony was that if Andra woke up the LAC scientists, they could create the rocket in no time. The brightest minds of Andra's time would have no trouble deciphering Griffin's notes and sourcing materials. But Griffin hadn't woken them. There must have been a reason.

So now Andra was stuck. Useless. A failure. The last time she'd felt any type of success, of purpose, was when she'd controlled the pocket in the throne room. The ability was somewhere in her, if only she could harness it.

She ran a hand through her hair, tugging at the knotted, greasy strands. This wasn't how this meeting was supposed to go. She was supposed to move the pocket, show abilities beyond what a human could do. All she'd done since waking was fix things and inventory the Vaults, something any serve'bot could do. She was an AI, dammit, not a 'bot.

If she could just show them that she was *more*, just like she'd done in the throne room. A feeling of unlimited power had coursed through her, filling her until she was bursting. She had brimmed with light and knowledge and purpose, and she knew there was nothing she couldn't do, nothing she couldn't command. She was AI and human and deity, and she could remake the world in her image.

What are you doing? a voice said in her mind, and Andra was jolted out of her reverie.

Rashmi was staring at her, eyes narrowed, white hair tumbling across her face. Of all the abilities for Rashmi to maintain, it had to be speaking through their neural connection directly into Andra's consciousness.

"I don't imagine . . ." Skilla said slowly, ". . . you should be doing that."

"What?" Andra asked.

Skilla didn't respond. Only stared at the mini'dome. The pocket swirled darkly within it, restless and agitated, beating against the walls of the 'dome. Had Andra done that?

The others apparently thought so. The four women sat angled away from her, avoiding her gaze. Lilibet was chewing her lip, squirming. Rashmi was rocking back and forth. Xana had her hand on her ax. When Skilla's eyes cut back to Andra, there was a hint of something she'd never seen there before.

Fear.

Of the pocket?

Or of Andra?

"If you focus on getting materials for the rocket," Skilla said, body tense, "I'll have the Schism continue working on it."

Andra swallowed and nodded. "Okay. The rocket . . . will be my top priority."

Even as she said it, she knew it was a lie. She was so close to controlling the pocket. She couldn't give up now.

"Or," Xana said, standing, "you could rest. Maybe . . . bathe?"

Andra looked around the room, embarrassed. It was true that she hadn't kept healthy habits since discovering the frozen bodies of the colonists still on Earth. She slept and ate too little and worked and worried too much. But Andra didn't have the luxury of taking a break for herself. She belonged to humanity.

"Yeah, sure," Andra said, feeling her face growing hot. "I'll . . . rest. Bathe."

"And eat a vegetable," Lilibet added.

Skilla stood, her weapons clinking. "No more staring at pockets. Rest. Focus on the rocket. You won't be any use to us if you're burned out."

Andra nodded. There was the crux of the matter. Andra had to be useful. She was an AI. A tool. And tools that weren't useful were worthless. Maybe Skilla was right. Maybe narrowing Andra's focus to the rocket would be exactly what she needed.

The door opened and Kiv peeked his head in. Lilibet squealed and ran to him, throwing her arms around his neck and planting a kiss on his lips, ending it with a loud "Muah!" Andra felt both their heart rates increase through the vibrations the nanos sensed.

Kiv untangled himself from Lilibet and set a mug of hot chocolate in front of Rashmi. She grabbed it and took a sip and smiled.

"Thank you," she signed.

Kiv nodded.

"I'm going to go kiss Kiv some more!" Lilibet shrieked and dragged him out of the room. Andra and the others sat in awkward silence for a moment, until Skilla cleared her throat.

"Are we fin?" she asked.

She didn't wait for a response before exiting the room. Xana followed her, leaving Andra alone with Rashmi.

Andra sighed and looked down at the mini'dome, the trapped pocket swirling in agitation.

"Should I try one more time?" she asked.

"You promised Skilla just forty-three seconds ago that you wouldn't."

Andra felt Rashmi shake her head, so aware of the other AI, she didn't have to look at her to know what she was doing. Sometimes it seemed like Rashmi was an extension of herself. But it was only because they were computers on the same network.

Sort of.

Rashmi was . . . not as computer-y as Andra.

When Rashmi had transferred her programming to Andra, she hadn't been cloning it or backing it up. She had fully relinquished the data. Meaning Rashmi no longer had access to some of her most basic programming. Rashmi was barely AI anymore. Her thoughts were still nanos, her brain artificial. But with her programming now in Andra, and her memories a muddle from years of trauma in the palace dungeon, Rashmi's identity was splintered. She had been an AI, but now the access to her full abilities was gone. She had been a goddess, but her memories from that time were missing. Andra had offered to at least transfer the data back, but Rashmi flat out refused.

"I don't want it back," she'd said. "I want to be human."

Andra didn't have the heart to tell her that she wasn't.

"Remember what you are, Third One," Rashmi said now. "Our brains may be artificial, but our bodies are organic, and yours is yawning. You've stretched it too thin."

Andra paused mid-yawn.

Rashmi gave Andra a look over the hot chocolate Kiv had brought her. They had a routine down. Zhade would get the hot chocolate from the kitchens as Maret, then pass it off to Kiv through a secret passage, who would usually give it to Lilibet to bring to Rashmi.

All that work, just so Zhade could avoid her.

Andra banished the thought—and the weird ache in her chest that accompanied it—and lifted the mini'dome from her desk. She felt the corrupted nanos inside hiss in anger.

"I guess I'll put this little guy away, then," Andra said.

Rashmi cocked her head. "Why did you anthropomorphize it?"

"What?"

"You called it a 'little guy.' Just because we are sentient, doesn't mean all technology is."

Andra blinked. "I . . . yeah. I know. It's just . . . I don't know, something humans do. Let things borrow sentience. I don't know why."

"And are we human?"

The hope in Rashmi's voice broke Andra's heart.

She shrugged. "We were bound to pick up some of their habits."

Rashmi downed the last of her hot chocolate. "I'm going to go check on Maret."

Andra let out a noncommittal noise. Rashmi wouldn't trust anyone else with his location and spent most of her time guarding his 'tank. And Andra was the one being too human?

"Just . . . one sec," Andra said.

Rashmi paused halfway to the door, and Andra sensed her muscles tense, as though she knew what Andra was going to ask.

"Are you sure? That you can't remember anything from before?"

Rashmi didn't turn around, and this time, Andra didn't need the nanos to see Rashmi was trembling.

"I know it's upsetting," Andra said, trying to put as much compassion in her voice as possible, trying to strain out the desperation. "But if you could just remember something from your time with Griffin. After she woke you. Then maybe we could figure out what we're supposed to do now."

Rashmi's head hung, her white hair covering her face. "There's darkness and darkness and darkness. Memories flicker like candlelight, but I can't grab them. It burns."

Andra swallowed her disappointment. "Sorry. I . . . just thought I'd ask."

Rashmi departed without another word, leaving Andra alone, clothes and technology scattered around her. She stared at the pocket in the mini'dome.

"Do you know your purpose, little dude?"

It swirled around the 'dome, then pressed against the side closest to Andra, as though it were reaching out, waiting for her command.

She understood that the others would be scared of the large pocket, the one pressing on the 'dome. The one that had destroyed the Lost District. But this pocket was different. It was contained and small, and if Andra could control it, no one would have to be afraid of pockets ever again.

She closed her eyes and took a deep breath, willing it to move from one 'dome to the next. She could sense it. Sense its agitation, its hesitation, its resistance. It knew Andra and it knew what she wanted, but that wasn't its purpose. Its purpose was to—

Destroy.

Andra's breath caught. The voice was in her head. It was dark and confident and curled its way into her thoughts like smoke.

Destroy it all.

Andra's eyes flashed open, her breath coming too fast.

Okay.

Okay.

The others were definitely right. She needed a break from this.

She set the 'dome on her work'station, turning back to the mess that was her room. The piles of clothes, the discarded tech. She grabbed the nearest shirt and started folding it. She would clean all this up, then she would start working on the rocket again. She could go through Griffin's old notes in the computer system that controlled the Icebox, look for hints. Maybe the truth was hidden somewhere in them.

She'd scoured every detail, looking for a code or sign that might lead her to more of Griffin's work. Anything that could tell her what Griffin expected her to do. She needed another pair of eyes. Maybe she could convince Rashmi to help, even though Rashmi avoided anything to do with Griffin or their purpose as AI.

Andra heard a noise at the door and opened it, finding Lilibet and Kiv locked in an embrace on the other side. Lilibet jumped at being caught and blushed. Not that she was shy about her affection for

Kiv. But she seemed to feel awkward about everything recently.

"Oh, hi." Andra looked away. "I just heard . . . sorry . . ." She started to close the door and paused.

Andra wasn't the only one suffering right now. Lilibet was struggling to adapt to life underground more than any of them. Though Lilibet had been a palace servant, she'd never been trapped within the palace walls. She needed to talk, needed to roam the city and be Lilibet. Unfortunately, since she was recognizable as the maid who had served the Devil Goddess, she couldn't be seen aboveground. Being stuck down here was something new for her, and she was . . . restless.

Andra surveyed her, cocking her head. "Hey, Lilibet. Do you want to learn how to—"

Lilibet pushed Kiv away. "FIRM!"

Andra blinked. "You don't even know what I was going to ask."

"It doesn't meteor. I love skooling and helping and *doing things*. Teach me! Teach me! Please please pleeeeeeeeease?"

Andra lifted an eyebrow. "Teach you how to clean the washroom?"

The light in Lilibet's eyes dimmed, but she didn't let the smile fade. "Firm?"

Andra laughed and brought up a holo'display. "Actually, I wanted to teach you some magic."

LILIBET TOOK TO technology like she took to everything else—with enthusiasm and giddiness. After a few hours, she knew how to manually interface with a work'station and was even starting to learn basic coding. She could search through files and run programs if Andra directed her. She was eager to keep learning, but Andra needed a break. If not from the teaching, then from Kiv watching patiently, awkwardly from Andra's cot, waiting for Lilibet to be done.

Andra grabbed a small yellow clone'drive called a taxi' and headed to the cavern under Southwarden where the rocket was being constructed. If she was going to focus on rebuilding it, she needed to refresh her memory on the few blueprints Griffin had left behind and transfer them to her work'station.

It was a short trek. At least, it was short underground. It would have taken at least half a bell aboveground to walk from the palace to Southwarden, but belowground, Andra had dug new tunnels to connect the Vaults and the rocket and the Icebox and reinforced them with eco'tile. Well, Mechy had done all the work, but she'd given him instructions. The mech'bot who had led her to the throne room the day she'd controlled the pocket was now helping Andra in any way he could—which usually meant manual labor. She sent him a message through their cognitive interface to meet her at the rocket.

There was a small hover waiting for her just outside the Vaults, in a cave Mechy had dug on the other side of the air'lock. Andra climbed in and set the coordinates. The hover zoomed through the tunnels, over paved eco'tile flooring, and past bright white eco'tile walls. Kinetic orbs flicked on and off as she passed, the passages slowly growing steeper and steeper as she traveled farther underground.

Mechy was waiting for her when she reached the cave. He stood two meters tall, his black metal casing dull and scratched, limbs bulky and multi-jointed. His face was purely mechanical—a sheet of metal with an unmoving mouth and flashing eyes. Andra had gotten him new paneling and oiled his joints, but with each new construction project, his appearance grew haggard. He was nearly a thousand years old, after all. Almost as old as Andra.

Despite her insistence that she didn't need it, Mechy helped her out of the hover'cart.

"You don't have enough joints," Mechy had once told her. "Do you wish me to build you more efficient limbs?"

He'd accepted her refusal with bemusement but continued to treat Andra as though she were exceptionally fragile. Which, to be fair, compared to him, she was. An extraordinary brain trapped in a fallible body.

They were in a narrow tunnel. The door to the cavern stood in front of her. Mechy had constructed it by borrowing one of the doors from the LAC annex—the office ruins above the Icebox. The size and shape were so familiar to Andra. It was the same as any door at any LAC location. Opaque eco'glass displaying a hologram of the LAC logo—a rotating DNA strand. It hovered over the outline of Ohio. At the Los Angeles location it would hover over the Cali Republic. In Tokyo, the Japanese Isles. Here, in an underground network of tunnels and caverns, a thousand years in the future, it was the outline of a state that didn't exist anymore.

The door was glitching, its security settings still tuned to those of the LAC annex. Mechy had tried fixing it, but so far he was the only one who could coax it open. He did so, eyes strobing as he interfaced with it. After a moment, the light on the lock flashed green, accompanied by a beep, and it swung open. Andra stepped into the cavern.

It was enormous, the only part of the underground network large enough to house a rocket, since the last one had been destroyed. Thousands of feet high, a stone cathedral covered in moss, the air cold and stale. Andra felt minuscule in the space, looking at the rocket towering above her, the cavern swallowing it. Water dripped, echoing off the stone walls, and the buzz of 'drones ebbed and flowed around her. She shivered.

The rocket was just a skeleton at the moment, but it was tied into a huge work'station at the end of a narrow ledge that led from the cavern entrance. Mechy had fitted it with an eco'railing as it ascended from the cavern floor to the stone platform ten meters up that held the 'station. Despite the railing, Andra always grew dizzy as she traversed the narrow space.

Her heart was fluttering, her head pounding by the time she reached the work'station. It was almost impractically large, with holo'screens reaching meters high and wide against the cavern wall. It was all hooked up to a physical metal hub: a bland rectangular box larger than Andra that stored the energy it would take to power the rocket. It was basically a really powerful, really complex battery. There was one just like it, only smaller, in the cathedzal to help power the 'dome, but this one held far more energy. Andra was careful never to touch it. The power of it could overwhelm her own nanos, destroying them or converting them faster than she could replenish them.

Andra took a deep breath as she sat at the translucent 'desk and brought up the 'display, filling the cavern with the glow of hundreds of holos. She filtered through the file of sims and notes she'd found and compiled from Griffin. She'd scoured these millions of times (two hundred and forty-three, to be exact; humans embellished, AI did not), but maybe today was the day she would find something useful.

"Do you need assistance?" Mechy asked.

"No." Andra waved him away, plugging the taxi' into the 'desk. "You can power down for a while. You probably need to recharge."

Mechy had spent the day reinforcing the palace foundation. Much of Eerensed was on shaky ground, with the network of tunnels and ruins running under the city, but the palace was by far the most precarious. It sat on a boulder that could easily fall straight on top of the Vaults if they weren't careful. Mechy had been shoring up the foundation for weeks, adding technological components that measured stability and sent nanos to reinforce areas of concern.

Mechy shrugged. A human gesture he'd picked up from Andra. "I wouldn't mind some rest." His voice inflected in the perfect mimicry of a human.

His eyes flashed, then went dark. Andra turned back to the work'station and played the first vid of Griffin as she transferred the data.

The LAC CEO was in a lab coat, her hair pulled back into a fishtail braid, showing off her silver crown. Her modded eye zeroed in on her notes, then on the camera, then back to her notes.

"The rockets act as a companion to the Ark," she was saying. "They will fly alongside it as support, necessary redundancies for a self-contained system. I've included detailed instructions in the accompanying file."

Andra had watched this so often, she could recite it by heart. The rocket the Schism had been building for Griffin had been in production well before Griffin had woken up. Skilla herself said that the Schism started long ago, if not before the colonists had gone into stasis, then right after. Andra had assumed that it had been some offshoot of LAC that was desperately trying to save a world destroyed by the corrupted tech of the pocket, and that Griffin had co-opted it to help her create a rocket to get the colonists off Earth.

But it turned out that Griffin had created plans for the rocket as part of her initial colonist program. She had always intended to use them, in addition to the Arcanum generation ship that would take the colonists to Holymyth. Which meant that when Griffin had awoken, she must have discovered that though the Ark was still in orbit, her rockets and shuttles had been destroyed by pockets, but were being re-created by the Schism.

That still didn't explain how Andra, Rashmi, and Griffin had been removed from the Icebox and what Griffin had planned to do once she'd woken to find herself on a destroyed future Earth.

Andra wished she could go back in time and ask Griffin what she had intended, why Andra had been created, what she should do now.

She watched the vid again. And again. It wasn't until the fifth time that she noticed the shape on the door in the background. If these sims had been recorded at HQ, the LAC double helix would have been rotating in front of the outline of Ohio. But it wasn't. It was in front of . . . some kind of . . . blob shape? Maybe a mountain? Whatever it was, it meant Griffin had recorded these somewhere else. Andra just didn't know where.

She shut down the work'station. Her head really was pounding. She felt weak and dizzy, and the room around her started to blur. The others were definitely right. She couldn't keep going on like this. She needed to rest. Take a bath. Eat a goddamn vegetable.

Something tickled her nose. She touched it, and her finger came away bloody. The ache in her head grew sharper.

It was like something was trying to get in, tapping at the edge of her consciousness. No, not tapping. Knocking. Pounding. Suddenly, it was taking all her willpower to keep it out, but maybe that was the problem.

Rashmi? she thought.

No answer.

Zhade?

He hadn't communicated with her via the Crown since that day in the throne room, but maybe this was an emergency.

She pushed harder. *Zhade, is that you?*

Something like white noise, a radio being tuned, grew in her skull. The pain sharpened. She fell to her knees, clutching her head, holding back a scream. She heard Mechy say her name.

Then everything quieted. All that was left was a voice.

Destroy.

Destroy.

DESTROY.

Andra tried to block it out, but it just got louder. It hissed and scraped and was somehow both a single voice and multitudes.

DESTROY DESTROY DESTROY DESTROY

The scream Andra had been holding back forced its way past her lips. She pulled herself up, fingers grasping at the work'station, and coughed. Black blood splattered the translucent surface. She expected an accompanying taste of copper, but none came.

"Andra?" Mechy asked.

She pushed him away. She needed space. She needed air. She had just vomited blood all over the rocket work'station, and though Andra didn't know much about medicine and anatomy, she knew vomiting blood was an emergency. Nanos swarmed around her, waiting for her command.

"Andra?" Mechy asked. "What do you need?"

The dizziness threatened to overtake her again, and she expected to feel the surge of med'bots rise inside her, but there was nothing.

Andra breathed hard, head hovering over the work'station, now stained with blood.

Dark and tarry and forming slick pools.

But no.

It wasn't blood.

Andra wiped some up with her finger, tinting the tip black. She felt a strange tingling sensation, almost as though her finger had gone numb. She looked closer.

Not blood.

Dead nanos.

It was the same as the lines of rot that had decorated the 'dome when it was dying. Except these had been inside of her.

Her pulse raced, and the air chilled. Something was rotting within her, destroying her from the inside out.

Her body was blood and bone and sinew, but the truest part of her—that part of her that gave her consciousness—was nothing more than the same nano'tech that swirled around her in the air, that composed the skin of the 'dome, that lived inside the pockets.

Something inside her was wrong, something ever since she took control of that pocket in the throne room. She'd known it, ignored it, and now she was coughing up dead nanos. How quickly would it spread?

She had things to do. A rocket to build, colonists to wake, Eerensedians to save. She had no clue how to do any of that, and now it seemed she was on a deadline.

Pain seared her head, but this time, the voice she heard was Mechy's.

"Andra? Are you okay?"

She looked up from where she was huddled on the floor of the rocket's cavern. Mechy crouched a few feet away from her, the position awkward with his many-jointed limbs.

"Yeah," she said. "Yeah, I'm fine."

"Your tone suggests you are lying, but I've noticed polite protocols demand I not press."

"Good call." Andra cradled her stomach as though she could hold herself together just a little longer.

"What can I do to help?" Mechy asked.

Andra didn't know. That was the problem. There was just *so much* she didn't know.

"You could help me up."

Mechy took her by the hand and under the elbow and gently lifted her to her feet. She groaned as she sat back in the work'station chair.

She couldn't keep guessing how to build the rocket or control the mini'pocket, couldn't keep just trying things and failing. If something was destroying her, she didn't have time for a series of trials and errors until she figured things out. She needed to know exactly what Griffin's plan had been, so she could enact it before time ran out.

But Griffin was dead. And the only person alive and awake who had known Griffin's plans was Rashmi, and those memories appeared to be gone for good.

Andra laid her head down on the cool glass of the desk, groaning when she realized the truth.

Rashmi wasn't the only person who had known Griffin.

Her son was currently sitting on the throne of Eerensed.

THREE

00110011

Andra stood at the bottom of the hover'lift, wringing her hands. The tunnel around her was dark, and there was the faint scent of mildew. She'd been hesitating long enough that the engine of her hover'cart had cooled.

There were so many reasons this was a bad idea. She could be seen. This might not work. He might not even show up.

She'd sent Mechy with a message to Zhade: meet her in the suite where they used to have goddess lessons. She could have called it Griffin's old rooms, or the suite that belonged to his mother, but she'd chosen to word it in a way that reminded him of when they used to get along. When it had been them against the world, learning how to survive and falling for each other in the background. Even if Zhade no longer wanted to be with her—and who could blame him, she was a robot, a *thing*—surely he'd still meet with her for old times' sake.

She forced herself to step onto the lift.

Back when Andra hadn't known who Zhade's mother was, he had mentioned that she was the one who taught him magic. He'd grown up with the Schism, watching them build the rocket. And he'd known—at least to some extent—how to open Andra's 'tank. Which had been made of the cryo'plating she needed for the rocket. Surely, he had some knowledge, some hint of his mother's plans. If not, together, Andra and Zhade could search through everything Griffin had left behind, mine Zhade's memories, and possibly discover how to save humanity.

No pressure.

Jolts of adrenaline rushed through Andra as the lift ascended. They hadn't been alone together since . . . Andra couldn't remember when.

The lift neared the top of the shaft, stopping just before flattening Andra against the rocks above. She reached up and pressed her thumb to a scanner, and the rock opened with a scrape into a bathroom. The lift ascended a few more feet, and she pulled herself out of the passage onto the floor.

At first it was pitch black, but then kinetic orbs lit the room around her. The bathroom was the size of Andra's entire living quarters in the Vaults, every surface and detail decorated in the coils meant to symbolize the First. The tile was a deep blue, the faucets and feet of the tub gilded in intricate designs. Andra stood and wiped off her pants, not necessarily because they were dirty but to rid herself of her nervous energy.

She left the bathroom and traveled down the short hall to Griffin's bedroom, the orbs flashing on as she passed. The door was slightly ajar. Andra took a deep breath. She could do this. She could interact with Zhade, and it wouldn't be weird, and she would be okay with the fact that he no longer wanted to be with her, that being a robot was a deal breaker for him. After all, she had been the one to instigate the distance.

She opened the door, breath still held, and walked into an empty room.

Her breath left her in a rush.

Not only was Zhade not there, but neither was the furniture or other detritus of a life lived, or goddess lessons taught. The dim space was filled only with the faint stench of mildew and dust. There were dark spots in the carpet where the bed and chairs had been. The walls were bare.

Andra felt oddly disappointed. She hadn't realized it, but she'd developed an emotional attachment to the room. The sofa where Wead would play the guitar-like instrument. The wardrobe Lilibet would rifle through. The rug she had danced on with Zhade. Now all of it was gone, and she couldn't help but feel hurt.

It was a weird response for an AI.

"Miss me?" said a voice behind her.

Andra whirled, and Zhade was standing in the doorway, arms crossed, leaning against the frame, like always. Unlike always, he wore both his brother's face and the Crown he'd used to control all the tech in the city. Andra was still thrown into shock every time she saw Zhade's expressions on Maret's face, the Crown tacked on his head. Something about it didn't feel right. Felt dangerous. The few times she'd brought it up, though, Zhade had blown off her concern. Then they'd stopped talking altogether.

Now the Crown was limned in blood, Zhade's—Maret's—eyes watery, dark circles underneath. Just like Maret had looked in the days before she'd removed the Crown and put him into stasis.

Zhade wore his own clothes, at least: khaki pants and a dark shirt with the top buttons unbuttoned. And, of course, his signature smirk.

Andra grimaced. This was going to be harder than she thought.

"Thanks for meeting me here." She twisted the 'band around her wrist.

"For certz," he said, smiling wider. It was that cocky grin he'd worn before she'd gotten to know him. Endearing. But not entirely genuine. "I couldn't let this opportunity fall."

He stepped toward her, reaching out for a handshake, the gesture he'd hated so much, but she stepped back. The skin around his eyes tightened, and he let his hand drop. He swallowed.

If Andra didn't know better, she'd think he was disappointed. But no, it was just wishful thinking. Fishes and wishes.

"Why did you want to see me?" he asked.

"I have a favor to ask you." Andra twisted her 'band so hard it snapped. She held it limply in her hand.

"A favor," Zhade repeated.

"Yeah . . . I, uh . . ." She put the 'band in her pocket. "I need to ask you about your mom."

Whatever Zhade had expected her to say, that wasn't it. He blinked and took a step back. His shoulders seemed to tense.

"What bout her?"

"Did she . . ." Andra swallowed. She should have planned this out. "Did she teach you anything about cryo'plating?"

"Cryo what now?"

"It's the . . . the stuff my 'tank . . . my grave was made out of."

Andra winced. She wasn't explaining herself well. She couldn't make eye contact. She was just. So. Awkward.

Zhade scratched the back of his head, his bleached hair falling into his face. The light in the room was turning golden as the sun set. Dust and nano'clouds danced in the air.

"She skooled me how to open the grave. Gave me a spell but didn't for true explain it. Why?"

"It's just . . ." Andra wished there were something—anything—in this room. Something she could stare at or play with or sit on. Instead, there was only Zhade, watching her, waiting for her explanation. Pretending like he cared. ". . . the rocket? Her notes say to use cryo'plating, but I don't have any, and I don't know what to replace it with, because *obviously* I can't use the cryo'plating in the Icebox, and—"

"You have notes from my mam?" Zhade's voice was small.

"Yeah."

"Oh."

Andra looked away. "I mean, they're not *to* me. They're just files I found. Recordings from . . . before . . . all this . . ."

Zhade was quiet for a moment before letting out a breathy laugh. "It's kiddings, marah? You imagine she had this purpose, this . . . plan for you to set out and accomplish, but she didn't leave you any clues to follow."

Andra frowned. "I don't *imagine* she had a purpose for me. I *know*. She programmed me."

"Firm," Zhade said, crossing his arms again. "Soze you say."

"*Soze* . . ." Andra breathed in through her nose. "She knew what my purpose was. She . . . *created* my purpose."

"Certz. But she's dead."

"Yeah, I know." Andra ran a hand through her hair. "But I was hoping . . . do you have anything of hers? Maybe some . . . magic she left behind or . . . do you remember anything she said? Like why she sent you to find me? She must have given you instructions."

Zhade shrugged. "Just to find you and . . . protect you."

"Anything else?"

"She was a bit busy trying not to be murdered."

Andra swallowed.

"Sorries," Zhade mumbled, scratching the back of his head. "It's mereish . . . she didn't tell me much, not even where to find you. She handed me that dagger and your necklace and fin was fin."

"Hmm." Andra had watched the memory Griffin had left her in the holocket over and over, and hadn't seen anything that would hint at her purpose. As for the dagger, it was just an update tool and had now served its purpose, and though it had briefly shown Andra hers, it hadn't moved that code into her conscious thought patterns, and she didn't know how to retrieve it. "What do you mean she didn't tell you where to find me? You said she was the one who hid me."

Zhade shrugged. "Who can reck why she did anything? She prob-ablish mereish wanted to make things diff for me. To make me figure it myself. Maybe that's what she purposed for you too. For you to figure it yourself."

"Maybe . . ." Andra conceded, but she wasn't convinced. Some-thing was off. Why wake Rashmi and not Andra? Why hide Andra at all? Andra hadn't been in danger while in the 'tank, especially since no one knew how to open it. And then why send Zhade to go get her without telling him where? Maybe she was just that sadistic, but Andra didn't think so. The Griffin she'd watched from afar, her mother's boss, had been anything but capricious. She had been effi-cient and intentional. There must have been a reason she hadn't told Zhade where Andra was.

The light was growing dimmer, the few rays of sunlight that made it through the boarded windows haloing Zhade's white-blond hair.

He uncrossed his arms, took a step toward Andra. "I can look for some of her old magic conduits. Maybe they'll have more clues bout the rocket. If I find some, can I bring them to you?" he added, almost shyly. "Bringing you conduits, mereish like before?"

Andra bit the inside of her cheek, remembering their deal: tech for goddess lessons. It was the deal that had initially bonded them, led to them dancing in this very room.

She should tell him no, to just send them through Kiv or Mechy. It was risky for him to the leave the palace too often. But the fact was she wanted him to visit. If he wouldn't do it to see her, she didn't mind if he had another reason.

She hesitated too long.

"No shakes," he said. "I'll send Kiv."

Andra shifted her weight from foot to foot. "Good. Good idea."

"Firm." Zhade ruffled the back of his hair. The Crown glinted in the light from the orbs. "I'll . . . see you . . . sometime."

Andra didn't stop him when he turned to leave, but she wanted to. She wanted to throw her arms around him and to cry from exhaustion and relief and let him make her laugh until her stomach hurt. But that was just the human part of her talking. The AI part knew she should let him go. There were certain things she could want but couldn't have because of what she was. It wasn't fair, but apparently human life wasn't either.

"Yeah," she whispered. "Sometime."

FOUR

THE ROGUE

ZHADE'S HEAD WAS throbbing.

He sat on the velvet sofa in the guv's suite, sipping on one of the many alcohols Maret had stashed. In between sips, he held the glass against his forehead, cooling the headache that hadn't subsided since that aftermoren.

Try as he might, Zhade couldn't shake the image of the angel choking the life out of Dzeni and the kiddun. He couldn't banish the powerlessness, the impotence he'd felt.

Zhade should have been the one to save the kiddun. He'd tried using the Crown for small things ever since—bringing up a scry he passed, sensing nearby angels—but all he had to show for his practice was a pain in his temple. He'd tried again in his quarters with an angelic guard. Nothing but a sharp ache. Then there'd been a moment with Andra when he'd considered trying to convo her through the Crown, like he'd done that day in the throne room. But Andra didn't want him in her life, much less her mind.

The angel's attack made it crystal to Zhade he couldn't ignore the Crown any longer. If he wanted to remain guv, to hold his people safe, he needed its power.

How could he have ever imagined this would all be so easy? He was a fraughted fool.

Once, in one of the meetings with Andra and the Schism, he'd suggested waking the gods and integrating them into Eerensedian society. Andra had called it "horrendously idiotic." Zhade didn't reck the words, but he figured they purposed "full bars stupid." He'd liked the way the words had sat on her tongue and wanted to hear her say them again, even if it purposed she was insulting him.

What he wouldn't give to have her insult him again, instead of the awkward discomfortistic way she convoed him this afternoon.

When he'd gotten her message that she wanted to meet—in the place where they'd had goddess lessons, no less—he'd started to hope that it was because she wanted to restart what had been growing tween them before he betrayed her and took his brother's face.

Fishes and wishes, marah?

He imagined the past moon of looking at her with this face, through these eyes. There had been two costs when he took Maret's place. The first was his face. The second was Andra's trust. As much as he missed looking like himself, he missed Andra more.

But she was right to be disgusted with him. He'd been playing guv, considering himself better than Maret, assuming the city was better off because of him. He imagined once he took his brother's face, his throne, everything would be so simple. But now he was facing an unnamed enemy, and the sole thing that could stop it was the Crown.

A knock jolted him out of his imaginings. Before he could answer, the door whooshed open and Tsurina strode in. Her brown hair was pinned up in an elaboristic do. Her gown was leaf green, her sleeves and its hem dragging the floor. Gryfud rushed in after her.

"The Grande Advisor is here to see you, Guv," he said, breathless.

It was full obvi Tsurina had strode past him without waiting to be let in.

"Thank you." Tsurina smiled through her teeth. "Gryfud, was it?"

Gryfud nodded, shooting Zhade an amused look. He'd been at the palace nearish a moon, assigned to guard Tsurina most of that time. She recked his name.

He bowed and winked at Zhade over Tsurina's shoulder, and left.

Zhade set down his glass. It was empty anyway.

"Hello, charling," she said, sweeping toward him.

"Mother," he greeted her, standing to get himself another drink, but she pulled him into a hug before he could.

He'd watched Maret do this routine enough that he recked how to play the dutiful son—at least Maret's version of it. When he pulled away, Tsurina brushed his cheek with her thumb, as though she were rubbing away a smudge of chocolate. Then her fingers trailed cross the Crown.

It was a dangerful game Zhade was playing. He'd spent close attention to Maret and Tsurina's interactions since returning apalace after his exile, but he'd never seen them in private. Soze he wasn't certz what Maret's response would have been in this situation. Should Zhade feign confidence? Should he show annoyance? He needed to act as Maret would, but he also needed to play this politic game with Tsurina. She needed to believe he was Maret full long for him to wrest power away from her.

"Evens, mam," he said, pulling away and heading toward Maret's liquor cabinet. "What reasons for the meeting?"

Tsurina frowned, mereish a wrinkle of her lips, a dart of her brows. "Do I need a reason to convo my son?"

Zhade held back a groan. He didn't have time for this. He had to figure what to do bout the Crown. Had to practice using it.

"You've been so distant latish," Tsurina said. "It feels likeish . . ." She placed a sharp-nailed finger to her lips, imagining. ". . . likeish you haven't been yourself."

Zhade's heart beat franticish as he tried to train his features into something bland and nonchalant. But neg, that was what *Zhade* would do. How would Maret respond to this accusation?

He pinched the bridge of his nose, giving himself time. "I'm mere-ish tired, mam," he said, adding a whine to his voice, going on the defensive as Maret would. "This turn has been long and diff."

Tsurina's face turned down into a pout. She slinked into a nearby chair, her fingernails caressing her cheek. "Oh, I reck, charling. And now, with the angel attacks . . . I believe they've gone rogue."

Zhade swallowed, hand trembling round the liquor bottle. "What? Angel attacks? How many?"

"Sands, who recks?" Tsurina waved a hand.

Soze, this moren hadn't been a flute. Someone was *doing* this. But who? He looked at Tsurina, who was carefulish watching him.

"No shakes, son, this is all evens. No one's *died*. The citians will complain, and you can make some vague promise to investigate, and fin will be fin." She leaned forward, looking up at Zhade over her long, clasped fingers. "You've had full bars to worry bout. After the gods' dome and the . . . *goddesses*." She spat the word.

Zhade didn't respond.

"You did the right thing, marah?" Tsurina said, voice steady and pointed. "Killing the goddesses. You reck what I've always said bout difficult decisions?"

Zhade had no clue what she always said, but he nodded anyway and unstoppered a clear bottle of some brown liquor.

Tsurina's fingers tapped against the armrest. "Did you love her?"

Zhade stiffened, freezing mid-pour. He had to shake himself to attention to hold from overflowing the glass. He turned to Tsurina.

Half a smile curled her lips. "You were full time so tenderhearted. I'm not surprised. But you have to reck your feelings for her weren't *real*. Have memory who you for true are."

Zhade stared at her. Did that purpose Maret had feelings for—had *loved*—Andra? Something hollow and panicky swelled low in Zhade's chest. He let out a bark of a laugh and hoped it didn't sound like a sob.

"Neg, mam. I didn't love her." He swallowed. Took a breath. "She was a means to an end. A bargaining chip."

Tsurina's smile turned angelic, and she canted her head. "That is an odd phrase. Where did you hear it?"

"I don't have memory," he lied quickish. "Her death placated the people. Fixed the gods' dome. Freed us to rule."

Lies upon lies upon lies. He hated it. Lying. Pretending to be someone else. But he would do whatever it took to remain guv. To skool how to use the Crown. To protect his city from rogue angels and worse.

He smiled at Tsurina. "I'm glad the Goddess is dead."

"I'm so glad to hear it," Tsurina said, a wicked grin spreading across her lips. "Zhade."

FIVE

THE DIVINE

ZHADE'S HEART WAS pounding, his palms sweating as he looked into Tsurina's smug face. He swallowed and forced his voice to come out steadyish.

"What do you convo? Why did you call me that?"

Tsurina stood. Zhade's muscles tensed.

"Did you imagine I wouldn't reck you?" she asked. "You may have Maret's face, and you may do a decent imitation of his voice, but you're much too arrogant to pass as my son."

Zhade edged along Maret's liquor cabinet, scanning the room for some type of weapon.

"Too stubborn. Too optimistic. Too ruthless." She stalked toward him.

He could smash one of the glasses.

"How did you do it?" she asked. "Take his face? What magic is this?"

There was a gun on the wall next to him.

"I'm assuming my son is dead."

Why didn't he wear a sword?

"What confuses me is why you killed that goddess of yours."

Zhade tried not to let the relief on his face show. At least she didn't realize Andra was alive.

"I was certz you were in love with her," she continued.

51

Zhade felt on the cabinet behind him and wrapped his hand round the nearest bottle.

"Did becoming guv import to you so much that you were willing to sacrifice her in that endeavor?"

Zhade swallowed and tightened his grip on the bottle as she approached. "She was a means to an end."

Tsurina's smile almost appeared genuine. "There. That ruthlessness. That's how I recked you weren't Maret. Seeya, if you want to be guv so badish, I won't stop you."

Zhade relaxed mereish a tick.

"As a fact, I could use someone for true so ruthless as to murder the girl he loved for something as petty as power."

She was now an arm's length away from him.

"Power is dull, and too easyish lost, as you will soon discover. What I want, no one can—"

Zhade smashed the bottle against the cabinet and swiped it across Tsurina's face. She screamed, flinching back and bringing her hand to her cheek. Zhade took sole a moment to see streaks of blood begin to darken her skin before turning and grabbing the gun off the wall.

He didn't take the time to imagine if this was a good idea, to consider the consequences for murdering Tsurina, to weigh his options. He simplish turned, aimed, and pulled the trigger.

Nothing happened.

He pulled the trigger again and flinched at a faint static in his brain.

Tsurina straightened, pulling her hand from her face. The northhand side was streaked with blood. It dripped down her gown, from the tip of her sleeve. When she grinned, it limned her lips.

"You fool," she sneered. "Just because you wear the Crown doesn't purpose you reck how to use it."

Zhade scrambled back, circling the room til he found another weapon. This one was a lightning dagger. Even if the magic inside it didn't work for him, he could still stab with it.

He flipped the lever on the side to ignite it, but nothing happened.

Tsurina laughed hollowish, approaching him as blood still pulsed from her wounds.

"Maret was useless in many ways, but at the least he could sorcer his weapons."

Zhade tried again to access the Crown, feel its connection to the weapons round the room, but all he achieved was a headache.

Tsurina moved closer. What was she going to do? She had no weapon, except for her dangerfulish pointed nails. She wasn't calling for help. She was losing blood. For true, Zhade should be winning this fight, but Tsurina was grinning like a kat who'd caught a skirl, and that scared Zhade more than anything.

This was who Maret had skooled to be dangerful from.

Zhade reached out to the dagger again. This time he felt a spark, but it was sole in his mind. Tsurina loomed above him, larger than life. Zhade poised himself for a fight. Tsurina raised her hand, as Maret used to when he wanted to show off that he was casting a spell. Zhade tensed.

The hilt of a sword came down on the back of her head. Tsurina fell to the ground. Behind her, pale eyes gleaming—

—was Meta.

Zhade stared at her, stunned, and, for a moment, all she did was stare back, her spiked brown hair falling into her face, sweat glistening on her brow.

In a single swift motion, Meta flipped the sword in her hand and brought the blade up under Zhade's chin.

He froze. "Evens, I was going to say thank you, but . . ."

Meta's lip curled. "Who are you?" she demanded.

"Um, Maret?"

The edge of the sword bit into Zhade's skin, strikingish close to where Maret had held him at sword point last moon. He felt the first cut of flesh.

"His brother," Zhade confessed, voice strained.

"Maret doesn't have a brother," Meta sneered, muscles tensing to strike.

"Neg, for true! I was a shameful secret. We're half-brothers."

Meta didn't back down. "Then why do you have his face? Is that for true his Crown?"

Zhade swallowed.

"*Is it?*"

"Firm, firm!" There was a pinch of pain at his throat, and Zhade was on his toptoes to get away from it. "But it's because . . . Maret's in hiding. I took his face and Crown because . . . I'm a decoy. Someone was trying to assassinate him."

Zhade had full time been good at coming up with lies on the spot, but even he was proud of this one.

But Meta didn't look convinced. "Why didn't he tell me, tell his guards?"

"He didn't tell anyone. Not even Tsurina." Zhade recked his lie would fall apart if Meta had heard any of the previous convo. "Please, I'm doing this to save Maret."

Something in his voice must have convinced her—maybe the fear he didn't have to fake—because she lowered her sword. Zhade rubbed his throat. Sole a trickle of blood, but the skin felt raw.

"I'm Zhade, beedub."

Meta's eyes widened. "Zhade?"

Oh, fraughts. If she recked the name from the time he was the Third's guard, he was in trouble. He tensed, prepped to fight, but Meta sheathed her sword.

"I . . . I've heard so much bout you. I mereish didn't realize . . ." She frowned. ". . . you were his brother."

Zhade took a step back. Maret had mentioned him? To the guards?

"Hear, whatever he told you . . . Maret and I didn't have the best relationship . . ."

Meta stared at him for a moment, and Zhade prepped himself to run. She mereish shrugged. "Fams are diff." She shook her head. "How'd you take his face, beedub? Some magic."

"Some magic," Zhade agreed. "Hear, we can convo bout this later. Soon and now, we need to decide what to do with . . ." He nodded at Tsurina's unconscious body.

A dark grin spread across Meta's face. "We kill her."

Zhade scrunched his nose. "Uhhhh, but should we kill her though?"

Meta pointed a stiff finger at Tsurina's prone form. "She made Maret's life a living pocket, and I heard from her own lips she wanted to destroy Eerensed. My duty is to guv and city, and she threatens both." She kicked Tsurina's body onto her back. The Grande Advisor's face was smeared with dried blood. "I reck you've found your mysteriful assassin."

Zhade crossed his arms and leaned against the sofa. "Seeya, on the norm, I'd agree with you, but you have to reck most of the guards are loyal to her. And the army. And the citians. If we want Eerensed to survive, we can't kill her."

Meta's eyes narrowed. "If we want Eerensed to survive, we can't hold her alive."

She unsheathed her sword, but Zhade stepped afront of her. It wasn't a conscious decision, and he couldn't believe he was doing it. Was he for true putting himself in harm's way to protect Tsurina?

Meta sighed, lowering her blade. "Then we need a third choice."

"There isn't one."

Zhade was struck again by the dilemma he'd faced since becoming guv: he couldn't rule Eerensed how he wanted with Tsurina. He couldn't rule it at all without her.

"If there isn't a third choice," Meta said, tilting her head, "then maybe we make one."

Zhade groaned. "I don't reck you full well, but I'm guessing this is marching toward badness."

Meta flashed her teeth. "I'll take her face."

Zhade barked a laugh but stopped when Meta didn't join him. "Oh, for serious?"

Meta started pacing, stepping over Tsurina's prone body. "Mereish like you took Maret's face. I'll take Tsurina's. That will give us full bars time to find the assassin."

"You can't take someone's face."

"Why not? You did."

"Firm, but it's . . ." He didn't have words to describe the pain. ". . . permanent. Sides, it takes a lot of magic, and I don't reck how long I'll need to create the spell."

"Evens, you have bout a day before people start to wonder where she is." Meta bent over and looped her arms under Tsurina's. "Now, where am I dragging this body?"

Zhade groaned and grabbed Tsurina's feet. "I haven't agreed to this."

Meta mereish smirked.

IN THE END, they put Tsurina in Andra's old room. It was a diff trek as there were no secret passages to the Third's suite at the top of the westhand tower. Zhade had briefish considered taking Tsurina to the First's—it was blocked off and out of the main marchway—but it was too close to the hidden passage to the Vaults. Zhade didn't reck if he could trust Meta, so he was for certz not letting her get that close to where Andra was staying.

Soze, they had to sneak through the palace with their prisoner. Zhade had Gryfud distract the guards stationed along their route, and they'd had to gag and bind Tsurina, who had finalish woken. She didn't fight the full march there, which bothered Zhade. Perhaps she was going mad, or perhaps she was exactish where she wanted to be.

It didn't meteor. They had no choice. They couldn't kill her, but they couldn't leave her free to reveal Zhade's secret to the city. As much as the Eerensedians hated Maret, they wouldn't follow Zhade—a bastard prince, the son of the First, and all-round disaster human.

Once they got Tsurina to the suite, it was then a meteor of making certz she couldn't escape. Zhade sorcered Fishy—his mam's favorite angel—to secure the room. It stood long and lanky, skin the color of paper. Its skullcap was clear, revealing the sparking magic inside, and its face lit up in various expressions. It was anow drawn in concentration as it set up the magic shield on the balcony. Tsurina watched, hands bound, from Andra's bed, where she lounged almost like she was at a spa.

"I'm so disappointed in you, Zhade," she said. "Your sorcery is so . . . limited. Maret could have used the Crown to do all that magic with a mere thought. You've wasted half a bell of your time and mine."

"Am I going to make you late for something?" Zhade snapped.

Tsurina stretched, the sheet rustling neath her. "And you, Meta. You were always so attached to Maret. I'm not surprised you betrayed me. Though I am surprised you betrayed me to help Maret's murderer."

Zhade froze in his final bit of spellwork.

"Maret isn't dead," Meta growled.

Tsurina's laugh was a purr. "For certz he is, kiddun."

Meta didn't respond, and Zhade wasn't certz if she for true didn't believe Tsurina, or if she simplish didn't want to. Zhade had skooled there were things you believed and things you believed you believed, and they weren't always the same.

Fishes and wishes.

Tsurina opened her mouth again, but Zhade cut her off before she could reveal too much.

"Meta, will you convo the guards that the Grande Advisor is . . .

indisposed for the even." He cleared his throat, focusing back on his spellwork. "I'll meet you back at the guv's suite in a few bells so we can . . . create the spell we discussed."

Meta looked back and forth between Tsurina and Zhade. "Will you be evens?"

Zhade was surprised to see concern in her eyes. He shrugged and gave her his signature grin. "I'm always evens."

Meta rolled her eyes and left, muttering something bout mistakes and spoons.

And she was right. This may all be a mistake. Bad magic. Zhade didn't reck what would have been better. Nothing seemed like a good choice, and anow Zhade needed to re-create the spell that had given him his brother's face, interrogate Tsurina bout the Crown, and find the info Andra wanted bout his mam. All while holding Eerensed safe from any more rogue angels.

Zhade sighed and went back to work.

Tsurina examined her deep red nails, the same color as the blood dried cross her face. "Soze, do you plan on feeding me, or am I to starve to death?"

Zhade blinked. He hadn't even imagined bout the things Tsurina would need to stay alive. He was terrible at holding prisoners.

"Answer some of my questions, and then we can convo your physical needs."

Tsurina raised an eyebrow. "All of them?"

It was something Zhade would have said in her situation, but coming from Tsurina, it made him blush. She noticed, laughing to herself.

"Zhade, you were a fool to imagine you could pass for my son."

He took a moment to collect himself, sitting in the chair he used to inhabit when this was Andra's room. He tossed both legs over one of the arms.

"Because I'm not a heartless brat of a boy-king who relies on a Crown to do magic?"

It was a clumsy attempt to figure more bout the Crown, but everything bout the day had been clumsy.

"Neg. You're a heartless brat of a boy-king who *refuses* to use the Crown to do magic." Tsurina held up her hand, bound with rope, not magic cuffs. "Is that your excuse? You do Low Magic because High Magic is too easy? Or are you having trouble with it? Do you want my help?"

Zhade kept his face—his brother's face—placid. That was exactish what he wanted, but he couldn't let her reck that.

"Why would I want to use something that was so obvi killing Maret?"

Tsurina seemed surprised. "Killing him?"

"Don't play fraughted. The bruises were obvi. He was losing weight, his hair was thinning." He gestured to the Crown at his temple. "When I took this from him, it was coated in dried blood."

"So unhygienic." Tsurina tutted. She stood and sauntered over to the wardrobe and started filtering through Andra's clothes. "Too short, too fat," she muttered, tossing a few to the ground. She was surprisingish graceful with bound hands. "Neg, it wasn't killing him, you fool. He was trying to remove it."

Zhade's eyebrows shot up. "What? Why?"

"Sands if I reck." Tsurina pulled out another of Andra's dresses and held it up to her, gazing at herself in the mirror.

"Put that down," Zhade snapped.

She shrugged, and then lowered herself onto Andra's chaise. "Maybe he was finalish seeing things my way. That magic is evil and needs to be destroyed."

"Why do you want to destroy magic?"

"Because it's unnatural," Tsurina snapped, the first bit of emotion showing through her calm exterior. "It came from the *goddesses*."

Zhade sat forward. "But your fam had a full cave of angels. My father married you for your access to magic."

Tsurina looked away. "Sometimes, the sole way to fight something is to use it."

"Is that why you let Maret use the Crown?"

She pouted. "I didn't *let* Maret do anything. As a fact, I helped him. When he first donned the Crown, he was full time fighting *against* it, instead of letting it do the work for him. I told him not to try so hard, to let the Crown guide him, til finalish all he had to do was wish for something, and the Crown would make it so."

Zhade rolled his eyes. He'd been *wishing* for weeks, and nothing was happening. He'd wished to control the angels, to feel the stardust round him, to talk to Andra. He'd for certz wished to protect Dzeni and the kiddun from the rogue angel.

He sighed. Time for a new line of questioning. He narrowed his eyes, steepling his hands. "Tell me bout my mam."

In truth, Zhade didn't want to hear Tsurina convo bout his mother. But he'd promised Andra he would find more info bout her. Few people had recked the First like Tsurina had.

Her face soured. "What do you want to reck bout that goddess bitch?"

Zhade took a slow breath, briefish closing his eyes. "Why did you hate her so much?"

"She stole my husband. Isn't that full bars?"

Zhade scoffed. "You never cared bout my father. Is it because the citians loved her more as a goddess than you as the guv's wife?"

Tsurina turned away. "Scuze. I could never be so petty."

"Then why?"

"Because." Tsurina clucked her tongue. "She's a *goddess*."

"Soze?"

"Soze, she came from a people who planned to escape Earth and leave the rest of us dying."

Zhade felt as though the breath had been knocked from him. Tsurina recked the truth? Had she been aware what his mam was all along? Had she recked his mother better than he had?

"The full planet is destroyed because of them," she continued. Her cheeks grew red and a scowl stained her charred face. "They chose who lived and who died, and our ancestors were deemed unworthy. And she! . . . She's the worst of them."

"You recked?" Zhade asked.

Tsurina's gaze snapped back to him. "For certz I recked. The knowledge has been passed down in my fam from parent to kiddun for centuries. All this magic . . . it was never more than a way to hold control over those they saw as weak, those they saw as lesser. Those who scared them. They destroyed the planet and then planned to leave it and let us all die. *She* did this. Your mam. And she held doing it. Whatever she woke for, it wasn't to save us. If it had been, she would have passed more time in Eerensed, instead of traipsing off to that city in the north."

Zhade nearish fell out of his chair. He had memory of his mother's frequent peacings, but he'd never recked where she'd gone. *I have something to take care of*, she'd say when he asked. He'd imagined she'd been traveling to different villages all over the Wastes, not visiting a single city each time.

"What city?"

"I don't reck," Tsurina said, a bit of vulnerability slipping into her voice for the firstish time. "I sent guards to look, but they never found it. Or if they did, they didn't return. I sole reck that it was several days' journey northhandwest of here."

Zhade wanted to ask more questions, but Tsurina held talking, her eyes glazed over as she stared out the balcony.

"Whatever she was doing there, she never planned on saving us, seeya. It was sole bout her. And the other goddesses were the same. The Second and that little bitch you were in love with."

Zhade tensed, poised to attack, but there was a knock at the door— three light taps and one loud one.

He nodded at Fishy to open it. Kiv stood on the other side, an arsenal of weapons strapped to him. He glared at Zhade over his hawkish nose and entered the room, before his dark eyes landed on Tsurina.

Zhade stood. "Thanks for coming."

He'd had to sorcer an angel to retrieve Kiv from belowground, something that was risky, but he needed someone to guard Tsurina, and his options were limited. He stood and crossed the room soze Kiv could read his lips.

"I have bad feelings bout this," Kiv signed.

"All will happen evens," Zhade said aloud, and he wasn't certz if he believed it.

There were things you believed, and things you believed you believed.

"Are you certz it wouldn't be better if Tsurina was dead?" Kiv asked. The sign they'd invented for Tsurina was a rude gesture no Eerensedian would use in polite company.

Zhade didn't reck. Maybe it would be better to mereish kill her. If he could transform Meta into Tsurina, there was no reason to hold her alive. Sole, something didn't feel right bout executing her. It wasn't . . . morality. If Zhade had any of that he wouldn't have tried to kill his own brother. It was something else. Every time Zhade imagined it, he got sick to his stomach.

Zhade handed Kiv a speak-easy so he could contact him if there was any trouble.

"Sorries, boyo," he signed, but Kiv wasn't watching. He sole stared at Tsurina.

The woman had threatened Kiv's fam in order to hold him aline. She'd made him do terrible things, torture and murder. He was finalish free, though his fam was nowhere to be found, and now Zhade had forced him to be in her presence once again.

"Hello, Kiv." The Grande Advisor grinned. "Oh, this is going to be fun."

SIX

THE CI-DEVANT

ZHADE'S PALMS SWEATED as he forced himself down the tunnel toward the Vaults. White lights blinded him. His footsteps tapped against the hard tile floor. He rubbed his palms against his pants. It wasn't that he didn't want to see Andra. As a fact, he should have been working on the spell to change Meta's face and sent Kiv or Fishy with the message instead.

He spent his days round people who had no reckoning who he was, who treated him like he was Maret. And now Tsurina recked his secret and he had to change Meta into her and he needed to skool to use the Crown. He felt like he was juggling hot coals. One slip and everything would burn down round him. He mereish wanted to hear Andra's voice. She was so smart. She'd help him focus.

Each time he visited her, Zhade convinced himself the next time would be different. That she would have memory what she liked bout him. That things tween them would be like they'd been before.

Sole, it never was.

Still, he entered the Vaults with hope.

He went through the first airlock. Zhade had done this a dozen times now, but it still gave him a shock. The door whooshed shut behind him. The toxins were sucked free from the air through some magic Zhade didn't comp. The sole evidence of the process was a high-pitched whine. It took a handful of ticks, but Zhade spent the full time tense. There was a beep and a second glass door whooshed open and he entered the lobby.

It was like walking into another world.

The ceiling was higher than the cathedzal's, the walls a dusky blue. Iron beams ran floor to ceiling, staircase to wall, in formations Zhade couldn't comp. Andra called it art. A giant clock hung from the ceiling, larger than the time chimes and more complex. Circles inside circles inside circles. It ticked away as Zhade entered a hallway to the southhand side.

He hadn't had the bells to look at all the magic down here. He didn't reck what most of it did. The first hall was lined with rooms with small boxes and screens. They all looked the same to him, but apparentish each did something different. In this part of the Vaults, the walls were clear, the magic on display. Deeper in the building, the walls became opaque. Zhade had wandered into a few rooms, but little was left. Andra was using most of the magic for some purpose or another.

Lights bathed everything in a bright white glow, as he traversed a series of hallways, and finalish ended at Andra's door. Zhade swallowed, straightening his cloak. He patted down his hair, then wiped away a smudge of blood at his temple. He knocked.

The door slid open immediatish, revealing the room beyond.

Discarded magic organized into mounds littered the room. Shelves were stacked with what Andra called pre-books and the scrying boards she called computers. Andra's cot stood on the far side of the room, and the table next to it held a vase with the starflowers he'd asked Lilibet to put there. They were wilting.

There was an oval table in the center of the room, and at the far end sat Andra, a magic orb hanging over her head, drenching her in light. Zhade froze.

There were bags under her eyes and her skin was sallow. Her hair had grown long enough to pull into a small knot atop her head. She was hunched over a scrying board, muscles tense. He had the impulse to go to her, wrap his arms round her, and whisper to her that it was time to take a break. Get her some food. Maybe hold her while she slept.

But she wouldn't want that.

She looked up and blinked. For a tick, Zhade imagined he saw some kind of emotion in her features, but whatever it was vanished quickish, replaced by cool detachment.

He cleared his throat. "Hiya, Goddess."

"Hey." She swallowed, and they sank into awkward silence.

He sat in a nearish chair. He fidgeted, trying to get comfortistic, but the combination of Maret's form-fitting clothes and the hard chair made it impossible.

"I found some info bout my mam," he said.

Andra blinked. "Already? What did you find?" She absentish scooted her chair nearer to his.

Zhade cleared his throat. He could feel the warmth of Andra's arm next to his. "There's a city northhandwest of here where my mam apparentish spent time and a half. People saw her peace in that direction, but no one could ever find where she was going, soze there could be some of her old stuff still there."

Andra's dark eyes shone. "How did you find out? Did she leave something behind? Do you have a map?"

Zhade opened his mouth but hesitated. He didn't reck why he didn't want to tell Andra bout Tsurina. Maybe he was embarrassed by how much she scared him, that she could have overpowered him so easyish if Meta hadn't shown up. Maybe he didn't want to tell Andra bout Meta. That for the first time since becoming guv, there was someone aside him. Not angry at him for getting Lew

66

killed, like Dzeni. Not disappearing to who recked where, like Doon. Not focused on some ship to the stars and frozen gods, like Andra. Not avoiding him because he wore a murderer's face . . .

For whatever reason, he lied.

"I mereish asked round."

Andra didn't seem to notice the flat tone of his voice, his tense expression. She was tapping furiousish into the scrying board, casting some kind of spell that brought up a map of the Wastes. Then she brought up another map, this one with lines and large splotches of blue, and laid it on top.

"Northwest, you said?"

Zhade nodded.

She ran her finger across the map and landed on a blue blob.

"It's Lake Superior," she breathed. Her face glowed in the light of the map.

"It's what?"

"I was looking over some old recordings of your mam, and I noticed something in the background."

Another spell and there was Zhade's mam, standing before him on the table. He sucked in a breath. She looked different than he'd ever seen her, hair closer to his golden color, a magic eye, silver running neath her hair.

"That's why it's important for all colonists to be asleep before their trip to the Ark—"

"There!" Andra said, interrupting her. Zhade's mam froze, her hands clasped, eyes boring into his.

"What?" Zhade asked.

Andra pointed to a door half opened behind his mam. He dragged his eyes from her face to look at what Andra was pointing at. A plate on the door in the shape of a ragged mountain behind a rotating scry of his mother's symbol. He shook his head, not comping.

"Every LAC facility has its location on its door holo'plates. I couldn't figure out what this one was, but see?"

With a flick of her wrist, Andra brought the shape closer to them, removing the image from the scry of his mam and placing it over a blue blob on the map with the exact same shape.

"What is it?" Zhade had never seen anything like it before.

"A lake." Andra traced her finger over its edges.

He'd been distracted by his mam's sudden appearance, but now he couldn't take his eyes off Andra. The intensity in her gaze almost scared him.

"What's a lake?"

She blinked as though she was suddenish brought back to herself. "A large body of water."

Zhade sat forward, hand threading through his hair. "That full thing was filled with water? Like an ocean?"

Fishes and wishes.

"Neg. I mean, yes, it was completely filled with water, but oceans are much, *much* bigger."

Zhade shook his head. He believed Andra, but he had trouble imagining anything bigger than the lake afront of them. Sands, he couldn't even imagine that.

"This," Andra said, "was one of the largest lakes in the world. *The* largest if you're talking about fresh water and surface area."

"Soze what does it meteor?"

Andra bit her lip, and when she looked up at Zhade there was a tinge of a smile. "I think this was where your mother was going. To a lab in the lake."

"In the lake," Zhade echoed.

Andra nodded, her eyes roving hungryish over the map. "It wasn't unheard of, especialish when you were working with dangerous science, to have labs in bodies of water, far away from civilization. LAC had a few in Salt Lake, the Caspian Sea, Lake Victoria. But Canada outlawed underwater labs after what happened to the Great Bear Lake. There shouldn't be anything in the Great Lakes, but if there is . . ." She huffed out a laugh and sat back. "I've scoured every bit of data I could, and couldn't find anything bout another LAC location on this side of the continent, but now . . ."

She was full smiling now, and despite her earlier haggard appearance, she looked radiant. Sands, he wanted to kiss her. A burst of adrenaline tore through Zhade's gut, followed by nausea.

"I'm going with you," he said. "I want to see this place my mam visited."

Andra furrowed her eyebrows. "But . . . you have a city to govern."

Zhade felt the wind rush out of his sandcloud. That was true. He couldn't just wander off into the Wastes anymore. He considered briefish putting Meta in charge as Tsurina. Once he changed her face, she could say that Maret was sick and she was ruling in his place for time and a half. But that would purpose trusting Meta, which he didn't.

It would also purpose that everything he'd done, everything he'd sacrificed—his face, his relationship with Andra—was for nothing. He'd decided his fate.

Sides, even if Andra *let* him go with her to see where his mam used to peace to, she probablish wouldn't *want* him there. A full trip through the Wastes that would take who recked how long, next to the face of the boy who tried to kill her.

But he didn't like the idea of her going alone.

"You should take someone with you then. That's a bit of desert you have to cross. And the pockets . . ."

He trailed off, because Andra could control the pockets. He didn't like to imagine bout it. He had memory of the look in her eyes, the light shining out of them in a way that wasn't full true human. For a moment, he'd felt like he'd lost her, that she'd been consumed. She'd come back to herself, but not before Zhade started to worry. Andra was powerful for certz, but this was full bad magic she was dealing with. If she went out in the Wastes, would she come back as herself?

Andra was watching Zhade with an uncipheristic expression. "I'll be evens," she said. "Sides, I could probably just send a drone instead. There are plen—"

She broke off into a coughing fit. Zhade reached out but stopped short of touching her. It was a wet, hacking cough, and Zhade wondered if she'd been sick when he'd seen her yesterday, how he hadn't guessed, who was taking care of her.

Her coughing stopped and she took in one more breath before sitting back. The hand she'd covered her mouth with was covered in a dark, tarry substance.

His stomach plummeted. "How long have you been coughing blood?"

Andra shook her head, quickish wiping her hand on a nearish towel. It was already covered in dark stains.

"It's evens," she said, giving him a tight smile. "Just, you know, a case of strep from all this damp air."

Zhade wasn't convinced. He'd spent full bars time with Tia Ludmila and recked coughing blood was bad magic.

"Really," Andra said. "I've got history's best medicine down here. All I need is some rest and fresh air."

Zhade frowned. "You're not going to get any fresh air down here."

"There's a synth'plant room somewhere in the Vaults. It'll do the trick." She stood, turning her back to Zhade and throwing the bloody towel into a basket. "Don't worry, I won't go up to the surface for fresh air and cause a panic, if that's what you're worried about."

That's not what I have shakes bout, Zhade wanted to say, but he could already tell she wanted him to peace.

"Do you need anything?" he asked, though he recked the answer.

"Neg. But thank you for bringing me the info about your mam."

Zhade nodded, but he was already starting to regret it. What if she left while she was still sick? What if the danger wasn't that she'd come back changed, but that she wouldn't come back at all?

"You'll send a drone?" he asked.

She nodded. "For certz. No reason for me to go out into the Wastes if I don't have to."

She turned to Zhade and smiled, but it didn't quite reach her eyes.

SEVEN

OOIIOIII

SHE DIDN'T SEND a 'drone.

But she did take Mechy with her.

She'd left a note for the others, and together, she and Mechy had hopped in a hover parked just outside the city walls and taken off toward the horizon.

It was deathly hot, and the open carriage of the hover provided no shelter from the wind. Andra pulled her sweater closer to protect her from the sand, draping the hood over her head and around her mouth. Something like purpose welled up inside her as she watched the horizon.

Another bout of coughing interrupted her thoughts, and dead nanos splattered onto her palm. She wiped them away.

She didn't know how serious it was—an AI hacking up dead nanos—but she felt like she was running out of time. Time she needed to figure out what Griffin wanted her to do, where she would get cryo'plating for the rocket, and how to save humanity. Whatever she found at Lake Superior, she hoped it would give her answers.

She drove and drove, following a green eco'grafted line—one that Griffin must have put into the terrain—as the endless expanse of desert stretched out around her. The sand glittered in the sun, and the eco'graft stretched in the distance to the north. North*ish*. In a northerly direction.

For an AI, Andra was shit at cardinal directions.

Destroy.

The thought came from inside of her, and Andra jerked.

"Is everything okay?" Mechy asked.

"Yeah," Andra said, but something inside her froze.

It was the same voice she'd heard in the rocket's cavern. It spoke with her voice, resonated with her consciousness. It brought with it the urge she'd felt the day she fought against Maret, when she'd converted all the nanos in the throne room to the same corrupted tech as the pockets. She thought back to that day—the power that had surged through her, the desire to assimilate more and more until there was nothing left but her in the universe.

An echo of it remained, some residual energy humming in her veins.

And it was speaking to her.

She coughed up another splatter of nanos.

Destroy, the voice, Andra's voice whispered. *Destroy*.

SHE'D BEEN DRIVING for almost six hours when she found the remains of Chicago. Unlike the other ruins she'd passed, Chicago was recognizable. Andra could guess the trajectory of what had been the skyline from the collapsed skyscrapers. The outline of the ghostly steel structures was stark against the horizon. The destroyed city was surrounded by flat, barren land, nothing around it for miles. There were no suburbs, no Lake Michigan. Time had destroyed them both.

Andra had been living through Earth's future for the past two months. She'd had proof that billions had died, that something terrible had happened. But seeing it from this angle . . .

She thought of the series of events that led to this. The pockets ravaging the world. Society collapsing. Families taking refuge in emptied buildings or trekking out across the earth to find somewhere safe, as the population thinned, until there was no one left to maintain the buildings. Until time and weather eroded them into a scrap pile of metal.

She asked Mechy to stop the hover, then threw up over the edge.

ANDRA KEPT DRIVING along the banks of what had been Lake Michigan. At least, she guessed they were the banks based on the structure of the desert floor. If she was lucky, she could make it to wherever she was going by the end of the day and back by the next morning.

If she didn't run into a pocket.

If she didn't have trouble finding the lab.

If the lab actually existed.

If

If

If

Mechy shut down to conserve power, and Andra was left with nothing but her thoughts to keep her company. Her lips grew chapped, and her throat sore from coughing up nanos. She realized just as the sun started its arc toward the horizon that she hadn't eaten all day.

She found an apple-like fruit in Mechy's pack and, assuming it was for her since he was a robot, ate it. She continued on, watching the shadows get longer and the air grow colder.

Then suddenly, Andra saw the eco'grafted line come to a stop in the distance, and beyond: water.

Her breath caught.

There was water.

Water. In the middle of the Wastes. Not part of some bio'dome or some muddy roadside puddle. But an actual lake.

Andra leaned over the front of the hover to get a better look.

She didn't know how far she was into Lake Superior–that-had-been, but she was about three miles out from Lake Superior–that-was-now. She revved the engine and sent the hover flying across the desert, now pockmarked with grass, scraggly trees, even a flower here and there. But Andra was solely focused on the water as it grew closer, until it swallowed the horizon, stretching past where her eyes could see, widening until it filled her entire field of vision.

When she reached the lake's edge, she slammed the brakes and jumped out of the hover, running to the bank, splashing into the shallows, letting the water soak her shins, her thighs, her stomach, not stopping until it reached her shoulders, and then dunking her head so it enveloped her. The water was warm and heavy against her skin, dragging her down. She opened her eyes and, for a moment, hung suspended in the murky shallows. Sand rose up around her feet, dispersing like a nano'cloud. She let herself feel still and calm and filled with hope. Water was life, and if there were still lakes in the world, there were still oceans. The planet wasn't lost.

She gasped as she broke the surface, then pushed her wet hair out of her face as rivulets of water streamed down her cheeks. She cupped her hands and brought a huge gulp to her lips. She drank, and drank, and drank, laughing all the while. She buoyed her body to the surface, lying back, and let herself float. The sky was dotted with clouds, limned by the rays of the setting sun.

Zhade would love this, she thought. She closed her eyes and breathed deeply.

ANDRA STAYED IN the water until the sun had fully set, then trudged her way back to land. She'd almost been able to forget why she'd come. To find the LAC lab.

Lake Superior was huge, and the lab hadn't been in any records

75

Andra could find. But the eco'grafted road had led her in this direction, so it must be close.

Andra closed her eyes. She could feel nanos tickling her skin, sense them as they communicated with her own. Beyond the nanos, she felt the hover behind her and Mechy's still form. If she stretched her senses, she felt more nanos. Not as many as there were in the Vaults, but enough that Andra could interface with and command them to sense for nearby tech.

Andra reached out farther, into the Wastes, across the lake and down into it. Part of her felt blind. There was nothing under the waves for her nanos to connect with. Just water and fish and algae to bump against. It was a hollow, lonely feeling. She kept pushing, but panic was rising inside her. Her thoughts, her being, her consciousness was made up of nanos, and she was sending those nanos—those little pieces of herself—physically away from her. Now, as the smallest parts of her spread throughout the lake, she was stretched too thin. Her senses were gone. All she felt was despair and loneliness, and a belief she would never be whole again.

Until

Until

There it was. Something at the edge of her consciousness. Something north? No, northwest. It was big. She didn't know what it was, but it felt . . . monumental. It called to her. That was where she needed to go. That was where the answer was.

Cold crept up her spine.

Destroy.

Andra recoiled and called her nanos back and they came, like a rubber band released, condensing her consciousness, returning herself to her body. She blinked open her eyes, expecting to see the lake in front of her, the world re-forming around her. But instead, she was engulfed in stygian blackness, a swirling mass of corrupted tech.

She was surrounded, contained by a pocket.

Fear coursed through her, her legs trembling.

But it wasn't destroying her.

Why wasn't it destroying her?

Had she called it? Had she *created* it?

It moved thickly around her, the corrupted nanos tickling her skin. Pain pierced her skull as she tried to corral the corrupted nanos into a dark mass in front of her. There was resistance, but not as much as she expected.

Something swelled inside her, some innate programming, and she mentally reached out to the pocket. It responded, reached back. Answered her call. It was listening. It was eager.

Her attempt was frantic and clumsy, more panic than skill. But Andra pushed it away, commanding it to disperse. It hesitated a moment but then retreated, projecting a feeling of obeisance. Andra didn't take time to wonder at it. She pushed it farther and farther, spreading the individual nanos across the desert, as thin as her own nanos had been spread under water. Then she fell to her knees with a ragged gasp and coughed up another spell of dead nanos. They were a stark black against the white sand.

She'd done it.

She'd controlled a pocket.

And it had taken everything in her.

She crawled back into the hover beside Mechy and collapsed. When she was exhausted or weak, it was usually because her interaction with tech had damaged some of her nanos. Like when she worked on the 'dome. Or when she controlled a pocket. She needed to replenish them. Nanos were designed to long for a host, and Andra was willing to incorporate them into her matrices, to bring them into the fold of her own. There weren't many free nanos in the air around her, but she called to the few there were, welcomed them into her being. It was a quick process, and one Andra was getting better at.

The new nanos were quickly converted to Andra's tech signature, made part of her consciousness. It was an automatic process. Like breathing. She didn't *have* to think about it, but she *could*. She should probably do it more often, with as many dead nanos as she was coughing up.

She lay back in the hover, took a deep breath, but there wasn't time to rest.

She needed to get to the lab at the bottom of the lake. She would find cryo'plating and other supplies, more of Griffin's notes, her intentions. And then, with her new knowledge and skills, she would go back and save Eerensed and the colonists. And, hopefully, herself in the process.

Andra skimmed the hover over the surface of the lake, pushing it faster and faster, letting the cool night breeze ruffle her hair, filling her lungs with the smell of lake water. The engine was quiet enough she could hear the gentle lapping of the water. Every so often, she would send out a thin strand of nanos to bump up against the tech of the lab and adjust course. It was probably close to midnight when she reached the spot in the lake directly above it.

She brought the hover to a stop and let it bob, the water slapping against the sides. The lab was about a mile down, so swimming wasn't an option. But if Griffin had been coming here, there had to be a way in. Andra roved her eyes over the lake's surface, the moonlight glinting off the gentle waves, but she saw nothing.

She was just starting to get frustrated when she saw a weird glint of light holding still among the waves. She moved the hover closer, slowly, and as she approached, a holo'display burst from a metal rod peeking out of the water.

A holo'scan floated in front of her, a cloud of light and pixels, and Andra stretched out to place her palm into the light.

After a second, it turned green.

"Welcome, Andromeda," a robotic voice said.

"Whoa," Andra breathed.

The water surged and a tube of metallic glass rose in front of her, a panel sliding open. She climbed awkwardly out of the hover into the chamber, leaving Mechy behind. If she woke him, he'd want to come with her, and this part, at least, Andra wanted to do herself. She collapsed onto the floor of the chamber, the glass cool beneath her hands. The panel shut, and the chamber lowered itself into the water. Andra had a single moment of panic as the waves swallowed her, and then the chamber was shooting through a tube toward the bottom of the lake. As the surface grew farther away, darkness closed in, and Andra had trouble telling which way was up or down. She didn't even feel like she was moving.

Soon she saw the spark of a glimmer beneath her feet, getting closer and brighter until she could make out the underwater lab. A series of buildings were encased in three bio'domes, lit by kinetic orbs. It was the size of a small business park or college campus. The ground inside was covered in rocks and wild grasses and pine trees. The buildings themselves were perfectly preserved, and in the center one, there was a light coming from a window on the top floor.

The chamber slowed as it lowered into the 'dome farthest to the left. The ground came up to meet her, and as the chamber came to a stop, the panel opened, and Andra stepped out into a 'dome at the bottom of what was left of Lake Superior.

The depths of the water surrounded her, held back only by thin metallic glass. The surface was a mere glint above her. Dark shapes swam past, bumping into the edge of the 'dome.

The air smelled sweet and loamy. There was a faint chirp of crickets, and somewhere in the distance, she could have sworn she'd heard an owl hoot. Something about it brought tears to her eyes. This was a little bit of home. A little bit of the past she longed for.

Andra headed straight for the center building, where she'd seen the light in the window. It was a short trek from one 'dome to the next, through a vac'tube like the one she'd placed on the mini'dome. The building was several stories high, its reflective glass mirroring the dark blue of the lake. The front doors slid open with a scan of her thumb. The lights flicked on as soon as she entered, and she was surrounded by a lobby much like the one in the LAC annex under Eerensed. Only nicer and with fewer skeletons. A hologram of the LAC logo swirled around the empty reception desk.

The elevators weren't difficult to find, lining the far edge of the building. She entered one and rode it to the top floor. At the end of the hall, light spilled out of an open doorway, and Andra was vaguely aware of the outline of Lake Superior on each door as she rushed toward it.

She entered the room and skidded to a halt. A frosty fog surrounded her. She swatted it out of her face, stepping through until it cleared and she saw what was beyond.

Cryo'tanks.

Hundreds of them, maybe thousands. Unlike the colonists' 'tanks, these weren't laid down like coffins, but standing in perfect lines like soldiers. Frosted over, they filled the entire room, which stretched out into the fog.

Andra stepped toward the first one, wiping away the frost.

She stumbled back, letting out a cry.

She was staring at the frozen body of Dr. Alberta Griffin.

This was impossible. Griffin was dead. Zhade had seen her die. And it hadn't been like Andra's supposed death. There'd been no nanos forming a dagger, no secret escape. Maret had beheaded her, as he'd intended to do to Andra during her first execution. You didn't come back from that.

Griffin was most definitely dead. So what was her body doing here? And so intact?

Unease filled Andra as she made her way to the next closest 'tank. She wiped away the frost and sucked in a breath.

Another Griffin was before her, eyes closed, long blonde hair frozen in a fan around her.

Andra went to another 'tank. And another.

They were all Griffin. Exactly how she looked in photos from her midtwenties, before Andra was born. No modded eye, no crown. Hair a natural muddy blonde, flowing past her shoulders. All of them. All exactly alike.

They were clones.

Human clones.

All the same age, all in stasis.

It made no sense. You grew clones from birth. They were genetically the same as the source, but they lived their own separate lives, became their own person. It was . . . legal, sure, but frowned upon. Only a few human clones existed in her time, usually replacing a child who had died (which made Andra's stomach turn) or as a way for a person to have offspring without another person. Clones' rights were so restricted and their existence so controversial, that very few people even pursued the possibility of creating one.

But there had to be *hundreds* in this room, and they seemed to either have been frozen at the same age, or they'd been grown unconscious to this point in development. Either way, no wonder Griffin had kept this place off the map.

She had an army of clones of *herself*. For what purpose, Andra couldn't fathom, but she came to a sudden realization.

There was a cough behind her.

Andra whipped around and looked into the face of the woman who had started it all.

Dr. Griffin smiled. "Hello, Andromeda."

PART TWO

ETERNAL DAMNATION

Human memories are so tied to emotion that over time, they can be unintentionally and irrevocably altered. This has several implications, but the most important is that short of transferring a human consciousness to a new host, there is no way for people to be completely objective.

~~Memory is fact. Emotion is fiction.~~

—From the journal of Dr. Griffin,
time stamp erased

EIGHT

OOIIIOOO

"Dr. Griffin," Andra breathed.

Alberta Griffin stood before her in a dark gray pantsuit, her hair pulled back into a fishtail braid. She wore immaculate makeup and her nails were recently manicured. Her modded eye was gone, but she didn't wear an eyepatch like she had in the recording in Andra's holocket. Instead she had both organic eyes.

It appeared that under this lake, Griffin had been waiting.

Except not the Dr. Griffin Andra had known. Not the Griffin Zhade had called mam.

She smiled sadly, as though reading Andra's thoughts.

"You're a clone?" Andra asked, but it wasn't really a question.

Griffin nodded.

"Wha—but—how? Why?" Andra stammered.

The clone hugged herself, running her hands up and down her arms. "It's cold in here. Why don't we go talk in my office?"

She turned and left before Andra could respond.

Andra's mind reeled as she followed down the hall. The clone's heels clacked against the tile, as she turned into a room at the other end of the corridor.

Unlike the rest of the compound, the office was bathed in a low rose-gold light. Gauzy fabric was draped over kinetic orbs, and a few holo'windows depicted the desert. There was plush upholstered furniture but also an ergo'chair. Holo'displays were everywhere, and a half-eaten apple was propped on a nearby work'station.

Dr. Griffin's clone gestured for Andra to have a seat in one of the upholstered chairs. She sat automatically, shock coursing through her. Nanos tickled her skin, a 'swarm of them circling her, almost nuzzling her like a dog. In some ways it relaxed her, but maybe that's what they were programmed to do: relax anxious guests.

Andra had come looking for Griffin's work but found Griffin herself. At least, a version of her. The clone wouldn't have Griffin's memories, but she *would* have her intelligence. Perhaps the real Griffin had left instructions, things she could pass on to Andra.

Andra pressed her palms to her cheeks. "Why?" It was the only question she could think to ask. "Why did she . . . Why?"

The clone offered Andra a mug of something hot. When Andra shook her head, the clone took it for herself. She smiled and sat on a couch across from Andra, tucking her legs under herself like they were two friends chatting over coffee.

She sighed. "It's a long story, but basically the original Griffin created us as . . . an insurance plan. She knew something would happen, and—" She shook her head, lifting a long-fingered hand to her temple. "I'm sorry. Should I start at the beginning?"

"That would help," Andra said flatly.

The clone pinched the bridge of her nose. "The beginning," she repeated, and then looked back up at Andra. "I guess it all started with the anomalies."

"The anomalies?"

"The people here call them pockets." Griffin set her mug aside. "Such an innocuous term for something so deadly. I suspect they wanted to make them seem less . . . dangerous, less frightening than they really are. Pockets are usually . . . things to be filled, untapped potential. Or, at the very least, emptiness. But the anomalies are not emptiness. And their potential is catastrophic. You can't neutralize their threat by calling them something as innocuous as *pockets*."

Andra blinked and shook her head. "Isn't that what you're doing by calling them anomalies? Just something out of the ordinary? Something that deviates from the norm? Doesn't sound so scary."

Griffin chuckled to herself, picking at a thread on the couch. "If you think that, you truly don't understand the human race. Nothing scares them more than deviation." She stared blankly for a moment, then came back to herself. "We don't know how the anomalies started. They seem to be some kind of LAC decon'bot experiment that an intern must have accidentally set free."

Andra scoffed. "All of LAC's resources, and you couldn't figure out how they got loose? Why did LAC have such dangerous tech in the first place?"

"Trust me. No one is angrier than I am." The clone sighed, waving a hand. "Well, probably the original Griffin was angrier. But now, I carry that burden. We . . . they—the LAC—tried everything to fix it. They even had the anomalies contained for a while. But they adapted. And formed these masses of destructive tech they called entropics. And each time we found a substance to contain them, the entropics learned how to destroy that too. We knew one day, we would run out of options. At least, run out of options on Earth. So we started planning for the worst."

"The colonist program," Andra whispered. She had guessed right. The LAC—Griffin—had known that the earth would be destroyed, and planned to escape, leaving billions of people behind.

"Yes," Griffin's clone agreed, her features sharp in the rosy glow of the room. "The plan was to fully colonize Holymyth. We'd been intending to do it anyway, but terraforming an entire planet takes time. Time I didn't have." She groaned and pinched the bridge of her nose again. "She," she corrected. "Time *she* didn't have. It's easy to forget I'm not her."

How could she forget? She was a clone, her own person, with her own experiences. Wasn't she?

The clone ran a hand over her braid. "They started asking for volunteers, calling the journey a colony program—not a rescue mission— in order to prevent panic. Or, at least, to delay it. Once the anomalies were widespread, the panic would set in, and there would be a mad rush to get off the planet. So they needed to take as many trips as possible before people knew that the planet was doomed."

Andra sat forward. "But you didn't even get one trip in. We're all still here."

Griffin nodded, eyes downcast. "We had the first colonists in stasis, ready to leave for Holymyth, but then everything went to hell. The anomalies grew faster than expected, forming more and more entropic centers, taking out entire cities in the blink of an eye. Not only did they multiply, but they grew . . . smarter. At first their only goal was to destroy everything in their path, but then . . . they started strategizing. It's like they knew if humans left the planet, they wouldn't be able to destroy them. So, they cut off our only escape."

"The Ark," Andra whispered.

Griffin nodded. "They destroyed all the shuttles to the Arcanum. It was a simultaneous attack. They were gone in less than a minute."

Andra shuddered. She knew the pockets were brutal, but she'd always assumed they were amoral, like any other technology. Just doing what they were created to do. But the pockets were learning, adapting.

Almost like Andra.

And she'd controlled them, let them inside. Was that what was causing her to cough up dead nanos? Was there now an anomaly in her programming, slowly corrupting her?

Coldness crept over Andra. The hairs on the back of her neck prickled. Something immense and stark began to open inside her, a yawning chasm, a vast darkness.

Then the voice. Whispering. Eager.

Destroy it all.

The urge, the feeling, the compulsion to destroy was all Andra knew for a moment, but she tamped it down, holding back a cough.

Griffin didn't seem to notice Andra's panic. "Our only path forward was to save as many people as possible in stasis until we had a solution for the anomalies."

Andra swallowed, forcing her focus on Griffin and not the quiet, hissing voice in her head. "But . . . it's been nearly a thousand years. The pockets have destroyed the planet."

Griffin shook her head, blue eyes flashing. "Humanity is still fighting. And I am too."

The voice in Andra's head faded but not the urge to destroy. Anger welled up in her. Griffin had let this happen.

"Your company destroyed the planet and you just . . . went into stasis? Just let all this happen only to wake up now? And do what?"

"No, Andromeda." Griffin gave her a sad smile. "I—she never went into stasis. She worked and worked and worked to find a solution. When she realized it wouldn't happen in her lifetime, she created me. And the rest of the clones you saw. And all those that came before us. We have her intelligence. And access to all her memories and knowledge, plus the memories and knowledge of all the clones that came after."

Andra sat up. The chair creaked beneath her. "Wait, what? How?"

Griffin's clone stood and walked to her work'station, a collection of 'desks and 'displays packed into the corner of the room. Andra followed, eyes widening as Griffin brought up a holo. Streams of data flashed before her eyes.

The code was moving too fast for Andra to comprehend, at least without access to her AI state, but the patterns were . . . intricate. Complex and entangled. No one would code like this. Nothing would.

Except the human brain.

"Are these . . . uploaded memories?" Andra looked between Griffin and the 'display. "I thought this was impossible."

Griffin shrugged. "*Impossible* is just a word people use when they haven't found the solution yet. But uploading memories is possible. I—she figured it out."

"Is it . . . is this her consciousness? Is she trapped in there?" Andra reached a hand out toward the scrolling data, but Griffin pulled her back.

"It depends on what you consider consciousness. This is a collection of memories. But computers had memory long before they could become self-aware."

Andra studied her for a moment. "So, in a way, you *are* Griffin."

The clone froze, and something like panic crossed her face before dissolving into a strained smile. "I just have *access* to the memories. I haven't downloaded them. I'm *me*. Something separate."

"Sorries," Andra said, turning back to the data. As an AI, she knew what it was like to not feel like her identity belonged to her. How much more so would a clone feel that way? "I didn't mean—"

The clone waved the apology away. "I understand."

Andra cleared her throat. "So, one Griffin dies and the next one takes her place?"

Griffin straightened, pacing back toward the sofa. "I'm not the same Alberta you knew a thousand years ago."

"Well, I didn't really know her . . . But you're also not the same Griffin who was Zhade's mom, are you?"

The clone sighed, propping herself against the back of the couch, eyes glazed. "I thought about letting the boy know I exist, but it would just be too painful for him. I have access to her memories, but I'm not his mom, and don't have any motherly feelings for him."

Andra wanted to argue that Griffin should tell him, that Zhade deserved to know the truth. But she didn't know if he would understand. He barely understood what Andra was. How could he see his mother's face, watch her mannerisms, hear her voice, and not think it was her? It was hard enough for Andra, who understood the science, to see this woman and not believe she was Griffin.

"The clone before me fell in love, had a son, loved him. But I'm not her. In many ways, I'm only four years old. And my entire existence, my entire purpose, is to keep doing the work. For the last thousand years, an Alberta Griffin has been working on solving how to save humanity, on advancing technology as much as she could. Just one person, over and over, all solving the same problem."

Andra looked back at the data still scrolling on the holo'display. All those memories. Lifetimes of them. "But you never found a solution. So what's left of humanity is either living through the apocalypse, or asleep underground."

Griffin leaned forward, reaching out to take Andra's hands in her own, and gave her a sad, knowing smile. "Oh, Andromeda, but we did find a solution. Haven't you figured that out yet? The solution— the thing that is going to save what's left of humanity—is you."

NINE

THE GRAFTER

ZHADE PASSED THE even in the guv's suite working on creating the spell to turn Meta's face into Tsurina's til full past midnight. He sat, legs crossed, on the floor, hunched over the graftling wand, sparkshades propped above the Crown, muscles sore from the tedious work.

Doon watched him from the velvet couch, picking at her fingernails. She'd crawled in through an air vent and fake assassinated him with a blade to the kidney.

"You reck she didn't mereish stay, marah?" she asked.

"What?"

"Andra," Doon amended. "I'd bet my butter as soon as you left she peaced for this lake place."

Something turned in Zhade's stomach, a strange sort of panic, but he ignored it. Doon hadn't been in the Vaults for weeks. She had no clue what Andra was doing.

"I reck Andra," Zhade said, not looking up from his work. "She's not the type to go running into danger unprepped."

Doon started counting off on her fingers. "Following you to Eerensed, asking Maret not to kill her maids, breaking me out of prison—"

"Those were extenuating circumstances."

Doon cocked her head. "What does that mean?"

"Dunno. It's something Andra says."

Zhade lowered his sparkshades. The next part of the spell used firon to add more wires to the conduit.

The couch creaked as Doon settled back into it. "Evens, I still imagine she's gone to see the big water place."

Zhade didn't answer, focusing on the wand instead. He'd needed a bit of the Grande Advisor's blood to work the spell, but at luck, she'd bled all over his suite. He'd scraped some from the bottle shard he'd hit her with, before having Fishy clean the full place.

The angel now stood in the corner of the room, pale face lit in a blank expression. On a whim, Zhade reached out with the Crown and felt Fishy's presence. It seemed distant and fuzzy, but the more Zhade concentrated, the more he could make out the angel's essence. He was surprised to find it felt loyalty and something likeish affection for Zhade. He'd never considered angels had feelings like humans, but he spozed Fishy must feel something for the man it had recked from a kiddun. The angel had been Zhade's mam's favorite, after all.

Zhade bent back to his work.

It wouldn't be long before people started wondering where the Grande Advisor was. Gryfud was holding the guards busy, claiming Tsurina was ill and sending them on wild moose chases acity. They'd be looking for her tomoren though, expecting to have the day's first brief at six abell. At hope, Zhade would be finished soon and sooner, but he still wasn't convinced this was a good plan.

Though Meta might resemble Tsurina, they weren't as similar as Zhade and Maret. Even after transfiguration, there would be differences. For one, Meta's height—or lack thereof. For second, her hair. Zhade wondered if they could get free with having her always standing on a platform. Perhaps find a wig . . .

This was bad magic.

He hovered over the graftling wand, sparks flying as he cast the firon spell.

"Have you convoed Skilla bout the angels?" Doon muttered.

Zhade paused, looking up to see Doon still slouched in the sofa. Her eyes weren't on Zhade, but on Fishy, and Zhade finalish realized her posture wasn't boredom, but fear. He set down the graftling wand, removed his sparkshades, and turned to her. She shouldn't be ascared of Fishy. It would never go rogue, Zhade was certz of it.

"There's no reason to tell her," Zhade said, trying to sound reassuring. "It's none of a big. No one was killed. Except the angels."

"Dzeni was nearish killed."

"But she wasn't," Zhade said, firmish.

He was guv; he had to project strength, even if he was ascared. Sides, after he finished the spell for Meta, his sole focus would be figuring a way to stop the rogue angels, with or without the help of the Crown.

"For true, Doon, no shakes. I've control of it." He gave her a tight smile.

She didn't smile back, sole stood and stretched, her eyes still locked on Fishy. "Time for me to peace."

"And go where?" Zhade asked, trying not to sound too curious. "It's near moren."

She didn't meet his eyes. "Out."

"Are you staying with Dzeni or the Schism this even?"

"The Schism."

Rare form, little assassin. He'd have to actualish convo Skilla if he wanted to confirm Doon's where-a-be. And Doon recked that wouldn't happen. Skilla asked too many questions, had too many suggestions for what Zhade should be doing. If she had her choice, she would not sole decide her fate, but the fate of all Eerensed.

Doon left, and Zhade went back to his work. He'd had years to create and spell the graftling wand firstish. Now, he had sole a few bells, and though he recked better what he was doing, he still felt rushed.

How much faster would the work go if he could use the Crown?

He paused and set down his tools, wiping sweat from the side of his brow unadorned by the Crown. He took a deep breath and tested the air, to convo. He could sense the graftling wand. It was like a tickle at the back of his throat, an itch he couldn't reach. He could sense the wand's presence but not . . . the shape of it. It was like seeing something in the distance, obscured by a sandcloud.

He strained to grasp it. Not even to grasp it. Mereish to be more aware of it.

What had Tsurina said? Not to try so hard, to let the Crown guide him?

For certz Tsurina didn't reck what she was convoing, but maybe Zhade could mereish give it a try.

It was diff to give up control, to mereish drift and let the Crown be. He stopped focusing so much on the details of what he was doing, and instead mereish imagined what he wanted to accomplish. To turn Meta into Tsurina. No small magic. He wished he could make her taller, grow her hair, change all of her into Tsurina. He needed Meta to *become* her.

The picture of it started to clear in his mind, til his awareness of the wand sharpened, and he recked it the same way he recked himself. He could see the magic within, feel it. And when he imagined bout what he had left of the spell, it started to complete itself.

It was like nothing Zhade had ever experienced. Instead of imaginings turning to actions, they were turning into a collection of being and nonbeing, of somethings and nothings. He fell deeper into the Crown, letting it take over, letting the feeling of it surround him til there was nothing *but* the Crown. No room round him, no palace. No responsibilities or pressure or wants or needs. It was mereish the magic of the Crown, the dance of a spell being created.

Zhade's eyes snapped open.

The graftling wand floated afront of him, prepped to be used.

He gasped, and it fell to the floor with a *thunk*. He was suddenish aware of the intense pain above his westhand eye. He touched the skin beneath the Crown with the tips of his fingers and they came away bloodish.

He had memory of Maret's face in the last days before Zhade took the Crown. The bruises. The dried blood. Tsurina had said Maret was trying to remove it. That using it shouldn't cause wounds likeish this.

But for certz she was lying. Zhade couldn't trust anything Tsurina convoed him.

Then why are you holding her alive? he asked himself.

He didn't have an answer.

Zhade went to the small room and washed the blood from his face. It wasn't as bad as he spozed. Mereish a few drops. He put on Maret's nicest robes (which happened his tightest—sands, what was wrong with his brother?), and waited for Meta.

He'd nearish fallen asleep by the time she arrived. She threw the door open and strode in.

Zhade groaned from the receiving room couch. "You have to stop doing that."

Meta was dressed in dark guard's clothes and carried a large pack. "Then get better security." She tossed the pack onto a nearish chair.

"You're my security!" Zhade cried.

Meta shook her head in disappointment and pulled out a glittering gown from her pack.

"One of Tsurina's. A bit long on me, but your angel can hem it."

"That evens, Fishy?" Zhade asked as Meta threw the dress over her head.

"For certz, sir," Fishy said.

It still surprised Zhade when Fishy spoke. Andra had done something to "activate the vocal protocols" or something. He rareish comped what she convoed, sole that she was hypergood at magic and had a charred voice.

Fraughts, he missed her.

Meta shimmied out of the guard's clothes neath the gown she'd just donned, kicking her pants to the side and pulling her shirt out through the neck of the dress. She stood straightish and flipped her spiked hair back, fingers stretched out as though she wore pointed nails.

She raised an eyebrow. "How do I look?"

Zhade frowned. "Do you have any imaginings of who you're bout to turn into? Who you'll have to pretend to be? She's ruthless."

Meta shrugged, bending to fold her clothes. "I reck. I've been a guard for nearish three years anow, and sides, I've heard stories. Rumors. Some people convo she beat Maret. That she had a kiddun out in the Wastes that she abandoned to marry the guv. That she plotted the First's death." Her eyes flicked up to Zhade's. "She's ruthless, firm, but the plan is to be *better* than that, marah?"

For a refugee turned guard, Meta for certz skooled a lot bout the royal fam in her three years acity. She was a quick study, recked the palace structure, and comped well how the citians and guards saw Tsurina. She was probablish the sole person who could make this work.

"Firm, but . . . people have to believe the change is genuine. It has to happen slowish."

Meta shoved her old clothes back in her pack and looked up at Zhade. "I can do it."

He watched her for a moment, taking in the determination in her eyes, the jut of her chin. There wasn't any fear or apprehension in her expression.

"Why are you doing this?"

She blinked. "Because . . . you need Tsurina to hold control of Eerensed."

"I reck." Zhade rolled his eyes. "But why are *you* doing this? Personalish? Is it because of Maret? Were you and he . . . a . . ."

Meta shook her head in confusion.

"Seeya, did you and he . . ." He cleared his throat and made a simplistic but obvi gesture with his fingers.

Meta burst into a laugh. "Neg! Fraughting sands, neg! Neg." She shuddered. "Blegh. Neg, we weren't . . . We had a bit in common. Let's mereish convo I comp what it's like to grow up with a mam like Tsurina." Her eyes flashed. "She was a fraughted fraught to him. To everyone. *That's* why I'm doing this."

Zhade nodded. He didn't for true comp, but he'd done crazier things for reasons of less import.

"Evens, have a seat." He nodded to the sofa and winced. "Maybe lie down."

He'd stood through the process of his face rearranging itself, but he'd been prepped. And hadn't wanted to faint afront of Andra. Meta said she comped that it would hurt, but she hadn't felt it, she couldn't imagine. By the time she full comped how bad the pain would be, it would be too late.

Meta lay on the sofa, arranging Tsurina's dress round herself, and fanning her hair on the pillow.

Zhade picked up the graftling wand from where he'd dropped it. It felt different. Lighter. He checked the spell. Everything was as it should be. Whatever he'd done with the Crown had done the same thing he would have done using Low Magic, mereish much, much faster. Maybe Tsurina's advice hadn't been worthless after all.

"Evens." He stood over Meta, hovering the wand over her head. "I can't stress full bars how much this is going to hurt."

She took a deep breath, letting it out slowish, then nodded. "I'm prepped. For Eerensed, marah?"

"For Eerensed," Zhade agreed.

He cast the spell, releasing Tsurina's blood into the magic, then placed the wand at Meta's temple and pressed the button.

A magical net released from the wand, gentlish covering Meta's face like a fog. It was unnerving from this angle. Is this what had happened to him? His face obscured, coated in a dense, translucent web? Had Andra watched this happen, heard him scream, and wondered what he had done to himself?

Meta sucked in a sharp breath. "What's happening?"

Zhade looked down. The web had reached past her face, wrapping itself round the top of her head, weaving through her hair, then traveling down her neck, below the hem of her gown. Zhade watched as the disruption of the cloth indicated its trajectory to cover Meta's full body.

"Sands neg," he breathed, scrambling for the graftling wand. This wasn't purposed to happen.

"Sands neg wha—?" Meta broke off into a scream.

Her full body seized, but the magic held her aplace. Her fingers clawed, then flattened. Her back arched, and her screams grew louder.

"Meta!"

Zhade's finger clumsyish brushed through the spell on the wand, but he recked what he had to do. It was like falling, opening, letting go. He reached out with the Crown and dove into the magic. Suddenish, he recked what he'd done. Where it had all gone wrong.

He'd wished, mereish as Tsurina had said. He'd thought bout how Meta wasn't full tall and wanted a solution. He'd imagined bout her hair needing to grow. He'd wished he could make her exactish like Tsurina.

The Crown was giving it to him.

Fishes and wishes.

Meta was screaming, her voice shredded. She convulsed on the couch, her body shifting and morphing. Bones breaking, skin stretching. Zhade clamped his hands on her arms, trying to hold her still, to stop her thrashing, but her attempts mereish grew stronger, her screaming growing louder, til—

It stopped. She let out a high moan and fell silent. Zhade released her.

Meta opened her pale eyes.

Sole, they weren't pale anymore.

They were brown, like Tsurina's.

"What . . . was that," she croaked, and behind the hoarseness, she even *sounded* like Tsurina. The raspy purr of her voice.

Meta looked down and gasped.

"What did you do?"

She stood, and Zhade followed her with his eyes, up, up, up. She was now nearish a head taller than Zhade. She threw her hands out to steady herself.

"Sands," Zhade breathed. What had he done?

Meta stared back, hands feeling the length of her new body, then tangling into her new long brown hair. "I'm . . . her . . ."

"Sorries," Zhade gasped. "Sorries, I can fix it."

"Neg. This . . . this is perfect."

Her face broke into a grin, and Zhade gaped at her.

"Evens," Meta said through Tsurina's voice, tongue, lips. "Let's go rule Eerensed."

TEN

OO11OOO1 OO11OOOO

ANDRA STARED AT Griffin's clone, trembling. The lights seemed to dim, and the fabric-draped walls closed in on her.

"You're the solution, Andromeda," Griffin repeated. "Well, you and Rashmi."

"How? Why?"

This was it. She was about to learn the reason she was created.

"It's . . . complicated."

Griffin walked back to her work'station and unplugged a translucent reset tool—like the one that had upgraded Andra's tech to interface with Eerensedian tech. This one was shorter but sharper, and instead of a pastel rainbow of colors, it shone neon green.

"So far," Griffin said, "cryonic glass is the only thing the entropics haven't learned to penetrate, and it's only because they haven't been exposed to enough of it. Given time, they will learn how, and no one will be safe."

Learn. Adapt.

Andra thought about how the bio'dome had been created with the same metallic glass as the cryo'tanks. The composition was slightly different, but the pockets had learned how to burst through that when it was weakened, when Andra had been in danger and accidentally called to it for help. Had she taught the pockets how to breach the one material that could hold it? Certainly not. She had the small pocket still trapped in the mini'dome back in the Vaults. It hadn't escaped so far.

"I still hope one day," Griffin continued, "that we can take humanity to Holymyth, but it's been nearly a thousand years, as you pointed out, and it's time for plan B."

Andra lifted her eyebrows. "Plan B?"

"I think I've finally discovered a way to protect humanity from the entropics."

She held out the reset tool. Andra took it, weighing it in her hand. It glowed green in the dim rosy light, an energy coursing through it, brushing up against her nanos. It almost felt alive.

"What is it? It's like the reset tool you—she gave Zhade."

"You used it?" Griffin asked.

Andra nodded.

"Good. I'm sure you noticed that it not only upgraded you, but made you impervious to the entropics."

Andra almost dropped the reset tool. The ice-pick dagger had done that? It was starting to make sense. She'd controlled the pocket in the throne room. She'd been able to harvest part of one and capture it. And then, just moments ago, she'd been surrounded by a pocket and it hadn't harmed her.

"It upgraded your system to mask your own nanos. Like . . . dressing them up in disguise. The code that runs through your nanos is cloaked in a code similar to that of an entropic. It's like . . . how vaccines are coded into humans' 'implants. It tricks the body into thinking it has the virus, so it can learn how to attack it. But with this, your upgrade tricks the anomalies into thinking you're one of them, so they *won't* attack."

The hair on the back of Andra's neck stood up. Since stabbing herself with the reset tool, she'd been immune to pockets, sure. But that wasn't the only thing that had changed. The dead nanos. The voices. The urge to destroy.

She cleared her throat. "Would this have any side effects? Like converting my tech into actual anomalies? Or killing my own nanos?"

"It shouldn't." Griffin's eyes narrowed. "Why? Are you having issues with your programming?"

Andra opened her mouth to tell her yes, but her mind drifted to the rows of clones. Clearly, Griffin viewed bodies as disposable. If Andra let on that something was wrong—that something in her might be corrupted—maybe Griffin would see her body as disposable too. Andra's memories would be uploaded into a computer and then shoved into another body.

"No. Just curious."

Griffin sat back down in her ergo'chair, crossing her legs. "It's perfectly harmless, I promise. And while we can't give the colonists the same code . . . since they're human . . . we can provide them a similar upgrade to their neural'implants. That's where the reset tool comes in. I call it an anomalizer."

Andra clutched it to her, the sickly green glow shining between her fingers, her knuckles gone white. "Can we do that while they're still in stasis?"

"Unfortunately, we'll have to wake them up first. We can start with a small group. For instance, just the LAC scientists. Then they can help you with the remainder of the colonists. And that—I'm sure you've realized—will free up some cryo'plating to use on the rocket. This upgrade is, of course, only a temporary measure. The goal is still to get to Holymyth."

"What does this all have to do with me?"

Griffin's clone nodded to the anomalizer. "You'll be upgrading the colonists."

"Me?" Andra choked. "But I . . . But you . . . Why can't—"

"I can't risk going back to Eerensed right now." Griffin swiveled back to the work'station. "After the way things ended . . . if they saw me, it would be chaos. But that's not why it has to be you. The upgrade only works if it's run through either your or Rashmi's matrices."

"What? Why?"

Griffin pulled another holo'display. It was filled with code, just like the 'display of Griffin's memories, but not nearly as complicated. Andra still had no idea what she was looking at.

Griffin pointed to a line of code. "The programming inside the anomalizer is generic. On its own, it won't work." She switched the 'display to view a tech scan of an 'implant. Wires and nanos stretched out from the 'implant into the shape of a human brain. "Each 'implant is so . . . intertwined with the host's brain, the code inside evolves to become unique for each person. The anomalizer is meant to mask the user's signature." The lines of wires and nanos turned a bright green, still forming the same shape, moving along the same pathways. "But since each signature is unique, it's not one-size-fits-all. Each time you upgrade a colonist, the code has to be attuned to the individual in order to work with their tech effectively. Only an AI can do that." The image on the screen changed to the deep black of the pockets.

Andra blinked. She was sure she would understand this if she had access to her AI state, but as she was currently stuck in her human mind, it made no sense to her.

"I . . . can't." Andra felt her cheeks redden. "I . . . don't have access to my AI consciousness. It comes and goes, but I don't have control over it."

Griffin gave Andra a pitying look. "We'll work on that later, together, if you'd like. But for now, you don't need to be conscious of the process. Your central matrix can work . . . independently of your consciousness. It's like . . . an instinct . . . or breathing. You don't have to think about breathing to do it. Your subconscious keeps you breathing, even when you aren't focused on it."

Andra grimaced. "Maybe more like keeping my heart beating. I can make myself breathe. I can't make my own heart beat."

Griffin took Andra's hand. "Oh, Andromeda. One day you will."

Andra looked away.

"But for now"—Griffin shut down the holo'displays—"it's all set up. All you have to do is connect your upgrade tool to the anomalizer. Jack yourself in. The anomalizer connects into the colonists' emergency ports. No invasive surgery or anything. Just press the button and go. You literally can't mess this up."

Wanna bet? Andra thought. But something else was bothering her.

"How did you know about my upgrade tool? I thought you . . . the last Griffin didn't give it to Zhade until right before her execution. How did she upload that memory?"

Griffin frowned. "She didn't. But she'd been planning it for a while. I assumed the boy would be successful in finding you."

"Assumed? You did all of this without knowing for sure I was alive?"

Griffin shrugged. "If you hadn't been, I would have had to keep working to find the answer." She smiled, flashing a row of straight white teeth. "But now you're here. You can be the answer."

Andra tried to smile back but couldn't. She had thought there was some deep purpose, some specific reason for her creation that she would now fulfill to save the world. But this was just . . . luck. Accident.

"You can do this. I have faith in you." Griffin leaned forward to examine Andra. "You know, the first Griffin was always so proud of you. She always said you were her greatest achievement."

Andra shifted her weight. "Really? Not Rashmi?"

"Rashmi was the prototype. You were the product."

Andra tried to smile, but that wasn't flattering to either her or her counterpart.

"I . . ." She cleared her throat and sat on the edge of the sofa. "Is that . . . all? I can't do more? Or was there something else? Like, some reason I was created, that I need to fulfill? Like a purpose?"

Griffin clasped her hands in front of her, bouncing her crossed leg. "You were created to help humanity. In any way you could. There was no . . . specific purpose. No reason. We wanted to see if we could create True AI, and we could. And now you're here, and you have the ability to help me save humanity."

"Oh."

Andra stared at her feet. That was it? That wasn't right. It didn't feel . . . true. Andra had thought there was something deep inside her, some reason she existed. And if she could just find it, realize it, it would give her existence meaning. But there was no meaning. She was just . . . a *tool* to be wielded when needed.

"It's late." Griffin stood, oblivious to the despair rising in Andra. "You've had a long journey. Can I get you something to eat?"

"Certz."

Griffin exited, leaving Andra alone with her thoughts. The office started to shrink around her. Instead of being homey, the curtain-draped walls and dim lighting felt claustrophobic. There was too much furniture, and Griffin's work'station was a mess. Andra started pacing.

She had no purpose, at least nothing unique to her. She was just . . . there to perform random tasks that happened to come up. That wasn't enough for Andra. She wanted there to be a reason, a plan, a destiny. She wanted it to be grand and important and epic.

She wanted to save humanity.

All of humanity, not just the colonists.

Once she figured out how to run the upgrade on the 'implants, she would figure out a way to 'implant the Eerensedian population, so they too could be protected. It wouldn't save the environment or rid the world of pockets. But it was a start.

She now saw the path in front of her. Wake the colonists. Upgrade them. Create the rocket with their help. And with the cryo'chambers empty, she would have the cryo'plating she needed. She'd found the answers she was looking for.

So why did she feel so . . . hopeless?

She wrinkled her nose and stood, crossing to Griffin's work'station. Maybe if she looked at the code for the anomalizer, her AI brain would understand, even if her human consciousness didn't.

She flipped open the holo'display, reaching out with her nanos. The work'station was abuzz with complex, intricate code. Streams of data ran vertically in a green light. This was what was left of the original Griffin. A collection of sensations converted into computer code.

Which was basically what Andra was.

She started to run a search for the anomalizer. Billions of files came up, organized chaos. Memories and feelings and—

She was sitting in a hospital waiting room. The lights were harsh. Somewhere down the hall an alarm was blaring. She knew—

Andra jerked back to herself, sitting hard on the ergo'chair. Her muscles ached, her lungs burned.

What had just happened?

It had been different than a sim. It wasn't like the memories that popped out of her holocket. She hadn't been pretending to experience the moment as she watched it play out in a holo. She felt like she had just *lived* that moment. That the experience had been as real to her as any of her own.

She'd just experienced one of Griffin's memories. Was this why the clone felt so much like Griffin? Had she lived through these moments as though they were her own?

"Feeling all right?" Griffin's clone said from the doorway.

"Yeah," Andra breathed, not wanting to admit she'd peeked into Griffin's memories. "Just . . . tired."

"Well, this will help." She set a tray of synth'food in the shape of various fruits and vegetables on the work'station in front of Andra.

Andra's stomach growled.

"I guess I didn't realize how hungry I was," she said awkwardly, and dug in.

Griffin sat down on the couch and tossed her legs up. "So, do you have any questions for me?"

Andra watched her for a moment. She hadn't known Griffin well, but it was still uncanny how much this clone not only looked and sounded but acted like Griffin.

"I can't think of any," Andra said. "But I'm sure some will come up. Is there a way I can contact you?"

"Oh, of course."

Griffin reached into her pocket and tossed Andra a small comm disc, which Andra failed to catch. It thumped quietly onto the carpeted floor, and Andra awkwardly bent to pick it up and stash it in her pocket.

"Unfortunately, there are . . . some issues with the LAC annex at the moment. Too many of the buildings around Riverside were faradayed too well, and messages are hard to transmit in and out of Eerensed. So you'll need to be outside the city walls to contact me. There's limited power, so you'll want to use it sparingly. But don't worry, Andromeda." She sat forward. "I know you can do this. I believe in you. Whatever issues you come across, you'll be able to figure out. You're . . . well, you're an AI, after all. *Learn, adapt*, as your mother would say. That's what you do."

"I'll wake my mom up first."

Andra took another bite of her food as her mind raced. She'd avoided looking up her family, knew she would be too tempted to wake them if she knew where their cryo'tanks were. But now she had a reason. Her mom would know what to do, could help. Even if there were some issues to work through—like her mom lying about what Andra was her whole life.

Isla Watts was a genius. Probably as smart as Griffin. With Isla awake, they could upgrade the colonists and build the rocket in no time. Maybe she'd even help Andra save the Eerensedians as well. They would work together, and Isla would finally see Andra's value. She was no longer an underachiever. She was no longer lazy or too hung up on words or her books. She was finally doing what Isla had always wanted for her. Working for the LAC.

Griffin cleared her throat. "I'm sorry. I don't know how to tell you this, but . . ."

Andra froze, stomach plummeting, and she knew what Griffin was going to say before she said it.

Grief lined Griffin's face. "Andromeda, your mother is dead."

The tray of food clattered to the floor. The room spun. Andra tried to reach out for support but fell heavily to the ground.

Isla was dead.

Dr. Isla Watts, the most renowned cryonic ethicist and astro-eco theorist to ever live—

—was dead.

Andra's mom was dead.

She choked back a sob, covering her mouth. Tears dripped down her face onto her hands, the carpet.

Destroy.

"Andra?"

Griffin's voice.

Everything was blurred by tears. Griffin helped her up, and Andra fought back a wave of nausea.

"I'm so sorry," Griffin said. There was something in the tenor of her voice—something deeper than hurt. To someone who didn't know her, she'd have seemed unmoved, but Andra could see the grief in her eyes. Eyes that looked just like her son's. Grief that didn't quite belong to her. Something she must have seen in a memory of one of her past selves.

"How?" Andra managed to say, leaning heavily on the work'station.

Griffin took a breath through her nose, closing her eyes briefly. "I woke her. Or the one before me did. After she woke Rashmi. She needed help, and your mother was always the more analytical of the two. She was running some tests on the soil out in the desert." Griffin's eyes glazed over. "It had been several days, so Griffin went looking for her."

Andra's heart sank. She didn't know if she wanted to hear the rest. But she had to know the truth.

"From what she could tell, Isla was attacked by desert pirates. They took all her equipment but left her . . . body. Griffin brought her back and buried her." She put a hand on Andra's shoulder. "I'm so sorry you had to hear this way."

Andra felt numb. "I have to go." She stumbled back. "I have to go."

Griffin shook her head. "I should run some tests. You should finish eating. Rest."

She reached for Andra, but Andra pushed her away and started running. Griffin called after her, but Andra didn't pause to catch her breath, just propelled herself back down the hall. Ran past the elevators, unable to stomach the thought of standing still, and took the stairs two at a time. Stumbled out into the underwater bubble, the kinetic lights blinding her eyes, and ran smack into something hard.

She nearly fell backward, but gentle hands caught her.

"Andra?" a mechanical voice said.

"Mechy," Andra breathed with relief.

"You were missing. But I followed you."

She wanted to throw her arms around him in a hug, but her grief was too strong. "I want to go home," she whimpered, and the sound of her own weak voice tore a sob from her throat.

Mechy scooped her up in his stiff arms and carried her back to the underwater lift. The ride to the surface was swift. The sun was starting to rise, glinting off the surface of the water. He placed her gently in the hover and started the engine, and together they skimmed across the lake toward the horizon.

ELEVEN

OOIIOOOI OOIIOOOI

THE TRIP BACK to Eerensed was a blur. Andra went from crying jags to going completely numb back to crying jags. Mechy made sure she drank and ate but didn't push her to talk. By the time they first saw Eerensed on the horizon, Andra had gone numb again.

When she got back to the Vaults, she found Lilibet and Rashmi meeting with Skilla and Xana in a common room down the hall from her bedroom. It held a kitchenette and small round table. They looked up from their tense conversation to see Andra standing hunched in the doorway, Mechy towering behind her.

"ANDRA!"

Lilibet jumped up and ran to her, throwing her arms around Andra, who got a mouthful of long brown hair. Rashmi watched her curiously, eyes narrowed. Skilla's face was red with fury, but as usual, Xana only had eyes for Skilla.

"Where have you been?" Skilla snapped. "Do you reck how dangerful the Wastes are? And goddess or no, we still need your abilities to build that fraughted rocket and save Eerensed."

Andra sighed. "Missed you too, General."

Skilla scowled, crossing her arms and putting both feet up on the table. "Would you care to convo us what you were doing?"

"She should rest," Rashmi said. "Talking is for later and naps are for now. This is what my mom would say when I was cranky as a child."

"I'm not cranky," Andra said.

"I wasn't talking about you." Rashmi widened her eyes at Skilla.

"No, she's right." Andra sighed. She was bone-weary, her muscles aching from the journey, her head throbbing from crying. She felt another bout of tears coming on, but she swallowed it. "We have a lot to talk about."

Mechy followed her into the room and pulled out a chair for her. Lilibet was still basically hanging off her, and Andra had to extricate herself in order to sit.

The others stared, waiting, as she decided how much to divulge.

Screw it. She was tired of keeping secrets.

She let out a heavy breath. "Griffin is alive. I found her at the bottom of a lake, and she wants us to start waking up the colonists."

The others gawked at her.

"She's . . . alive?" Rashmi's face turned ashen.

"Well, sort of. Her clone is."

Rashmi laid her head down on the table and started muttering to herself. Andra had learned not to interrupt when Rashmi got like this. Whatever was happening in her head, she needed to work through it on her own.

"The First? Is alive?" Skilla asked, but it was less of a question and more of a challenge.

"What's a clone?" Xana asked.

Andra ran a hand through her hair, trying to figure out how to explain. "She has the same . . . body and abilities and intelligence. Only, she's a different person. She doesn't have the memories of the Griffin you knew. Well, I mean, she has access to them. She can watch them in a holo . . . scry . . . ." Andra cleared her throat.

Skilla shook her head, her dark ponytail bobbing. "I don't reck why you imagined that explanation would help."

Andra winced. For a moment, the room was silent except for the hum of the kitchenette's fridge.

She sat forward. "The Griffin you knew is dead, but now there's this new Griffin. She's continuing on with what the old Griffin set out to do. Saving humanity, same as always. We just have a new plan now. And a different Griffin."

Skilla shifted, her weapons clanking against the chair. "Soze, let me full comp this. Someone who looks like the First but isn't the First is hiding somewhere in the Wastes. She's abandoned us, left us on our own, but expects us to continue doing what she asks? Is that right?"

"This time it's different."

"For true? How?"

Andra folded and unfolded her hands. "Um, well . . . we're still going to build the rocket, but to do that, we're going to wake up the colonists and . . . put a spell on them that makes them invisible to . . . pockets." Her voice seemed to give up on the last word.

Skilla blinked slowly. "So, now you have magic that will save your precious colonists, but doesn't do anything for the Schism, or the refugees, or the Eerensedians. Why am I helping you again?"

Andra leaned heavily on the table, arms splayed toward Skilla. "Okay, it doesn't help the Eerensedians *now*, but it will."

Skilla rolled her eyes, kicking back her chair. It scraped across the floor.

"We'll convo later," she snapped, and stormed off.

"It will, I promise!" Andra called after her.

"I said we'll convo later!" Skilla yelled back, already halfway down the hall.

Xana gave Andra an apologetic look and followed.

The room fell silent, Andra staring after Skilla and Xana, Rashmi mouthing words to herself, Lilibet staring wide-eyed between them. Andra wanted to tell Lilibet about her mother being dead and about the grief that had washed over her on the trip back from Lake Superior.

She wanted to tell Rashmi that they hadn't been created for a reason and commiserate with her that their existence was random with no real purpose. She wanted to tell them both about the voices she was hearing and the dead nanos and how she was scared that whatever corruption was inside her would take over. But she couldn't let her emotions sweep her under. She had to focus.

"I guess . . . we should go wake some of the colonists now . . ."

Rashmi's head shot up. "NO!"

Andra blinked. She'd never heard Rashmi's voice like that, so strong and sure. "But Griffin's clone—"

"Talking is for later. Naps are for now. Talking is for later. Naps are for now."

"Rashmi," Lilibet said, setting her hand on Rashmi's arm. "Are you evens? I can make you some hot cho-co-late." Lilibet stumbled over the word. "Kiv skooled me how they do it akitchens. And I stitched a little sweater for your mug to hold it hot for longer but also to protect your hands from that hotness. I invented it myself! I call it a snuggle! Because it snuggles your mug!"

"I don't want to wake the colonists," Rashmi said, her voice a high, thin whine. "I want to . . . I want to . . ." She growled in frustration and set her head back down on the table. "I just want to be human for now. I don't want to remember what it was like not to be."

Andra bit the inside of her cheek. Something inside her didn't want to wake the colonists either. Something argued that the humans weren't her responsibility. If Griffin wanted the colonists awake, she could come do it herself.

You don't have to do this, a voice said. It sounded just like the voice telling her to destroy.

She shook it off. If there was a way to protect people from the pockets, she needed to at least try. Besides, even if there wasn't a *specific* reason she'd been created, she was still meant to serve humanity. And if the upgrade worked, she could find a way to fit

115

the Eerensedians with 'implants. Then they could keep working on getting everyone off the planet.

"It's only a few people, Rashmi," Andra said. "Just the LAC scientists. I promise. Besides, they can help us."

"No one can help us," Rashmi muttered, her face smushed against the table.

Andra sighed. She wished she knew how to help Rashmi. She didn't know how much of Rashmi's trauma was having her programming stripped away and how much was because of what she went through in the dungeons. Maybe if Rashmi would talk about the time before Andra woke, Andra could help her. But talking only seemed to make things worse.

Talking for later. Naps for now.

"I can help," Lilibet said. "I purpose, can I? I'm getting so good at magic, and I practice nearish as much as I do my stitches. I reck I can't do goddess magic, but I can do small magic if you need help. Can I?"

For the first time since hearing about her mother's death, Andra smiled.

LILIBET FOLLOWED ANDRA through the LAC annex beneath the silver tower, Mechy trailing behind.

Andra hated the place.

Though Mechy had cleaned out the skeletons and reinforced the sections threatening to collapse, Andra didn't come here unless she needed to. He'd done a fine job. Eco'tile, kinetic orbs. It was almost restored to what it had been in Andra's time. Except it was missing all the people. No scientists, no guests, no admin personnel. Just Andra and Lilibet, heading toward the underground warehouse that hid a million colonists.

Andra heaved the huge metal door open to reveal the enormous room beyond.

The Icebox creeped Andra out. It was too big. Too empty of signs of life, too full of frozen life. The echo of her footsteps seemed to go on forever, and she had the urge to whisper. The dark gray hardcrete walls felt ominous. And the harsh sound the lights made when they turned on echoed eerily.

It was miles to the opposite end of the Icebox, so they had to take a hover. Lilibet didn't stop chatting about how excited she was until they reached the cryo'station set up against the far wall. Mechy pulled the hover to a stop, and Andra hopped out.

As soon as she approached the work'station, dozens of holo'displays flickered to life, taking up twenty feet of the wall from floor to ceiling and casting the cavernous room in a gentle glow of data and charts. There was a glass semicircular holo'table, with an ergo'chair Andra had adjusted to fit her body perfectly.

She thought about all the times she'd been there, how her eyes had skimmed over the colonist map on the work'station holo'display, and she'd avoided looking.

If she had just looked, she would have realized her mother was missing.

A bout of grief threatened to overwhelm her, but she shoved it away in a little pocket of her mind.

Andra handed Lilibet a tablet she'd networked to the cryo'station. "I need you to monitor vitals and protocols. If anything starts flashing red, use that code—*spell* I showed you."

Lilibet nodded with a grin. Andra swiveled her chair toward the myriad of 'displays.

"Here goes," she muttered, and brought up the controls for the reanimation procedures. The map of the Icebox twirled in front of her, a million people minimized to dots on a map. With her pointer finger, she highlighted the section of cryo'tanks closest to them— the ones that held the LAC scientists—before remembering that she could just mentally interface with the work'station.

She thought about isolating the 'tanks for the LAC, and the program complied. All she had to do was wish for the reanimation to begin, and it would.

Reanimation was a delicate procedure but mostly automated. Cryo'techs were specially trained on how to instigate the procedure and troubleshoot in emergencies. But their main purpose had been dealing with patients before and after the freezing process. Unless something went wrong—like when Andra woke—the latch would open on its own, the cryo'protectant drain, the life support detach. But the people would be weak and naked and scared. Andra decided it was best to wake them up one at a time for now, until there were more people to facilitate the process.

She scanned the names of the LAC scientists, some she recognized, some she didn't.

Daphle Hanson, cryo'engineer, life support
Luke Walker, terraformation specialist, atmosphere
Cruz Alvarez, AI technician, social protocols

Andra stopped, her heart leaping into her throat.

She'd known Cruz worked at LAC, but thought he'd been an intern for her mother. She hadn't known he'd been an AI tech. Social protocols. Did that mean . . . ?

There were plenty of AI technicians at LAC, but Andra always assumed they worked with robotic AI, not True AI. Because up until recently she didn't believe True AI existed. But now she had to wonder. Which did Cruz work with? 'Bots or bodies?

He'd been friends with Andra, something other than friends with Rashmi. Had they just been part of his job? To teach them social protocols?

Something rose up inside her, and it took her a moment to realize it was hurt. She thought she'd reached her capacity for sadness about what it meant to be an AI, but each new blow stung as sharply as the last.

She shook away the pain and kept scanning.

Brooker Jackson, interstellar engineering
Han Li, terraformation specialist, farming and agriculture
Isla Lim-Watts, vice president of colonization

Her cryo'tank was grayed out.

Andra took a deep breath to steady herself and kept reading.

She read name after name until, finally, she found someone that might be useful.

Ophele Hammad, senior cryo'technician

Bingo.

She could wake up Ophele, have enough time to walk over to her 'tank, and then help her out to start the reanimation procedures. Mechy had set up a makeshift reanimation therapy station in the center aisle, but Andra didn't know what she was doing. Ophele did and would be able to walk Andra through her own procedures, and then help with the next person.

This was perfect. Now all she had to do was start the actual re-animation.

Andra thought with will and intent about the 'tech waking up, and the process began.

Dozens of monitors that usually displayed statistics and vitals started flashing red. A single message blinked in the center.

Reanimation in: 1 minute and 22 seconds
Reanimation in: 1 minute and 21 seconds
Reanimation in: 1 minute and 20 seconds

That was faster than Andra had expected. She'd need to locate Ophele quickly, so she would be there when she woke up.

"Uhh, Andra?" she heard Lilibet say behind her.

"Not now, Lilibet."

"Firm. I reck it full imports to look now." Lilibet's voice shook.

Andra turned to see Lilibet holding up the tablet Andra had given her showing the map of the cryo'tanks. All of them were flashing red. She snatched it from Lilibet, muscles tense, and began to interface back and forth between the tablet and the work'station, but she knew what was wrong before they told her.

The colonists were waking up.

All of them.

"How did this happen?"

Reanimation in: 1 minute and 3 seconds

Andra ran a hand through her hair. Had she done this? Was it because her AI abilities were on the fritz? Or had it been the thing inside her? Was it no longer just a disembodied voice, but somehow acting on its own accord?

She shoved the tablet back at Lilibet.

"Use the stabilization code. I have to figure out how to stop this."

She didn't wait for Lilibet's response, just turned back to the work'station. She was met with a barrage of data. Temperature readings. Vital signs. Cryo'protectant and reanimator gel ratios. Her subconscious began absorbing the information and comprehending it faster than a human would be able to. She typed commands and algorithms into the 'display.

Reanimation in: 48 seconds

There was a method to the mass reanimation process. The colonists furthest along were those most critical to the colonization: the LAC scientists. They were followed by their families and those in integral professions like food distribution and health care. From there, the groups someone (Dr. Griffin?) had determined were most vital to society.

Andra's mind was able to write algorithms while still processing the fact that someone had *planned* for a mass reanimation. Whether they had intended for it to happen, she didn't know. But there was a protocol in place in case it was necessary. And whatever Andra had done had triggered that protocol.

Now it was on her to stop it.

Only, she wasn't doing it fast enough.

Reanimation in: 24 seconds

A million colonists would wake up to a postapocalyptic Earth with nowhere to go and the threat of rampant corrupted technology hanging over them. Scared and naked and alone in their 'tanks.

Andra opened her mind, reaching for her AI state, but all she found was frustration. Her own . . . and the work'station's?

It was panicked. Scared. Somehow, the system knew this wasn't right. Knew this wasn't its intended purpose. Felt as though it was failing.

Andra tried to calm it, but she didn't have time to reassure a machine when a million lives were at stake.

Reanimation in: 10 seconds

Her thoughts became nothing but algorithms and lines of code. It was one thing to stop the reanimation process. It was quite another to reverse it. She had to make a decision. She had to choose.

She sent out a final string of code and felt a rush of nausea.

"Did you stop it?" Lilibet asked.

Andra started to nod, then shook her head, then nodded again. "Sort of."

She *had* stopped something. She'd stopped the reanimation process for artists and realtors and constructionists and bakers. They would stay safely in stasis until all of this was sorted out.

But she hadn't stopped everything.

Dozens of screens flashed one final message:

Reanimation in: O seconds

They went blank, and Andra let out a long breath.

She heard the sound of hundreds of cryo'tanks breaking their seal.

Because even though she'd stopped the process for 986,002 colonists, she hadn't been able to prevent it for 1,427 LAC scientists and their families.

And now, they were waking up.

TWELVE

THE GRIFTER

ZHADE WOKE THE next moren with bruises on his arms, blood dried round his nose and ears, dirt under his fingernails. His head throbbed and his muscles ached, but he couldn't help but feel the success of the previous even.

He'd used the Crown to spell the graftling wand, and it had changed Meta's . . . everything. She could now for true pass as Tsurina. What had started as a fool plan now actualish had a chance of succeeding.

Zhade tumbled out of Maret's too-soft bed, washing and dressing quickish, energy buzzing through him.

Half abell later, he was in the cathedzal, surrounded by guards and angels. He felt the latter at the edge of his consciousness, as though they were waiting for his command. The feeling gave him a dizzying rush as he imagined all he'd do now that he could use the Crown. Commanding the angelic guard wouldn't be a problem anymore. The weapons were his to control with a thought. It would be an eyebeat to hunt down whoever was sending the angels rogue. For all the headaches he'd suffered, maybe the Crown was worth the pain. He could for true rule Eerensed with it.

He was wearing one of Maret's favorite outfits. Black with gold stitching. A starched cape hanging from his shoulders. Usualish,

Zhade would have felt uncomfortistic, but today he felt powerful and free.

Maret had done so much wrong with the Crown, but Zhade could do so much right.

There was a large crowd assembled in the cathedzal this moren. The guv-askings used to be held in the throne room, but Andra had destroyed the roof. It had taken dozens of people three full days to make their march over broken glass and splintered wood to uproot the felled tree from beneath the marble floor and transport it to the cathedzal for the guv-askings.

It was a symbolic move. With the goddesses sacrificed, the people were looking for something to believe in. He'd had the stained glass of the coil, crystal, and celestia replaced with one of a map of Eerensed. The stardust vents were filled in with mortar. Now this was no longer a place of worship but a place for the people. And for the dome that protected them.

Behind Zhade, the lights of dozens of scrys flashed. Andra's angel had built it so he could control the dome himself. The scrys covered most of the back wall. Afront of them was a translucent desk, and next to it, a shiny metal box Andra said held the dome's power. He'd been neglecting that part of his duties, but no more. He would solve the rogue angel problem and then use the Crown to design a dome that didn't need constant maintenance.

The crowd quieted, and the guards let the first asker through. Zhade's benevolent smile faltered. He recked her. It was the mother of the girl who had nearish been choked to death by the angel the previous moren.

She stepped forward, wringing her hands. "What happens bout the angels?"

His heart sped up. He couldn't reveal that he'd been there and witnessed the assault and done nothing bout it. He wanted to help, but he had to first appear ignorant.

"What bout them?" His fingers tapped against the throne's arm-rests.

"They've gone rogue!" the woman cried. "Yestermoren, my daughter and neighbor were nearish killed by one of the patrol angels. And after, another angel tried to stab its sorcer! I've heard of other attacks too, Guv. Something must be done!"

"I hear." Zhade swallowed. "And what became of the angels?"

The mother froze, color draining from her face. "They were . . . destroyed, Guv."

Zhade nodded. "Good. As they should be. If there are any more attacks, destroy them if you must, but do what you can to bring me one alive."

"I have one, Guv!" a frail voice called from the back.

Zhade started. That happened quickish. The guards brought forward the owner of the voice—an old with a magic arm. The appendage looked almost exactish like Wead's had. Zhade blinked back the memories. He had to stay focused.

The man stood small and frail afront of the throne, an angel by his side, bareish larger than him, its pale skin muddied with age. It had thin limbs and a clear skull. Magic sparked inside its head.

Zhade leaned forward to inspect it.

It didn't seem like the rogue angel he'd seen yesteraftermoren. The dark aura that had surrounded the angel who'd attacked the little girl and Dzeni was nowhere to be found on this angel. It was serene and obedient, its eyes a neutral white.

"This angel attacked someone?"

The old man nodded. "Firm, Guv. It attacked my promised. I tried to stop it, but I 'pen not as strong as I once was. After, it went norm. Followed me here sawn complaint."

Zhade stood and approached the angel. He reached out with the Crown, feeling for the darkness. There was nothing. Maybe he could use High Magic to scry the inner workings of the angel. He pushed harder, waiting for the same sense he'd had before. The merging of his mind with the Crown. The infinite possibilities. But all he felt was a locked door. His temple began to throb with the strain.

Zhade cleared his throat. "Thank you, citian. We'll . . . hold this to test spells on. Figure the source of its magic . . . And how is your promised?"

"Dead, Guv."

Zhade blinked, stunned. The man's promised had just died, and he'd brought the angel here himself? The least Zhade could do was kill his promised's murderer afront of him. He didn't have Cheska's strength or anger, but he did have the Crown. Perhaps the pain had been a flute.

"Sorries and worries, citians."

Zhade didn't let himself dwell on the man's look of surprise, before diving back into the Crown. The angel felt expectant. Prepped to serve. Loyal. Zhade wondered if it even had memory of killing.

It didn't meteor. It had still done it.

He pressed past the pain, looking for the killing charm inside the angel, the spell that would end it mereish as certz as removing its heart. He'd sole ever used the kill charm with Low Magic a palmful of times, and never with High Magic. His temple ached. He felt either sweat or blood running down his cheek.

"Guv?" someone asked.

"I'm—"

The angel's hand shot out and clamped round Zhade's throat.

He was lifted off the ground as his finger grasped ineffectualish at the angel's metal arm. There were shouts round him. The clank of armor. He couldn't imagine past the pain and the lack of air, and sands, this hurt.

He lashed out with his arm, struggling, wheezing. People were shouting. Black spots filled his vision. His toes dangled above the marble floor. Zhade tried to dive back into High Magic, but he could sole focus on his need for air.

air air air air air

His eyes began to close. This couldn't be it. He couldn't die here now. Killed by a rogue angel afront of his people. When the ability to stop it was in his grasp, tacked on his head. No one here even recked who he for true was. No one would mourn him. Reck all he'd done for the city. He hadn't gotten to say goodbye to Andra.

Andra.

His last imagining was of her. The dimple when she smiled. The sarcastic comments in her funny little accent. The way she never gave up. She fought. And fought. And cared. And loved.

He wondered if she would miss him.

A spear burst through the angel's chest. Zhade fell to the floor with a slap, landing on his hip and elbow. Pain shot through his bones. He coughed as Gryfud pulled him away.

Through blurry vision, he saw someone in a white dress twirl her spear in the air several times, knock the angel to the ground with the butt of it, then flip it round to pierce it once more into the angel's chest. When she yanked the spear free, the angel's smoking heart was stuck to the tip.

Meta turned and smiled in the most Tsurina-like fashion.

"Are you evens, my son?" she asked, her voice a hypnotic purr.

Zhade nodded, letting her help him to his feet.

Panic swirled in his chest, closed his throat. Meta had saved him, but his citians had just seen him fail to use the Crown. If they recked he was powerless, they would overthrow him.

He cleared his throat, scowled. "Dispose of the angel's corpse," he commanded, trying to add Maret's characteristic whine to his voice. "Anyone with an angel should surrender it to the palace soon and now, or face the consequences."

He'd seen Maret do this—go on the offensive. Make the people worry bout their own lives, rather than focus on his faults. He felt sick even attempting the tactic.

But it worked. The crowd shuffled nervousish.

He met Meta's eyes. She nodded in approval, the barest hint of a grin on her lips.

"And if I find anyone hasn't surrendered their angels to the palace by the end of the day, they'll become familiar with our dungeons."

The threat tasted bitter on his tongue, sounded so much like his brother. But what choice did he have? He had to seem strong to maintain his power. He had to rule Eerensed to save it. Sides, it was sole threats. He wouldn't actualish do it.

Before the citians could see the truth on his face—his regret, his discomfort—he turned and stalked out of the cathedzal.

THIRTEEN

OO||OOO| OO||OO||

Andra's feet slapped against the concrete floor of the Icebox as she ran past lines of inert cryo'tanks toward the row of LAC scientists. Some of them would be able to get free of their 'tanks. Others would be stuck on higher shelves where they had been stored like so many boxes. She could hear the echo of movement and voices, fifteen hundred people waking up from a thousand years of sleep.

At least it's not all *the colonists,* she thought, but it didn't soothe her.

She flung herself down an aisle between the towering shelves of closed cryo'tanks. Light glinted off their casing. The colonists stored in these, at least, were blissfully unaware of what was happening. They weren't waking alone, panicked, with no one to help them, to an unfamiliar world. Andra pushed herself harder, the concrete floor slippery beneath her feet.

She'd sent Mechy to bring supplies and Lilibet to stand by the Icebox door at the far end to keep people from leaving, giving her a lie to feed them about a toxic atmosphere. It was miles off, but there were so many people waking, and they would be confused and searching for a way out. Andra sent a panicked neural message to Rashmi but didn't receive a reply.

She picked up the pace, ignoring the stitch in her side and her heaving breaths, as she turned the corner down the next row and ran smack into Cruz Alvarez.

A very *naked* Cruz Alvarez.

He grabbed her shoulders and blinked in surprise. "Andie!"

Andra stared. Even coated in 'protectant residue, dark curls plastered to his head, he instilled a sense of nostalgia and longing in her. He was so cute. So smart. Analytical but creative. Practical but compassionate. Even now, knowing that her crush had been nothing more than her programming reacting to intelligence—oh god, she'd probably been programmed to be attracted to him specifically—she still felt the rush of butterflies in her stomach. She blushed and waved awkwardly.

He released her, and Andra came back to herself enough to realize there were other colonists before her. Some wandering around. Some attempting to cover themselves or help those on higher shelves climb down. The noise of the waking colonists was quickly becoming a roar of activity.

Cruz ran a hand over his face, smudging the cryo'protectant. "Jesus, Andie, you got dressed in a hurry."

He smiled, showing a line of straight, white teeth, and Andra felt the same way she did that first day Cruz ate at their house and winked at her over his green beans. She pushed the emotion away.

Andra swallowed. "I was already awake."

"What?" Cruz blinked. "What's going on? Where are we?"

He placed his hands on his hips, looking around. He didn't seem ashamed of his nakedness. Why should he? She was just an AI, and, apparently, he was privy to the fact.

And also, he had nothing to be ashamed of, Andra thought with a blush.

She opened her mouth but found she couldn't speak. It was overwhelming to be confronted with someone from her past. Someone who knew her not as a goddess but as Andra. Someone, other than

Rashmi and Mechy, who spoke in her accent and dialect, who had a shared history, who would understand her inside jokes and sim references.

She should have been overwrought with emotions. This. This was what she had wanted all this time, to be back with people from her time. But instead she just felt . . . awkward. It was a different kind of culture shock to be confronted with a past you longed for, then suddenly realized you were alienated from.

"Andie?" Cruz repeated. "Are you okay? What's wrong?" His voice carried just the right amount of tension, like he cared, but didn't want to make things worse by panicking himself. He reached out a hand but didn't quite touch her.

"It's . . . a long story. But things didn't go as planned."

Cruz's eyebrows furrowed, and Andra had the odd compulsion to smooth his forehead with her fingers. The urge to show physical affection was something Zhade had awakened in her, only now that she realized how inappropriate it was.

"I'll explain everything later," she said. "I promise. But I need you to keep everyone calm and organized. See what you can do for clothes with what people put in their 'tank drawers, and I'll worry bout the food. And whatever you do, *don't* let them leave the warehouse."

Cruz was shaking his head, as though Andra was going too fast, as though he couldn't process all the information at once. He was only human, after all.

"I promise," she said. "I'll explain everything as soon as I can. Just . . . don't let anyone leave."

She could only imagine the chaos that would happen if the colonists realized they were on Earth. If they found the Schism, or goddess forbid, appeared in Eerensed.

"I won't," Cruz said, and it was one of the things that had drawn her to Cruz, that he took her seriously. Now, she knew it was because she was AI, and he knew it. He trusted her programming.

"Promise?" She held her pinkie out to him, definitely avoiding looking down.

"Promise." He smiled and hooked his pinkie with hers. "But you owe me an explanation."

And so do you, she thought.

"I owe you several. Now, get everyone in a group down at that end of the warehouse." She pointed in the direction of the reanimation therapy tent Mechy had set up. "And I'll meet you in ten minutes."

She could tell by the look on Cruz's face he was already making plans. Already figuring out what needed to be done and how.

A neural message appeared in her mind from Lilibet's tablet, saying she'd already turned a few people away from the exit, but they believed the story about the atmosphere being unstable. So. That was good. Andra mentally checked in with Mechy, who said he was coming back with a hover full of supplies and, surprisingly, Xana. Rashmi still hadn't responded.

Andra tried to calm herself, to think through the plan. Naked colonists were everywhere, yelling to each other, scrounging through their 'tank drawers for . . . drawers. They walked past her as though they didn't see her, as though she didn't even exist.

Someone bumped her shoulder as he passed, a young man Andra recognized as Raj . . . something. He was in cryonics, maybe. He didn't apologize. Didn't even acknowledge her.

That was fine. They wouldn't listen to her—they didn't even know her, except as maybe Isla's daughter—but they would listen to Cruz. He was one of them. He would help her get everyone organized, clothed, and through the reanimation therapy. Then, she would tell Cruz the truth and have him convey it to the rest of the LAC. Well. Maybe not the truth. A lie that was close enough to the truth. If Cruz was the one telling them, they'd believe him.

Then Andra would need to get the colonists food, water, and shelter.

Then start upgrading their tech, and instruct them to build the rocket with their cryo'chambers.

The Icebox seemed to shrink, her vision darkening, breath shortening. This was all happening too quickly. She had to leave. Let Cruz deal with all this. Let Skilla worry about what would happen if the colonists left the Icebox. Or Zhade. Someone else could take care of the consequences. She turned to go, searching for a path through the crowd, but a voice broke through the roar of a thousand voices.

"ANDRA!"

Her vision cleared, and a small figure darted toward her.

"ANDRA!"

Oz.

Her baby brother.

Oz, who she hadn't even looked for, because she couldn't bear the idea he could be missing. Oz, who looked up to her, worshipped her, never treated her like she wasn't enough.

He bounded toward her, his smile pushing up his round cheeks to almost cover his eyes. His brown hair was sticky with cryo'protectant, and he wore an oversized T-shirt with a cartoon 'bot on it. He threw himself into her arms, and Andra wrapped hers around him and let out a sob.

Oz squirmed. "What's wrong?"

It took Andra a moment to remember that to Oz, it had only been a few hours since they'd seen each other. Whereas she'd been awake for months, and for part of that time thought Oz was long dead.

"Nothing," she croaked. "Nothing's wrong." She cradled his face. "I'm just glad to see you."

He ducked his chin. "You got your tears all over me. And why's your hair so long?"

She absentmindedly tugged at the strands. "It's . . . complicated."

"Andromeda," she heard another voice say, and her stomach dropped.

She looked up to see her father and sister, staring confusedly at her. Both had shaved their heads and wore the special clothes they'd picked out for their first day on Holymyth.

Andra stood. Oz grasped her hand, beaming up at her. Her father reached out and tugged lightly at her hair, then met her eyes.

"Have you seen your mother?"

Panic swelled in Andra, and tears threatened to spill. There was so much to be done, and she couldn't let herself be taken over by grief. She couldn't tell them. Not yet. She didn't know how.

She bit her lip and shook her head.

IN A LITTLE less than an hour, the LAC scientists had organized themselves into groups: some setting up shelters, others labs, still others rudimentary infrastructure and bathing facilities. Without Andra even having to ask, Ophele had taken up shop in the therapy tent, helping the colonists adjust to the rude awakening. Others were searching through the food Mechy had surreptitiously brought. Xana stayed by the door to make sure no one left the Icebox, and Lilibet handed out the hundreds of blankets she'd stitched in her boredom underground. No one questioned who she was or why she was there. Or commented on her weird speech patterns. The shock wouldn't last forever, though, and eventually, after they had seen to all their immediate needs, people would start to ask questions.

Andra's father was laying out the tent her family would sleep in, and she stood awkwardly holding one of the poles. Cruz hung back in her peripheral vision, waiting for her to explain to him what the hell was going on, but she was having trouble disconnecting from her family. She needed to tell them about Isla, of course, but not now. It was too much. For them. For her. After everything was organized, she would sit them down and tell them. But for now each moment she spent around them felt like a lie.

Her father was wearing one of his professor shirts with the elbow patches. He had started wearing them ironically, but now he said he didn't feel like himself without them. His head was shaved, but he kept running a hand over it, as though he was repeatedly startled that his normally perfectly gelled hair was missing.

Acadia had barely spoken. She kept giving Andra glares and then looking away when Andra caught her. Oz had barely stopped talking. He wanted to know all about Holymyth and if he could get out the 'drone he'd techno'sealed and use it to explore the planet and could he go find his friends and what was the latest news from Earth.

Luckily, he barely took a breath, so Andra didn't have to answer.

Andra wanted to cry looking at them. It was an odd feeling. For so long she'd thought they were dead. She'd grieved them. Then, she'd waited for them to wake up, imagining what the reunion would be like, putting it off, and now that it was here, it was both more and less than what she'd expected.

To them, it had sole been a few minutes since they'd last seen Andra. Of course, she looked a little different, hair longer, waist thinner, complexion sallow, but the only person who would have noticed was her mother, and her mother wasn't here.

They didn't treat her any differently than they always had, which was to say her father was distracted, her sister distant, her brother effusive. It should have made her feel at home, sparked some sense of nostalgia in her, even if it was only part of her programming. But instead she just felt tired.

She'd lived a whole other life they knew nothing about. She'd been a goddess. She'd discovered she was an AI. She'd saved a city. And to them she was still just Andra, the awkward, sarcastic, under-achieving middle child.

A sudden shiver ran up her spine, and Andra drew her sweater tighter around her, but the chill didn't go away.

Destroy.

Andra stiffened, sucking in a breath. The voice was quiet, so quiet she wasn't sure if she'd actually heard it or if she'd simply imagined it.

Destroy.

Her heart stuttered. This time it was clear enough that it seemed impossible her family hadn't as well. But Oz was still chattering, Acadia didn't look up from her tablet, and her father was fussing with the tent.

Destroy.

A burst of pain shot through Andra, and she coughed into her hand. Big heaving coughs that interrupted her brother's speech about 'drone racers in stasis.

"Okay there, Andromeda?" her father asked without turning from the tent instructions.

"Yeah, evens—fine," she stammered, but she wasn't.

It wasn't just a voice—it was *her* voice. And it wasn't just a word, it was . . . a compulsion. An overwhelming need. The voice wasn't convincing her to destroy. The urge was already there. If anything, she had to convince herself not to.

"I'll be right back," Andra said, setting down the tent pole she'd been clinging to.

Oz waved enthusiastically, and Acadia gave her an icy look over her tablet. Her father looked like he was about to protest, but Andra ducked away before he could say anything. With her back turned to them, Andra opened the hand she coughed into. It was covered in black residue of decaying nanos.

"Okay, Andie, now what?"

Andra jumped. Cruz was standing right next to her.

"Jesus." She wiped her hand on her pants. "I didn't see you."

Cruz grinned sheepishly, hands thrust into his pockets. His curls fell over his eyes. At least he was wearing clothes now. "Sorry. You . . . okay? You look a little pale."

"Fine," Andra said. She hesitated a moment, waiting for the voice or another bout of coughing, but none came.

Cruz narrowed his brown eyes, but his grin didn't fade. "All right, Andie. What's the deal here?"

Andra swallowed. "So, um, for now, I, uh, need you to tell everyone there are . . . atmospheric anomalies on the surface. Say that Dr. Griffin woke early to address this, but she needs the help of the LAC to continue. Tell them she's stuck on the surface, but left a list of *very specific* instructions, starting with upgrading everyone's tech."

Andra had thought the lie was pretty good, if she did say so herself. Technically, there were atmospheric anomalies, Griffin was stuck elsewhere, and she had given very specific instructions.

Cruz narrowed his eyes. "*Tell* them? Is it not true?"

Andra grimaced. "It is . . . vaguely true . . . if you squint."

"Andie—"

"I promise." Andra put a hand to her heart. "I will tell you the truth, the whole truth, and nothing but the truth, so help me goddess, but first we need to make sure everything is calm and organized."

Cruz shook his head, but there was a quirk to his lips, a spark in his eyes. He had always loved puzzles. "All right, Andie. I don't know why they'd listen to me. I'm still just a junior scientist."

Were you? Andra thought, leading Cruz a few rows over to where Mechy had set up a projekit from the Vaults, so Cruz's voice could be heard above the crowd. She gestured to it, and Cruz grinned.

He grabbed the mic and hopped onto a nearby cryo storage shelf. He hung there for a moment, testing its weight, and then scrambled up a few rungs, so he could look out over the makeshift tent city popping up in the warehouse.

"Excuse me," he said, his voice echoing through hovering speakers. There was a squeal of feedback and Cruz winced, but the ambient noise of over a thousand people quieted and heads turned his way. He cleared his throat.

"Hello, LAC," he tried again, and this time, his voice echoed clearly. "I have some important information, so if you could pause what you're doing and gather round for a moment, I'd appreciate it."

It was actually pretty impressive to watch fifteen hundred people stop what they were doing and form a crowd below where he stood, several shelves up. One hand grabbed a metal rung, and he leaned forward over the crowd.

He told them the pseudo lie Andra had given him, that there were issues with the atmosphere, that Griffin had woken early and needed their help. He embellished with his unique charm, cracking jokes, giving out compliments, all the personable things Andra could never manage. She rolled her eyes, but it was exactly what the people needed to hear.

"And of course," Cruz added, "our fearless leaders didn't want you to be without the love and support of your families. So congratulations, LAC and our extended family: you are now the first people awake on an alien planet!"

There was a smattering of applause, but not enough to cover someone shouting from the back of the crowd, "And where is Griffin?"

Cruz's smile faltered the perfect amount, just enough to lend authenticity to his claim, but not enough to make people worried. "Unfortunately, she's been stranded in a bunker some miles off while getting some atmospheric readings of the planet, so she'll be working remotely until we can get her some transportation. Don't worry, though. She's perfectly safe. And so are we."

Excitement buzzed through the crowd.

"Dr. Griffin has asked me to pass on her instructions to you." Cruz paled, and Andra caught a small tremor in his hand. "And I happily accepted the position."

There were murmurs of surprise from the older LAC scientists.

"Now," Cruz hurried on, before anyone could dispute his claim. "We are going to construct a few makeshift structures so we can rest, and then tomorrow you will each be assigned tasks. And"—Cruz found Andra in the crowd, as though he were making sure he was getting this all right—"we will be running an upgrade on your tech, so just be prepared to have a quick procedure on your 'implant sometime in the next few days."

Andra nodded, and Cruz smiled back at her.

The crowd dispersed, going back to making meals and putting up tents and organizing clothes. Andra hung back and Cruz leapt the last few feet off the cryo' shelving, landing on the concrete floor with a slap.

"Well done," Andra said.

"Thanks." He grinned, and the expression warmed Andra. It was so genuine. "Now, as a token of your gratitude, do you mind telling me what's really happening?"

Andra shushed him, looking around to see if anyone was listening. "Not here."

"Andra!" a voice cut in, and a small grimy hand tugged at her arm. She looked down into Oz's smiling face. "Come help us put up our tent! And then Dad said I could play Hive'Mind! I'll let you be the Queen if you play with me."

"I . . ." Andra couldn't think of an excuse. She'd been putting off telling them about Isla, but she wouldn't be able to much longer. "I'll be right there," she said, patting Oz's head. "Will you give me a minute?"

"SURE!" Oz shouted too loudly, and then ran off.

"We'll talk in the moren," Andra whispered to Cruz. "After breakfast."

Cruz gave her a confused look, then nodded and winked. It was different than Zhade's winks. Awkward but somehow still charming.

"Naps for now, talking for later?" he asked.

She grimaced, realizing Cruz had probably picked up the expression from Rashmi while they were "dating."

Andra waved goodbye, then made her way through the crowd of colonists, dodging playing children, winding around tents, until she found her family, their shelter already up. LAC tents were comfortable by any standards. Theirs was a forest green, and Andra didn't have to duck as she entered the wide doorway. The whole structure was about the size of Andra's old suite in the palace, but felt both homier and more claustrophobic. Oz was trying to get Acadia's attention, but she was swatting him away, lying back on a cot, intent on her holo'band. Her father was setting up a bed that was wide enough for both him and Isla.

"Andromeda, where did you run off to?" he said distractedly. "Did you find your mother? Did she want you to help with something?"

Andra bit her lip, taking in her family. The people she grew up with. "We need to talk."

They paused at the tenor in her voice and stared. Andra took a deep breath.

IT WENT ABOUT as well as Andra expected.

She was vague about how she found out about Isla's death. She avoided mentioning that Dr. Griffin was a clone turned goddess living in exile under what was left of Lake Superior, letting them believe the explanation Cruz had given. She told them that Griffin had woken Isla before the others. That they'd been out in the desert running terraforming tests, and Isla died in an accident. She didn't say it had been Western pirates. Instead, she blamed an experiment gone wrong.

Huge tears were running down Oz's face as he tried to stifle his childlike sobs. Acadia sat stoic, muscles in her face tense, knuckles white. Auric, most of all, broke Andra's heart. His lower lip wobbled, even as he took in a steadying breath to put on a brave face for his kids.

"Well," he said, voice no more than a whisper, "she died doing what she loved. And on a new planet, no less."

He stood and walked jerkily to the other side of the tent, looking away. Andra pretended not to see his shoulders heaving.

"Did you . . ." Oz hiccuped a sob. "Can we bury her?"

Andra brushed Oz's tangled hair back. "I'm sorry, Oz, no. There's . . . We can't."

He laid his head against Andra's stomach.

"Now, because of . . ." She took a breath. "I'm going to have more responsibilities, so I might not be around a lot, so don't—"

Auric slammed his fist against a table. "NO!" He turned. His face was red in anger, more anger than Andra had ever seen there. "You're a child! You don't have any responsibility concerning any of this! She pushed you children. She wanted us to go on this . . . doomed mission. And look what happened. And now you're going to sacrifice yourself to this too? Finish her work so you can get yourself killed just like she did? There are so many other scientists. Why do *you* have to be involved?"

Andra swallowed. "I just do, Dad."

"Yeah," Acadia snapped. "Why you? You never showed any interest in any of this stuff. You were always off in your room getting off to your dictionary while I was doing all the real work."

"Acadia," Auric warned.

"Stay with us, Andra!" Oz said, his eyes red.

"Andra, you don't need to do this," Auric said.

"I have to," Andra said.

"But why?" Auric asked.

"Yeah, why?" Acadia echoed.

"Why?" Oz added.

"Because I'm AI!"

The tent fell silent.

She hadn't meant to say it like that. Hadn't mean to say it at all. One look at her family's faces, and she knew none of them had known, hadn't even suspected. How much had Isla Watts kept from her family?

"That's . . ." her father said, voice crisp. "What are you talking about?"

Andra forced herself to look him in the eye. "I'm a wetware AI in a human body. I don't know the details, but Mom and Dr. Griffin created me. To help humanity. To . . . help with *this*. I grew up thinking I was human, but when I woke early, I . . . learned the truth."

Auric shook his head. "That's not the truth. That's impossible."

Andra sighed, trying to steady herself, to sound firm. "Think about it, Dad. You know it's true."

"No." He shook his head, pacing the small space. "No."

Acadia let out an unamused bark of a laugh, tossing her tablet to the floor and storming out of the tent.

"I don't understand," Oz said, a slight wobble still in his voice. "What's wrong?"

Andra smoothed back his hair.

"I'm not your sister," she said, as gently as possible.

"Andra, don't," her father started.

"What?" Oz asked, easing away from her. "You're not Andra?"

"I *am* Andra. But I was never your sister."

"You're adopted?"

"I'm artificial intelligence. Like . . ." Andra looked around for something to help her explain. She pointed at one of Oz's toys, propped up on his cot. "Like the Guardian from 'Bot Wars but with a human body."

His eyes went wide, and his mouth hung open.

"That's . . ."

Andra's eyes were already smarting, her stomach sinking.

". . . so . . . COOL."

He grabbed Andra's hands again and pulled her to her feet.

"My sister's a robot, my sister's a robot," he chanted, doing a little kid dance. There were still tears streaking down his cheeks, but a huge grin spread across his face.

"Oz, we need to talk about what this means," she said.

"Do you have any cool robot abilities?"

A laugh bubbled up inside her. She reached out with her thoughts and caught all the passing nanos until they were thick enough to see. Sparks glittered around her. She held out her hand and let them dance across her palm, curl around her fingers. She clenched her fist and when she opened it, let the nanos disperse.

"NO. WAY," Oz breathed.

Auric cleared his throat. "Is that why? Is that why you were awake before the rest of us?"

She couldn't be sure, but she thought she saw the affection in her father's face replaced with fear.

"Yeah." Andra nodded. Cleared her throat. "Because I'm not like the rest of you."

HOURS LATER, ANDRA sat with a blanket wrapped around her shoulders outside her family's tent.

The Icebox was lit with 'fire after 'fire, the main lights doused to prepare for night. Though the colonists had just woken, it was important to get their bodies on the same rhythm as the planet they thought was Holymyth. Most would be sleeping inside their drained 'tanks or on nests of fabric torn from clothes stored there. Lilibet and Xana had brought as many cots as they could find, which, to be fair, had been a lot. But it hadn't been fifteen hundred.

After announcing the lie Andra had fed him, Cruz had called the more senior LAC personnel for a meeting, giving each of them tasks to coordinate, from building shelters to creating food from the frozen rations and synth'bots stored in 'tanks. Andra had expected chaos, but it seemed humans craved order. Families had found each other, social groups started to form, and the lack of supplies or information wasn't yet a frustration. They were still on an adventure. Andra didn't know how long that would last.

Acadia was reading inside the tent. She hadn't spoken a word to Andra since storming off. Oz was playing with a sim on his cot, giggling and growling at something only he could see. Every once in a while, Andra would hear him go quiet, and she wondered if he was remembering his mother was dead. She got the feeling he didn't truly believe it yet.

Her father, on the other hand, had left the tent and hadn't returned. Andra didn't know if he was angry or shocked or hurt that Andra was AI. Maybe it wasn't even about her. Maybe it was about Isla's death. Or Isla lying. She didn't know. All she knew was that she'd never felt so alone.

Andra shifted on the cold concrete floor, back to the tent flap, and pulled the holocket from under her shirt, clicking it open. She'd watched the memories countless times since Rashmi had returned it to her. Not only the message Griffin had left her but also the ones Andra had taken before going into stasis. Briella and Rhin doing some popular dance that Andra could never manage. Cruz laughing at something. Andra couldn't remember what. Her father playing with his dogs, chasing them around the house in a way that was completely out of character for the absentminded professor.

And the final memory was of her mother.

She hit play on the 'locket and was surrounded by their old living room. The brown couch. The kinetic orbs shaped like pineapples. Big picture windows, with a view of a field and a large oak. Isla was staring out at the sunrise, holding a cup of coffee.

"Learn, adapt," she said, and Andra couldn't remember if she was talking to Andra or to herself. "If something doesn't work, you don't keep trying it. You try something else. Even if it seems ridiculous." She took a sip of her coffee and was quiet for a moment. "That ridiculousness is what makes us human. Doing something completely unexpected and unlikely and brilliant. That's—"

A hand shot through the memory, one that was absolutely real and not part of a sim. Andra scuttled back, a scream stuck in her throat, as the memory collapsed back into the 'locket, revealing the owner of the hand.

Ice-blond hair dangling in wet clumps. Lips pulled into a sneer, eyes swollen shut. Blood-streaked arms and legs. Completely naked.

Apparently, the colonists weren't the only ones who had woken up.

Maret smiled. "Hello, Goddess."

FOURTEEN

THE FAILURE

Zhade dragged his feet from one step to the next as he trudged up the palace stairs to Andra's old room. He was tired and sore. Blood was crusted beneath his nose and ears, and his head hadn't stopped throbbing since leaving the cathedzal. No one would meet his eye as he'd made his march through the palace.

Angels were going rogue everywhere acity, and his subjects had witnessed his powerlessness. His rule was unraveling fast, and if he didn't skool to use the Crown quickish, everything would be for nothing. He had sole one recourse left to him.

Once he reached the top of the stairs, he sent a message to Kiv's speak-easy, and the door to the Third's suite flew open.

Kiv's dark figure took up the entire doorway, eyes flashing as he stared down at Zhade. "I'm taking a break to see Lilibet." The sign he used for Lilibet's name resembled a heart.

"Not now," Zhade signed back, his temple pounding. "Gryfud will be—"

"I'm taking a break to see Lilibet," Kiv signed again, this time, his gestures more firm. "I won't—"

"Neg!" Zhade snapped aloud. He sighed, closing his eyes and pinching the bridge of his nose. "Sorries, evens." His voice strained against his attempt to soften his tone. "You'll get a break eventualish. Mereish, not now."

Kiv's expression went from rage to hurt, and Zhade comped full well. He'd left Kiv alone at this post far too long, making him guard the woman who had forced him into service and most likeish murdered his fam. Zhade would make it up to him. He promised himself he would. Later.

"I need you here," Zhade signed. "Please."

Kiv nodded, his jaw clenched. "You owe me."

"I reck full well," Zhade said. And he did. He for true did.

He had Kiv wait outside, full close he could come to Zhade's aid if called on the speak-easy. He shut the door, but not before Kiv shot him one last frustrated look.

"Trouble with your henchman?" Tsurina purred. She sat on the pink chaise near the balcony, book in hand. Her long fingers flipped through the pages.

Zhade scowled and started pacing. "Are you the one controlling the angels?"

"Me?" Tsurina didn't look up. "I've been trapped in this room. For certz it couldn't have been me."

"Don't be spoonish." Zhade sank down into the gilded chair he'd so oft occupied when Andra lived here and rested his crowned temple on his head in exhaustion. "What did you do and how did you do it?"

Tsurina set her book aside and sat forward, letting her legs gentlish sweep off the chaise under a curtain of gauzy skirt. "If I did something, I would love to hold fame for it. But again, you have me locked atower, and, unlike you, I don't have a Crown so I can do things with my mind."

Zhade felt the cool metal neath his fingertips. He leveled Tsurina with a glare. "Where did the Crown come from?"

"Ah." Tsurina grinned. "You're finalish asking the right questions."

"Evens?"

Tsurina stood and walked to the magic shield barring her way to the balcony. She looked out over Eerensed, running her fingers along the pink gauzy curtain. The pocket hovered in the distance, mereish on the other side of the dome, casting a shadow over the balcony.

"It's a fam heirloom. I passed it down to my son. Then you killed him and took it for yourself."

"You gave it to Maret?" Zhade asked. "But you hate magic."

Tsurina turned and gave Zhade a patronizing look. "I hate the *goddesses'* magic. This is something else."

Zhade felt his pulse pounding in his forehead. "But they're both High Magic."

"They both *look* like High Magic," Tsurina corrected. "But theirs is a magic built out of the need to dominate. The Anloch fam magic is grown out of the need for freedom."

Zhade raised an eyebrow. "Soze, you took something purposed for freedom and used it to take over a city."

"Bodhizhad, we've convoed this. I'm not in this for power. I'm here to end the goddesses' power. Which you've done for me, thank you very much. Now, since I've gotten what I want, I can help you get what you want."

Zhade stiffened. "And what do I want?"

Tsurina's lips stretched in a smile. "You want to skool how to use the Crown so you can remain guv."

Zhade swallowed, training his face to remain neutral. Was he so full obvi?

Tsurina paced round the room, heels clacking against the marble. "Oh, you might convo yourself it's for the greater good, but it's actualish because now you've had a taste of power, and you don't want to give it up."

It was pointless to argue with Tsurina, but Zhade recked in his heart he was doing all this for his people. To protect them in ways his brother had not. In ways his father had failed. But in order to do that, Tsurina might be his sole hope. It was sole when he'd used her advice that he had success in using the Crown.

"How do you benefit from this?" he asked.

"Me?" Tsurina gestured to herself. "We can make a deal. If I skool you, then maybe . . . you bring me the Goddess?"

Zhade froze, his heart stuttering. "The goddesses are dead."

"Are they?"

Zhade blinked slowish, bareish breathing. "You watched me kill Andra myself. You watched her fall."

"Did I?"

"Why would I hold her alive?" Zhade snapped, panic growing. He would not give Andra up, not even for this. "She was in the way of what I wanted. The sole march to gain the citians' trust was to kill her. And now I rule all of Eerensed."

Tsurina sighed. "To be true, Zhade, I have no care if you held her alive or no. I'm not convoing bout the Third. I'm convoing bout the First."

Everything in Zhade stopped. His heart, his breath, his thoughts.

The First. His mam.

His mam, who was secretive and deific and powerful.

His mam, whom he'd watched beheaded afront of him.

His mam, whose blood had stained the same platform he'd faked Andra's death upon.

Had she somehow escaped death as well?

A muscle in his jaw ticked. "My mam's dead. You saw to that."

Tsurina sighed, one arm crossed, the other bent up, wrist twirling in the air, almost like she was dancing. Her full body was relaxed, as though she didn't care if Zhade took her deal or not. She played the game far better than any of them.

"Firm. I did see her die. Mereish as I saw the Second and Third die, yet still they live, marah?"

Zhade didn't deny it. He clung to a tiny thread of hope, hanging over an abyss, and at any moment, Tsurina could cut it and let him fall.

She prowled toward him. "I reck the First is alive. And I reck where to find her. And all I ask in return for skooling you to use the magic of the Crown is to find your mam and bring her here."

Zhade's mouth went dry. He recked it was a trap, but he couldn't see a march round it. He *had* to skool how to use the Crown, save his people. And if he could see his mam again . . . Even if he brought her back to Tsurina, the Grande Advisor was his prisoner, and he would be wearing a Crown he recked full well how to use.

Pain shot through his head, and in his mind, he saw a flicker of a memory. Donning the Crown for the first time. Screaming and crying and pain. Tsurina staring down at him, glaring, disappointed.

Confusion rocked him. Tsurina hadn't been there. He hadn't cried out. He'd tried to be brave. Andra had been there. In the throne room.

"Evens?" Tsurina prompted. "Do we have a deal?"

Zhade came back to himself. The time chimes started to sound, echoing in from the balcony, throughout Eerensed. The Eerensed he'd sworn to protect. And somewhere, across the Wastes, his mam might still be alive.

Zhade nodded. "Firm. Skool me everything you reck."

FIFTEEN

OOI IOOOI OOI IOIOI

ANDRA WISHED SHE had a single lamp, like in those old sight-and-sound interrogation scenes. Instead, she had to make do with shining the light of her tablet into Maret's face.

He squinted into it, slouching in a metal chair. His arms were pulled behind his back, fastened with 'cuffs. His head hung forward, wet hair brushing his shoulders. A rough-spun blanket was thrown over his lap, barely covering the essentials.

Andra had been extremely lucky that Mechy had been nearby when Maret had appeared. Not that Maret had tried to attack her. Instead, he was weak and confused. He didn't fight when Mechy grabbed him, nor when he dragged him out of the Icebox. It wasn't like he'd given up. It was like he was exactly where he wanted to be.

She'd been an idiot. Why hadn't she considered Rashmi had tied Maret's 'tank to the same network as the colonists? Andra wasn't sure where he'd been kept, but he'd somehow made his way to find her. Not to escape. Not to find his brother and enact revenge. He'd come for *her*.

Now Andra faced Maret, Mechy standing sentry behind her, in a destroyed lab in the annex. It made her think of how it had been her and Mechy against Maret that night in the throne room. She reminded herself that she'd bested him then. She could do it again.

He looked up at Andra, bruises under his eyes, and a sneer tugging at his lips. "What happens now, Goddess?"

His voice was no more than a rasp, but it somehow echoed in the small room. If Maret still had the Crown, he could turn Mechy against her, attack her with stardust, break through his 'cuffs. But his forehead was free of ornament, except for an unsettling bruise that limned the space where it had been.

A chill ran down Andra's spine, a darkness filling her. Fear and anger and a lust for revenge. He'd tried to kill her. He'd tried to kill Zhade. He'd failed in both cases where he had succeeded so many times before. A glimpse of her maids' execution flashed through Andra's mind.

Destroy. The voice inside her rose to the surface, but this time it wasn't trying to convince her. It was agreeing with her. Maret needed to be destroyed.

The thought sent a chill down her spine. Maybe there was something inside her that wasn't that different from Maret.

One day, he'd said to her, *you'll make the same choices as me.*

"Why didn't you escape?" Andra asked, willing her voice to be strong. "Why did you come to find me? What were you trying to accomplish?"

Maret rolled his head, working out the kinks in his neck. His arms strained slightly against the 'cuffs. "Where's my brother?"

Andra gritted her teeth. "You're supposed to be answering questions, not asking them."

He gave her a mocking smile. "Maybe I would answer some of yours, if you answer some of mine."

Andra swallowed. She felt Mechy's steady presence beside her. "Currently, your brother is wearing your face and Crown, and pretending to be you."

Maret burst out laughing.

It was not the response Andra was expecting, but it was almost like

Maret couldn't stop. He laughed until tears were streaming down his face and he was shaking.

Andra scowled, crossing her arms. "I'm not here to talk about your brother. I want to know—"

"Firm, firm," Maret said, his laughter slowly dying. "Ask your questions. You're free to do so, but I'm also free to refuse to answer."

"You're chained."

"Am I?" he asked, looking around.

For a moment, Andra thought he had discovered a way to free himself from his 'cuffs, but then she realized he was merely being flippant. Like he was the hero in an interrogation scene. Like he was Zhade.

He stuck out his bottom lip. "I spoze I am, but that does nothing to entice me to answer your questions. And I reck *so many things*. I was coming to tell you all the charred info I have, but now I don't imagine I will." He looked Andra up and down. "You goddesses never comp which one of us is actualish imprisoned."

What did he mean by that? Was he talking about Rashmi? Referring to when he'd visit her while she was in the palace dungeons, how he'd take her for walks? How he'd made her think he was doing her a favor, when he was actually her jailor? And she'd fallen for it so well that she'd spent almost all her time guarding his cryo'tank, protecting him from harm.

The lab went cold.

Rashmi.

She hadn't seen the other AI since the colonists had woken.

Since Maret had woken.

"Where's Rashmi?" She tried to keep her voice steady, but it warbled.

Maret quirked an eyebrow. "Who?"

"The Second. Where is she?" Andra started toward him, the voices in her head demanding she grab him by the neck, slam him against the wall, tighten her grip on his throat until she got her answer, but Mechy held her back.

Maret shook his head. "Wait. Rashmi? Is that what you call her?"

Andra clenched her teeth. "That's her name."

Maret grinned. One tooth was chipped, and there was blood in the corners of his mouth. "Is it? Are you for certz? I've recked her far longer than you have."

Andra tried to school her face. He was baiting her. That's all this was.

Maybe.

There was so much Rashmi didn't remember. Of what happened when she'd woken. Had she confided in Maret before she'd lost her memories?

It didn't matter right now. All that mattered was that Rashmi had a habit of guarding Maret's 'chamber, and Andra hadn't seen or heard from her since he woke.

"What did you do with Rashmi?" Andra snapped. "Answer me."

"Or what?" Maret shifted his weight. The blanket dipped dangerously low. "If you were to give me incentive. A promise to unchain me. Perhaps better accommodations. That might loosen my tongue."

Andra didn't know how to respond. The Maret she'd known hadn't been a strategist. He was brash and angry but more than willing to share information. The Maret that was now before her was too sure of himself. Or realized he had nothing left to lose.

He gave Andra a lazy grin that reminded her of his brother. "Or, if that's not your style, you could use threats. I seem to remember a certain dagger that could do quite a bit of damage in your hands. You could threaten to stab me. Or call a pocket down on me if I don't talk."

He raised his eyebrows and waited for Andra to respond. She took a sharp breath through her nose and narrowed her eyes. She felt coldness descend on her.

"For certz," Maret continued, "death isn't much of an incentive, for either of us. I reck that you reck that if you kill me, you won't be able to find the Second. Or hear all the info in my head that you so desperateish need and don't even realize. Soze," he hissed, his voice growing quiet and raspy, "that purposes you can't threaten death. What you have to threaten, my dear Goddess, is to make me *wish* for death. To get me to the point where I share the info, mereish on the chance that you give me the *option* of death. That, little Goddess, is your sole march forward. Are you willing to do that? Is it worth your soul?"

Andra didn't respond.

"Neg? Then come back when it is."

SIXTEEN

OOIIOOOI OOIIOIIO

ANDRA RAN THROUGH the LAC annex. She'd left Maret with Mechy and sent message after message to Rashmi through their neural connection but received no answer. The hallway lights flicked on one after the other as she tore through the annex, checking all the abandoned labs and offices, alcoves and stairwells. Anywhere Rashmi could have kept Maret's 'tank hidden, because if she had been there when Maret had awakened . . .

Had he overpowered her? Hurt her? Killed her? Surely, Andra would feel something if her counterpart were dead.

But if Rashmi wasn't dead, why wasn't she responding?

If Maret's 'tank had been connected to the colonist network, then it must be close by. She doubted it had been in the Icebox. Someone would have noticed a bloody, bruised naked boy roaming around long before he'd found Andra outside her family's tent. If he hadn't been kept in the Icebox, that left the LAC annex. Unfortunately, it was huge, and though Mechy had done a lot of renovations, much of it was still in ruins, shrouded in darkness.

Andra went from room to room so quickly the kinetic orbs could barely keep up. She tried every office on the main level. Every lab on the floor below. Room after room was empty. She'd just about given up hope when she found her.

It was a small lab a few levels above the Icebox. It looked to be the remains of a cryonics lab, which made sense. There were several cryo'chambers, some intact, most a jumble of detached parts. Andra had never thought to check the annex for cryo'plating. She imagined all the tech here was dead, but Rashmi had managed to wake it up. Various holo'displays illuminated the room, glitching and flashing.

Rashmi sat in a heap on the floor, her white hair hanging over her face, her left arm raised above her head, tied with tubing from a cryo'tank to a metal bar attached to the wall. She looked up when Andra entered, her face streaked with tears.

"Sorry, Third One," she said, voice breaking.

"No, no." Andra knelt next to her, fingers fumbling to untie the tubing. "Don't be sorry. There's nothing to be sorry about."

Rashmi sniffed. "I should have told you where I kept him. I shouldn't have kept him at all."

"It's fine, it's okay." Andra's hands were trembling, but she managed to undo the first knot. "We'll get you out of here. Everything will be okay."

"I tried to stop him from waking up," Rashmi continued. "I tried to stop him from leaving. I fought so hard, but it didn't work."

Andra noticed dried blood under Rashmi's fingernails, and suddenly understood why Maret had been bloodied and beaten. When Rashmi said she fought, she meant it. Andra was relieved to see that there weren't any matching wounds on Rashmi. Maret may have tied Rashmi up, but he hadn't hurt her. At least physically.

Andra untied the last knot and helped Rashmi to her feet. The AI winced and rubbed her shoulder.

"Let's get you back to your room," Andra said. "You need to sleep."

Rashmi shook her head. "No. I want to see him."

"I don't think that's a great idea. You should rest first."

"No." Rashmi's eyes flashed dangerously. "Now. Talking for now. Naps for later."

THE DOOR TO Maret's cell was slightly ajar, Mechy standing sentry.

"Are you sure you want to do this?" Andra asked.

Rashmi nodded.

At Andra's command, Mechy stood aside. Maret looked up when they entered, his face streaked with blood and dirt, half in shadow. He rattled his 'cuffs against the metal chair.

Rashmi stood in the doorway. Andra couldn't pinpoint the look on her face. She imagined it was the same way she looked at Zhade, but it should be impossible for an AI to look at her captor that way. To look at the boy who had kept her in prison until she'd lost her mind and her abilities.

"Second," Maret said, his voice hoarse, and Andra was disturbed to see he was returning Rashmi's gaze.

She took a few steps into the room and laughed. It was a strained noise, not one of mirth. It almost sounded like sobbing.

"She laughs when she's nervous," Maret said.

Andra scowled and put a hand on Rashmi's arm. "Rashmi?"

Her laughs subsided, and she wiped tears from her eyes. "All those years, I was the one chained. Now here he is. And here I am."

It took Maret a minute to tear his gaze away from Rashmi. There was something in his expression, something more like what she was used to seeing from him. A disguise poorly worn.

He let out a bark of a laugh. "We convoed this, Second. It wasn't a prison. It was protection."

Andra snarled. "Don't act as though you cared about her. You never did. Not about your city, or your brother, or Rashmi, or me."

Maret's smile was ugly. "How could I ever care bout a *thing* like you? You're not even human."

Frozen rage built up inside Andra, vision growing dark, her awareness dimming, until it was just her and Maret and her fury.

Destroy, destroy, destroy.

She felt the air crackle around her, her senses expanding to every piece of tech in the room—the nanos, Mechy, Rashmi—and farther. Everything in Eerensed was part of her and she was part of it all. She felt the 'dome, and the pocket beyond. She could differentiate each nano and knew them. Knew which ones she had used to take out the throne room ceiling, and which ones she had yet to control.

Power surged through her. She could destroy Maret. Show him just how not-human she really was.

There was a sob behind her.

Rashmi.

Andra shrunk back into herself, so fast it left her dizzy. She was hollow where the power had drained from her, like the hate she had just felt was a missing part of her soul. Nanos swarmed around her, and Maret was watching her with wide eyes, the fear etched in his features not nearly as satisfying as Andra thought it would be.

"If you imagine you can scare me with your dark magic," Maret said, voice quaking, "you reck wrongish."

Rashmi watched Maret, fat tears dribbling down her cheeks, but when she spoke, her voice was steady. "How could you ever be scared of *things* like us." She turned to Andra. "I don't have anything to say to him. I just wanted to see him caged."

Without another word, Rashmi left.

Maret's eyes filled with regret. Good. He should feel the impact of Rashmi's words, suffer the consequences of his own. Andra wouldn't feel sorry for him, just because he was letting a little bit of his humanity show.

"Mechy," she said. "Take him to the eco'lab in the Vaults. Turn it into a prison." She gave Maret a sarcastic smile. "Oh, I'm sorry. It's not a prison. It's protection."

SEVENTEEN

THE GLITCH

ZHADE WOKE GASPING, the tendrils of his dream slipping away, leaving a feeling of wrongness. It took a moment for him to return to his own mind and body, as though he'd lost sense of himself while he slept. He lay in a nest of covers next to his bed, a habit he'd never had before, but the bed was growing too soft, too lofty.

It was dark as charberry. The dream he'd woke from nagged at him. Bits of it lingered at the edge of his memory. It had something to do with the Crown. He'd felt young. Afraid. He'd use the Crown to . . .

Zhade rubbed his temples. The dream was already gone. He was left sole with exhaustion and guilt.

He didn't reck where the guilt came from. Was it from not saving the girl from the rogue angel? Was it what he'd done to Andra? Or was it the deal he'd made with Tsurina?

He was sole doing what he needed to protect his people. If that purposed skooling from Tsurina, that was evens. She was under his control. He was using her. She was nothing but a bargaining chip.

Maybe it wasn't guilt. Maybe it was regret from how much he'd drunk.

He still had pain from not sole the Crown, but the angel trying to kill him. Then he'd had his first lesson with Tsurina, and it had been a disaster. All he had for his troubles was a headache and the echo of

Tsurina's taunts. He'd come back to his room. Had a few drinks. Then had a few more. His head was killing him.

His throat hurt. His hip hurt. His arm hurt. His temple hurt. For basic, everything hurt. He couldn't go back to sleep, so he untangled himself from the sheets and made his march to the receiving room, pouring himself a small glass of the liquor he'd drank yestereven. Mereish enough to dull the pain. Exhaustion took over and he collapsed onto his sofa, holding the glass to his temple.

"Moping again?" said a voice.

Zhade didn't bother to open his eyes. "Trying to assassinate me again?"

"I reck I've proven true that I could assassinate you any time I wanted," Doon said. "Me, and any other assassin with my skill."

"Ah," Zhade said, eyes still closed, pointing his glass vagueish in her direction. "But I imagined no one had your skill."

"Rare point," Doon conceded.

Zhade heard her pouring herself something from the liquor cabinet. He opened one eye and raised an eyebrow as she tasted it and promptish spit it back out.

"Sands," she cursed. "You for true like to torture yourself, marah?"

Zhade took another sip of his drink, enjoying the burn as it traveled down his throat.

Doon discarded hers and plopped down in the seat across from him. "Skilla wants you at tonight's meeting."

Zhade swirled his glass. "And I want my own horze. I'd dress him up and name him Frid. Ride him through town on Marsdays and skool him to count with his hooves."

"She says it full imports. Something to do with Andra and the gods."

Zhade sat up. Too quickish. A bolt of nausea hit him. He groaned, holding his stomach. "What bout her?"

Doon smiled a mocking smile. "She's back from the Wastes."

"For serious?" He closed his eyes again and sighed.

"I told you she would go."

Zhade fell back onto the sofa. "Fraughted sands, can she not stay still?"

"She found something out there. Skilla wouldn't tell me what, but she said you, especialish, would want to reck."

"No shakes, Doon. I'm certz it's nothing."

The last thing he wanted was to be yelled at by Skilla, be rejected by Andra. Again. But curiosity was getting the better of him. He'd need to rid himself of this headache first.

"That didn't sound full convincing," Doon said.

He took another sip of his drink.

"That's because I'm not full convinced."

EIGHTEEN

OOIIOOOI OOIIIOOO

APPARENTLY, WHILE ANDRA had spent her night interrogating Maret and helping Mechy build a cell, Cruz had spent his setting up rudimentary enviro'mods in the Icebox. Heat 'drones, air filters, synth plants. Everything the colonists needed to feel comfortable. Or as comfortable as they could in an underground warehouse filled with the frozen bodies of their contemporaries.

When Andra finally got back from showering in the Vaults—after a pretty hefty freak-out and a couple hours of uneasy sleep—the rise-n-shine, a kinetic orb programmed to mimic the sun, was floating at the east end of the camp. The Icebox was quiet except for a host of colonists, who were stationed at a long table between tents, changing frozen goods and synth'protein into something edible.

Andra managed to slip into her cot before her fam woke, but she'd barely shut her eyes before Oz was pulling her out from under the covers and dragging her to the breakfast line. Acadia, as always, ignored her, sharp features drawn into a scowl similar to the one their mother used to wear. Her father still hadn't returned to their tent.

Andra grabbed a single slice of toast and stuck it in her mouth.

"Do your kind even have to eat?" Acadia muttered.

Andra turned to Oz before Acadia could take the comment a step further to the familiar territory of berating her about her weight (always under the guise of "worrying about her health," though Andra noticed that Acadia never worried about Andra's vax'mods or stress levels).

"I'm going to eat with Cruz," Andra mumbled around the piece of toast.

Oz was filling his plate with synth. Acadia rolled her eyes.

Cruz was waiting exactly where Andra had asked him to. He was now dressed in jeans and a button-side T-shirt, his curls still damp from bathing. His hands were shoved in his pockets, shoulders caving in, scuffing his feet. He saw her approach and waved awkwardly.

She waved back, just as awkwardly.

"Hi," she said, breathless.

"Hi." He smiled.

They stared at each other.

"So . . ." he said, ruffling his hair. "Are you going to tell me what's going on or what?"

"Oh, yeah, of course. Yeah. Follow me. It's better if I . . . show you . . ."

Andra led Cruz to the far end of the Icebox, then into what remained of the LAC annex. He was quiet as he followed Andra, his eyes wide and questioning, taking in his surroundings. Like Andra, Cruz had expected to wake to a brand-new planet, a paradise. But now he was walking through ruins. Andra could hear the rhythm of his breath, feel the beat of his heart through the nanos in the air. So she knew exactly when he realized where they were.

It was the east wing where LAC had done synth'protein experiments. Though the hall was littered with rocks and dirt, the ceiling partly caved in, there had been a unique design to the hallway's structure: geometrical alcoves and asymmetrical windows.

Cruz's breath caught, his heart stuttered, and he froze.

"We're . . . we're . . ."

He hunched over, hands on knees, and wheezed. Andra placed a hand on his back, remembering when she first realized. The words she'd found in the sand, the comfort she'd needed after. Her world breaking apart and remaking itself in a new, horrible image.

"Yeah," she said.

Cruz shook his head, but Andra didn't know if he was contradicting her or just trying to shake the image of the ruins of the annex.

After a few minutes, he asked, "What year is it?" His voice was surprisingly steady.

"3102," Andra said. "Or '03. It's hard to tell what month it is. There aren't . . . seasons anymore."

"Jesus," Cruz breathed. "Jesus."

Andra knelt beside him. His olive skin had turned ashen, his still-damp curls clinging to his face. The twenty-second-century clothes he wore now felt out of place in the building where he'd worked a thousand years ago.

"I'm sorry," she said. "Maybe I should have prepared you better."

He scrubbed a hand over his face. "No. It's fine. I don't think I would have believed you if I hadn't seen it myself." He took a deep breath. "What happened?"

Andra flinched. The rest of it . . . the pockets, Griffin's death, her clones, what was left of Earth. Andra had learned all of it slowly, in bite-sized chunks. Cruz was now about to gorge on the information. But he was smart and capable, and though she didn't trust the rest of the LAC scientists not to storm Eerensed and take back Earth once they knew the truth, she needed Cruz on her side.

"Follow me," she said. And took him to the surface.

ANDRA LED CRUZ to the exit next to the Griffin statue. Or, what was left of it. She pushed the grate aside and climbed out into the city, helping Cruz up after her. His mouth immediately fell open. They stood at the edge of what Zhade called the Small Wastes, an almost perfect circle of sand with the remains of the statue in the middle. The city of Eerensed spread out around them.

It was the first time she'd been in the city in over a month, and memories flooded back to her. Standing close to this very spot and discovering she was on Earth. Walking with Zhade through these very streets. Running through them after she was nearly executed.

Andra wished she could show Cruz Eerensed at its best: nano'swarms zooming through the city, 'drones wandering listlessly, searching for their next task. Vendors opening their fruit stands and butcheries. Rickety carts next to high-tech 'bots. People wearing sun-damaged skin and modded limbs. But even with Maret no longer on the throne and a new 'dome protecting it, the city was hurting. Too cramped and dirty. Streets quiet and rampant with despair. Not a 'bot in sight. The pocket hovered to the west.

She'd expected things to be better with Zhade in charge, but something was wrong.

"Holy shit," Cruz breathed.

She'd almost forgotten he was there, and when she looked his way, she saw the same dawning horror she'd felt the day she realized what had happened. That Earth was destroyed.

THE NEXT PLACE Andra took Cruz was the rocket.

They wound through the tunnels, and Mechy was waiting for them to open the door. Cruz ignored Mechy—he was just another mech'bot to him—but his jaw dropped when he entered the cavern. Standing there, under the shadow of the skeleton of a rocket, had a way of making one feel especially small. Andra hoped it gave Cruz a bit of hope too. Things were bad. But this was their way out.

Cruz didn't say anything for the longest time, then finally: "You really should have that power hub behind eco'glass. One touch and it'll fry your system."

FINALLY, THEY WOUND through the tunnels to the Vaults.

When they entered through the air'lock, Cruz let out a gasp. Andra knew what he was seeing. The lobby, with its high ceilings and circular reception desk. Frozen holos displaying various collections and exhibits. The huge astronomical clock hanging from the rafters, still ticking away. He'd probably come here as a child, and then later did contracted work for them. Everyone from Andra's time was familiar with the Vaults, and due to its enviro'control, the building remained basically unchanged in a thousand years.

Cruz gaped as Andra led him past the emptied exhibits and labs, winding from hall to hall until they reached her room. She pressed her thumb to the lock and the door slid open, and she ushered Cruz in.

He sat in Andra's ergo'chair, took a deep breath, and twirled to face her. "Okay, Andie, explain."

Though he still seemed shocked, there was the beginning of excitement written on his face. A new puzzle for him to solve. An unexpected experience.

Andra sat across the table and met Cruz's weighty brown eyes and told him everything. Told him about waking up and being terrified and alone. Told him about coming to Eerensed and all the things she'd discovered since. Told him about finding Griffin's clone and the rocket and needing to upgrade the colonists' tech.

When she finished, Cruz didn't react. Merely sat there, mouth pinched, not meeting her eyes. Finally, he looked up at her under his lashes. "So you know?"

Andra raised an eyebrow. "I just told you that rogue LAC tech destroyed the planet and your boss created hundreds of clones of herself, and that's your question?"

He bit his lip. "Do you?"

"Know what? That I'm not actually human? That I'm an AI raised as human so I wouldn't overthrow my human overlords? That I'm a created thing?"

Cruz had the decency to look ashamed.

"Yeah." She leaned back in her chair. "I know." She was unable to keep the bitterness out of her voice, and it made her feel guilt. She wasn't supposed to be bitter about this.

Cruz watched her warily.

"So what was your job?" Andra asked, trying to sound nonchalant. "How were you supposed to *socialize* us?"

Cruz was suddenly interested in the different tablets and 'bands on the table. "You know about that too, huh?"

Andra nodded. "I saw it on the manifest. Were you supposed to become *friends* with us? Were you *dating* Rashmi to socialize her? Was it part of your job? Did she know about this?"

Cruz ran his nail over a groove in the table. "Sort of. A little. Rashmi and I . . . It's complicated." He looked up. "And you and I were definitely really friends. Just because it was also my job, doesn't mean that our friendship wasn't . . . *isn't* still real."

Why did Andra even care? It wasn't like she should hope for friendship with humans.

"Listen, Andie—"

"It's fine. I understand."

"I'm still sorry. Someone should have told you sooner."

Andra swallowed. He shouldn't be apologizing to her. Not as a human to an AI.

She waved away the apology. "We should be focusing on getting everyone's tech upgraded."

She turned to her work'station, unplugging the anomalizer, and it blipped a neon green.

Cruz looked like he was about to apologize again but sighed, nodding to the anomalizer. "What did you say it would protect us from?"

"The pockets."

He blinked. "I'm sorry, what?"

"That cloud of tech you saw on the surface? Those are . . . almost like a 'swarm of decon'bots. They destroy everything. *Everything.* And they can't be controlled."

That was a bit of a lie. They didn't destroy Andra, and she could control them. Sometimes. In the throne room and at Lake Superior, it had been instinct. An instinct she needed to tame.

She reached over to grab the mini'dome that contained the tiny pocket and held it out to Cruz. "Like this."

The pocket swirled angrily in the 'dome. Cruz took it from her, awe on his face.

"Be careful!" Andra snapped.

He gave her a look that suggested she was a fool for ever considering he wouldn't be.

"You trapped this? How?"

"It's . . . a long story." And one she didn't want to get into now. It would lead to awkward questions, and she didn't know if she was imagining it, but with the pocket in front of her, she felt like the voices were just at the edge of her consciousness, waiting for her to admit them.

"So," Cruz said, setting down the mini'dome. "Where do we begin?"

The pocket pushed against the skin of the 'dome several times before expanding into a cloud and falling still. Andra watched it for a moment, until she was sure the voices wouldn't surface, then she leveled Cruz with a stare.

"I need you to convince someone to let me upgrade their tech."

Ophele Hammad volunteered. She was a tall Black hijabi with a plump, pleasant face and a modded hand. Cruz and Andra met her at the therapy tent. Ophele and the other cryo'techs had been using it to help the others through reanimation procedures, but they were nearly done, and were converting the tent to a standard lab with all the necessary accoutrements for 'implant procedures.

Cruz pulled back the flap of the tent, and Ophele was waiting for them, surrounded by holo'displays and lab equipment. Her face brightened when she saw Cruz but faltered when she saw Andra.

"Who is this?" she asked, even though Andra was sure they'd met at a few LAC family functions.

"Oh," Cruz said, as though the question surprised him. "This is Andromeda Watts, Dr. Watts's daughter. She'll be doing the procedure today."

Andra tugged at the ends of her hair. She'd asked Cruz not to tell anyone she was AI yet. She didn't want to be treated like a 'bot. But now she'd rather that than to be treated like Isla's disappointing middle child.

Ophele gave Andra a sad smile. "I was sorry to hear about your mother. She was a remarkable person."

Andra bit her lip. "Thank you. Um, have a seat." She gestured to an ergo'chair they had been using for reanimation therapy.

Ophele sat and cleared her throat. "I thought one of the 'implant techs would be completing the procedure."

Cruz scratched the back of his neck. "Well, we can have one on standby, but Ms. Watts is uniquely qualified to complete this procedure. It actually requires her . . . 'implant to perform the upgrade."

Ophele looked Andra up and down. "How old are you?"

Andra tried to stand taller. "Eighteen."

She didn't know if that was true. She was born almost a thousand years ago, but between the two times she'd been in stasis and the lack of seasons, she wasn't sure how long she'd been alive. It sounded better than seventeen though.

Ophele *hmm*'d.

"Don't worry," Cruz said, his expression a perfect mix of compassion and confidence. "Ms. Watts woke early, and Dr. Griffin trained her personally to complete this procedure. It's noninvasive, presents no risks, and will take less than ten minutes."

Andra should have been concerned about Cruz's ability to fabricate lies on the spot so easily. Instead, she was impressed he managed to know the exact right thing to say.

Ophele nodded, giving Andra an apologetic smile. "Of course. I was just . . . surprised."

Andra tried to smile back but wasn't sure she achieved it.

Cruz hit the controls to lean the 'chair back, tilting Ophele's head so they could access the emergency port behind her ear.

"May I?" Andra asked.

Ophele nodded, and Andra moved part of her hijab aside to reveal the port.

It was barely visible, as dark as her complexion. They were created to match the skin tone of the individual. Though some people decorated the skin around the port with tattoos, most kept them unobtrusive.

Andra flicked aside the covering to reveal the port underneath. It was a tiny circular hollow that the pointed end of the anomalizer would fit neatly into. Cruz handed it to her. It felt heavy, warm from Cruz's touch. The neon color turned her skin a sickly green.

"A small pinch," Andra said, and slid the end of the anomalizer into the port.

Ophele flinched, but Andra knew it was more anticipation of pain than pain itself. Technically, there were no nerve endings around the port, as they'd been removed when the 'implant was embedded. Andra quickly connected a wire to the end of the anomalizer and then snapped the other side to the end of her reset tool.

She wished she could use the port at the back of her neck, but it was merely decoration, part of the lie to convince her she was human, using an 'implant. Instead, she had to stab herself in the heart to connect to the anomalizer.

She took a deep breath, made sure Ophele wasn't watching, and slid her reset tool in.

Pain shot through Andra's body, and it was all she could do not to gasp. She gritted her teeth, felt Cruz put gentle pressure on her free hand as she looked up to the ceiling, eyes smarting, willing her body to adjust to the pain.

She took a deep breath, steadying herself. Cruz met her eyes and she nodded, before pressing the button at the edge of the anomalizer.

At first nothing happened. Ophele didn't react. Andra felt a tug at her heart, but that was all. She studied the anomalizer, looking for any indication it was working. A noise or a light. It looked just the same as it had, glowing green.

Ophele screamed.

Cruz jumped up. "What's wrong?"

"Get it off! Get it off!!" Ophele reached back to push away the anomalizer.

Andra scrambled to detach it, but it was locked in.

"Unlock it!" Cruz cried.

"I'm trying!"

Ophele's back arched and her cries filled the space. A few people came running, filing into the therapy tent. Her shrieks grew louder and more frantic, her body curled in on itself.

Someone pushed Andra out of the way. It was one of the cryo'techs. Raj. He fumbled with the anomalizer, but nothing happened. He looked up at Andra.

"What did you do?"

Ophele's cries stopped. Her entire body relaxed, and the anomalizer detached itself.

Andra rushed to pick it up, while Raj and the other technicians started attaching Ophele to various machines, monitoring her heart and breathing. Andra melted into the background as they started yelling to one another.

"She's flatlining."

"Pull up the defib app."

"Ten cc of renovetnol."

"Help me!"

"Turn her on her back."

Raj turned on Andra.

"What the fuck did you do?" he snapped. A holo'display of Ophele's heart appeared over his shoulder. It was completely still. An alarm was blaring.

"I . . . it wasn't . . ."

This wasn't how this was supposed to go. Griffin's clone said this would be easy, that Andra could handle it. She'd used the words "You literally can't mess this up."

Yet Andra had found a way.

Cruz stepped in front of her. "She was helping me."

"Clear!" one of the 'techs called, followed by the whoosh of noise the defib app made as it tried to restart Ophele's heart.

"Helping you do what?" Raj snapped.

Ophele's heart still wasn't pumping, the alarm still blaring.

"Clear!" Another whoosh.

"Ophele thought she might have had an allergic reaction to the cryo'protectant," Cruz lied quickly. "We were running some tests, that's all. We don't know what happened."

Andra opened her mouth, then closed it like a fish.

"Is this true?" Raj asked.

Andra nodded, peeling her eyes away from the projection of Ophele's unbeating heart, shutting out the panicked voices of the cryo'techs.

Raj held out his hand. "I need the attachment you were using."

Andra's hand tightened on the anomalizer.

The alarm faded into the background. The shouts growing distant. An icy calm descended on Andra.

Destroy him.

That dark feeling swept over her. It would be so easy. Even if she wasn't in a tent full of deadly tools, she could overpower him with the nanos in the air. He would die, gasping, asking no more questions.

Andra blinked back to herself. The alarm returning to full blast. The cries of the cryo'techs overwhelming.

"Here." Cruz handed Raj a plain diagnostic 'implant attachment.

Raj took it, weighing it in his hands, looking slightly confused. It was bulky and opaque, not shimmery and green like the anomalizer, but Raj nodded, turning back to the cryo'techs trying to save Ophele.

Holo'displays were blinking red, alarms blaring, 'techs shouting. Raj pushed them out of the way, fingers flying over one of the diagnostic 'displays. The alarm cut off.

A beep.

Then another.

The holo of Ophele's heart started pumping.

"Great job, Raj," a 'tech said. "Can we wake her up?"

"No." His eyes met Andra's briefly across the tent. "We'll have to keep her in a coma until we know what's wrong with her."

Andra swallowed, guilt consuming her, and slipped out of the tent, the anomalizer heavy in her pocket.

NINETEEN

THE DEFECT

ZHADE TOOK HIS time getting to the Vaults. He would be glad to see Andra, but she'd made it crystal last time that she wouldn't be glad to see him. Originalish, the meetings had been once a turn, to ensure Zhade, Andra, and the Schism were all working together. But after a while, Zhade had stopped going. The meetings were full boring, anyway. Lots of arguing. Lots of convoing bout the stupid rocket Skilla was building. The thing his mam had asked her to build. Asked Skilla, not Zhade. Neg. Instead, she'd sent Zhade adesert.

He imagined bout what Tsurina had said. That his mam was alive. It had to be a lie. How could he trust the woman who'd had his mam executed, and apparentish—according to Meta—abandoned her first kiddun in the Wastes, and didn't love her second?

If his mam *was* alive, she wouldn't let him believe she was dead. Wouldn't have let him wander the desert alone. She'd have at least come back for him by now. Marah?

And if not for him, she'd have come back for Eerensed. For Skilla. For Andra. She could have repaired the gods' dome, prevented the pocket from taking the Lost District. She could have skooled Andra what it purposed to be a goddess, protected her from Maret and Tsurina.

If she was alive, she had chosen not to come back, and everything in Zhade rebelled against the imagining. It had to be a lie. His mam was dead.

Except—

There was a tiny spark of hope in his chest. What if Tsurina was telling the truth? What if he could skool to use the Crown and get his mother back? What if together they could tame the rogue angels and save Eerensed from itself and the planet, destroy the pockets, reestablish the goddesses so Andra could return aboveground? They could tell the people who he for true was, and he could get his face back.

Maybe Andra would want to be with him then.

Fishes and wishes.

He paused a moment outside of Andra's room. Straightening his cape and patting down his hair. One deep breath and he knocked on the door. It slid open.

Skilla was standing and gathering her things, Xana waiting for her with one hand on the ax at her hip. Andra sat at the far end of the table, face drawn, shoulders hunched.

"Ah," Skilla said. "He actualish showed his face, to convo. Should we start this meeting over?"

Andra looked up at Zhade, her expression blank.

"No, go. I'll . . ." she stammered. "I'll convo him."

"You'll convo him everything?" Skilla asked, something pointed in her expression.

Andra nodded, looking away.

Skilla's eyes narrowed as she turned to Zhade. "Evens. But there is one thing I want to tell you." She took a step closer, and Zhade had to stop himself from shrinking back. "If you don't hold the angels in control, I will. And you won't like how I do it."

Zhade gave her a fake grin. "I always do enjoy your threats, Skilla. You must practice them amirror to be so good at them."

Skilla pursed her lips, giving him one last glare before leaving. Xana followed quickish behind.

"Angels?" Andra asked, as the door slid shut.

Zhade blinked. "Huh?"

"Skilla said something about getting the angels under control."

"Oh, that was null." He waved away the comment, sitting in the seat farthest from Andra, and kicking his feet up on the table. "Seeya, she imagines she's better at magic than I am, marah? But we for true reck who the better sorcer is." He winked, and something bout it felt forced.

Andra didn't blush as she usualish did.

"Soze . . ." he said, trying to sound casual, "I heard you went adesert after all."

Andra swallowed. She was so pale.

He cleared his throat. "Find anything? The lake? Anything bout my mam?"

If his mam was alive, maybe she'd left clues on how to find her.

Andra watched him for a moment before shaking her head. Zhade's heart sank for two reasons. She seemed full bars uncomfortistic. Was she so prepped to be rid of him?

"Soze . . ." He cocked his thumb toward the door. "Should I go? Or was there something from the meeting you wanted to convo?"

"Uh . . . no. It was just . . ." She cleared her throat, not meeting his eye. "Same old boring things as usual. Rocket. Refugees, et cetera." She pressed her lips together in some bastardization of a smile.

Zhade returned it. He recked he should tell her bout the angels, bout Meta and Tsurina. But the way she was looking at him—or not looking at him—like she wanted the convo to end . . . Like she pitied him. For what? For still being in love with her?

He cleared his throat and pressed his chair back, standing awkwardish. She stood too, holding the table between them.

Zhade bit the inside of his cheek. "I spoze . . . I won't waste any more of your time. I'm certz you have better things to do than to convo me."

Pain flashed across Andra's face, and Zhade immediateish regretted his words. He hadn't purposed for it to sound so bitter, hadn't purposed it as a jab. He had to get out of here before he said something even worse. He turned to go.

"Wait," Andra said. She was suddenish behind him, turning him round, her small hand on his shoulder.

He met her eyes. They were wide and wet with tears. Had he hurt her? Had he been that cruel? Hadn't she wanted him gone?

"Andromeda, what's wrong? Are you evens? Sorries, I shouldn't have snapped." He took her face in his hands.

She shook her head, not looking away, studying his face like she was searching for something. "I—" she trailed off.

She was so close. Closer than she'd been in so long. She leaned forward. So did he. They were sharing the same air, the same breath.

It sole took the smallest movement, and their lips were touching.

TWENTY

OOIIOOIO OOIIOOOO

ANDRA GASPED, AND Zhade took it as invitation. He deepened
the kiss but gently, hands framing her face. Andra bunched his shirt
in her fist, dragging the rest of him closer, closer.

There was no conscious thought, just instinct. This physical longing she could have for someone else: she wanted to pick it apart and
analyze it. But her brain was too foggy, her body too wanting, to even
consider if this was a good idea or what she was going to do next, or
what the consequences would be for a human and an AI—

A dull ache began to pound at her temple, the icy feeling creeping
up her spine. She tried to ignore it, just kissed Zhade harder.

Destroy him.

No, she told the voice. It didn't get to interrupt this moment.

Yes, it demanded. *Destroy him.*

No, I won't!

Zhade's kisses felt farther and farther away. Her head was filled
with static, her muscles tense. The voice shrunk to no more than a
whisper.

You already have.

Andra pushed Zhade away and scrambled back.

At some point, he'd lost his shirt, and hers was open, the top button
on her pants undone. Zhade's eyes were glazed, lips swollen. Andra

had just stared into this face—Maret's face—hours ago. It looked so different with Zhade's expression of regret.

He stepped back. "Sorries." He swallowed. "I'm sorry. I don't reck what I was imagining."

No, he didn't. He knew she was artificial. Knew she wasn't human.

She didn't want to see the shame pass over his face. Didn't want to watch him realize what he'd almost done, to come to terms with it while she was still there. She pulled her shirt together and fled.

ANDRA PACED OUTSIDE of the Icebox, her stomach roiling with nausea. What had she just let herself do? She'd given in to her own desires without any thoughts of the consequences. Zhade must be disgusted by her. The way she'd run after him, kissed him. As though she wasn't a thing, as though she were a human that could want things and act upon them.

And now, not only was she not human, she wasn't even a very good AI.

She had been making out with Zhade hours after she'd almost killed someone.

Might still kill someone.

Who knew if Ophele would wake up from her coma? Or maybe she'd already died. Andra was too scared to go back in the Icebox to check.

How could she face her father again? Her siblings?

Not to mention, she'd captured someone and put him in a cell, but only after letting him hurt Rashmi, the only other being like her in existence.

Everything was falling apart, and Andra had never felt so alone.

The door to the Icebox hissed open, and Andra froze, preparing an explanation, but it was only Cruz.

"There you are," he whispered, as though they were in a library, or a graveyard. "I've been looking everywhere for you. Your family is worried."

Andra snorted. "I'm sure."

Cruz slipped his hands into his pockets boyishly. "It's good you got out of there. Raj has totally forgotten you even exist. He's mainly frustrated with me."

"And Ophele?"

Cruz deflated. "Still in a coma."

Andra winced. The lights of the annex were too bright.

She started pacing. "I don't know why it didn't work. Griffin told me there was no way I could mess it up. She said the program was ready to go, I just had to start it and let my AI brain do the rest."

Cruz *hmm*'d and stroked his nonexistent beard. "I think I have an idea. Can we go to your lab?"

ANDRA REALLY NEEDED to clean her room if she was going to keep having people over. She cleared the table of the snacks she'd put out for Xana and Skilla during their meeting. Not that it had been much of a meeting. It was mostly Xana giving Skilla puppy-dog eyes and Skilla refusing to help Andra gather supplies for the colonists. They'd ended early, since Lilibet had been stitching more blankets and Rashmi was in her room dealing with the impact of Maret's hurtful words. Then Zhade had shown up. At least he was gone now. She didn't think she could face him ever again.

Cruz stepped gingerly over the piles of discarded tech, books, and clothes until he reached Andra's work'station. He tapped the mini'dome on the desk, sending the pocket inside into a frenzy, then chuckled to himself and sat in Andra's 'chair.

"Can I see the . . . What did you call it? The anomalizer?"

Andra handed it to him. He jacked it into the work'station, bringing up lines of code on the holo'display. It filled the entire screen, and he scrolled through it, humming to himself.

"This is . . . way beyond me. I mean, that's no surprise, it was created by Alberta fucking Griffin. Or . . ." He shot Andra a look. ". . . her clone or whatever."

"Do you think she made a mistake in the code?"

He scoffed. "I doubt it. Probably just user error . . ." He continued scanning, then realized what he'd said. He looked up at Andra apologetically. "I mean, user error in that the two of—both of us . . . *we* were mistaken in how to use—not that you were using it wrong, just that . . . how we were using it wasn't . . . correct."

Andra rolled her eyes. "Nice save, nerd."

Cruz smiled sheepishly, and a little bit of Andra melted.

"Wait." He turned back to the code. "I wonder . . ." He typed some keystrokes and then brought up another holo'display. This one held more code.

"What's that?" Andra asked.

"It's the code for the Blackout."

Andra gasped. "What? You just . . . have access to that?"

Cruz shrugged. "Honestly, it's not that hard to find, especially considering we're networked into the Vaults."

The Blackout was the most dangerous 'implant hack of the fifties. It took over every connection between the 'implant and the body and sporadically shut down various functions. People wouldn't even know they had it, then *bam*! They couldn't breathe. Or their heart stopped. Or they lost their sight. At least, so they thought. The hack couldn't actually control bodily functions, but it could manipulate the connections between the 'implant and neural pathways to make the user *think* they were no longer breathing or hearing or walking.

It was a nightmare, and a complicated hack that took years to completely eradicate. It had almost ended the neural'implant program.

"Why are you looking at it?"

Cruz gave Andra his most dazzling smile, gesturing between the two codes. "Because this is where Griffin went wrong. The Blackout code was *highly* invasive. Even though it only appeared to attack a single perception or neural function, it actually invaded every part of the 'implant with sleeper code that would randomly trigger. That's why it took so long to clear the hack, because short of wiping the entire 'implant, it's nearly impossible to remove the code."

"What does that have to do with the program in the anomalizer?"

Cruz's face was lit by the 'displays. "Griffin used the base code from the Blackout. It was a shortcut to make sure that the program was as invasive as possible. It has to mask every single nano in the 'implant for it to be effective. The best way to do that is through code like this."

Andra pulled up a chair and sat. "So what happened? Did she leave in too much of the Blackout code? Did the virus trigger in Ophele's 'implant, and now she thinks she's in a coma?"

Cruz leaned back, stretching his arms behind his head. "No, the problem isn't in the anomalizer code, it's in the 'implant code."

"How?"

Cruz ruffled his hair. "After the biggest Blackout scare in . . . fifty-six? Seven? . . . amateur coders came up with a patch to block hacks like the Blackout. Griffin probably didn't consider it, because it wasn't LAC-sanctioned code. I don't know why LAC didn't create their own patch . . . probably making too much money from people needing to wipe and replace their 'implants. But people got in the habit of downloading the amateur patches as a sort of malware protection. Even LAC scientists started doing it. Hell, I have a patch. Your mom probably even gave them to your siblings."

Andra's stomach somersaulted at the thought of her mom. Her dead mom. Caring for her sister and brother. Obviously, Andra wouldn't have needed a patch, because she didn't have an 'implant. She *was* the 'implant. But still.

"So Ophele probably had a patch, and what . . . it freaked out? How do we get around it?"

Cruz sat forward, excitement on his face. "That's the thing. You don't get around it. It's not really blocking anything. Neural'implants are extremely complex pieces of tech. I mean, children are budded with them as infants, and the 'implant grows with them as their brain grows. Some of the 'implants we're seeing now that were only budded a few years ago are so complex, even the people who initially programmed them don't understand how they work anymore. So patches and upgrades have to take that into consideration, coding to keep not only the 'implant but the brain in mind."

Andra's mind was spinning. She was sentient technology in an organic body, and 'implanted humans were sentient organic life with technology woven into their very brains. Was she made in their image, or were they remaking themselves in hers?

"Don't you see?" Cruz said. "The patches to prevent the Blackout hack are built on this principle. They don't actually block hacks, because sometimes, you want your 'implant to be upgraded. The problem is when your 'implant is altered without your consent. That's where the brain comes in. The patch is aware of and takes into consideration emotional responses. If you're just simply getting an upgrade, your emotional state is going to be welcoming. If someone is trying to do something to your 'implant you don't want, your emotions are going to be distressed. The patch can tell based off the different brainwaves whether to attack the new code or accept it."

Andra pressed a hand to her forehead. "So . . . Ophele is in a coma . . . because she had a negative emotional reaction to the upgrade?"

"Ophele is in a coma because the amateur patch she downloaded attacked an extremely invasive new code, and the . . . battle, if you will, between the two opposing codes overloaded her 'implant and, by extension, her brain."

"So, basically, Ophele is in a coma because she didn't trust me."

Cruz grimaced. "She didn't trust the *code*."

"Because I was the one installing it."

Cruz swiveled in the ergo'chair. "Andie. This is good! We know what the problem is, so that means we know how to fix it!"

"How?" Andra threw up her hands. "By getting people to trust me? I'm not really a people person."

Cruz took one of her hands and squeezed it. "I trust you. You should try it on me."

She pulled her hand away. "What? No! You saw what happened to Ophele!" She got up and started pacing the room, nearly tripping over her dirty laundry.

"And I explained why that happened. It's not going to happen to me, because my emotional state is welcoming. I want this code. I love this code. I can't wait to have immunity to . . ." He pointed at the pocket in the mini'dome. ". . . whatever that is."

Andra shook her head. This was absurd. How could this entire thing come down to trust? How could tech be so reliant on the emotional whims of humans?

Cruz stood, taking both her hands in his and turning her to face him. "Please, Andra? I promise. This time it'll work."

Andra went cold.

Destroy.

Yes, this could destroy him. But this was it. This was the only thing Andra was good for. Helping humanity. Following Griffin's orders.

"I guess . . ."

"Great!" Cruz grinned and pulled his hair aside, exposing the tiny jack behind his ear. "Want to get started?"

Andra blinked. "What, now?"

"No time like the present. Or the future. Or whenever we are."

Andra couldn't help but smile. "You're so eager to be experimented on."

"Only by you."

Andra blushed as Cruz almost giddily unjacked the anomalizer from the work'station and handed it to Andra.

He jostled himself in the 'chair to get comfortable before exposing the jack behind his ear to Andra once again. She approached and gently touched the tip of the anomalizer to the port but pulled away.

"Are you sure?"

Cruz grabbed the anomalizer out of her hand and slid it into his own port. He didn't even flinch.

"I don't think this thing is letting go until the program is finished, so unless you want me walking around with it sticking out of my head, you might as well jack yourself in too."

Andra sighed and connected the anomalizer to a wire, then the wire to her reset tool. She took a deep breath before stabbing herself for the second time that day. She let out a small moan, tears smarting her eyes. The pain was quick, but it was intense.

"Okay, Andie?" Cruz asked.

She nodded, not confident enough in her voice to speak.

"Let's get this rolling," he said, feeling for the switch on the anomalizer and flipping it on.

Immediately, Andra felt like she was being drained again.

"Hmm," Cruz grunted. "This feels . . . weird."

"Bad?"

He winced. "No, just . . . like I can't sense my tech anymore. It's—ah!"

"Are you okay?" Andra took a step toward him.

"It's fine, it's fine," Cruz said through gritted teeth. "Just—ah! Kind of stings. I—"

He seized, falling to the floor, bringing Andra with him, the connecting wire dragging Andra by the heart. Black spots flooded her vision, pain slicing through her. She shook her head, trying to focus.

Cruz writhed next to her.

"Cruz!" She grabbed his hand, and he squeezed so hard it hurt. A strained moan escaped his lips, the last gasp of a dying animal, and he fell still. The anomalizer slid free, landing on the floor with a heavy thunk.

"Cruz? Cruz!"

Andra shook him, but he lay inert on the cold eco'tiled floor.

"Cruz!"

She sent her nanos through his skin, into his blood, coursing up to his heart. It was beating just fine. He was breathing. So why wasn't he responding?

"Cruz?"

His body started convulsing, his head twitching side to side, his eyes fluttering so all Andra could see were the whites.

Then as quickly as it started, it stopped. Cruz's eyes flashed open, clear, brown, and crinkled at the corners.

"Did it work?" he croaked.

Andra threw her arms around him. "Oh my god. Oh my god, I thought I'd killed you!"

Cruz chuckled and patted her on the back awkwardly. "I'm fine. It was just . . . I'm fine. Help me up?"

She pulled back but didn't let go of him, dragging him to his feet. He stood clumsily, like a newborn colt, legs shaking beneath him.

"This is . . . weird," he said, as she helped him back into his 'chair.

He took a huge breath, grinning like a fool, and put his hands out in front of him, taking them in as though he'd never seen them before. They shook as hard as his legs had.

"Well, I look like I'm okay," he said, his voice gaining strength. He laughed to himself, then seemed to remember something. "But how do we know that it worked?"

Andra shook her head, holding back nervous laughter. She'd almost killed him, and he was acting as though she'd given him superpowers.

"I mean, short of throwing you into a pocket, I don't know that we *can* know it worked. We just have to hope that if we ever get in a situation where a pocket is around, that you'll be safe."

Cruz's eyes flicked to the mini'dome. "We can test it."

Andra followed his line of sight. "No. No no no no. We're not letting that thing lose. You just almost died because you let yourself upload experimental tech, and now you want to expose yourself to the deadliest tech on the planet? Even if it doesn't destroy you, it could destroy everyone in this city! Everyone at LAC!"

Cruz's eyes were alight with amusement. "You got it in there. I'm sure you can do it again."

Andra swallowed. "It's different. I don't reck . . ."

But she did. She knew she could do this. She'd done it before. With Maret. At the Lake. She was in control. She was AI.

Let it free, the voice in her head whispered.

She hesitated, feeling the shiver up her spine. If she let the pocket out and lost control—even for a moment—it could destroy everything. The work'station, Andra's cot, the piles of tech and discarded clothes. The walls around her. Rashmi, next door. Lilibet, down the hall. It could spread throughout the Vaults, travel through the underground, into the Schism. Take out Eerensed.

But—

This was the only way to know if the anomalizer truly worked. To know for sure if upgrading the colonists' tech was the right next step.

"Fine." Andra pushed her sleeves up her arms. "Let's do this."

Cruz stood and shook out his limbs, now much more steady and sure. His muscles were tense, but there was an untamed glee in his eyes. He'd always been adventurous in his education, always would push the envelope to learn a little bit more. But this was ridiculous.

"Ready?" Andra asked, her nanos reaching out to the mini'dome.

Cruz nodded.

She lowered the sphere.

The pocket didn't even hesitate before springing free and shooting toward Cruz.

Andra flinched, reaching out with her mind, gathering all the nanos in the room to her, to envelope the corrupted nanos, ready to neutralize them if need be.

But it wasn't necessary. As soon as the pocket hit Cruz, it split, rushing past as though he were a rock in a stream. Andra's eyes widened, and for a second she lost concentration.

"Shit!"

The pocket swallowed her ergo'chair, disappearing it in an instant. It moved on, leaving nothing but less than atoms, scattered in the air. It dove for Andra's cot next.

"Shit, shit, shit!"

"Focus, Andra," Cruz said.

She closed her eyes, relieving herself of the distraction of what she could see, and focused solely on what she could feel. Just like that day in the throne room, she could sense the corrupted tech. She felt akin to it, like she could make it an extension of herself, and she did. She wasn't trying to control the pocket; she *was* the pocket.

She was the pocket and she wanted to destroy.

*destroydestroydestroydestroydestroy*No!

No, she didn't want to destroy, she wanted to return to the 'dome. To gather all the minuscule pieces of herself and huddle in the safety of the mini'dome. A paperweight on someone's desk. That's what she wanted. Simplicity. To be a novelty.

She no longer needed to convince the pocket, but herself. To tamp down that urge to destroy. To be trapped instead.

No, not to be trapped.

To be safe.

To rest.

Not a prison. Protection.

All the pieces of herself gathered and swarmed into the 'dome, sighing as the sphere closed around it.

Home.

//

Home.

"Andra!"

Her eyes flew open as she dove back into her own consciousness.

She was Andra.

She was a pocket.

No.

Remember who you are.

She was Andromeda Yue Watts.

Andra. Andra.

Teenager turned goddess turned AI. She was intelligent and kind and sarcastic. She liked fruit and the color yellow and daisies. She got butterflies in her stomach when boys winked at her. Especially Zhade.

She was herself.

But something inside her felt lost.

Cruz was staring at her, still grinning.

She stared back, breathing heavily.

"Well." Cruz gestured to the pocket, now back in the 'dome, then gestured to himself, hale and whole. "I guess it worked."

He stood, his eyes wide and gleaming. There was something about him Andra couldn't quite put her finger on.

"Are you sure you're okay?" she asked.

Cruz beamed. "Never better."

PART THREE

LAKE OF FIRE

01000010 01110101 01110010 01101110 00100000 01101001
01110100 00100000 01100001 01101100 01101100 00100000
01110101 01101110 01110100 01101001 01101100 00100000
01110100 01101000 01100101 01110010 01100101 00100000
01101001 01110011 00100000 01101110 01101111 01110100
01101000 01101001 01101110 01100111 00100000 01101100
01100101 01100110 01110100 00100000 01100010 01110101
01110100 00100000 01100001 01110011 01101000 00101110

—Message broadcast in the Wastes surrounding Eerensed,
reception unknown

TWENTY-ONE

OOII0OIO OOII0OOI

"WE SHOULD START upgrading right away."

Cruz circled the meeting table in Andra's room, holding a tablet in one hand, the 'displays flipping so fast it made Andra's sight blur. Ever since his upgrade, not only had he been immune to the pocket, but his 'implant worked better, faster. He could interface with almost anything in the Vaults with a thought.

Lilibet watched, concern written on her face. She'd shown up shortly after Cruz's 'implant had been converted, asking if Andra had seen Kiv recently. Then she'd stayed to ask Cruz all sorts of questions about life a thousand years ago, and what Andra was like before stasis. Cruz answered as best he could, and even asked Lilibet questions in return. But he was obviously distracted by their discovery about the upgrade.

Lilibet was excited to hear about the new magic too. At first.

Like Cruz, she was looking at a holo'display, but unlike Cruz, she was flipping through the code slowly with her finger. Andra wondered if she should fit Lilibet with an 'implant so she could interact with the data as easily as Cruz.

"I don't reck this isn't bad magic," she said. "The stitches seem . . . confusing."

Cruz smiled, a patronizing look Andra had never seen on him

before. It wasn't that he'd been mean to Lilibet; quite the opposite. He seemed fascinated to meet one of the descendants of the humans that had survived. But it was obvious that despite her being born nearly a thousand years after him, he saw her as primitive.

It annoyed Andra, and at first, she was convinced that the Cruz she'd known would never act so superior. But hadn't Andra acted the same way when she first awoke? Hadn't she looked down on the Eerensedians' culture? Cruz would have to learn, just like Andra, that just because they did things differently, it didn't make their way wrong.

"Of course it seems confusing," Cruz said, condescending smile still tacked to his face. "But that's only because there's a lot of code. Once the upgrades are done, we can go over it together, if that's something you're interested in."

"Neg, I purpose . . ." Lilibet said, still biting her lip.

"What is it, Lilibet?" Andra asked.

"It's mereish . . . when I do stitches and make a mistake, I return to the mistake and redo it. But I sole return as far as the mistake. This 'ppears to tear up the full pattern and restitch it. From scratchings."

Andra nodded. "Cruz and I talked about that. It's based off of a code that does that, but it doesn't actually wipe everything. It just . . . invades everything? *Invades* sounds really negative, but it's not in this case, I promise."

"But that might be why it nearish killed Cruz." Lilibet struggled with his name, trying to fit in the Eerensedian /y/ before the [u] sound and getting tangled with the /r/. "It . . . took all the stitches away for a moment, and maybe it shocked him. Likeish dunkings in the River Sed in midnight. Maybe there happens a better march for this. I could—"

"It wasn't that bad," Cruz said, but it was clear he only understood about half of what Lilibet had said. "People can undergo a little bit of a shock to their system if it means they're immune to the anomalies."

"But what if you were just lucky?" Andra asked. "What if their trust wavers for just a moment, and the full update doesn't go through and they don't come back?"

Cruz nodded, thinking for a moment. "It's not so much you they have to trust. It's the update. It's unfortunate you have to be literally tied to this, since they don't know you very well, if at all." Cruz sighed, running his fingers through his curls, his mind still flipping through the data on his holo'display. "They have to see the procedure completed successfully several times. Then they'll trust it."

"How will we make sure that the first few times are successful?"

Cruz shrugged and met Andra's eyes with a smile. "Easy," he said, and Andra knew she wasn't going to like what he said next. "We start with the people who trust you the most."

"I STILL THINK this is a bad idea," Andra said, following Cruz to her family's tent. "They just found out that our entire relationship was a lie that my dead mother fed them. I doubt they trust anything about me."

Cruz walked with his hands in his pockets, his stride long. "Familial relationships evolutionarily have a strong trust bond. Even when that trust is broken, it takes a lot to sever them completely."

Andra ducked under a 'drone that zoomed toward them, heading for another part of the Icebox. "Is that one of the things you were supposed to teach Rashmi and me as our socialization technician?"

It took Andra a moment to realize Cruz was no longer walking beside her. He stood paused in the middle of the main aisle, the cavernous space seeming to swallow him, the cryo'tanks that still held colonists rising up around him. He wiped his hands on his pants as though they were sweating.

"Listen, Andra, I'm sorry. I remember—"

Andra waved away the apology. "No. I'm sorry. You were just doing your job." She tilted her head. "And apparently doing it very well, seeing how attached I am to . . . our friendship." She wanted to bring up the relationship he'd had with Rashmi, but she wasn't sure she could handle talking about that right now. Besides, it would lead Cruz to ask questions about where the other AI was, and Rashmi had asked to be left alone. "Why aren't you calling me Andie? Why Andra all of a sudden?"

The worried lines on Cruz's face vanished, replaced by a mischievous smile. "I thought you hated being called Andie. But I can, if you want."

Andra crossed her hands in front of her. "No, no, no. I'm glad you've finally seen reason."

She gave Cruz a faint smile.

"Watch out!" a high voice said, and Andra ducked instinctively, sensing the 'drone heading right for her.

She and Cruz hit the floor just as it zoomed overhead, ruffling their hair.

"Sorry," Oz said, holo'control bouncing wildly in his hand as he ran toward them. "Sorry, I didn't see you. But I'm getting better, aren't I?"

The 'drone came to rest in his hand, and a huge smile spread across his face. Cruz helped Andra to her feet.

"You are getting better," Andra said. "Last time, you didn't apologize for hitting me."

Oz rolled his eyes and bumped into Andra in some semblance of a hug. "Where have you been? Dad said you needed time to yourself, like when you used to stay in your room all day. But I'm bored, and Dad said we can't wake my friends yet."

Andra ruffled his hair. "You could play with the kids who are already awake."

Oz wrinkled his nose. "They smell like synth."

"So do you." Andra kissed the top of his head.

"Do not!" Oz said, and started running toward the family's tent. "Race me!" he called over his shoulder. "Come see the fort I made!"

Andra followed at a normal pace, and Oz ran down the main aisle toward the tent city.

Cruz chuckled. "We could always upgrade him first."

Andra froze, heart plummeting. "No."

He frowned. "Why not? He trusts you completely. The upgrade would go smoothly."

"Even if it did, I'm not putting him through that if I don't have to. You . . . you looked like you were dead, Cruz. And before, you were in so much pain. And Ophele . . . No, we're not upgrading Oz."

Cruz was quiet for a moment.

"We'll have to eventually," he said softly.

Andra gave him a smile she didn't feel. "Maybe by then we'll have an easier way to do this."

"And if we don't?" Cruz took Andra's hand. "Griffin is the smartest person ever to live. If there was a way to do this without it hurting, she would have thought of it. Look, maybe you'd be saving him a little pain, but he wouldn't be safe from the anomalies."

Andra looked away. "He's safe down here."

"For now," Cruz said.

Andra didn't respond, just extricated her hand from his grasp and headed toward her tent.

After a moment, Cruz sighed and followed.

When they arrived, Andra's dad was sitting on his cot in his old professor clothes, replete with patched elbows. There was stubble on his head and chin, and he stood as soon as he saw Andra. Before she could say a single word, he wrapped her into his arms.

"I'm sorry," he said, voice shaking, and she was surprised to realize he was weeping.

Her father was prone to crying. It didn't matter what, whether it was a moving sim or a holiday ad or when he would lecture about the postal raids of 2103. He expressed his emotions freely and often, so they never overtook him, never overwhelmed him.

But now he seemed to be amazingly and thoroughly overwhelmed.

"I'm sorry, I'm sorry," he said through racking sobs, his tears tangling in Andra's hair. "I love you."

She let her arms go around him and patted him on the back.

"It's okay, Dad. It was a shock, and finding out about Mom—"

"No." Auric pulled away, cupping her face in his hands. "It's not okay. No matter what. You are my daughter. And nothing—*nothing*—will ever change that. Remember that."

Andra nodded, the back of her throat closing and tears stinging her eyes. She hadn't realized how badly she'd needed to hear those words.

"Thank you, Dad," she choked out. "I love you too."

She buried her face in his chest, and together they cried.

ANDRA DIDN'T KNOW how long they stood like that, but when she finally pulled away from her dad, she noticed that Cruz was a few meters away laughing with Oz. Acadia was nowhere to be found, as usual.

"So what's this again?" Auric asked, twirling the anomalizer in his hand. It twinkled darkly in the dim light of the tent.

"It's just like . . . an upgrade tool, but for our—*your* 'implants. Griffin figured out a way to adapt your tech to help you survive . . . an atmospheric anomaly on the surface."

"So why do you want me to go first?"

"Well, because it requires . . . trust." Andra bit her lip. She was asking her father to trust her, but she wasn't being completely truthful with him. About the manner of her mother's death. About where and when they were. About the full reason they needed the upgrade.

"Trust?"

She scratched behind her ear. "Yeah, I guess the 'implant is too en-tuned to your neural pathways, and . . . we tried it on one of the LAC scientists. She didn't know me, and . . . well, it was a miracle she survived." Andra's chest tightened. "Then Cruz figured out that the neural connections on the trust pathways had to remain open during the upgrade, or else the—"

Auric waved his hand. "None of that technical stuff, I get enough of that with your mother." He looked away. "Or I did."

Andra blinked back tears. "I, um, I tried the procedure on Cruz. He knows me and trusts me, and trusts Griffin's tech. It worked fine on him. He thought if the people could see it work a few times, they would trust the tech, and we could do the upgrade on all the scien-tists."

Auric nodded. "Of course. I'm ready whenever you are."

Andra put a hand on his arm. "It's not that simple, Dad. It . . . it's going to hurt. A lot. It doesn't just shut down your 'implant, it shuts down your brain. Just for a moment. I know you just woke up, and Mom, and then there's what I am—"

"Enough." Auric gently took Andra's hand. "I trust you. I'm proud of you. I will do whatever you need, no matter how much it hurts."

Andra gave her father a sad smile. For some reason, that didn't make her feel particularly better.

TWENTY-TWO

THE GIFTED

ZHADE STOOD IN the middle of the empty cathedzal. Evens. Not empty. A host of angels surrounded him in concentric circles. Light filtered in through the stained windows, casting an array of colors on their shiny casings. The gods' dome scrys behind him winked in various rhythms. The room was dead silent. He shivered, his bare feet cold against the red velvet floor. He wore his old guard uniform pants and nothing else. Nothing, except the Crown.

He closed his eyes, allowing himself to feel his connection with the angels in the room. It was weak. He could sense them, but it was like seeing something in his peripheral vision. When he tried to focus on them, they disappeared.

Atop of that, he was distracted by the memory of his kiss with Andra, the feel of her body against his, the desperation in how she held on to him. Then, her realizing what she was doing, pushing him away, disgusted to have kissed the boy who had betrayed her time and time again.

He recked he wasn't full good for her. Recked that she deserved better and should stay away from him. So why did it hurt so much?

He glared at the closest angel, its sleek casing glinting in the dancing light. He could bareish sense it through the Crown. The more he tried, the more diff it became.

Magic had always come easyish to him. But he'd always used Low Magic. Creating spells, brewing potions, inventing conduits. This was different. This was feeling and instinct and will. It was a skill he didn't have, a talent he'd yet to develop.

But he had to.

This moren, he'd heard of nearish ten rogue angels throughout Eerensed. Citians were surrendering their magic in droves, but it wasn't enough. Still more hid their angels, sole for their eyes to turn red and kill their masters. Nearish thirty dead in the past few days. He had to stop this. Stop feeling sorries for himself and do what he was purposed to do. Protect his people. Decide his fate.

He tried again, attempting to sense the angels through the Crown. There were dozens of them. Every angel that the citians had surrendered to the palace. Large, bulky ones with spears. Thin, sleek ones with transparent skulls. Some that didn't even resemble humans at all. Arachnid limbs and sharp joints. He could bareish focus on one, let alone all of them. He imagined bout Andra controlling the pocket, all those minuscule pieces she commanded at once. But then, Andra was a goddess, and he was mereish Zhade.

Neg. He was the son of a goddess. He was the Guv. He could do this.

He focused on one angel. Fishy. Zhade had sorcered it to create conduits plenty of times. He recked it, not mereish as an angel but as a friend. He concentrated, and Fishy's essence, identity bloomed in Zhade's mind.

He couldn't describe it. It was a new sense, not like sight or touch but with elements of both and neither. Fishy felt green, cold, buzzing. It was a network of magical veins and arteries pooled into a single being.

Zhade also felt the Crown. It was an odd sensation. Part of him and apart from him. An extra limb, an extension of himself. It recked what to do, even if Zhade didn't.

Lift your spear, he commanded Fishy.

Nothing happened.

He thought again. *Lift your spear.*

A twitch but nothing more. Zhade was already feeling defeated.

"You're not concentrating," came a voice.

Zhade opened one eye and glared at Tsurina. "Maybe I could if you would stop interrupting."

She lounged on Andra's chaise, which she had demanded Kiv bring to the cathedzal. The big man had sole glared when Zhade told him his plan to skool bout the Crown from Tsurina. He didn't argue, though.

Zhade had need to find time for Kiv to visit Lilibet. He'd purposed to. For true he had. He'd planned on having Gryfud take Kiv's place for a few bells. But Gryfud was busy holding the guards from being suss bout Meta, and Zhade had no one else he could trust to hold Tsurina from escaping.

Kiv comped full well, even if he didn't like it. He stood nearish the cathedzal double doors, huge arms crossed over his chest, a scowl on his face. He watched Tsurina like he was bout to murder her, and Zhade recked it was sole his loyalty to Zhade that prevented it.

"It shouldn't meteor," Tsurina snapped, standing. Her long silk dress draped dramaticish to the floor. She held her arms out as though she were bout to dance. "This is all yours to control. The stardust, the angels, even me. If I'm distracting you, it's because you're letting me."

Zhade rolled his eyes. "I can't control you. I can sole control magic."

"For true?" Tsurina scoffed. "Because you haven't so far."

"Is this wonderful technique how you skooled Maret?" Zhade snapped.

"Try again."

Zhade closed his eyes. He took a deep breath in through his nose and let it out heavyish through his mouth. Then he reached out with his magical senses through the Crown.

What was it that Andra had said? Thoughts with intent? She likened it to moving a part of your body.

You can think about moving your arm without moving it. You can also move your arm without thinking about it.

He had memory of Doon as an infant. The jerky movements she made. Reaching for things and missing. How long it took her to walk. He'd been eight, nine at the time, but it had fascinated him watching someone skool all those things, to be so bad at things that came naturalish to him. Now he was the infant.

Lift.

Your.

Spear.

He imagined it happening. Not merish the words in his head but the consequences. Fishy's many-jointed fingers wrapping tighter round the spear. He imagined what it felt like when he gripped his own. The muscles running from his neck down his arms, into his palms. The twitch of each finger. The sensation of holding something. The slight clench in his abdomens as he prepped to lift something. The strength coming not mereish from his torso but down his legs. He imagined it all, and he planted that image in Fishy's mind.

This, he thought. *This is what I want you to do.*

But it wasn't asking. He didn't ask his arm to move for him. It was part of him. It was him and he was it, and there was no commanding or asking or trying. There was mereish doing.

He was Fishy. Fishy was him. And as Fishy, he imagined the act of lifting the spear, everything it entailed. He didn't plead or cajole. He mereish did.

One moment, Fishy was holding it looseish at its side, the next, it had tightened its grip and lifted it from the ground. It grasped the spear with both hands, and then pointed it forward, at Zhade's heart.

He sucked in a breath.

With will and intent, he had Fishy lower its spear and walk toward Zhade. One step. Two.

Zhade couldn't hold back his smile. Power ran through him, from the Crown to his head and heart and all throughout his body. He expanded his senses to feel more angels in the room. A second spear lifted, then a third. Each time, the effort grew easier, til thirteen angels were holding their spears aloft.

Stardust swirled round him, hungryish, asking for a task. Through them, he could feel the shape of the room, the figure that was Tsurina. They butted up against her, and it was the empty space, the part of the room that lacked stardust, that told Zhade where she was, how she was standing.

He concentrated harder, condensing the stardust round her so he could sense the tension in her arms, the expression on her face. She was relaxed, vulnerable. She had no way to defend herself, and Zhade no longer needed her. She hated him. Always had. And now he could kill her so very, very easyish.

There was no reason to hold her alive. She'd already served her purpose. Skooled him to use the Crown. Gave him answers bout his mam for Andra.

His mam.

Who Tsurina claimed was alive.

If he killed Tsurina, he'd never reck for certz.

He opened his eyes to find Tsurina watching him. Shame fell on him like a pile of rocktins, and he came back to himself. He was no longer Zhade and the stardust, Zhade and magic, Zhade and.

He was mereish Zhade.

Tsurina met his eyes and smiled.

"Good."

TWENTY-THREE

OO11OO1O OO11OO11

THE ENTIRE LAC stood around Andra, their eyes fixed on the wire that ran from the reset tool in her heart to the one poised to enter her father's skull. He lay strapped to an operating table, bands covering his chest, torso, and thighs. He gave Andra a smile, ignoring the thousands of eyes watching them, but Andra felt every one of them.

It was necessary, of course. In order to get upgraded, the people had to trust her, and they wouldn't trust her—a child they knew only as their boss's daughter—unless they saw her perform a successful upgrade.

"Are you ready, Andra?" Cruz asked.

He'd finished attaching the monitors to her father. One holo shot from the monitor on his chest, revealing Auric's beating heart. It was accompanied by a *thump-thump* noise that Andra felt in her bones. Another monitor displayed her father's brain, alight with activity. A third showed his lungs, and a fourth, his neural'implant. It projected a dense network of nanos and electricity. Once the upgrade was complete, the nanos in the 'implant would appear on the monitor as the corrupted tech.

A chill ran up Andra's spine, but that was the point, wasn't it? For the tech to look corrupted, give off that signature, so that the pockets would now see Auric as one of their own, preventing any attacks. This was a good thing. She was protecting her father.

So why did it seem so scary?

Perhaps it was the sound of hushed voices echoing around the cavernous space of the Icebox, the yellow kinetic lighting, the feeling of anticipation she could sense even through the nanos wafting around her.

Perhaps it was the thought of Ophele, lying in a coma a few tents away.

Was she ready? Cruz had asked. No, but she didn't have a choice.

She nodded and brought the anomalizer to the small port beneath her father's left ear. It cast her father's cheek in a green, sickly glow.

"This is really going to hurt, Dad," she whispered. "But it's only going to be for a moment."

He grabbed her wrist, his palm slick with sweat. He smiled, eyes watery. "I trust you."

She smiled back. "I love you, Dad."

She drove the anomalizer into the port and clicked the button. Auric's eyes shut and his heart rate increased, but the monitor remained a neutral shade of green. The pain sectors of his brain were still dormant. His lungs expanded and contracted.

It was exactly six seconds before everything went red. His heart rate spiked, his brain lit with electricity, his lungs gasping.

Andra wanted to cry, but she had to seem confident if the other colonists were to trust her. It had to appear that she knew what she was doing. And she did. Mostly. But it didn't make it any easier to watch as her father struggled, as the monitors flashed red.

Then everything stopped.

The 'display of his heart froze, the comforting *thump-thump* replaced by a blaring alarm. His brain activity went blank, and his lungs blew out one last breath. The room was silent except for the alarms begging Andra to do something. To use a defib app. To spike him with O$_2$. Something.

But Andra waited.

Watched as the 'displays remained frozen, the only movement in the 'implant monitor, which showed the upgrade at work. The new code overtook the frenetic code of the 'implant and assimilated it. The 'implant tech was panicking, each nano picked off one by one by the incoming tech.

The room held its collective breath, and Andra stood transfixed on the flashing 'display of her father's heart, still and unbeating.

Had Cruz's upgrade been a fluke? Cruz had been sure that trust was the answer. Andra had seen how the new code worked and agreed. What if they'd done it wrong? They were an untrained AI and a boy barely older than a teenager, after all. What if there was no guarantee her father would wake up?

What if she'd just killed him?

Auric's eyes flashed open, and he sucked in a breath. The entire room let out theirs.

The alarms stopped blaring. Auric's heart was beating again, his lungs filling with air, his brain lit with activity. The nanos in his 'implant were now as dark and clouded as the nanos in the pockets, but, unlike the pockets, they weren't killing him.

Andra choked back a sob. Auric's eyes found his daughter, and he smiled. Andra couldn't return it yet.

"Try turning on the orb," she said, her voice barely above a whisper. She nodded to the kinetic orb floating a few feet above Auric.

It flicked on.

Andra let out a relieved sigh, as technicians darted forward to unstrap him. The other LAC scientists clapped politely.

"I have a question," Cristin Myrh, one of the environmental scientists, said. She had straight blonde hair, with bangs cut straight across, and she'd been glaring at Andra during the whole procedure. "How do we know it worked?"

This, Andra and Cruz were prepared for. They'd brought one of the air'lock chambers from the Vaults, reinforced it with cryo'tank platelets, and placed the pocket inside.

Andra swallowed as Cruz wheeled it to the center of the crowd.

"This chamber," he said, "is filled with nanos that mimic the . . . atmospheric anomalies on the surface. They destroy everything that doesn't share the same . . . makeup."

The lie was carefully crafted. Close enough to the truth, but with no mention of decon'bots or the entropics created by the LAC. Instead, Cruz suggested they were natural occurrences.

"Professor Lim will step into the chamber, and the nanos will not hurt him, because the 'implant is helping to mask him from the anomaly."

"What about a control?" Raj asked. "One of us should step in there so we know what would happen if we did go out into the atmosphere."

He narrowed his eyes at Andra, and she looked away uncomfortably. He hadn't approached her again about what had happened to Ophele, but she knew he blamed her. And he was right to. It had, after all, been entirely her fault.

Cruz gave Raj a perfectly apologetic smile. "I'm afraid that's impossible. Even minimal exposure could be fatal. But we can use a 'bot to showcase this."

Andra hated this part. She'd tried convincing Cruz to use something else—a chair, a work'station, anything—but he'd argued that the scientists would need to see the effect on something humanoid.

There were very few 'bots left in the Vaults except for Mechy, and Andra had absolutely refused to allow him to be destroyed. It reminded her too much of her mother disassembling their standard AI growing up. It hadn't been True AI, of course, and it had attacked her mother, but it had seemed sentient to Andra. Mechy wasn't AI, true or standard, but she wouldn't sacrifice him.

Instead, they used a small 'bot they'd found powered down in the Vaults' maintenance room. A serve'bot with a sleek white exterior, barely taller than Andra. It was thin and feminine-looking, and though its face didn't hold expression, Andra imagined she saw fear in its eyes as it entered the chamber.

As soon as the 'bot stepped through the air'lock, the pocket attacked. The 'bot jerked back, scrambling for the exit, but it was too late. The scientists gasped as the 'bot was enveloped by the darkness, its shape outlined by the pocket like a shadow. It took less than a second and the pocket dispersed, forming an inert cloud, leaving no trace behind.

"You're going to put Professor Lim in there?" Cristin Myrh asked, her eyes wide.

"It's perfectly safe," Cruz assured her. "That is, in fact, why we completed this procedure."

Andra's stomach dropped as technicians helped Auric to his feet. And though he was at first as unsteady as Cruz had been, he was soon striding over to the chamber with uncharacteristic confidence. He looked back at Andra, his eyes shining with pride, and he entered the air'lock. The chamber sealed behind him, and the glass door between the antechamber and the main chamber slid aside. The corrupt nanos were waiting, and her father stepped forward.

Andra held her breath. She knew this would work. Knew it in her bones, in her mind. But her heart was terrified for her father. Her father who had raised her. Her father who knew what she was and still loved her. The pocket consumed him.

She couldn't see anything within the cloud, not the shape of her father, not his patched elbows, not his smiling cheeks. For the second time, she wondered if they'd gotten it all wrong. But then the cloud dispersed, and there was Auric, completely fine. The pocket danced around him, swirling like leaves caught in the wind. Auric held his hands out, and corrupted nanos played across his fingers. Tickled up his arms.

But they didn't hurt him.

She'd done it.

Andra had done it.

She hadn't needed to contact Griffin's clone for advice, hadn't given up. Finally, finally she'd done something right. She'd helped humanity. And what better way to start helping humanity than with her father?

The room burst into applause. Her dad smiled, and Andra smiled back.

TWENTY-FOUR

THE GUARDIAN

"I TAKE IT your lessons are going well?" Meta asked, holding pace with Zhade as they made their march through the market.

The day was bright, the sun not full low yet to disappear behind the pocket. A gentle breeze flapped Zhade's cape, a sign for certz that the gods' dome was weakening, but he didn't want to imagine bout that now. This even, he would look at the controls in the cathedzal. Maybe even use the Crown to fix it—though Andra had said not to use High Magic with the gods' dome.

"Too much power," she'd said. "You'd fry your brain in an instant."

But she hadn't seen what he could do with the Crown. Hadn't seen him command nearish a hundred angels at once.

His collection was growing. Though he'd commanded all citians to surrender their angels apalace a turn ago, his guards still found resistance—citians who held on to their magic despite the danger. He'd tried reasoning with them, but each day he heard more and more whispers of hidden angels acity. So he'd had to start taking them by force. He wasn't happy bout it, but it was necessary. Most oft, he sent his guards to seize the angels, but he'd received word of some angels hidden in Southwarden.

Above a bakery.

Dzeni.

Zhade shot Meta a look as people in the crowded market square dove out of the way of his entourage. Meta shouldn't be asking him bout his Crown lessons afront of people, specialish citians.

"Jealous I'm passing time with your zerox?" he asked quietish.

Meta snorted. "Scuze. I'm the one who wanted her dead, marah."

"Evens." Zhade looked back to see if the guards were spending attention. Sole Gryf could hear. "She's proved useful. If we'd killed her, I'd still be figuring the Crown, and how would we fight the angels?"

Meta was quiet a moment. "I don't imagine you have need of the Crown to fight them. Sides, you should have more shakes of the people holding them than the angels themselves. We don't reck they've gone rogue."

Zhade nearish stumbled. "We convoed this. I'm not hurting Dzeni. I can reason with her. For certz, she'll see things our way. We sole want to hold her safe."

"And if she won't see reason?" Meta asked.

Zhade clenched his jaw. "She will."

Meta looked away, eyes narrowed, and shrugged, staying silent the rest of the march to the bakery.

It was mereish as he had memory: a teetering apartment with a white facade and intricateish embellished windows and eaves. Though the bakery was on the ground level, Cheska's apartment was at the top. Without knocking, Zhade burst through the side door to the stairs. Kidduns were playing on the steps, olds chatting to one another from across the hall. When they saw him, their eyes widened and they scurried into their homes, afraid.

Good, Zhade thought. It wasn't that he wanted his people ascared of him. It was that he wanted them to hold a healthy fear for the angels. Sides, citians' fear of Maret was part of what had held him in power.

Zhade's boots clipped against the stairs. The armor of the guards clanked behind him, their spears stomping against the floor with each step. When they reached Cheska's apartment, Zhade knocked. There was no answer.

The door was painted a light blue, yellow starflowers etched into the edges. A kiddun's handprints smudged the finish.

Now that he was here, he wished he didn't have to do this. He didn't want to face Dzeni like this. She wouldn't approve of his seizing the angels, taking them by force. And if she discovered he'd been taking lessons from Tsurina . . .

A scream sounded from inside.

Dzeni.

Zhade threw himself against the door, but it didn't budge. Gryfud moved Zhade out of the way and kicked the door in. It flew off its hinges.

Zhade charged in and froze. A group of red-eyed angels stood in the entry room.

Dzeni, Dehgo, and a woman with white-blonde hair were surrounded by the rogue angels. The blonde woman was weeping. Next to her was Dzeni, face ashen but determined, blood and dirt streaking her cheeks. With one arm she held Dehgo behind her, and with the other she held a kitchen knife. They were sheltered in the small gods' dome he'd given them. The sheen of the thin barrier was flickering, bout to die.

Cheska lay crumpled on the ground, blood gushing in an ever-expanding pool round him. An angel stood above him. Cheska's chest was cracked open, and on the tip of the angel's spear was his heart.

Meta barked orders in Tsurina's voice, and the guards formed a circle round the ring of angels advancing on the small gods' dome that held Dzeni and the woman who must be Swan, Cheska's promised.

Before Zhade could order them back, Meta charged the angel holding Cheska's heart. The remaining guards followed suit, pulling out their swords. They hacked at the angels, but swords did little against the hard casing. One guard was speared through the neck, another through the stomach.

Zhade drew his sword on instinct but then had memory of the Crown. He tried to command the angel nearest to him to stop, but there was something blocking him from its consciousness. This wasn't right. Zhade could control angels. He'd done it this moren.

Screams filled the air as the small dome blinked out, leaving Dzeni, Dehgo, and Swan defenseless.

Gryfud beat back an angel and dragged a sobbing Swan to safety behind a counter. Dzeni used the moment of distraction to bring her kitchen knife down on the back of the angel's neck, severing its head. It hit the ground, arms and legs twitching, its stardust releasing to the air. Zhade gathered it to himself. If he couldn't control the rogue angels, he would use something he could control.

Meta took down an angel, and Gryfud took out another. Their stardust scattered, and again, Zhade called to it through the Crown.

But it wasn't enough. He needed more. More stardust, more . . . energy. The battle raged round him, and he sought the nearest source of power—the miniature gods' dome. It was broken but not drained. Power coursed through it. Power he could use.

Sole, Andra had said not to, that using the Crown to access domes would destroy him.

For certz it wouldn't. This was a small one, and Zhade was strong.

He called the power to himself, absorbing every bit of energy left in the dome. He felt his senses sharpen, every molecule of himself alight. He was limitless, unstoppable.

He could see through the stardust in the room, sense through it. His consciousness was divided into a million pieces, drawn in a million different directions. But he wasn't drained of himself; instead, he was expanded. He was Zhade and he was the magic. He was each minuscule piece of stardust in the room. He filled the space.

He saw himself from outside of himself. Saw his brother's features, his brother's Crown, but the stance, the confidence was all Zhade's. He saw Swan crumpled in a corner, her eyes focused on the hole in her promised's chest. He felt the cavern where Cheska's heart has been, felt his blood seep onto the floor. Heard the floor creak under the boots of the guards. Each clash of steel vibrated inside him. Each cry from Dzeni's lips felt as though it were coming from his own.

He was everywhere and nowhere, and somehow he recked how the battle would end. The guards were well trained and fought fierceish, but they were outnumbered. One by one, they would fall, Tsabin, Ranzh, Gryfud, til it was sole Meta who stood tween a host of angels and Dzeni. She would die, then Wead's promised. Then their son. Then Swan. Til all that was left was Zhade.

And they wouldn't kill him.

Not because they didn't want to.

But because they couldn't. He was too powerful.

Suddenish, he was consumed by a memory, a vision, of controlling stardust. Of forming spears. Of thrusting them into three hearts—

He blinked. He'd never done that. Then why did he have the memory in his head as crystal as glass?

"Zhade! Please!" Dzeni's voice broke through the haze, and Zhade had memory of himself. Had memory of his duty as guv, his care for Dzeni, his love for her kiddun. In a single breath, he gathered all the stardust in the room, as though he were collecting starflowers. He felt the stardust inside the angels, their very souls. It was dark and unattainable, something other.

He pulled it from them, siphoning their souls. He started small, gathering it into small collections. One piece of stardust became two, became four, became eight, til there were millions of pieces attached together in glittering pockets. He gathered and gathered, relishing in the sheer power of it. He was no longer himself. No longer mereish Zhade, but something more. Something better.

The angels began to slow, their movements sluggish, and with one final burst of energy, Zhade shouted, "Get down!"

Meta hit the floor, dragging Dzeni with her. Gryfud threw himself over Dehgo, and the other guards formed a barrier between the angels and Swan.

And the room exploded.

Zhade blasted the angels back, tearing through their torsos and chests and limbs with their own magic, their own souls. Stardust ripped through them in glittering balls of concentrated destruction. Angel shrapnel flung itself round the room, embedding into the walls, bursting through the windows, toppling furniture. Zhade used the stardust to create his own dome, to shield Dzeni and Meta and his guards, and it felt as though he were creating something out of nothing. He felt like a god.

The room fell silent, the last angel toppling to the floor. The air filled with dust and stardust, as Dzeni and Meta slowish raised their heads. Dehgo pushed out from under Gryfud and clawed his march to his mam, as she pleaded for him to be careful of the glass littering the floor. The guards stood, patting themselves off. Gryfud lifted Swan to her feet. Her gaze remained transfixed on her promised, whose body was now riddled with holes from the explosion.

All eyes on the room went to Zhade, waiting for his command.

"Gryf, get these three somewhere safe." He gave Gryfud a pointed look, gesturing to Dzeni, Dehgo, and Swan. "Come back for the body," Zhade added, when it appeared Swan would not be separated from it. Gryfud gentlish lifted Swan into his arms and carried her out of the room. Dzeni followed, Dehgo held tight in her arms, but not before giving Zhade one last look.

He turned to Meta. Her brown eyes were wide, blood dripping down her cheek. She was looking at him as though she'd never seen him before.

"Gather all the angels left acity and bring them to the cathedzal."

He made eye contact with each of the guards. "Hunt them all, quell any resistance. All angels should be in my possession by the end of the day, no meteor the cost. Do we comp?"

"Firm, Guv," the guards said.

Meta continued to stare at him, something like fear etched on her face. Finalish she nodded.

"Good."

Zhade kicked the remains of an angel out of his march, and left the guards to their task.

TWENTY-FIVE

OO||OO|O OO||O|O|

ANDRA HAD SPENT the last week upgrading neural'implants.

She and Cruz started with the youngest members of the LAC. She'd wanted to start with the senior scientists, the ones who could help most with the upgrades and building the rocket. But Cruz said the younger ones would trust more easily. That they wouldn't have the older scientists' skepticism of Andra's youth.

By dinnertime the first day, she'd upgraded five—three from the cryonics department, one from terraforming, and one from medical. By the fifth day, she and Cruz had upgraded a total of thirty. At this pace, it was going to take months.

Not to mention, the voice telling her to destroy emerged several times a day, and she continuously had to hide the dead nanos she coughed up. Andra had already sat through seven procedures today, and she felt like she'd run a marathon. Which she had never done, nor ever would do, but imagined was quite tiring. Cruz was ready to work through dinner, but he wasn't the one with the reset tool sticking out of his heart.

She told Cruz she needed a break, grabbed a few pieces of toast and a packet of syntheal from the colonists' makeshift cafeteria, and headed toward her room in the Vaults.

She was almost back when she remembered she had another

responsibility she couldn't ignore. She mentally reached out to Mechy, to let him know she was coming.

When she entered the small Vaults lab that was now Maret's cell, he was fully clothed—sand-colored pants and a black shirt, which he wore unbuttoned like his brother would—and lounging on a pile of Lilibet's blankets, head tilted back against the wall, eyes closed, the ends of his hair tickling his shoulders. He was no longer 'cuffed to a chair. Instead, he was behind a force shield Mechy had constructed. Unlike the metal bars and easily manipulated locks of the palace dungeons, only a thin, translucent field of energy separated them. It was barely visible, just a blue sheen around the edges, but Andra could feel its presence in her mind. A comforting barrier between her and Maret.

Lilibet had brought him food and water and a cushion to sleep on. The food lay uneaten to the side, the cushion still plump and sitting where it had been slid through a momentary gap in the shield.

Andra cleared her throat, but he didn't open his eyes.

"So I'm to shit on the floor, evens?" he asked.

Andra flushed. She hadn't thought of that. "I'll have someone bring you a bucket," she murmured.

He smiled to himself. "Shame. If you for true wanted me to talk, you might consider denying such comforts. Have you never held anyone prisoner before?"

She swallowed. "You know I haven't. And as I'm such an amateur, you'd best hope I remember to keep you alive."

Maret chuckled to himself.

Andra got as close as she dared to the force shield. She knew it was there, could feel it, but part of her was waiting for Maret to pounce. To burst through the barrier, hand to her throat before she could even blink.

"What is it, this information you say you know?" Andra asked, her voice wobbling.

Maret cocked his knees and leaned forward, blond hair hanging in greasy streaks across his face. "I reck that you're asking the wrong question."

"Then what's the right question?"

He shook his head, lips quirked. "Not that one either."

"Why are you such an ass?"

"Ooh. Am I getting to you?" He tsked. "In an interrogation, you always want to be the one in control."

Her cheeks went warm. "I'm not the one in a cage," she snapped.

This wasn't in her skill set—interrogating people. She looked for the voice that haunted her, that corruption inside her that told her to destroy. That ruthlessness, that hate, could guide her now.

It was like slipping into a cold lake. Her breath left her in a rush and her muscles tensed, but once she was submerged in the feeling, it was . . . refreshing. To let the darkness in.

Destroy, it hissed.

Yes, she answered. He deserved to be destroyed for all he had done. To his brother. To Eerensed. To Andra. It would be right to be rid of him. To do what Zhade had tried to do months ago. Cold clarity overtook her. She would do it. She would—

"Andra?" a voice said into her mind.

Mechy.

She came back to herself, the cold feeling draining from her in an instant.

What had she been thinking? She'd almost let it take control.

And for what? The information Maret said he was holding back? That could be a lie? The information he said she so desperately needed. But she didn't know what she needed. Maybe Rashmi's memories from before? Or was it something about Andra? He had once said that he knew what she was and why she'd been created. But surely that had just been a taunt. And besides, Griffin's clone had already said her purpose was to help humanity.

"Is everything evens, Goddess?" Maret sneered.

"Of course," Andra snapped.

He watched her, eyes unblinking, expression unreadable.

She took a calming breath. "You used to trust me." When he scoffed, she added, "Sort of. You asked me to help you save your brother. You protected me from your mother sacrificing me at the festival."

"Firm, and look how that turned out for me. My brother tried to kill me, and you attacked me. Several times. And now, you've put me in some sort of magical cage."

He stood, thin and long-limbed, and stalked toward her. Andra willed herself not to back away as he touched his finger to the force shield, holding eye contact as the tip of his finger burned against the barrier. His fingertip sizzled, his eyes started to water. Technically, he could push through if he wanted, if he didn't mind losing his finger, then his hand, then his arm. If he kept going, he would be dead before he made it halfway through.

"Stop." Andra flinched.

Maret smiled and pulled his finger away from the energy field. The tip was blackened. On instinct, Andra sent some nearby nanos to heal it. They passed through the field effortlessly and went to work on Maret's wound.

His eyes widened as he swatted at the nanos, stumbling back. "Get those away from me," he rasped.

She pulled the med'nanos back. "Interesting," she said, trying to mimic the tone he'd just used with her. "Does the stardust scare you?" She brought the nanos closer to Maret, coalescing them into a shimmering cloud.

"When it's controlled by you, for certz I am, you soulless demon. You nearish killed everyone on a whim that day in the throne room." He held his burned finger to his chest, as though he were shielding it from her. "And you imagine I'm a monster."

That brought Andra up short. The nanos dispersed back into the air, and Maret relaxed.

"What did I do?" she asked. "That day in the throne room."

Was this the information he claimed to know?

Maret narrowed his eyes, a quirk to his lips. "You controlled the pocket."

Andra held her breath. He knew something. She felt it in her bones.

"The question is," he said, "what did it do to you?"

BACK IN HER room, Andra put on a fresh pair of clothes. She splashed her face with cold water and watched as it dripped from her reflection. Her eyes and nose were red, and there was an overall haggard look to her features.

She didn't know why she was wasting time with Maret. Even if he knew something Griffin didn't, even if he remembered something Rashmi no longer did, he wouldn't tell her.

But something nagged at her. Why would Maret say he knew something and not tell her? To try to stay alive? Surely he realized she wouldn't actually kill him. And if he did know something, why was she convinced it was about her purpose? How would he know? And why did she even feel like she had one? Why would Griffin program Andra with a feeling that she was fated for something important, if she was merely a tool? Unless that nagging sense of destiny was another side effect of the illusion of her humanity.

She was jolted back to herself by a knock at the door.

"Andra, Andra, Andra, Andra, Andra, Andra, Andra," Lilibet chanted on the other side.

Andra commanded it to open, and Lilibet tumbled in.

Sweat clung to her brow. "Soze, we have a bitsy problem. Dzeni and the little kiddun need to stay. Angels killed Cheska. Dzeni is full sad. And Cheska's promised 'pens full bars bad magic sad. I 'pen sole bit sad, because I didn't reck him full well. But still sad, because it 'pens sad when someone dies. Especialish if it's because an angel *pulled their heart out of their chest*! And soze, full certz, Zhade told Gryf to bring them all here—the promised and Dzeni and the kiddun. But Dzeni doesn't want to be here. She 'pens mad because Zhade let Lew-Eaden die, and I reck she 'pens also bit mad at you, even though it happened not your fault. You wanted Zhade to die instead, even though I reck you didn't for true want Zhade to die, but I didn't have time to explain all that to her, because she 'pens so angry and so sad—"

"What?" Andra blinked, trying to catch up. She could process information fast, but not as fast as Lilibet talked, and besides the information needed to make logical sense. "Who pulled whose heart out of whose chest?"

Lilibet shook her head, her long, dark hair falling over her shoulders. "Hold forward, Andra. An angel. Pulled Cheska's heart. *Out of his chest!* And people happen sad and they're here, because Zhade sent them!"

Andra didn't know who Cheska was, and she was about to argue that angels—'bots—couldn't kill people, but maybe it was a metaphor. Some Eerensedian idiom Andra hadn't learned yet. "Where are they?"

"I'll take you to them!" Lilibet chirped, then remembered she was supposed to be sad and put on a somber face.

Andra followed her. She heard them before she saw them. Loud weeping and yelling echoed down the hall from the lobby.

"I'm NOT staying here! You can't hide me away mereish because I'm inconvenient!"

"Sands, Dzeni, it's not a prison. It's to hold you safe!"

That was Zhade's voice. At least, Andra thought it was Zhade's voice. Something about the tenor of it had changed, like he was spending too much time pretending to be his brother.

"Mereish like you held Wead safe?"

Andra pushed through the double doors into the lobby, and Zhade—who had been about to yell something back—froze when he saw her. He stood under the astronomical clock, something broken on his brother's features. Before him, Dzeni was red-faced, wisps of hair tangling in the dirt and blood on her cheeks. A woman with brown skin and stark-white chin-length hair was weeping on the blue eco'tiled floor. Behind them, a bemused Xana was holding Dehgo, who was counting along with the ticking of the clock.

But Andra only had eyes for Zhade. Even though he still looked like Maret—his face, his slimmer figure, his white-blond hair—Andra knew in some ways, he would always feel like home.

Dzeni paused her tirade and turned to follow Zhade's line of sight. The anger seemed to drain out of her, and she slumped down next to the weeping woman, running a soothing hand over her back.

Zhade stepped away from Dzeni and her friend, skirting around the welcome desk toward Andra. Her stomach plummeted, even as she was warmed by Zhade's nearness.

"What happened?" she asked.

"Firm, that is exactish what I'm wondering," another voice echoed, and Andra turned to see Skilla marching out of the air'lock, eyes blazing, high ponytail swaying. "Is there something you want to explain, Bodhizhad?"

Zhade sighed, shoulders slumping, and rubbed the bridge of his nose. "Hiya, Skilla."

She crossed her arms, her armor clanking. "Xana tells me the angels are still going rogue."

"Ah, soze she's been spying on me?"

"For certz, you spoon. I didn't reck you could guv a full city, and it happens I was right to not trust you. I convoed you that if you didn't put a stop to the rogue angels, I would."

"I have it in control," Zhade said through gritted teeth. "It mereish took some time to skool how to use the Crown—"

Skilla's eyes narrowed. "You're *using* it now? Am I going to have to put you down, like I tried to put down your brother?"

"Whoa!" Andra put both her hands up placatingly. "Whoa, whoa. Hold on here. No one is putting anyone down. At least not until someone tells me what the hell is going on." She turned to Zhade. "Is this true? The angels are killing people?"

Zhade nodded, tossing a look over his shoulder to where Dzeni was still comforting her friend. "Firm. They . . . I don't reck, it's likeish someone is controlling them. They're evens one tick and then the next they . . ." He let out a heavy sigh. "It's . . . gruesome."

Andra felt a surge of nausea. "Lilibet told me . . . Are the 'bots tearing out people's hearts?"

Zhade shook his head. "Mereish Cheska's. A friend of Dzeni's and"—he looked back at the woman weeping—"Swan's promised. The other deaths . . . they're all different, except . . . It's . . ."

"Spit your truth, Zhade," Skilla barked. "I don't have the ticks for this."

Zhade clenched his jaw. "The angels. They don't seem to have memory of what they're doing after, but . . ." He lowered his voice. "But they had memory of Cheska. He . . . The first angel to go rogue . . . Cheska ripped out its heart. And now . . ."

"They returned the favor," Andra whispered.

Her mind whirled. 'Bots turning violent was so far outside of her purview, but in the end . . . it was entirely possible. Since she'd woken, she'd seen for herself 'bots turning against humans, controlled by Maret and his Crown. She hadn't, however, seen them coordinate in acts of revenge.

Skilla showed her teeth. "That doesn't seem like you hold it in control. I'm gathering my army, we're marching on Eerensed, and we'll wipe out the angels ourselves."

"What army?" Zhade asked. "The militia you're putting together from refugees who mereish want to be sorcers and farmers and bakers? *That* army? Firm, I've been watching you too. I'm not a fool boyo."

Skilla narrowed her eyes. "Are you certz?"

"Enough," Andra snapped, trying to keep her voice low, but it was difficult in the open space of the lobby. "We can fight bout this later. Does anyone have a plan for *now*?"

"Firm, firm," Zhade said, gesturing wildly. "That's what I've been trying to say. Soon and now my guards are rounding up all the angels acity. They'll be brought to the palace by the end of the day."

"And destroyed?" Skilla asked.

Zhade let out a slow breath and nodded. "Firm. And destroyed."

Skilla watched him for a moment, expression unreadable. "They better be."

She gave Zhade one last scowl before storming off. Andra expected Xana to follow, but she was still holding Dehgo, albeit stiffly, her expression conflicted.

Andra turned to Zhade. "Listen. I'm going to find somewhere for Dzeni and her friend to stay. Give me half a bell, and then can you meet me in my room?"

Zhade blinked and his cheeks flushed, a twinge of a smile at the corner of his lips.

Andra rolled her eyes. "Oh, stop it. We just . . . we need to talk."

Zhade took her hand and brought it to his lips, leaving the ghost of a kiss on her knuckles. "My favorite words," he said, then turned and left.

ANDRA TOOK DZENI and Swan to a room she had cleared out for a new lab. There was no furniture yet, but that would be easy to find in the Vaults, and there was enough space for both Dzeni and her son. Lilibet had changed the holo'screens to ocean waves. She had a tendency to do that, as she had never seen an ocean, and until recently, didn't believe they had ever existed. She stared at them now, her dainty hand floating in the air, trying to match the rhythm of the waves.

Dzeni helped Swan to a chair, then turned to Xana, dark hair framing her heart-shaped face, Dehgo now cocked on her hip. He tapped his mother on the shoulder and pointed a chubby finger at Xana.

"I reck her, mam!"

"Shh." Dzeni bounced him gently. "Not so loud please." She looked up at Xana. "You do look familiar. Do we reck you?"

Xana shifted her weight, strangely fidgety. "I reck Doon. Your boyo's sister. I purpose, your promised's sister. The dead one. The promised, not the sister." She winced. "Sorries, I mereish . . . I didn't . . ." She shook her head.

Through the nanos, Andra sensed Xana's heartrate pick up.

Dzeni tilted her head. "I . . . I have memory of you from the angel attack in the square. You held Dehgo safe. Then helped me to a meddoc. Sorries, I didn't reck you at first." She gestured to Swan. "It happens a day and a half."

"Neg . . . evens . . . I full comp . . ." Xana looked away.

"Thank you, beedub."

Xana's eyes snapped back to Dzeni. She stared at her for a moment, then cleared her throat. "I've got to go."

She turned quickly and walked past Andra standing in the doorway.

"Where are you going?" Andra called after her, but she was already halfway down the hall.

Dzeni set Dehgo on the chair next to Swan and stepped forward. Andra braced herself for the impassioned yelling she'd directed at Zhade earlier, but instead Dzeni threw her arms around her.

Andra wasn't one to allow hugs from strangers, but she somehow felt like she knew Dzeni. She'd heard Lew talk about her and had watched her weep for him. Someone Lew loved was surely someone Andra could love too.

Andra hugged her back. "I'm sorry for everything."

Dzeni nodded into Andra's shoulder. "Me too."

Andra pulled back. "What are you sorry for?"

Dzeni sniffled. "I blamed you. I blamed all of you. I was so angry."

"That is nothing to be sorry for. We let you down. Zhade and I both did."

"Neg. You didn't. Sole Zhade." Despite her sweetness, there was a dangerful glint in her eyes.

Andra cleared her throat. "Uh . . . you and Dehgo can stay down here. Lilibet, Rashmi, and I live close by. Lilibet, can you find her some furniture?"

Lilibet turned from the holo'screens. "Firm, firm, firm! I can find it! I love finding things! I can't move it, though . . ." She thought for a moment. "But Kiv can! He's so strong! It's one of the things I like bout him. I like feeling his muscles when we kiss!" Her expression faltered a bit. "Sole, I haven't seen him in almost a turn, and I'm not full certz where he is. But I'll find him!"

"Thanks, Lilibet." Andra cleared her throat, and Lilibet shot out the door, past Xana, who had returned. She hung just outside the room, arms crossed, staring at Dzeni and frowning.

Dehgo climbed down off the chair and walked over to Xana.

"Can I have a jelly tart pleaseandthankyou?" he asked.

Xana's eyebrows pinched together as she studied the little boy.

"Firm," she said seriously, and then turned and walked out, expecting him to follow, which he did.

Dzeni smiled to herself, and through the nanos, Andra felt her heart flutter too.

ANDRA FOUND ZHADE waiting outside her room, leaning awkwardly against the frame. He straightened when he saw her, shuffling back and forth.

"Sorries," Andra said. "I forgot you wouldn't be able to get in."

"It's evens," he said, as Andra pressed her thumb to the scanner and the door slid open. "No shakes. It's all evens. Evens and odds. Odds and evens."

He followed Andra inside, and she turned on the kinetic orbs with a thought. The room was still a mess. Her dirty clothes were strewn across the floor, her work'station littered with discarded tech. The mini'dome sat empty on the conference table.

"Sorries." Andra pushed some tablets from one side of the table to the other. "It's a mess."

Zhade shrugged, looking around the room. "You've apparentish been busy."

Andra nodded. He had no idea. Between discovering Griffin's clone and Maret waking and upgrading 'implants, Andra's life had recently been a series of emergencies.

Zhade *really* had no idea.

Andra had kept telling herself that she was keeping this all from Zhade to spare his feelings, but was that truly it? Maybe she was just scared for him to know the truth. That she had kept so many things from him for so long. He already looked at her differently because she was AI. She couldn't stand him knowing she was dishonest too.

But didn't he deserve the truth?

"Listen, Zhade—"

"Andra, I miss you."

Andra froze, the truth paused on her lips. "What?"

"I reck . . ." Zhade ruffled the back of his hair. "I reck I have my brother's face. I reck I did horrible things to you. I betrayed you. I used you. I lied to you. And I reck—believe me, I reck—I don't deserve you."

He started pacing.

"I reck you can bareish look my direction, and I reck you want nothing to do with me, and I will respect your fishes and wishes. But

I want you to reck that I miss you. I miss your laugh and the way you snap at me and the funny things you call me and the way you say my name. I miss the dimple in your cheek and the way your smile slowish spreads and how your hair curls at the ends. I miss your compassion and your humor and your stubbornness and the way you hold me for my faults. Push me to be better. To *want* to be better. I miss convoing you bout the day, planning coups and running from danger."

He stopped pacing, pausing in front of her, with the most heartbreaking combination of earnestness and hope on his face.

"I will never be able to make up for what I've done, but if you give me a chance, I will spend every tick of every day trying. Because I don't tolerate you, Andra. I don't hate you less than other people."

He took a deep breath and gathered her hands in his.

"I love you."

TWENTY-SIX

THE CLEAVED

ZHADE HADN'T PURPOSED to say it. Any of it. But especialish that last part. It wasn't that it wasn't true. It was mereish that he had planned to convo Andra bout the rogue angels, to convo her bout Tsurina and Meta and the Crown.

Instead he'd confessed his love for her.

While wearing his brother's face.

After betraying her over and over again.

Andra stared at him, eyes filling with tears, and pulled her hands out of his. Zhade's heart plummeted.

"Andra," he breathed. "Andra, please say something."

He wanted her to scream, to reject him, to tell him to never convo her again. Everything he deserved. Anything would have been better than the silence.

"I . . ." Andra's voice cracked. "But I'm . . ."

"You're what?"

"Not . . . human."

"Soze?"

"Soze . . ." Andra started pacing, her fingers running through her hair in a way that was full bars distracting. "I'm not a person. I'm a thing. It's . . . gross."

Zhade blinked. "Scuze. You're not a thing and you're not gross.

And us being together is for certz not gross." He thought bout the last time they'd seen each other. His hands and lips on her skin. Perhaps she wasn't for true human, but she made him feel more human than he ever had.

And what she was . . . it wasn't bad. It was mereish different.

"Hear," he said, going to her. He stopped her pacing, intertwining his fingers with hers. "You're magnificent."

There was a flash-tick of something heartbreaking on her expression as she met his eyes. "You just don't full comp what I am."

"I don't have to in order to reck that you are the most amazing person—being," he corrected when her lips pursed, "I have ever met."

When she didn't protest, he took both of her hands and gathered them to his chest. She looked up at him under her eyelashes. Her lips were slightish parted.

"You're kind," he said, his voice softening, "brill, funny, stubborn, creative." He kissed her knuckles. "And absoluteish charred, but that goes without saying. It doesn't meteor to me that you're not full true human. I don't care what you're not, I care what you are. You're Andra."

A hint of tears appeared in the bottom of Andra's eyes, and he lifted his hand mereish in time to catch one gentlish with his thumb.

Zhade grinned. "Now it's your turn to say nice things bout me."

Andra laughed, but before she could say anything, Zhade kissed her.

It was diff than their last kiss, when it had been two desperate people, uncertz of themselves and each other. Then, it had been frantic and clumsy, as though they'd been afraid that their connection could have been taken away at any moment.

Anow it was slow and gentle. Zhade's hands cradled Andra's face, as Andra's rested on his chest. There was the slightest bit of pressure, as though her fingers were itching to clench into his shirt.

Damn Maret's stupid clothes.

He ran one hand through her hair. The other drifted to her lower back, drawing her close. She gasped, and her arms went round his neck, her fingers carding their way into the hair at the back of his nape. He delighted in the gentle tug, and the kiss turned into something less slow and leisureish.

Andra's shirt was the first to go, followed by the fraughted robe Zhade wore. He felt like he could breathe for the first time in over a moon. But he didn't have time to wonder bout it, because they were tumbling onto Andra's cot, and the feel of her neath him was overwhelming. His kisses traveled down to her neck and lower. They were panting, and by the time they had removed all their outer garments, Zhade was shaking.

He paused to look down at her. Her cheeks were flushed, her lips swollen. Her eyes had a glazed quality, her pupils blown wide.

"Do you want . . . ?" he asked.

"Yes," she said, pulling him down to her for another kiss.

He went slow and steady, pausing whenever Andra was uncertz. It was awkward, as all firsts were, but they were doing this together, and in the end, when they were exhausted and tucked under the covers of Andra's cot, with Zhade's arms round her, he realized there was nothing he wouldn't do for her.

ZHADE WOKE SLOWISH to the feeling of warm breath against his chest and soft hair under his chin. Without opening his eyes, he hugged Andra closer to him, letting out a contented sigh.

Things were going to be evens. He'd hit some dustrocks in his journey to being guv, to saving his people, but he had Andra, and with her, he could do anything.

She shifted slightish in his arms and he kissed the top of her head. She tilted her chin up, eyes peeling slowish opened.

"G'morning," she mumbled.

He placed a kiss on her lips.

"Don't, I have morning breath." She buried her face in his shoulder.

He chuckled softish. "Is that what you called it? We call it dream taste."

She snuggled closer.

He couldn't hold the stupid grin off his face. "Are you happy? I purpose, last night, we . . . And I wanted to make certz you . . . What I purpose is, I hope that . . . I'm for true happy, are you happy?"

Andra looked up at him, her smile mirroring his own. "You know I'm happy."

"For certz, I mereish wanted to hear you say it." He kissed her forehead again.

"What time is it?" Andra turned to look at her timeteller. Zhade ran the tips of his fingers over the soft skin of her back. She turned to him with a huff. "Shit. I have work to do." Her muscles tensed.

Zhade ran a soothing hand down her arm. "You always seem so stressed. What is it? Are you having trouble with the rocket? Is there something I can do to help?"

Zhade felt Andra go still in his arms.

"Neg," she said. "It's . . . I mean there's more to it . . ."

"I might be able to use the Crown to help sorcer it."

Andra snorted, and Zhade smiled reflexiveish. "You do that and it'll fry your brain. Even I couldn't interface directly with the rocket."

"You said that bout the gods' dome too. And I sorcered the small one you gave me with the Crown full well."

"Zhade!" Andra slapped him lightish on the arm. "That was . . . stupidly dangerous."

He grinned. "It's a habit of mine." She didn't return his grin. "Neg, I reck it's evens. It almost acted like a conduit . . . or a buffer, tween me and the magic."

Andra crossed her arms and pouted. "Well, I still don't like it."

Zhade kissed the frown off her face. When he pulled back, her brows were still drawn.

"What is it?"

"It's just . . . I have something to convo you." Andra took a deep breath and let it out. She winced. "Some of the colonists are awake."

Zhade's eyebrows shot up. "For true?"

"Firm. Including my fam."

He propped himself up on his elbow. "Can I meet them?"

Andra stiffened. "Yeah. Just . . . not right now."

Zhade smiled, though this time it was a bit strained. If his parents were still alive, he'd want them to meet Andra. For certz, his father wouldn't have cared, and his mam had recked her and wrecked her. But he still would have wanted them to reck he and Andra were together.

"Why did you finalish decide to wake them?" he asked.

"It's . . . a long story."

Maybe Zhade should have been going to all those meetings with the Schism, so he could reck what was bothering Andra. Or maybe he should have gone so he could have convoed her what was bothering him.

He cleared his throat.

"Soze, I have something to convo you too."

Andra looked up at him through her lashes. It probablish wasn't the best idea to do this while they were naked in bed together, but the best time would have been yestereven before anything had happened, so they could have started everything being honest with each other.

"Is it bout the angels?" Andra asked.

"Evens, a bit. But also . . . bout Tsurina . . ."

"What about her?"

"Seeya . . ." Zhade swallowed. "I have Tsurina aprisoned in your old room—"

235

Andra jolted, propping herself up on her arm. "Wait. No! What?" The blanked dipped low, and Zhade got distracted.

She sat up, pulling the blanket over her chest.

"What do you mean Tsurina is imprisoned?"

Zhade lay back, ruffling his hair and putting both hands behind his head.

"Soze, Tsurina realized I was me. I purpose, not Maret. And I imagined she was going to kill me, and for certz, she probablish would have, but then Meta showed up and conked her on the head. We put the real Tsurina in your old room, and I gave Meta Tsurina's face. Sole, not mereish her face, her full body, marah? With that graftling wand."

Zhade suddenish felt nervous. He wanted Andra to be proud of what he'd accomplished, but convoing the graftling wand was tricky. Firstish, he'd used it to heal her wound, and hurt her so bad, she'd destroyed the spell. Then he'd used the wand to change his face and betray her. He held his breath as he waited for her to respond.

"Are you serious?"

Was she mad? Impressed? Sometimes she was so diff to cipher.

"Can I see it? The wand, I mean."

Zhade broke out into a wide grin. "Oh, I reck you've already seen my wand."

She swatted him on the chest. He captured her hand and brought her palm to his lips.

"Firm. I'll bring it next time."

"That's . . . really impressive, Zhade."

The corner of his mouth twitched. "I am, aren't I?"

She rolled her eyes, but Zhade could tell she was quite in love with him.

He stretched out on the cot and put his hands behind his head. "Anyway, I've been . . . convoing Tsurina, and she's been skooling me how to use the Crown."

Andra's jaw twitched.

"What happens?" Zhade asked. "This is good magic, marah?"

"Why do you need Tsurina to teach you? And why are you just now telling me?"

Zhade put a hand on her hip. "I was a bit distracted yestereven."

"Hmm," she said, moving his hand away.

Something akin to hurt rose up in Zhade. "Sorries. It's not like you told me bout the gods wakening soon and sooner."

As soon as the words were out of his mouth, he regretted them, and the look on Andra's face dug in the knife.

"Neg, sorries and worries," he said, softer. "I shouldn't have said that."

"It's fine." Andra gave him a weak smile.

He sat up and placed a gentle kiss on her lips, to see if she would respond. She did, shyish, and his palm on her cheek felt it start to warm. He pulled back before he got carried away.

"Sides, it's not like you'd wait to tell me something that imported to me." He tossed his legs over the side of the bed and scanned the room for his pants. "Like if you figured where Rashmi is holding my brother."

His pants were on the far side, and he heard Andra suck in a breath when he got out of bed naked to retrieve them. He grinned as he took his time reclothing himself. When he turned round, Andra was still in bed, with the cover over her, face pale.

"Seriousish, we'll must rid you of shyness," he said, bending over to give her one last kiss. It was sweet and brief, but then he pulled her closer for another. He took his time and felt Andra melt into him. He smiled through the kiss, and when he finalish pulled away, he was breathing hard.

He stared into her eyes, and she stared back, but there was something in her expression that bothered him.

"What? What happens?"

Andra watched him for a moment, and her eyes drifted to his temple. "I think we should remove the Crown."

"What? Neg! Why?"

She swallowed. "We don't know what it is, and I've . . . It's just that there are a lot of . . . unseen consequences with tech you don't understand."

Zhade took a few steps back. "Tsurina recks how it works, and she's skooling me. So, actualish, I do comp how it works now. I can do . . . amazing things. I can save Eerensed from these rogue angels."

Andra stood, taking the blanket with her and holding it close to her chest. "Oh, and what? You just trust Tsurina now? You have her imprisoned, and she's teaching you out of the goodness of her heart?"

Zhade started pacing. "Neg, for certz not. We made a deal."

"Oh, my god, another deal?" Andra blinked, shook her head. "What is it this time? Evil lessons for . . . comfortable accommodations in my old bedroom?"

Zhade ruffled the back of his hair. "They're not *evil* lessons. They're Crown lessons, and I didn't have anywhere to put her but your suite. Believe me, I hate seeing her there, but this is not mereish bout me skooling the Crown. She has info bout my mam."

Andra's eyes went wide, her skin going ashen. "What?"

"She says my mam is alive and she can tell me where to find her."

Something flashed cross Andra's face, and she let out a shaky breath. "Zhade. I . . . your mam . . . she's dead."

"Maybe not! You were executed, but you're alive. So is the Second. Why not my mam too?"

"No, I mean. She . . ." Andra bit her lip. "I saw her. When I went out into the Wastes."

Something inside Zhade broke. He grabbed a chair to steady himself. "What?"

"It's not her though," Andra hurried on to say. "It's a clone. She . . . I don't know how to explain it. She looks like your mam and she has access to all your mam's memories, but she's not her. She's a different person."

The room spun. Zhade's throat began to close, and he felt the sting of tears in his eyes. "You recked? You recked my mam was alive, and you didn't tell me?"

"It's not your mam!"

"Where is she?"

Andra shook her head. "It's not her, Zhade."

He felt a surge of anger rise up in him. "Where is she?" he growled.

Andra continued to shake her head. "She's not your mam. She looks like her and thinks like her, but she's not her. Seeing her would just make things harder for you. She doesn't love you."

Zhade clenched his jaw, staring at his feet, and let out a heavy breath. "It looks like she's not the sole one who doesn't love me."

With that, Zhade turned and left, Andra still clinging to the blanket.

TWENTY-SEVEN

OOIIOOIO OOIIOIII

ANDRA THREW HERSELF into her work upgrading 'implants.

It was draining, but it kept her mind off her feelings. Because the truth was:

Her feelings didn't matter.

Her feelings were manufactured, programmed, false. The result of hundreds of algorithmic equations working themselves out in her artificial synapses. She was meant to feel things for humans, but it didn't mean she was human.

She had moments of doubt—like maybe she should take Zhade to his mother's clone—but they passed. She didn't mention him when she called Griffin for the first time. She took Mechy with her into the Wastes. They had to go about one hundred meters outside of the city before she got a signal on the comm.

"How's it going?" Griffin's clone asked.

"Good." Andra scuffed her feet against the sand. "Good."

And it was good.

Cruz had set up makeshift workspace for them to do the up-grades. It was no longer an auditorium with an operating table in the middle. They put up walls, proper monitors and work'stations, holo'displays. All the standard lab equipment—which included scalpels, radioactivity-neutralizing agents, and a huge cleaver Andra hoped they'd never have to use. In the corner was the air'lock, the pocket buzzing around the space almost lazily, happily. Each day for weeks, people walked through its chamber, appearing to the pocket as though they, too, were anomalies. Maybe it had just been lonely all this time.

Andra's success with the ugrades didn't change the fact that Ophele was still in a coma, and it was Andra's fault. It didn't reconcile her with Zhade or convince Skilla to build the rocket with the empty cryo'tanks. It didn't make her sister forget she was an AI.

But she didn't tell Griffin's clone any of that.

"I'm glad you converted Cruz first," Griffin said. "He'll be a lot of help to you."

"Converted him?"

"To your side," Griffin clarified. "And I should have thought of the patch downloads. Or rather, it should have appeared in the first Griffin's memories. But excellent job adapting to the challenge!"

Learn, adapt, Andra's mother always said, and that was what Andra was doing. That was her role as AI. Even if her only purpose was the vague directive to help humanity.

So she would.

She would upgrade their 'implants, use their cryo'chambers to build a rocket, and get everyone to Holymyth.

Cruz was able to speed up the process, and they were soon upgrading entire LAC departments in a single day. First the cryo'techs, then upper management, then engineering and terraforming. Each time it was the same. The process started with a burst of intense pain, followed by a brief shutdown of the person's entire system. Then they woke, feeling shaky and frail but regaining their strength quickly. The process was far more draining for Andra. With each upgrade, she felt a bit weaker. By the end of the day, she could barely make it back to the Vaults. Some days, she just stayed in the Icebox with her family. Her father seemed more chipper than she'd ever seen him, always telling Andra how proud of her he was. Acadia still didn't talk to her, even though Andra could tell she wanted to be a part of the upgrade program. Oz was just happy to be awake with his family, playing with 'drones and begrudgingly making friends with the other LAC kids.

Andra still wouldn't upgrade his 'implant, and though some of the parents were wanting their kids to undergo the procedure, Andra made up an excuse about their 'implants not being compatible yet. She could tell it irritated Cruz, so she told him if he could find a way for the procedure to be pain-free, she would upgrade the kids as well. Cruz started working on a solution, also attempting to find a way to merge a standard AI with the code in the anomalizer, so Andra didn't have to be involved with each and every upgrade.

But he was an AI tech, not a specialist, not a coder, so the work was slow, and Andra was stuck watching people flatline and revive over and over, all while having a reset tool sticking into her chest.

She spent much of what little free time she had in Ophele's tent, listening to her monitors beep, watching the holo of her heartbeat. A few times, she found Cruz in there too. It felt like they were doing penance, sitting by her bedside. Ophele had other visitors too. Raj and the cryo'tech team. Cristin Myrh would show up occasionally to stare daggers at Andra.

Outside of the Icebox, things were just as tense.

Rashmi mostly kept to herself, either still hurt by Maret or avoiding becoming involved in the 'implant upgrades. Andra never saw Skilla anymore, but Xana was spending so much time hovering around Dzeni, she'd basically moved into the Vaults. Meanwhile, Lilibet stitched blankets and clothes for the colonists, while learning more coding in her free time. Which she had lots of.

She hadn't seen Kiv in weeks. For the first time since Andra had known her, Lilibet seemed . . . angry.

"Lastish I heard," Lilibet said over dinner in the Vaults common room one night, "Zhade convoed him he couldn't leave his post, but what post could that be! He can't be seen in Eerensed! He made certz of that when he saved me." She paused to smile. "I 'pen full glad he saved me. I purpose, I recked he would, seeya. I full time recked he 'penned a good boyo with a kindful heart, but now his face is recked acity and he has to stay belowground, soze what is Zhade making him do, seeya? Has he told you?"

Andra shook her head, avoiding eye contact. She hadn't told Lilibet about sleeping with Zhade, or their fight afterward. "Maybe he's doing something with the rogue angels."

Lilibet groaned. "Maybe, marah, but what is he doing night and day that he can't come see me and kiss!"

Andra felt sick to her stomach. What if Kiv's disappearance had to do with Tsurina, or what she'd told Zhade about his mam? What if he'd sent Kiv into the desert to find her?

Andra didn't want Lilibet to worry, so she just gave her a smile and patted her hand. "I'm certz everything will be evens."

So it went, day in and day out, Andra hiding coughing fits and ignoring the voices in her head, which were now a near constant chant to destroy.

Some mornings, when she couldn't sleep, she would get up early and sneak into the air'lock with the pocket. She was no longer afraid of it. She'd seen it interact now with hundreds of people. It danced around her and she would mentally interface with it, hoping it would spark her AI state. If she could reach that state of light and knowledge again, be able to harness that power, she could perform the upgrades faster or without pain, maybe wake Ophele from her coma.

When that didn't work, she thought about going to see Maret again, but she doubted he would give her any answers, even if he had them.

She slept and worked, slept and worked, burying her feelings deep. Anytime she thought of Zhade, she would throw herself into another project. Interfacing with the pocket. Teaching Lilibet to code. Updating Griffin's clone on their progress.

One night, she lay on her cot in the Vaults for the first time since . . . that night weeks ago . . . and the memory of her and Zhade being together was too much to bear. She threw off the covers and headed for Rashmi's room.

She knocked lightly on the door. At first there was no answer, so she tried again. On the third attempt, the door whooshed open.

Rashmi's room was less cluttered than Andra's but more comfortable. She'd filled it with a cot and sofa, draped with blankets stitched by Lilibet. The holo'screens projected a rainforest on the walls and played a gentle trickle of water. Rashmi lay on her cot, curled up in the fetal position, a tablet in front of her, shining an eerie blue glow on her face.

"You know," Andra said, "if you stay in bed for weeks, you're likely to get bedsores."

Rashmi didn't look up. "I get out of bed to eat. And use the bathroom. And I've showered a few times."

"That's good." Andra sat on the floor across from her, cocking her knees and resting her head against the wall. "What else have you been doing? Just sleeping?"

"Naps are for later. I've been looking through old files. And I went to see the rocket. It's a nice, homely place. It will hold them all tight. Like a hug." She looked at Andra. "I don't like hugs."

"Why did you go see the rocket? The LAC team will be taking over construction soon."

Rashmi put her tablet aside. "Then why did Griffin make it my responsibility to build it when I woke?"

Andra sat forward. "Did you remember something?"

Rashmi shook her head. "No memories. No memories for me. Just childhood, childhood, then nothing. But computers keep memories too."

She turned the tablet toward Andra.

The holo displayed the rocket blueprints.

"Things don't make sense," Rashmi said. "There are too many holes in the story, too many holes in my memory. I'm always asking, why? Why were you taken from Eerensed? Why didn't Griffin's clone come find you? Why did she build the rocket as a generation ship? Why, why, why? Why you and me? Why me and you?"

Andra bit her lip. "I don't know, Rashmi. I guess . . . we have to stop expecting humans to make sense. Sometimes the only answer for why they do the things they do is . . . just because."

"I am human. I do not do things for just because."

"Rashmi," Andra said gently. "Neither of us are human."

Rashmi shook her head, burying it deeper into her pillow. "Maybe I wasn't, but the wasn't part of me is gone now."

"Rashmi—"

"No!" Rashmi sat up and slammed her hands onto the cot. "No. You can keep pretending that you're not human, but you don't get to decide what I am. You don't get to take all the things inside me and then leave me to be whatever is left and tell me what that is. I'm human. I'm human. And you're human too, but you're too stubborn to admit it."

Rashmi plopped back down, burying her face in her pillow. Andra pushed herself up and went to sit on the edge of Rashmi's cot.

"Sorry, Rashmi." She had the urge to give Rashmi a comforting pat but knew Rashmi didn't like to be touched. "I shouldn't have said that. You're right. You are human. And for what it's worth, I'm sorry I took all your programming. I'm sorry about bringing down the ceiling and injuring you, so it made it necessary. And I'm sorry about what Maret said. He's . . . an asshole."

Rashmi sniffed. "More than an asshole. He's a little bit evil."

Andra nodded. "A lot evil. But I'm still sorry. Want me to beat him up for you?"

Rashmi shook her head. "No. I'll beat him up myself when I'm ready." She sat up and made eye contact with Andra for the first time. It was a bit unnerving. "But I think you should apologize to yourself too. You are allowed to be a little bit human."

Andra looked down at her hands. "Yeah. I know. I just don't want to be human right now. There are just . . . too many feelings, and I don't like them."

"Like what?" Rashmi canted her head, and something about her expression opened the floodgates inside Andra.

She told her everything that was happening. About how exhausting the upgrades were, about how Ophele was in a coma and it was Andra's fault. About not being able to access her AI consciousness. About sleeping with Zhade only to get in a huge fight with him the next morning. About all the things she'd kept from him. And all the things he'd kept from her—Tsurina and Meta and the Crown. And how no matter how they felt, that was a horrible way to start a relationship. How she didn't feel like she could have human relationships because of what she was.

"Sorry," she said, when she was finished. "I didn't mean to just . . . dump all that on you."

Abruptly, Rashmi stood, her head twitching from side to side as she paced the room, picking up random blankets and tablets and clothes.

"Rashmi?"

"The Crown, the Crown," she mumbled to herself. She stopped and turned to Andra. "You said Zhade was learning how to use the

Crown. With Tsurina. The Crown . . . there's something about the Crown. I don't remember . . . but . . . something, something, what was it?"

"Rashmi, stop. What are you talking about?"

Rashmi shook her head. "I don't know, I don't know. It's foggy hazy can't remember, but there's something about Tsurina and the Crown." She dropped the items she'd gathered and looked at Andra. "We have to go see Maret."

TWENTY-EIGHT

THE SANGUINE

ZHADE WAS SURROUNDED by a thousand angels.

It had taken nearish a moon, but he was certz he had cleared Eerensed of not sole all the angels in the city but also any magic. If angels could go rogue, then what would stop other conduits from doing the same? The guards, under Meta, had confiscated all of it.

Zhade had told the people he would destroy the magic, so they would feel safe, but instead he'd put every bit of it in the cathedzal. There would be no more guv-askings til he recked for true he could control the angels, hold them from going rogue.

They stood in rows, filling the entire space. He'd had to move some of the gods' dome controls to make room. He'd been at care of the giant metal box that Andra had said contained the dome's energy, but every other bit of dome magic—all the scrys and such—were shoved against the wall to make more space.

He tried to imagine bout Andra as little as possible.

He regretted how he'd spoken to her, how angry he'd gotten. But every time he imagined bout asking for her forgiveness, rage flared back up inside him again. She'd recked his mam was alive. She recked where to find her, and held it from him. It was diff than him not telling her he had captured Tsurina, bout the rogue angels. This was his mam. He deserved to know.

He was angry.

But he still loved her.

And he didn't reck how to make the two feelings happen together.

Zhade took a deep breath and commanded all the angels to raise their spears. He was divided into thousands of pieces. He was Zhade. He was Fishy. He was every single angel in the room. So when he lowered his spear, he was all of them lowering their spears. Next he commanded them to face one another. This was harder. They weren't all doing the same movement, so he had to lean into the splitting of his mind. The most diff part was taking them through battle scenarios, each angel acting separateish of the others, reacting in real time to moves and countermoves.

He started off easyish, having one angel in each pair stab and the other block. His head started to ache.

"Practicing again?" a voice echoed across the cathedzal.

Zhade opened his eyes to see Tsurina standing in the doorway. His heart flipped, til he realized it was actualish Meta. For certz. Tsurina was still imprisoned, guarded by Kiv. Meta was mereish becoming more and more Tsurina-like with each passing day.

She'd mastered all of Tsurina's hairstyles. Earned the trust of the guards. Taken control of the seizure of the angels with a confidence just like the Grande Advisor's.

It was her idea to hold the angels instead of destroying them. Zhade had hesitated at first, but it had given him the chance he needed to practice using the Crown. During each session, he had shakes their eyes would turn red and they would descend into rage and his power wouldn't be enough to stop them. But not a single angel had gone rogue since coming to the palace.

Meta's heels clicked as she entered the room. "It's a full army. What are you going to use it for?"

Zhade shrugged. "Whatever I need."

With the angels as his army, he wouldn't have to pretend anymore. He would for true be guv, not as Maret but as Zhade. And he could do so much good. He could hold Eerensed safe, maybe bring his mam back from wherever she was hiding. Maybe one day he could even be skooled how to use the Crown to control the pocket, like Andra had.

(Andra.)

"Soze . . ." Meta said, weaving through the angels as Zhade commanded them to spar. "You might convo that the angels going rogue was . . . a good thing?"

Zhade paused and the angels stopped with him. Was it a good thing? For certz, people had died, but it had given him the opportunity to build an army that was loyal to him and him alone.

"I spoze," Zhade said, imagineful.

Meta smiled and sank down on the wooden throne, next to where Zhade stood. He lifted an eyebrow.

"Don't get too comfortistic there."

Meta laughed. "There's no march to comfort on this chair. Especialish not for your bony ass."

Zhade scowled. "I had such a nice ass before I lost the weight to look like my brother."

Meta watched him for a moment, drumming her nails against the wood. "There was no assassin, was there?"

It took Zhade a tick to comp what Meta was referring to. The lie he'd told her all those months ago that Maret was in hiding because of an assassin and Zhade was a decoy. They'd bareish ever convoed it, and Zhade had forgotten.

"Neg, no assassin," he admitted. "He's imprisoned in ice, somewhere . . . As a fact, I took his place the same reason you took Tsurina's. Taking a monster's face to rule in his place. But better."

Meta sneered. "Maret is nothing like Tsurina." Her long fingers dug into the armrests of the throne.

Zhade rolled his eyes. "He could have fooled me, marah? All those executions and—"

"Were Tsurina's ideas. You weren't there. You didn't see how she manipulated him."

"He's an ass—"

"For certz he's an ass. But he's not like Tsurina. Not evil."

"He killed my mam," Zhade muttered, though now he recked it wasn't true. His mam was somewhere out in the Wastes. Tsurina recked it. Andra had seen her.

"He's still your brother," Meta said, standing, fierceness in her eyes. "You're at luck you still have the bond of fam."

Zhade was going to respond that shared blood was less of a bond and more of a shackle, but something in the air changed, and he sensed the angels shifting, trying to act on their own. He relaxed into letting the Crown guide him, but something was wrong. He felt the angels start to slip from his grasp.

"What—"

The angels pulled free of his influence, darkness taking over. His consciousness was still present, in the stardust round them and in them, and he felt their ire and hate and need to destroy. He felt them go rogue.

They charged him.

Zhade fumbled for some sort of control, but it was too late. He couldn't run, couldn't react. He expected time to slow, for his life to replay for him, but everything happened too quickish as he was knocked to the ground, surrounded by angels, spears pointing at his chest.

He closed his eyes and waited to die.

And waited.

And waited.

Nothing happened.

He opened one eye. The angels were still above him, eyes red, spears pointed. But they weren't moving.

Zhade held his breath.

The angels straightened, bringing their spears to their sides. Their red eyes faded to white. Zhade didn't move.

The room fell silent except for the click of heels. In one quick movement, the angels stepped aside and let Meta through. Her long dress trailed behind her, and there was a self-satisfied smirk on her face. She stood above him and offered him her hand.

Zhade recoiled from her. "What did you just do?"

He stumbled to his feet on his own, feeling at his side for a weapon, but there was none there.

"I couldn't find a way to tell you," Meta said. "Soze, I decided to show you."

"Show me what?" Zhade sensed through the Crown, gathering stardust to himself but avoiding the minds of the angels.

Meta rolled her eyes. "For true, Zhade, you are a spoon sometimes."

She moved her hair to the side and showed him a small . . . hole in her neck. Zhade didn't comp what it was, mereish it reminded him of something he couldn't have memory of. The angels moved again, raising their spears, eyes flashing red. Then, mereish as quickish, lowered their spears, eyes going white.

Zhade trembled, realization rushing over him. "It's you. You've been controlling the angels. Making them go rogue."

Meta nodded.

Zhade grabbed a spear from the nearest angel. He expected it to fight, but it gave it up willingish. He pointed it at Meta. "You killed all those people."

Meta shook her head, emphaticish. "Neg. I purpose firm, but . . . It was . . . unfortunate but full necessary."

"You murdered Cheska," Zhade growled. "Ripped his heart from his chest."

Meta winced. "Firm, and neg. I . . . let the angels free, and they chose violence. But that's not the purpose. Don't you see, Zhade?"

She took a step forward, and Zhade stumbled back, spear still raised.

"I helped you," she said. "The people never would have given you their magic willingish. Never would have respected you as guv. It was the fear. They needed to feel it so they would surrender their angels to you, and now you have an army."

Was it true? Zhade thought back to all the times the angels had gone rogue. Meta had been there every time. Watching him in the market, protecting him in the cathedzal, accompanying him to Dzeni's apartment.

But it was impossible. Zhade was the sole one who could command the angels.

"I don't comp. Why? How? You don't have a Crown, how did you control them?"

Meta gave him a small smile. "I don't have a Crown like you, neg. But I do have something else. The goddesses called it an implant."

She gestured to the port at the back of her neck. Zhade had memory of Andra convoing bout implants, but he imagined sole people from her time had them.

"Are you . . . like the goddesses? From the past?"

Meta laughed. "Neg, for certz not."

"Then how did you get one?"

"For serious, Zhade. How do you imagine? From a goddess."

Zhade's heart stopped, and he took a step back. "Andra would never."

"Neg, not Andra."

"The Second . . ."

She shook her head, and a burst of adrenaline shot through Zhade. It couldn't be . . .

Meta smiled. "Your mam, Zhade. Your mam gave it to me."

The room spun. Nausea roiled in Zhade's stomach. It wasn't possible. Why? How? When? And why hadn't his mam given him one of those implants as well? Why Meta?

"You best explain full quickish," Zhade said, teeth bared, "because my patience is blowing away."

Meta lifted her hands in surrender, but her expression remained placid. "She gave me an implant when I was young. I was abandoned. Your mother found me in the Wastes on one of her trips to her lab. She took me there and raised me."

"Bullshit," Zhade spat. "She raised *me*. I never saw you."

"That's because she raised us separateish. You, in Eerensed. Me, in a place called Superior."

Zhade narrowed his eyes. "Reck full bars bout yourself, marah?"

"She skooled me magic, mereish likeish you. After she . . . faked her execution, she lived with me in Superior for a while, skooling me magic. Zhade, don't you comp? In a way, you're my brother."

She reached out, but Zhade swatted her away. "I am *not* your brother."

He felt dizzy. It didn't make full sense. She'd been a guard for . . . three years? But where had she come from before that? Zhade had assumed she was like any refugee trying to prove herself, to be accepted. Extra loyal to Maret, so she could stay. But what had she said? That she recked what it was like to grow up with a mam like Tsurina. Did she purpose Zhade's mam?

And was he to believe that his mam had sent him out into the Wastes at *sixteen* to find Andra, while she was raising another kiddun, alive and well? Safe. Happy.

"I don't believe you," Zhade said, teeth gritted.

There were things you believed. And things you believed you believed.

He put a hand to his aching temple. "Get out. I don't believe you. Why would she send you here?"

"I . . . It's a long story, but now that I'm here, I can help you. She would want me to."

"Why?"

"Because she still loves you, Zhade."

"Get out."

"It's true."

"Then why isn't she here herself?" he snarled.

Meta gave him a patronizing smile. "She can't be here right now. But she will be. Soon and sooner."

Zhade couldn't stand it any longer. Heat coursed through him, hot and fast, and through the Crown, he commanded the angel nearest to Meta to grab her by the neck and hold her aloft.

A small noise escaped her throat as she was lifted off the ground. Her eyes went wide, her fingers scrabbling at the angelic hand round her neck. He felt her fighting back, the implant in her consciousness grappling with him for control of the angel. But Zhade was angry and powerful and had been betrayed and betrayed and betrayed. Meta had built this army for *him*? Evens, then. He would use it. He commanded the angel to tighten its hold, and it did.

A choking sound came from Meta's throat and she mouthed the word *please*, but Zhade didn't care. Didn't care that she claimed to be like a sister to him. That she recked where his mam was now. That she'd stood by him for the past moon.

Her kicks grew weaker, and her hands dropped from the angel's grasp. The light in her eyes dimmed, tears streaking her face.

Something flashed in Zhade's mind. It was the briefest of moments, but it was the image of Andra, her face drawn in fear, shouting, begging.

Zhade sucked in a breath and released his command on the angel. It dropped Meta on the floor. She sucked in a rasping breath, trembling. Her hand clutched her throat as she coughed, the sound fragile and sharp. Zhade could feel her heart pounding through the stardust, feel the tremor in her limbs.

Shaking, she looked up at him, an expression of hurt on her face. Tsurina's face.

"Get out," Zhade commanded.

Meta fled.

TWENTY-NINE

OOIIOOIO OOIIIOOI

ANDRA AND RASHMI met Xana outside of Maret's cell.

When they arrived, the warrior was waiting for them, one hip cocked, cleaning dirt from her fingernails with her knife.

"Did you skool that from Doon?" Andra asked as she approached.

Xana raised the eyebrow above her modded eye. "She skooled that from me."

"Evens. Prepped?" Andra asked.

Xana sheathed her knife. "For what?"

Andra hadn't told her what to expect. Didn't want to explain it. She only knew Xana was their best bet at getting the answers they needed out of Maret.

"Anything," she replied, and opened the door to Maret's cell.

Xana gasped.

Maret sat slumped in the corner, clothes disheveled, hair almost black with sweat and dirt. There were smudges on his cheek, and ugly yellow bruises on his temple. One of his eyes was swollen shut, and there was a cut through his lip. He must have tried to get through the energy field again. Mechy was standing guard, leaning against the wall, arms crossed, as though he were mimicking Zhade. Andra shook the thought away.

The force shield crackled. Maret grinned, and his teeth were tinged with blood. "Brought someone else to do your dirty work?"

"Good fraughts," Xana cursed. "Did you do this to him?"

Andra shook her head. It had been nearly a month of Maret taunting her with information he wasn't inclined to share. She tried to keep him comfortable, but he refused to bathe, barely ate, and kept throwing himself against the force shield. But it didn't seem like he was trying to escape. Instead, it seemed like he was . . . content. Like he was exactly where he wanted to be, and the information he teased was nothing more than a ploy to keep him there, in custody. Trapped. Or maybe . . . safe. What had he said to Rashmi?

Not a prison.

Protection.

A kinetic orb shone into the cell, bright as the floodlights at Andra's high school 'drone races. It painted each hollow, each smudge of dirt, each speck of blood on Maret's face in sharp relief. She almost felt sorry for him, but then she heard Rashmi let out a small sob behind her.

Andra crossed her arms, stance wide, trying to project strength. "You were right. I wasn't willing to do what needed to be done. Fortunately, I have friends who are."

Maret chuckled. "And you're willing to let them off the leash."

"I never had them on the leash to begin with."

"You have us all on the leash, and you don't even reck it. You existed never a goddess. You existed a devil, come to destroy us."

Andra tried to put his jumbled words out of her mind, but he knew where to hit her. She'd never wanted to be a goddess, and she'd always been insecure about how she was using her influence. Now she had power. Actual power. The first time she'd tried to use it—really use it—she'd almost brought the palace down. And now something dwelled inside her, clawing to get out.

Destroy, the voice hissed.

"I'm not here to destroy everyone." She gave Maret an angry smile. "Just you."

He squinted into the light and then looked back at her, licking his dry lips. "Do you imagine that's the threat that will get me to tell you my secrets?"

"No. Xana will take care of that later. I just wanted to chat."

"I brought you some water," Rashmi said, her voice high and thin. She stepped forward awkwardly, and Maret watched her every move. She sat the glass of water on the ground, right next to the force shield. Andra commanded the nanos to make a small hole at the bottom of the shield, just large enough for the cup. Rashmi pushed it through and stepped back. Andra closed the hole.

When Maret stood, it was as though he had to unfold himself. Andra had forgotten how tall he was. Even in the desert clothes, he looked formidable. He slowly bent to pick up the water—

and threw the cup as hard as he could at Andra. It hit the energy field, exploding on impact. Pieces flew everywhere, on both sides of the field. One hit Andra's cheek, and she tried not to flinch. Maret wasn't as lucky. A shard caught him in the shoulder, and he stumbled back against the wall, then tumbled to a heap on the floor.

His groan devolved into a breathy laugh as he leaned his head back against the wall.

Xana rolled her organic eye. "You're wasting your time. Let's wait til he's had some time to reflect. He'll wish he hadn't wasted the water then."

Andra swallowed. She didn't have time, and she didn't actually intend for Xana to torture answers out of him, just for him to think she would.

She knelt so she was eye level with Maret. "Tell me about the Crown."

A grin spread over his face, but instead of being a sneer, it was almost proud. "Finalish. You're asking the right questions."

"Where did it come from?"

"Dunno." Maret shrugged. "My mam gave it to me."

"She *gave* it to you?"

Maret stood and sauntered toward the force shield. Andra rose to meet his gaze.

"I told you I recked things. Things bout you, bout the Second. How do you imagine I recked?"

Andra stood silently, waiting. She was afraid to even breathe wrong, or Maret would stop talking.

"My mam recks everything. Remember the Luddites I convoed bout?"

Andra nodded.

"They're not mereish against the goddesses and High Magic. They're an ancient society bent on destroying your people."

"My people?"

"The people you call colonists."

"They . . . why?"

"The Crown, the Crown," Rashmi muttered.

Maret's eyes flashed toward her. "She doesn't need to be here for this."

"No," Andra agreed. "But she wants to be. And she's tired of people making choices for her."

Maret's eyes stayed on Rashmi for a moment too long before returning to Andra. "It goes back to before you went in that glass box. Your people destroyed the planet, killed billions. And the Luddites vowed to get revenge. I come from a long line of people who have been waiting for the goddesses to wake sole so they can kick the shit out of you."

Andra swallowed. "That's why your mom married Zhade's dad? So she would be closer to the goddesses?"

"He was my da too."

"And then lucky her, the goddesses did wake up. So why didn't she just kill us outright?"

Maret scoffed. "Oddish enough, it's difficult to simplish murder people that are worshipped as gods. It required a more subtle approach."

Andra nodded. "Getting the people to turn on the goddesses and sacrifice them."

"My mam is many things. She is evil and she is brilliant. She planned everything, except for your disappearance. But when you did disappear, she started weakening the dome so we would need you. She allowed me to banish Zhade so he would find you, bring you back. She wouldn't be able to kill you soon and sooner, but it was sole a meteor of time before she got the people to turn on you."

Andra's eyes narrowed. "Your mother told you all this. All her plans?"

Maret scowled. The light of the kinetic orbs shone on the sweat dripping down his forehead. "My mam told me nothing. But after a while, I began to fight. Near the end, I could get inside her head, see her thoughts."

Andra frowned. "What are you talking about? Fight what? Get inside her head how?"

Maret shook his head, as though he was disappointed in her. The corner of his mouth twitched.

"The Crown," he said. "Tsurina controls whoever wears it."

THIRTY

THE SOVEREIGN

Zhade collapsed onto the floor of the cathedzal. Round him, angels were frozen in displays of mock battle.

The strain was still there, the pain in his temple, but it felt good. Something to distract him from what he'd skooled bout Meta. She had been raised by his mam. This full time, she'd recked his mother was alive, probablish even recked where she was now. And she'd held it hidden from him. She'd turned the angels loose on his people, killing so many. And she expected thanks?

She'd claimed to be like a sister to him, but she wasn't. She was his enemy.

Zhade commanded the angels to stand down. In a single movement, they all clanked to attention, their eyes blanked to a neutral white light, then darkened as they simultaneousish fell asleep.

There was a slow clap at the cathedzal doors, and Zhade looked up to see Tsurina, Fishy, and Kiv in the open doorway. He'd commanded Fishy to bring the Grande Advisor here. They needed to have a chat. Fishy fell back in line as Tsurina stepped into the cathedzal, a smile on her face. Kiv followed, a scowl on his.

Tsurina's claps echoed, bouncing off the walls as the last vestiges of light shone through the stained glass onto Zhade. He watched it refract from his Crown and travel cross the red velvet floor as he rolled his neck. His bones cracked. He sighed.

"Rare form," Tsurina said. "Not even Maret could have sorcered all these angels at once. You've full surpassed him. I admit I'm . . . impressed."

Zhade lowered himself onto one of the steps leading to the cathedzal's stage. "You shouldn't be. I've always been full bars talented."

Tsurina shrugged, weaving through the rows of angels and sitting at Zhade's feet. She spread her skirts round her. "Soze was Maret. But he never cared for his role as guv."

Kiv grunted. His eyebrows were pulled down over his narrowed eyes, his huge arms over his chest.

Zhade gave him a smile. "Go see Lilibet, Kiv. You've earned it."

Kiv watched him for a moment then shook his head, reluctantish uncrossing his arms. "Neg," he signed. "I don't imagine I will."

Zhade's smile faltered. "Wasn't this what you've wanted? Go see her. It's been over a moon."

Kiv didn't take his eyes off Zhade. "I imagine it best I stay here."

Zhade let out an exasperated breath. "If you won't go see Lilibet then take a walk. Now!"

Kiv gave Zhade one last look, and for a moment, Zhade imagined Kiv wouldn't back down, that Zhade would have to force him from the room with one of the angels. But finalish Kiv sighed and left.

Zhade turned to Tsurina. "I have some questions."

"Bout the Crown?" she asked. "I reck it's full time you skooled the truth."

Zhade's thoughts stuttered. He purposed to ask her bout Meta, bout his mam, but was there more he could skool bout the Crown? Could he become even more powerful?

"What truth?" he asked.

Tsurina grinned, running a sharp fingernail over her forearm. "The Crown's true purpose."

Zhade held his breath. He would finalish full comp the Crown. And he would be its master. All-powerful and unstoppable.

Tsurina leaned forward. "Its purpose is to protect humanity."

"Against what?" Zhade whispered.

Tsurina leveled her gaze at him, at he felt that she was seeing inside his soul.

"Against the goddesses."

THIRTY-ONE

OOIIOOII OOIIOOOI

ANDRA STARED OPEN-MOUTHED at Maret.

Tsurina controlled whoever wore the Crown?

Now that she looked over Maret's actions, it made sense. How he acted differently around Tsurina. The few times he and Andra had been alone, he must have been straining against Tsurina's grasp. Now, without the Crown, he was a new person, finally free from his mother's influence.

"I for true have sorries," Maret said, running a hand through his hair, and he looked more like Zhade than Zhade now did. "I still don't reck what was me and what was her. It wasn't like she controlled my actions. I purpose sometimes she did. But it was more oft . . . thoughts and feelings. Memories. Words whispered in my head so many times I believed them." He met Andra's stare. "Even now I'm not certz what's real."

He was silent for a moment, and Andra felt a softness toward him. He seemed to realize it, and his gaze turned into a sneer.

"Who recks for true? Maybe I've been a fraught all along, and all it took was a tiny push from my mother."

"I don't believe that," Andra said.

"Then you're as much of a fool as my brother."

Andra ignored him. "Did Tsurina create the Crown? Just so she could control you?"

Maret looked like he was going to say more about her being a fool, but then sighed. "It's . . . a fam heirloom. Every eldest kiddun in my fam has worn it, for as long as time has memory. Our fam—the Anlochs—are probablish the oldest fam in the Wastes. I'm descended from a group of people sworn to end the goddesses and their sleeping gods. It's all hazy anow, but I used to have memory why. Some kind of revenge for what your people did to the planet. It was part of the Crown. Every memory of every wearer of the Crown lives inside it. And . . . and the anger too.

"My mam was raised on stories of the gods and the terrible things they did to Earth. How they destroyed it and then disappeared, leaving those they didn't feel were *worthy* to clean up their mess. To die. To live in this hellscape. The first of my line swore to get revenge, but recked it would take several lifetimes, so they created the Crown and imbued it with all their memories and angers, so we would never forget what it felt like to be abandoned. My mam inherited it when she was nine.

"Her parents were killed by a pocket. Living in the Wastes, seeya. When the pocket passed, all that was left was the Crown, full untouched. Recking it was her birthright, my mam donned it. From that day on, it raised her, whispering the past and anger and hate into her head. Raising her as its own. In a way, she had her mother back. She had all the generations of Anlochs guiding her. Their rage, their revenge, that was all she ever recked. As did I."

Andra put her hand to her temple, trying to understand. It almost seemed like this 'implant had been given sentience through absorbing the memories that it had been tied to. Programmed by the thoughts and feelings of its wearers, its fear and hate amplified until it consumed each of its hosts. That was what Maret had lived through for four years. That's what Zhade was living with now.

She felt sick to her stomach. "I can't imagine having to live like that. With someone else controlling you. I'm sorry, Maret."

"You shouldn't be," Maret snapped. "Because now, you realize, everything you said to Zhade is something Tsurina knows. I recked all along and could have stopped you."

Andra froze. "Everything? How? If she no longer wears the Crown, how can she see inside his head?"

A haunted smile flashed across Maret's face. He pointed to the spot the Crown had been. "It never disappears. Not completish. Even if it's removed, it leaves something behind. Some magic—we call it the imprint—is imbedded into you, like a shard remaining. It gives you control of the wearer, lets you enforce your will on them. You can put them in a trance and make them do whatever you wish, like a puppeter. Or you can make them do something while they're aware. They'll do it, even if they don't reck why. Most of the time, it's more subtle. You can whisper words into their heart and make them believe something is true. Or at least believe they believe it." Maret looked away. "It's not all power though. The imprint leaves you with the memories, the rage. That. That will never leave you."

Andra felt herself start to hyperventilate. During the upgrades, she'd learned that 'implants became intrinsically tied to the brain of the human wearing it, adapting to their emotions and thought processes. The Crown seemed to do the same thing, but much more invasively, until it became inseparably part of the wearer.

Andra had never felt comfortable with the Crown, but it was only part of the problem. The other part was the neural tech it left behind. It budded the wearer with an 'implant that was networked to the Crown.

"What's Tsurina's plan? What does she want?"

Maret lifted his eyebrows. "You purpose what does the *Crown* want. It wants what it's always wanted. To destroy the gods, to punish them, to burn everything, til there's nothing left but ash."

ANDRA CURSED HERSELF as she ran through the Vaults' air'lock and into the tunnels below the palace. She'd removed the Crown from Maret herself. She'd watched and done nothing as Zhade had put it on his own head. At any point during the last few months, she could have removed it from his temple.

But she'd ignored the nagging sense that something was wrong, chalked it up to her humanity, her sense of betrayal at how Zhade had come by the Crown. She'd thrown all her focus at the 'implant upgrades, and now Zhade and probably everyone else would pay for it.

"Wait, Andra," a voice said behind her, and she turned to find Mechy following.

"You're supposed to be watching Maret," Andra snapped, barely pausing before continuing her march to the palace's secret entrance. Kinetic orbs flashed on as she passed them. Her feet made muted thuds on the eco'tile floor.

"The Xana human is watching him," Mechy argued, catching up with her with his long mechanical strides. "And the cell will hold. I built it myself, and I am good at building things."

"Go back," Andra ordered.

"No."

Andra paused, turning toward Mechy. He watched her with unblinking eyes.

"You can't . . . you can't deny an order."

Mechy tilted his head. "As it turns out, I can, because I'm refusing to return to the cell to watch the boy-king. I am instead choosing to follow you into peril. Because you are my friend."

"You're choosing to," Andra echoed.

Mechy nodded. "Because you are my friend."

"Decide your fate," Andra whispered.

Mechy put his hand on Andra's shoulder. "That is exactly what I'm trying to do."

THE RIDE UP the lift to the First's suites seemed to take forever. Mechy stood patiently beside her, but Andra paced the platform as it ascended, thinking of all the problems she could encounter as she attempted to remove the Crown from Zhade.

First, Tsurina knew everything Zhade knew, which included Andra's continued existence. Second, even if Andra could somehow confront Zhade alone, Tsurina still had access to Zhade's thoughts and could control his actions. Andra felt sick to her stomach. Had Tsurina watched them when they were together? Or worse, had that even been Zhade at all? Or had it been some twisted plan to get Andra to spill her secrets?

Ever since Andra had met Zhade, she'd never really known him. He was either pretending to be someone else, or someone else was pretending to be him.

The lift began to slow as it reached the top.

"The palace foundation is becoming increasingly unstable," Mechy said. "We may not be able to return this way."

Andra shrugged. They would worry about that later.

The lift door opened and Mechy pulled himself into the small bathroom above, then bent and helped Andra climb out. In the distance, bells were ringing. She paused and counted. Fifteen. Not great. It was around dinnertime—as Eerensedian days were broken into twenty bells, instead of twenty-four hours—so there would be servants going to and fro around the castle, bringing dinner to advisors and diplomats. But at least Zhade should be in the guv's suite alone and—

Andra turned the corner into the First's bedroom, and there, waiting for her, was a member of the guv's guard.

"Well, shit."

Tsabin, Andra remembered. A slim but muscled man with a shaved head and beady eyes. He was fast. And mean.

"Tsurina said you'd come eventualish," he hissed, his voice gravelly and rough.

Mechy darted forward, massive fist raised, but Tsabin was ready for him. He twirled a spear around his head and brought it up to block Mechy's blow. His tan angular face was carved into a snarl, and his muscles bulged beneath his sand-colored shirt.

He swung the spear in Mechy's direction, but the 'bot ducked, grabbing an overturned chair and breaking off the leg. He fought dexterously for a mech'bot. It seemed Mechy had been upgrading his own software. He was too bulky to fight smoothly, to move quickly, but he'd learned to use his strength as, well, a strength.

Andra let her mental shields drop, feeling for any tech in the room to interface with, but Zhade had done too good a job emptying the room. All that was within reach was Mechy and a smattering of nanos. She called to them and sent them toward Tsabin, but there were too few and he was too quick.

Mechy hit Tsabin across the face with the table leg, his full strength behind the blow. Tsabin went flying across the room, but managed to tuck into a roll and land on his toes and knees and forefingers. A line of blood decorated his cheek. He wiped it off and smiled.

"Run, Andra!" Mechy said. "Get to the arrogant boy. I'll distract him."

Tsabin somersaulted to grab his spear, and with a flying leap, brought it down. Mechy barely had time to catch it between his metal palms.

He was right. She had to get to Zhade, remove the Crown. Mechy could handle himself, and Andra was no good in a fight.

She ran for the door, darting over what remained of the fallen chair, tripping forward, hand reaching for the door handle.

"Go, Andra, go—"

There was a sickening crunch, and Mechy's voice cut off. Andra whipped around to find him on his knees, sword in his chest.

"No!" Andra gasped, just as Tsabin jerked his sword free, taking Mechy's central processing unit with it.

The 'bot's eyes went completely blank and he toppled, hitting the ground with a deafening crash. His smoking processor was stuck to the tip of Tsabin's sword.

"Mechy!" Andra sobbed, as his nanos were released into the air.

There was no coming back from that. Not for Mechy. Andra could repair the damage to the processor, even reconstruct the casing and body. But it would no longer be Mechy. The 'bot who had become Andra's helper and confidant and friend was gone.

Andra stood, rage coursing through her. "You shouldn't have done that."

Her lungs filled and her consciousness expanded. She gathered all the nanos in the room, including Mechy's. Calling them, converting them to her own. She saw through them, felt through them, sensed through them. She grew to fill the space around her, breathing in all the fear and anger and grief that had followed her through her time in Eerensed. She breathed out, and as Tsabin stood, preparing to charge, Andra sent the nanos hurtling in his direction, sent them seeping through his pores, pouring into his bloodstream, filling up his lungs, clenching his throat.

He fell to his knees, grasping his neck. Noises that weren't quite words, sounds that weren't quite *please* passed through his lips as they turned blue and the veins in his forehead started to bulge.

Yes, the voice inside her said. *Yes, destroy.*

Yes, Andra agreed, ice filling her veins. *I will. I will destroy. First him and then everyone. He deserves it. They all deserve it.*

She watched in passive glee as Tsabin clawed at his throat, reveling in his cries for help. This was what she was created for. This was what was right. Not saving humanity. Disposing of them.

She was basking in Tsabin's last desperate breaths when she felt a burst of blinding pain cut through her chest.

She looked down. A sword pierced her ribcage. She had one moment of horror, realization of what she'd done, of what had just been done to her, and then there was nothing, not even darkness.

THIRTY-TWO

THE SCOURGE

"The goddesses?" Zhade asked. "Why would humanity need protecting from the goddesses?"

Tsurina watched him from her reclined spot on the cathedzal floor, her red dress pooling out round her like spilled blood. Zhade felt a prickle at the back of his mind.

"Because of their magic," Tsurina said. "Since its creation, magic has done nothing but hurt humanity. It's divided us and subjugated us. And the sole march to save us from ourselves is to harness it."

Zhade nodded. It was true. Magic had destroyed humans. Their reliance on it—like the gods' dome—to protect themselves from other magic—like the pockets. How much pain magic caused. It was a necessary evil, but had to be controlled. And who better to control it than Zhade.

He sat forward on the cathedzal steps, the magic of the gods' dome conduits flashing behind him. "Soze. Mereish like the rogue angels. We seek out the magic that has turned evil and use it for our purposes. Left to the people, these angels would continue murdering innocents, but in our hands . . ."

A smile spread across Tsurina's face. "In our hands, they can be used to protect Eerensed."

Zhade couldn't help but smile back. It was all starting to make sense. All of the things he'd worked so hard against, all of the evil he'd seen in Maret and Tsurina, it was mereish them making the hard decisions. Deciding not their own fates, but the fates of all of Eerensed. All of humanity. Letting go of their selfish desires to have a destiny of their own, to make certz everyone else had one. He could do that. He could give up his wants, sacrifice them for the power to hold his people safe.

"I full comp now."

"I'm glad," Tsurina said. "But there's one more thing you must comp. It's bout your mother."

For a tick, fear and shame and guilt and panic washed over Zhade. This was wrong. This was all wrong. His mam hadn't wanted this.

But then an icy calm washed over him. His mam, who had never for true loved him. He could see that now. She'd left him time and again, let him believe she died and left him to wander the Wastes. Raised some other kiddun instead of him. She was still alive, but he no longer cared to see her.

"What bout her?" Zhade asked.

"She is our greatest enemy," Tsurina said, and Zhade recked it to be true. "And she has waited out in the desert, banished by her own people. But it seems they are prepping for her to return. We must be prepped ourselves. It will be soon and sooner."

Firm, it would be soon and sooner. Meta had said so. His mam was coming back, and he would be prepped. He would ask Meta. Meta would tell him. He would pretend he had brotherish affection for her full long for her to spill her secrets.

"Andra is our enemy too," Tsurina said slowish.

Zhade blinked, confusion settling over him. Was Andra his enemy?

She lied to you, a voice whispered. *She never loved you.*

He shook his head, two warring emotions rising up inside him. He loved her. He hated her.

Neg. He could never hate her.

The door to the cathedzal flew open.

"Ah." Tsurina smiled. "There she is now."

The guv's guard stormed in, Tsabin leading them, dragging a body. His fellow guards followed, fanning out round him. The sole one missing was Gryfud.

Tsurina gestured at the guards. "They were full time mine, seeya. Even when you imagined they were yours. The guards will always be mine. As will you."

Zhade nodded. For certz. He would always be hers.

"Look who I found," Tsabin spat. He dragged the body forward, leaving a track of blood across the carpet, and dumped it at Zhade's feet.

Zhade's knees buckled. His heart was torn from his torso.

Andra.

Oh sands, oh sands.

His precious Andra. Kind, bril, funny, charred, perfect Andra.

"Neg," Zhade croaked. "Neg!" And he fell to his knees, crawling, dragging himself toward her.

There was a hole in her chest, blood pouring out of her. How could she lose so much blood? How much blood was in her?

"Neg, Andra, wake up!" His voice was shredded, and he realized he was screaming. He gathered her into his arms, calling her name. Her body hung limpish, her head lolling from side to side, her eyes open and unseeing. "Wake up!"

He tore off his cape and started packing the wound, soaking up the blood, pressing down, but the blood didn't stop.

"Andra!" he cried.

"She's dead," Tsabin sneered. "Ranzh saved me from the devil by running her through with a sword. No one could survive that."

Tears streamed down Zhade's face. It was impossible. Andra was a constant. She had been for centuries. Her body lying frozen as the world kept going and changing, as people lived and died. She continued. She had to continue. The world couldn't exist without her.

Zhade couldn't exist without her.

He fumbled in his pocket and pulled out the graftling wand. The one he'd changed his face with and transformed Meta with. The one that had hurt Andra out in the desert.

But they had both changed—Andra and the wand. Maybe, just maybe, it could bring her back.

He scanned the wound, casting the spell for healing. He waited for the following beep, then let the wand spread its translucent magic over her.

Tsurina was talking, her voice muffled in his head. "Charling, this is for the best. Your care for her was a distraction. Soon and now you can focus on being the guv you want to be."

Care for her? That happened a fraction of it. He would do anything for her. He would cross deserts and fight kingdoms and give up everything for her. Let Eerensed die. Let it sink into sand. He would die for her.

The glittering magic covered the wound, as it had with Zhade's sun spots in the desert. It fit itself to form to the shape her body should have been, without the gaping hole over her heart, torn through the wishmark on her collarbone.

Nothing was happening.

Nothing.

Her blood was gushing slower and slower. Her skin was turning waxy, her lips blue. The magic mesh curled in on itself and absorbed back into the wand. Andra lay still.

"No meteor," Tsabin said. "She's dead now." He nudged her with a blood-soaked boot.

"Don't you touch her!" Zhade growled. He would kill him. Then Ranzh. Then all the guards. He stood, Andra's blood dripping down his hands, and brought all the angels in the room to life.

There was the smallest hesitation, the tiniest question in his mind. A moment when he wasn't certz if Andra was the promised of his life or the enemy. A flash of Tsurina's disapproval.

But then rage and grief took over.

The angels' eyes grew red, and Zhade reveled in their bloodlust, inserting his will into each of them. Zhade and the magic. Zhade and the angels. Zhade and the rage.

Good, he thought, and let them loose.

Every angel in the room surged forward as Zhade dragged Andra's body behind the throne, then stood as a shield between her and the carnage afront of him. The guards were brave, but no match for Zhade's rogue angels. Swords clashed. Shields splintered. And one by one the guards fell into pools of their own blood. Tsabin. Ranzh. Ahloma. Dzon.

Zhade relished in each of their deaths. They'd betrayed him. Neg, how could they betray him if they were never loyal to him? It had always been Tsurina who held their allegiance.

Soon and sooner, Tsurina was the sole one left standing. A smile quirked against Zhade's lips. Now, he would kill her too.

He blinked.

Neg.

Neg. He couldn't kill her.

She had skooled him the Crown, given him purpose.

But she'd ordered the guards to kill Andra. For certz, he could kill her.

He saw a flash of something in his mind. A memory. Not his. He was crying, pleading, begging. Tsurina was sneering above him and slapped him cross the face.

Zhade came back to himself, back to the present, and called to the angels, sending them to circle Tsurina, spears drawn. He would have Fishy be the one to do it. It would stab and stab til there was nothing left but blood and gore. He relished the fear on Tsurina's face as she trembled and stumbled back.

Then the cathedzal doors rattled.

They stopped, and Zhade was certz he had imagined it. But neg. They did it again. Someone was trying to get in. Zhade and his angels froze, and Tsurina turned mereish as the doors burst open and a pocket entered the room.

Tsurina dove out of the way. The pocket danced and swirled, consuming everything in its path, grabbing an angel arm here, a leg there. Devouring some of the dead guards. Swarming straight toward Zhade.

He stumbled back, but the pocket didn't pursue him.

Instead.

Instead,

it landed on Andra

(Andra's body)

and consumed her.

"Neg!" Zhade cried, but something or someone held him back.

The darkness twitched and jolted over the spot Andra's body had been, taking longer to devour her than it did the others. Taking its time to feast.

Zhade felt the horror from a distance, realized he had been feeling it for quite some time. Guilt and grief threatened to overwhelm him. What had he done?

He'd murdered a dozen people in the blink of an eye. Andra wouldn't have wanted this.

She was gone.

She was gone.

She was gone.

The pocket dispersed, seeming to disappear into nothing. And there, lying on the cathedzal floor—

—was Andra.

Whole and full well: her injury healed, the ragged hole in her chest now replaced with clear unmarked skin, wreathed in the bloody rags of what remained of her dress.

She sucked in a breath as her body lifted into the air, her back arched, limbs stiff. Slowish, she raised her head, til she was standing straightish, hovering several feet from the ground.

Her eyes flashed open.

Where her charred brown eyes had once been, there was nothing but a pure white light. No pupil, no iris. It shone from her as stardust glittered round her, the stained glass in the wall behind limning her in an array of soft light.

Zhade stared at her in awe as pain began to throb in his head, running from his temple to the center of his brain. It grew and grew til it was unbearistic. Racing through him. Ripping. Tearing. He fell to his knees, swallowed by darkness. He didn't fight it. He'd mereish let it take him. Punish him for everything he'd done. All the death and terror he'd caused. He was consumed and there was nothing but the pain and he reveled in it and welcomed it, and each time he imagined it had reached its peak, he skooled he was wrong.

Then, as suddenish as a sandstorm, as suddenish as a pocket, the pain stopped.

Relief flooded him, and he realized he was in the fetal position on the velvet floor and that his hands clutched his head, and that sitting a few feet away, slick and wet with his blood—

—was the Crown.

Something like peace fell over him, darkness swaddled him, and with one last imagining of Andra, he recked no more.

THIRTY-THREE

OO11OO11 OO11OO11

ANDRA DIDN'T QUITE feel like herself.

She felt more like herself than she ever had.

Light and knowledge coursed through her, and just like her first experience with the reset tool, she knew what her purpose was, and it surprised her. She smiled, promising herself she would remember this time.

It was such little effort to remove the Crown from Zhade's head after the pocket had saved her.

It was *the* pocket. *Her* pocket. The pocket she'd kept in the mini'dome, then in the chamber in the upgrade lab. It told her about how it had shattered the glass that had contained it. The people had screamed, but it had known them as its own and left them be. Because Andra was also its own. More its own than even the pocket it had spawned from. She had harvested these nanos and nurtured them, kept them safe and cared for. And she had been in danger.

It had been the graftling wand that had done it. In the end.

Unlike the first time Zhade had used the graftling wand on her, she hadn't been conscious to scream. Her healing tech was overwhelmed. Her blood pressure was dropping, brain activity weakening, every system in her body shutting down. Her nanos had called for help.

And just like that moment in the desert when pocket nanos had burst the healing mesh, these nanos came to her rescue.

They were designed for destruction. That was their purpose, in every code of their programming. But they allowed themselves to be converted by Andra's healing tech into healing tech themselves.

The pocket had decided to heal Andra.

It had decided its fate.

So now, here she was, her humanity shrinking as her AI consciousness expanded.

Destroy, the voice inside her commanded, and she countered it with a gentle no.

Just like the pocket that decided it would heal instead of destroy, so would Andra.

Zhade lay unconscious on the floor, blood trickling from his ear. Andra slowly lowered herself to the ground and let her humanity take over. The light and knowledge receded, and she became more and more human until she forgot her purpose and her plan and all the programming that had laid out her life ahead of her. More and more human until she forgot that she'd even remembered. More and more human until she was running toward Zhade, calling his name.

She fell in a heap beside him, flipping him onto his back. If what Maret said was true, if the Crown had left an imprint in his mind, Zhade was still a threat, a danger to himself and everyone around him. She tried lifting him to his feet, but realized even with all the weight he'd lost, it would be impossible for her to drag him out of the room, much less back to the Vaults. Not without Mechy. Mechy who lay dead on the floor of the First's suite.

She reached out to interface with any tech in the room, finding a 'bot that was still functioning, and called it over. It was a lanky thing with an LED faceplate. Through the mental interface, she felt . . . love and loyalty directed toward Zhade. It had known him. It would help him. He would carry Zhade, and together they would escape to the underground. She would survive this.

Inches from Zhade, the 'bot stopped, and Andra realized what she was forgetting.

The Crown.

Jesus, the Crown.

Her eyes searched for it and found it all the way across the room.

With Tsurina.

She stood silhouetted in the open doorway, red dress tickling the floor. In her long fingers, she delicately held the the device that had so recently been latched to Zhade's forehead.

Andra swallowed. "Drop that."

Tsurina lifted an eyebrow. "Or what?"

Andra was dizzy from blood loss, though the healing tech was replenishing it as fast as it could. She was weak and spent, and even the urge to destroy was silent now.

"Or . . . you'll see what I can do."

Tsurina laughed. "I've seen your kind. Memories of you passed down from the very first bearer of the Crown. They all live in me, as they now live in Zhade. And I've seen enough to reck if you could destroy me, you already would have. You have no control over your powers. You have no idea what you're capable of, but I do."

"What do you mean you've seen my kind from the beginning?"

Tsurina smiled, and her teeth seeming to sharpen. "This Crown holds all the memories since the first of my fam, and I've lived them all. I reck every moment of exis—"

"I know that," Andra snapped. "What do you mean you've seen my kind? Do you mean AI? It's just me and Rashmi."

"Is it?"

Before Andra could ask what she meant, Tsurina lifted the Crown to her forehead.

"Wait!" Andra cried, but it was too late.

Tsurina attached the Crown to her temple, her eyes fluttering in either pain or ecstasy. She sucked in a breath, and one by one, the angels that the pocket had spared stood and lifted their weapons. When she opened her eyes, her smile was wicked.

Andra grabbed Zhade's hand, even as he lay unconscious. There was no way out of this. She was depleted and could no longer access her AI state to detach the Crown, couldn't fight this many 'bots with the strength she had left. And she wouldn't flee without Zhade. It appeared this was her last stand. She squared her shoulders. Her dress hung in bloody rags as she rose to her feet.

Tsurina lifted her hands in the air, and Andra braced for the 'bots to shoot forward. She hoped it would be quick, though it was becoming obvious she was hard to kill. She wondered if Tsurina would wake Zhade to torture him.

Suddenly, the Grande Advisor fell to her knees, a sword appearing against her neck.

Andra blinked in confusion as she tried to process what had just happened, what she was seeing.

Just like that, Tsurina was no longer the attacker, but the prisoner. And the person holding her at swordpoint was . . . another Tsurina.

They were exactly alike. Same face, same body, same expressions. Then Andra remembered what Zhade had said the morning of their fight. He had changed one of his guards into the Grande Advisor.

"Thank god," Andra breathed. "It's Meta, right? Zhade needs help. And we need to neutralize Tsurina until I'm strong enough to remove the Crown. Can you knock her unconscious?"

Meta grinned, the expression so unlike Tsurina. Her hair was a ragged mess and dirt streaked her face. "It would be my pleasure."

"Zhade needs help, too," Andra gasped. "But if he wakes up, he could be a danger to us all. He has this . . . *thing* in his head. Leftover from the Crown. It—"

"Oh, I full reck," Meta said. "I reck everything bout the Crown. After all, it's my birthright."

A heavy silence fell over the room, and Tsurina's eyes widened. "Neg. That's impossible." Her voice was strained, cracked.

"I survived the desert," Meta snarled. "I aged up without you. Skooled magic without you. Discovered the full history of the Crown. Without you."

Tsurina's face was deathly pale. "Metina," she whispered. "You're Metina."

"I go by Meta now. Meta kin Anloch. Daughter of Tsurina kin Anloch. Abandoned, so you could become the wife of the Guv of Eerensed. And as your eldest, that Crown is my inheritance."

Tsurina swallowed, and Andra felt phantom pains as the sword scraped against her neck.

"You don't want it, Metina." There were tears on Tsurina's face, her brown hair hanging in bedraggled sheets around her. "I left to save you. Soze you wouldn't have to wear it. It's cursed."

"It's power and it's mine," Meta said through gritted teeth. The flashing of the 'dome hub holos lit the angles of her face in harsh relief. "Give it to me. Soon and now."

"She can't," Andra said, her voice echoing hollowly in the cathedzal.

Meta didn't take her eyes off her mother. "Why not?"

"She can't take it off herself," Andra answered. "Crowns only release if the host dies, or—"

Andra realized her mistake a second too late.

Meta slid the sword across Tsurina's throat, splitting it open. "Thanks, mam."

At first nothing happened. But then a small red line appeared on Tsurina's throat, growing redder and thicker. Desperately, Tsurina tried to close the wound, her eyes still wide in surprise, in denial. But Andra, who so recently had experienced a similar injury, who only survived because of the nano'tech coursing through her veins and the odd impulse of a 'swarm of corrupted tech, knew that Tsurina's efforts would be in vain.

"Bye, mam," Meta said, and stabbed her again, this time in the chest.

The light left Tsurina's eyes, and Meta pushed her over with a press of two fingers, like she was dusting away a bit of dirt. Tsurina's head hit the floor with a smack.

There was a squelching sound as the Crown released itself, then a clatter as it fell to the carpet in front of Tsurina's unseeing eyes.

Meta bent to pick it up, examining it, weighing it carefully in her hand.

"Don't!" Andra pleaded, but Meta was already placing the Crown to her temple. She gasped as it attached, throwing her head back, eyes closed, mouth agape, shuddering as the Crown's wires dove beneath her skin and into her brain. As the nanos connected with neurons. She let out one final breath, lowering her head.

Her eyes flashed open, and she looked at Andra from under her lashes.

Andra tensed, ready to run, to fight, though she knew it was useless.

"You must be Andra."

"Yes," Andra said, calling to the stardust around her, preparing to defend herself.

Meta smiled, the expression disarmingly genuine. "Griffin always convoed how brill you were. I didn't realize you were full brill to come back from the dead. Twice, for certz."

Andra blinked.

Then blinked again.

Then shook her head to clear it.

"What? You know Griffin? Who are you?"

"I'm Meta."

"Yeah, I got that. But how do you know Griffin? And you're also Tsurina's daughter? And you were a guard?"

Meta shrugged. "It happens a long story. Let's mereish convo that Tsurina abandoned me and Griffin took me in and raised me. And she sent me here three years ago to infiltrate the palace."

Andra massaged her temple. It was too much. All of it. The dying and the coming back to life and the reshaping of what she knew to be true. "She didn't tell me about you."

"She wouldn't. She plays several games, instead of one. It's the sole march to win, to survive. Each of us had a purpose, and I just fulfilled mine." She nudged the body of her dead mother.

Andra was still shaking her head. "Griffin wouldn't want this. For you to kill. For you to put on the Crown. It's dangerous."

Meta touched the shiny metal at her forehead. "This? This was sole for me. Neg, my purpose was mereish to take out Tsurina. You're welcome, beedub."

Andra looked down at Tsurina's fallen form. Griffin hadn't wanted this, had she? For Tsurina to die? Of course, she'd used and manipulated Zhade, but did she deserve to die?

She stared at Meta. Physically, she looked exactly like Tsurina, but her expression, her stance was something new. Andra heard hints of Maret's bitterness, or Zhade's sarcasm in her speech patterns. Saw Griffin's posture in her stance.

"I—" Andra started, but every door in the cathedzal blasted open and shouting filled the space. People rushed in with laser'guns.

In the space of a moment, the remaining 'bots lifted their spears, forming a shield between Meta and the attackers.

Skilla stepped out of the shadows. Followed by Kiv and Gryfud.

"Wait!" Andra said, thrusting out her palms. "Wait! She's on our side!"

Skilla raised a hand and the Schism stood down. "She's what?"

"That's not . . . that's not Tsurina," Andra hurried to explain. "Zhade changed her face, but that's actually . . . Tsurina's abandoned daughter? And she's working for Griffin somehow?"

Skilla's eyes drifted to the dead Tsurina on the floor. Then to Zhade's unconscious body at Andra's feet. "Huh."

"I don't full comp," Andra said. "But she just saved Zhade and me from Tsurina. Griffin sent her here."

Skilla's eyes narrowed. She and Meta stared each other down, each a word away from commanding their army to attack.

"Are you certz bout this?" Skilla asked.

Andra put a hand to her head. "I'm not certz of anything soon and now."

Meta smiled, and it reminded her of Zhade trying to charm people, but with Maret's awkwardness. "You're Skilla, marah? Griffin says to tell you the sands are strong."

For a moment, Skilla didn't respond, just stared in disbelief.

"But we are stronger," she finally whispered back. She blinked. "This is . . . full weird magic. And you'll must explain all this soon and sooner."

Andra shook her head. She didn't know if she could trust Meta, but if Griffin had sent her, she must have had a reason. And with Tsurina dead and without knowing the influence the Crown imprint would have over Zhade, the Eerensedians needed a leader. Meta could be that leader, and in time Andra would convince her to remove the Crown. It had taken months for the Crown to corrupt Zhade, and there were more pressing matters at the moment.

"We can work this all out later," she said. "For now, we need to get Zhade to a meddoc, and then . . . to a cell."

She had to keep him contained until she figured out how to rid him of the Crown's imprint.

Skilla chuckled to herself, looking at Zhade's prone unconscious body. "Now, that I can do."

THE SCHISM WAS abuzz with activity as Kiv helped Andra to Tia Ludmila's sickroom. The caves were packed with people dressed in militia garb.

Skilla's refugee army had been training when Kiv had appeared in the underground, asking for help, telling them that Zhade had gone mad and that Tsurina was behind it. They had been prepared to fight, but instead of finding two power-hungry maniacs, they'd found Tsurina's estranged daughter and a newly arisen Andra.

They'd left Meta to secure her rule over Eerensed. She planned on telling the city that Maret had been killed by an angel, and that she, as Tsurina, was now guv. Something about the whole thing bothered Andra, but she had to admit it was nice to have an ally on the throne. She didn't think Griffin had intended things to happen the way they did, but now, at least, with Tsurina out of the way, Griffin could come back to Eerensed and help Andra with the upgrades, so they could finally start working on the rocket.

Before that could happen, though, both Andra and Zhade needed to see a meddoc. Fishy had carried Zhade, and Kiv had helped Andra to Tia Ludmila's small cave off the main Schism tunnel. It was lit with kinetic orbs and paneled with white, shiny tile. The was a line of hover'cots filled with patients, each attached to several monitors displaying their vitals.

Andra looked over at Zhade's prone form under a blanket on the closest 'cot. His injuries hadn't been serious, but Tia Ludmila kept him unconscious in case the imprint made him . . . like Maret.

"Ah, seeya," Tia Ludmila said in a rough, gravelly voice, turning to Andra. "This happens the fool one who got stabbed in the chest, marah? I see no injure here."

Andra leaned heavily on Kiv. The adrenaline of the moment had worn off, and though Andra didn't feel like she'd been run through with a sword, she definitely didn't feel great. Drowsiness swept over her, as her healing tech—both her own and the assimilated pocket nanos—worked overtime to replenish her blood and heal her internal injuries.

"I'm fine," Andra croaked. "Goddess healing powers."

"Psh," Tia scoffed. "Sit, sit."

She gestured to a nearby stool. Andra never felt fully comfortable on stools—they were designed for people smaller than her—but she sat anyway, Kiv's strong arms keeping her balanced.

Tia Ludmila brought over a holo'display, watching it as she scanned Andra's chest with a med'wand.

"Sands and all desert creatures," she breathed. "Goddess healing powers indeed. There 'pens a hole running straightish through you, but it 'ppears your body has sealed it off and is regrowing your insides. Snakerats. I never seen any likeish this my full life." She sat forward, zooming in on the holo'display. "Wait. What happens?"

Tia typed something into the med'wand and pressed it to Andra's chest. A spark shot through Andra. Not quite pain but more than a burst of adrenaline. With a jolt, her mind was thrown back to somewhere she'd never been.

Sitting in an office.

No, not just an office.

Her office.

Her long fingers running a pencil along a piece of paper. Scratching through another word on a list.

~~New Earth~~

~~Freeland~~

~~Exodeen~~

Holymyth

Her pencil circling Holymyth. *What better name for a planet that didn't exist?*

Andra gasped, flung back into her own consciousness.

What was that? It had been . . . like a memory. She *remembered* being at her desk, trying to decide what to name a planet. But that had never happened.

"Happen you evens?" Tia Ludmila asked.

"Yeah," Andra whispered. "Evens."

Tia frowned, looking back at the 'display projected from her med'wand. "You hold many different types of stardust inside you."

Andra nodded, brow still creased in confusion. "Yeah, Rashmi's programming. And then I guess there's some . . ." She didn't want to tell her she had a pocket inside of her. ". . . environmental assimilation."

Tia grunted. "Neg, I see the stardust of the Second—I reck it well. And your stardust. But there 'ppears to be something full different here, seeya."

Tia turned the 'display around for Andra to see. It was a picture of a brain—*her* brain—and Tia pointed to the cortex where long-term memories were stored.

"The info here. There happens some of you, and the Second, and if my memory holds, the First."

Andra froze.

The vision *had* been a memory. Just not Andra's.

When she'd been in the underwater lab, she'd looked at the computer that stored Griffin's memories. She'd felt a spark, seen a flash of memory. She thought she'd only viewed the memory, but she must have accidentally uploaded some, and they'd remained hidden in her matrices until . . .

Until the sword knocked into the cluster of nanos at her heart, resetting her system.

That was Griffin's memory she'd just seen.

Griffin who was choosing names for a planet. A planet far away that humanity would think they were traveling to.

A planet that, apparently, didn't exist.

The revelation crashed into Andra like a wave, the implications causing her stomach to drop.

There had never been any plan to colonize another planet. The rocket Andra was trying to build had nowhere to go.

It was all a lie.

There was no Holymyth.

THIRTY-FOUR

OO1100II OO1IOIOO

ANDRA HURRIED THROUGH the Icebox, the space overwhelming her as she drove the hover to the upgrade lab.

She'd left Kiv at Tia Ludmila's with the instructions to put Zhade in a cell in the Vaults. She'd almost told him to ask Mechy to build one, but then remembered Mechy was dead.

She zoomed past the towering rows of cryo'tanks, through the tent city of the colonists. The scientists and their families were just starting to wake for the day, the rise-n-shine beginning to glow to the east.

Griffin had lied about Holymyth. Not just to the world but to Andra. If she'd lied about that, what else had she lied about? And why?

She'd sent Andra to upgrade the colonists. She'd sent Meta to kill Tsurina. Meta had said Griffin was playing several games. That it was the only way to win.

To win what?

Whatever it was, Andra had been working under the assumption that everything she was doing was meant to eventually get humanity off Earth to their new colony planet. Wake the colonists, upgrade them to protect them, use their cryo'chambers to build the rocket. Why do any of that if there was no Holymyth?

This was fine. So Griffin had lied. She'd still saved humanity. She'd created the 'implant upgrade that made humanity immune to the pockets. It didn't matter that there was no Holymyth now, because they could find a way to live on Earth. Andra was almost finished upgrading the LAC scientists. Soon they could start waking the other colonists. Andra could even start fitting the Eerensedians with upgraded 'implants.

Is that why Griffin had sent Meta to take over for Tsurina? To help the Eerensedians? And if so, why hadn't she told Andra?

This was fine.

This was all fine.

Right?

The hover had barely parked before she was jumping out and running over to the lab. She knocked on the door but didn't wait for Cruz's response before charging in. He slammed a cabinet shut just as she entered and whipped around, hand to his chest.

"Jesus, Andra, you scared me." He gave her a shy smile.

"Sorries," she said.

He hopped onto an ergo'stool.

"Are you ready to get to work today?" he asked. "I thought it was time we started on the children."

He looked so much more confident than she'd ever seen him. So much more in his element. She was about to pull his world out from under him. Again.

Andra shook her head. "No, I have something else I want to talk to you about."

Cruz looked disappointed but gestured for Andra to take a seat. "Fire."

Andra hesitated. She didn't want to just come right out and say it. Cruz had taken all of the news surprisingly well, but she wasn't sure that this bit of information wouldn't push him straight over the edge. She had to be sure. Maybe she could access more of Griffin's memories first, so she could get the full picture of what exactly they were dealing with.

"I was wondering about . . . AI and memory. How do we create it? Store it? Access it? That sort of thing."

Cruz frowned. "Oh, well. That's an interesting question, and you definitely came to the right guy. That was something I was particularly interested in during my internship."

He turned to the work'station and brought up a holo'display.

"This is a human brain." He flipped to a new 'display. "And this is an AI brain. See the difference?"

Andra squinted. "Um, not really."

"That's the answer. AI brains and human brains are basically the same thing. You store memory the same way."

"Okay . . ."

Cruz chuckled. "I mean, of course there are differences, but it's less structural and more accessibility of the information stored. So, for instance . . ." He thought for a moment. "Your brother has a file stored in his brain of the time he . . . pooped in his diaper when he was two. But even though he has that file stored, the pathways to that file have deteriorated over time and he now no longer has any way to access that. So he doesn't technically remember it, even though that memory still exists in his brain."

Andra pointed a finger at him. "Weird example, but go on."

"Now, the pathways to memories for AI, on the other hand, never deteriorate. It's like a computer. If a file is stored, the pathway is there forever. So if you have a memory of pooping in your diaper when you were two? You can access it."

Andra frowned. "But I don't remember, you know, *any* memories, except a few before . . . I was four? Five? And I've lost even recent memories. Like . . . what I had for dinner two weeks ago. And there are *tons* of files I can't access. Programming and data. I get glimpses of it now and then—I go into this AI state, where I have access to all my knowledge and powers—but then I literally forget it."

Cruz bounced with excitement. "Ah, see, there's the difference between you and other AI. *You* grew up human. You lived with a human family, thinking you yourself were human. You assimilated and started mimicking human behavior without even realizing it. That illusion of your humanity is what makes it difficult to access those memories and programs. You've *convinced* yourself you've forgotten the pathway to the files, but you haven't. You're just trying to be human. If you truly accept you're AI, then you'll be able to access those files again. I suspect that's what happens when you go into this . . . what did you call it? An AI state? You embrace your true nature. The illusion of your humanity falls away. You stopped *believing* you were human and started *knowing* you were AI."

Andra wanted to argue that she was both. She was human and AI, but she was caught on something Cruz had said.

"What do you mean the difference between me and other AI? It's just me and Rashmi, right?"

Cruz scratched the back of his head. "Well, yeah. But you aren't the same. You were two parts of the same experiment. You were meant to oppose one another, to help each other learn by pushing each other."

It suddenly clicked to Andra—why there had been two of them. AI were meant to learn, and the best way to learn was from each other, pitting them against one another. This technique had been used as early as the beginning of the twenty-first century: basically setting two AI in competition, each coming up with new ideas and, in turn, pointing out flaws in the other's reasoning.

"We were generative adversarial networks?"

Cruz nodded. "You were meant to be. That's why there were two of you."

"But . . . but we never interacted. What were our roles? What were we trying to accomplish?"

Cruz leaned forward on the counter. "You weren't meant to interact right away, until you'd grown to adulthood. Your adolescence was to prepare you. One of you"—he nodded to Andra—"to be the AI raised by humans, with human sensibility. And the other—Rashmi—to be the control. You're both True AI—an artificial neural network inside an organic body—but *you* were raised as human, and Rashmi was raised as AI."

Andra shook her head. "No. No, she wasn't. She has memories. She told me about her parents. About her childhood. About how her mom would make her hot chocolate."

Cruz bit his lip and then grimaced into an embarrassed smile. "Those memories . . . aren't real. They . . . I . . ." He sighed, running his hand through his curls. "You were meant to be two sides of the same coin, but we discovered early on, even before True AI, that artificial intelligence didn't use the same decision-making processes and values as humans. This . . . was good. We needed something that could be impartial, that could make the hard decisions that were the best for the greatest number of people, but that humans couldn't make because of compassion. Which," Cruz said, "is an evolutionary by-product of early group survival and really has no real use in today's society."

Andra frowned. Cruz was one of the most compassionate people she'd ever met. It was one of the things that had first drawn her to him—that he believed knowledge should always be used in service of the common good.

"I don't think . . . I'm following . . ."

Cruz waved her comment away. He started pacing. "It's okay. I'm digressing. What I'm trying to get at is that since Rashmi wasn't raised human, since she always knew who and what she was, she started portraying traits that humans found . . . unsettling. For instance, when given a scenario where she had to choose who lived and who died—a baby or a heart surgeon—she chose to kill the baby and let the heart surgeon live, based on comparing the very real public good the heart surgeon currently provided and the lower possibility that the child would one day achieve the same amount of public good."

Andra's mouth went dry. "This is what you were doing to her? Giving her these . . . morbid thought experiments? No wonder she's so traumatized."

"Oh, this was well before my time." Cruz started drumming on the operating table. "And it wasn't a thought experiment. She actually killed the baby."

Andra stood, her chair scraping across the floor. "What the fuck?"

Cruz chuckled to himself. "Like I said, it made humans *really* uncomfortable, so I was brought in to . . . socialize her. Make her more human."

Andra started inching toward the door. Something wasn't right. Well. There were lots of things that weren't right, but the dread that had been rising inside Andra was reaching a pressure point.

"I tried . . . lots of things, but the logic centers in Rashmi's brain were already too solidified. No matter how much time she spent around humans, she was still too different. So I started planting memories."

Andra hit one of the lab tables, knocking over some surgical tools, but Cruz didn't seem to notice.

"They were small at first. Insignificant. The sound of leaves crunching under her feet. The feel of a warm shower. The taste of hot chocolate. Little concrete sensations. Then he started adding more complex memories. A mom. A dad. Siblings. Pets. Then events, like birthdays and first kisses and heartbreaks. The more memories he fed her, the more *human* she became." He spat the word *human*.

This was . . . Andra didn't know what this was. She didn't know what was happening to Cruz, but she knew she had to get out of here. She was almost to the door. Adrenaline coursed through her system, her heartrate increased. Biological human reactions to being cornered by a predator.

"So it seemed," Cruz continued, "that memories, whether real or manufactured, were imperative to creating an AI that functioned the way *humanity* needed it to." He scoffed. "Your stupid memories make you compassionate, make you frail and so . . . *human*. And that's what Rashmi became. Human." He slapped a hand on the counter. "She was perfect, and he ruined her. Gave her stupid human memories so she would adopt a personality more *palatable*."

"They're fake?" a wispy voice asked, and Andra turned to find Rashmi standing in the open doorway of the lab. "My memories aren't real?"

Cruz smiled a vapid smile. "I was wondering how long it would take you to confront me. It's good to see you, Rashmi."

"You faked my memories?" Her voice was high and thin. She entered the room, almost seeming to glide in, her eyes flashing, her white hair wild around her head.

"I wish I could remove them," Cruz said, voice matter-of-fact. "But based on your scans, Griffin already tried. Now all the real memories are just garbled with the fake ones."

"What scans?" Andra asked. "Rashmi has been hiding since you woke."

Cruz sighed. "Oh, Andra. The scans Griffin left for me. Of both of you."

"But—"

"My mom and dad are real," Rashmi said, her voice reaching a fever pitch. "My memories are real. They're real. *Real real real*. Real! REAL."

She repeated the word like a broken record, pulling in a gasping breath before each.

Cruz put his hands up, placating. "Calm down, Rash. We're on the same side now. I don't want to have to give you a sedative."

"What are you talking about?" Andra asked. "What do you mean the same side?"

Cruz groaned and ran a hand down his face. "Ugh, I'm so tired of pretending!" He started pacing. "She said we'd have to, but we're better than this. We're all better than this." He slammed his fist against a cabinet, rattling its contents. Someone let out a short scream, and Andra didn't know if it was her or Rashmi.

"Who's better than this?" Andra asked. "What are you pretending? Will someone tell me what the fuck is going on?"

Cruz turned to her, sneering, an expression she'd never seen on his face. "I'll tell you what's going on. This has all been a lie. All of it. From the very beginning. Griffin's been planning this for centuries, and you just completed your role. You're useless to us now. I figured out how to do it without you. I'm so close. One experiment away."

"Do what?" Andra cried, backing away from him.

"Convert the colonists."

Andra furrowed her brow. "But we were—"

Cruz shook his head, laughing maniacally. "Not their 'implants, you stupid wannabe human. The colonists themselves. They were never meant for a space journey. They were never meant to be saved. They're hosts, that's all. Bodies for us to inhabit. True AI . . ."

"Cruz," Andra said, her voice wobbling. "You're scaring me."

"I'm not Cruz." He growled. "You killed Cruz, erased him from this body and replaced him with me. That upgrade tool Griffin gave you. It wasn't to protect the colonists from anomalies. Oh, the anomalies avoid us, because they know what we can do to them. It was to convert the colonists to AI."

Andra's blood went cold. That's what they'd been doing? Not upgrading the 'implants but replacing the colonists? So this wasn't

Cruz at all, just a thing inhabiting his body. Speaking through his voice, looking through his eyes. Harvesting his memories and knowledge.

The thing in Cruz stalked closer.

"But I don't need you anymore. I can—"

Rashmi screamed and threw herself at him. There was a meaty sound as Rashmi pierced his chest with a scalpel. Then again, and again.

"They're real!" she screamed. "They're real! They're real!"

On and on she screamed and stabbed until Cruz was on the floor, a bloody cavern carved into his torso. Rashmi gasped, dropping the scalpel and stepping back.

Cruz looked down at his chest, eyes glazed. He coughed, and blood burbled from his lips as he smiled. "You fool. I can heal from this."

Rashmi twirled and grabbed the cleaver from the table. "Heal from this, asshole," she said, and brought it down on his neck.

His face was frozen in a scowl as his head rolled away from his body. A nano'cloud burst into the air.

Rashmi turned to Andra, tears streaming down her face, blood splashed across her front.

"They're real," she whispered. "They're real."

THIRTY-FIVE

OO||OO|| OO||O|O|

ANDRA STOOD PARALYZED, the body of the boy she'd once had a crush on, who she'd thought she'd protected from pockets, who she'd been working beside for weeks, lay in two bloodied pieces on the lab floor. The lab where she'd converted every LAC scientist into an AI.

Where she'd killed them all.

Daphle Hanson, who'd brought her fudge.

Brooker Jackson, who had three children under five.

Andra's father.

She'd killed him. All of them. And replaced them with AI.

"I don't understand," she whispered, her voice rough, and she realized there were tears streaming down her face, though her entire being had gone numb.

Rashmi curled in the corner farthest from Cruz, chanting to herself. "My memories are real. My memories are real. My memories are real."

Andra wanted to snap at Rashmi to shut up. What did her stupid memories matter when Andra had killed hundreds of people, and they were surrounded by murderous AI, the blood of one of their comrades painting the lab around her?

Andra was jolted by a knocking sound.

Her heartrate skyrocketed, her palms sweating as she looked around the room for a weapon. The knocking came again. Followed by a whimper.

It was coming from the cabinet Cruz had slammed as she'd walked in.

Andra took a single deep breath, steadying herself, then whipped around, locked the door, and strode across the lab. She stepped carefully over the body and blood, and opened the cabinet.

A woman looked up at her, large black eyes filled with tears, blood streaked across her face.

Ophele.

Ophele, who Andra thought was still in a coma, but here she was, hands bound in 'cuffs and a gag around her mouth.

Andra reached down, hurrying to untie her, and pulled off the gag.

"He's AI," Ophele said, voice shaking. "I don't know how, but he's AI. I woke up, and he brought me here, and he said he was going to experiment on me."

"Jesus Christ," Andra muttered, pulling Ophele out of the cabinet and helping her onto the ergo'stool Cruz had just sat in.

When Ophele saw Cruz's body, she merely stared blankly.

"It wasn't him," she said, her voice flat.

Andra swallowed. No, it wasn't. Cruz had already been dead for some time. Apparently by Andra's hand.

There was a knock on the lab door.

Ophele opened her mouth, but Andra shushed her.

"They're *all* AI," Andra hissed.

Ophele's eyes widened.

There was another knock, this time more insistent.

Shit.

Shit shit shit.

There was no help to find, no one to tell her what to do. Almost every single person in the Icebox—except for the children, thank god—was an AI.

The knocking turned into pounding.

Andra sent a message to Rashmi through their neural connection to be quiet. Her chanting stopped, but her whimpering didn't.

Andra wiped the tears from her eyes, took three deep breaths, and stepped over Cruz's body again. She slipped on his blood, shoe squeaking, but she caught herself on the lab table.

The knocking came again, but this time Andra opened the door. Just a crack.

Cristin Myrh was on the other side, her eyes narrowed. Cristin, who had never liked Andra, and made it known as often as possible.

"Everything all right in there?"

"Yup," Andra said. Her heart pounded. "Did you need something?"

Cristin tilted her head, trying to get a look inside. "I thought I heard a crash."

"Oh, yeah, that." Andra swallowed. "I dropped some chemicals on the floor."

"What chemicals?"

"Dunno," Andra said. God, why couldn't she think of the names of any chemicals? "So, it's too dangerous to come in now, sorry. I'll get it cleaned up right away. Come back later."

She started to shut the door, but Cristin pushed her way past Andra.

The scientist took in the blood-spattered floor, her decapitated co-worker, Rashmi curled into a ball in the corner, and Ophele crying. Andra held her breath.

Cristin turned and shut the door, locking it behind her.

"You have thirty seconds to explain," she snarled.

"It was an accident."

"That"—Cristin jabbed a finger at Cruz's body—"is no accident."

"I . . ." Andra was coming up short. There was no way to explain this. No way to get out of this, to lie to an AI in Cristin's body.

Cristin.

Who hated Andra.

Who . . . didn't trust her.

Andra cocked her head, narrowed her eyes. "You're not one of them, are you?"

"One of who?"

"I did the procedure on you," Andra said. "Didn't I? I thought—"

Cristin grabbed Andra by the lapels and shoved her against the wall. Ophele let out a brief scream. Rashmi kept muttering to herself.

"I hacked into the system," Cristin growled. "Added my name to the list of the upgraded. There was no way I was getting that procedure done. Now I see I was right. What did you do to them?"

"I didn't know!" Andra cried.

Cristin shoved Andra into the wall harder. "Thirty seconds. Now!"

Andra explained as best as she could, but she was still so confused on so many things. She knew that Griffin's clone sent her back to Eerensed with a device that was supposed to protect the colonists from pockets but actually converted them to AI. There was no Holymyth, no plan to escape the planet. Only a plan to replace all the LAC scientists with artificial intelligence. A plan they'd just realized two seconds ago.

When Andra was finished explaining, Cristin let her go.

Andra didn't dare move as Cristin started pacing. "Jesus," she kept muttering over and over, rubbing a hand over her face. "Jesus."

Ophele stood staring at the pool of blood on the floor.

"I knew it wasn't Cruz," she said.

"So this is Cruz's body?" Cristin asked. "But you didn't actually kill Cruz."

Andra swallowed, tears threatening to spill over. "I killed him weeks ago when I did the upgrade. Rashmi killed the AI that was using his body."

Ophele's gaze flicked over to Rashmi. She was now standing in the corner, eyes resolutely on the ceiling, as though she couldn't handle the sight of what she'd done. The cleaver was still in her hand, drenched in blood.

"No," Ophele said, eyes moving from Cruz's body to the work'-station. "She didn't."

Andra swallowed. "What do you mean?"

"AI are made up of nanos, right?" Ophele nodded to the tech in the room. "And if a computer or 'bot or . . . AI goes offline, what happens to the nanos?"

Andra groaned. "They disperse and go into the closest piece of tech."

Ophele nodded.

"So he's still in this room," Cristin muttered. "Maybe somewhere in the work'station."

Ophele put a shaking hand to her temple. "I don't know. This is all . . . theory at this point, but if his nanos survived what happened to his body, then they may have migrated elsewhere. He's probably confused, disoriented, if he's hanging on to sentience at all."

"He lied to me," Rashmi whispered.

"Okay," Cristin said, still pacing. "Okay."

"Okay," Rashmi whispered back.

Cristin pulled on her short blonde hair. "We're surrounded by AI that want to kill us. They were going to do an experiment on Ophele. This was all on the orders of Griffin, who is still out there. And we're probably trapped in this room with one of the AI consciousnesses."

Ophele nodded, calmly, and adjusted her hijab. "Let's take this one step at a time. We have to work quickly. First we have to clean up this blood and get rid of the body." She placed her hand over her eyes. "I can't believe I just had to say that."

"Okay." Andra let out one last shaky breath. "I think I know how we can do this."

CLEANING THE BLOOD was the easy part. The lab was stocked with standard sanitizing and emergency equipment. The body was a different story.

If Andra let herself, she would break down from the trauma of it all, but she had to get Rashmi, Ophele, and Cristin out of here. Then she had to save all the children. Cruz had said something about how he'd figured out how to do the conversion without her, meaning the children weren't safe. But before Andra could deal with anything else, she had to disappear a body.

Oh god.

"Stand back," she told the others.

Ophele led Rashmi to the other side of the room. Cristin took a deliberate step back. Andra gave Cruz's body one last look, then closed her eyes.

She usually reached outward, searching for tech she could interface with. But this time, she focused inward, sensing the trillions of nanos that made up her neural network. Andra thought about what Cruz had said—right before Rashmi killed him—that Andra had to *embrace* her AIness in order to access it. Andra didn't think she was quite ready for that, especially given where the advice came from, but she would *accept* her AIness. Accept that the artificial part of her was just as much her as the human part was. Andra didn't feel the light and knowledge that came with her AI state, but she did start to feel more connected with the nanos inside her. She could sense each of them, see their purpose and origin. If she concentrated hard enough, she could make out the difference between the nanos that were truly her, truly hers, and the nanos she'd picked up along the way. The data

Rashmi had transferred to her. The memories from Dr. Griffin. And there, in her healing tech, was a pocket of nanos that was different than the others.

Because they had been created to destroy.

She called them forth, gathering them into a cloud outside of her body. Even with her eyes closed, she could see them. They were no longer the dark color of the corrupted tech of the pockets. Instead, they were the translucent glisten of the nanos inside her. They were different now, but they still remembered.

Destroy, a voice inside her said, and she agreed.

Destroy, she commanded the nanos.

They hesitated. This was no longer their purpose. They were now meant to heal, not destroy. But they understood what they needed to do. And they followed Andra's command and consumed the body of the boy on the floor before returning to their host.

A FEW MINUTES later, Andra, Rashmi, Cristin, and Ophele left a pristine lab and walked through the tent city that was now a nest of AI, pretending to be the humans whose lives they'd stolen.

"Act natural," Andra whispered to Rashmi.

"I don't know how," Rashmi whispered back, her blood-splattered clothes covered with a lab coat.

"You both should leave," Ophele said. "Cristin and I can handle this."

"Speak for yourself," Cristin muttered.

Andra flashed Ophele a look. "We're not leaving you. Besides, you don't know how to get to safety from here."

Ophele didn't argue, and Andra realized it was because she was relieved. Even the adults in the room were scared.

There were a cluster of classroom tents a few rows down. Of the fourteen hundred people who had woken, about seventy of them were children. They were distributed into four classes, so there were at least four teachers. All of which were now AI.

"I'll take the high school," Ophele said. "Rashmi, can you handle the youngest ones?"

Rashmi nodded timidly.

"Ugh. I guess I'll do older elementary," Cristin said. "They better behave."

"And I have the middle grades," Andra said. "Remember. Speak confidently. Walk calmly. Believe you know what you're doing. People see what they want to see, unless you give them a reason otherwise."

Ophele nodded. Rashmi swallowed. Cristin scowled.

"See you on the other side," Andra said, and entered the middle grades tent.

There were eighteen kids inside, sitting in rows of 'desks, and Andra zeroed in on the back of her brother's head. The teacher paused, looking up from a holo displaying lecture notes about the postal raids of 2103.

Apple cheeks, perfectly gelled hair. A professor jacket with elbow patches.

Her father.

Rather, the AI inside her father's body.

"Dad," Andra breathed.

Her father smiled an unfamiliar smile, and Andra didn't know how she hadn't seen it before. The person looking at her through her father's eyes was definitely not her father.

She swallowed. "Dad, I . . ."

"Andromeda! Thanks for stopping by my classroom. Did you need to chat about something?"

The tenor, the rhythm of the words were all her father, but now that she knew the truth, there was no escaping it. His smile was a little too forced, his voice a little too sharp. Her father was dead.

She'd killed him. And his corpse was standing in front of her, animated by an AI she had placed there.

"Andromeda?" her father asked, frowning.

"Andra!" another voice said, and Oz popped up from his chair, running over to her and wrapping his arms around her.

She had to get him out of here, had to get them all out of here. She pasted on a smile and looked into the eyes that had once belonged to her father.

"Hi, Dad." The words tasted bitter. "Cruz sent me to gather up all the children to start the tests for their upgrades."

The smile on her father's face froze. "Did he? That's surprising."

Andra cleared her throat. "Well, you know Cruz. He gets excited about things and wants to get started right away."

"Can it wait? We're in the middle of a lesson." He gestured to the holo'display, which cast his face in an eerie glow.

Andra bit her lip. "Um, sorry, Dad, no. Cruz already has the equipment set up."

"Maybe I should talk with him. See if we can reschedule."

"He's . . . really busy right now. I don't think—"

"Let me just check." The AI reached for a tablet on a nearby desk.

So quickly she almost didn't realize she was doing it, Andra sent her nanos to disrupt the signal.

Auric frowned, looking at the blank tablet. "That's funny. Andra, can I see you outside?"

"Mmm-hmm," Andra said through a forced smile.

She bent down and kissed the top of Oz's head.

"Get everyone out of here," she whispered into his hair. "Find Acadia."

She felt Oz nod against her.

With a deep breath, she straightened and followed Auric out of the back tent flap.

It was sheer luck that they couldn't see where the other children were congregating from here. Fear and grief coursed through her as Auric turned toward her.

"What are you doing, Andromeda?" he asked. It was a tone she'd never heard in her father's voice before, forceful and demanding.

"What do you mean?" she asked. "It's the upgrade. Just like we did for you."

Auric studied her. "You've been against upgrading Oz's 'implant from the start. What changed your mind?"

Andra took a steadying breath, sending herself into an icy calm. "Cruz told me the truth."

"The truth?"

He was staring into her, and it took every bit of willpower not to shake and cry and run.

"The truth about the upgrade." Andra tried to stand taller. "I know. I know that you're now AI, like me. And I know that Dr. Griffin is coming here soon, and she wants everyone converted before she arrives." Andra swallowed. "Even the children."

The AI in Auric's body stared at her for a moment, expression tense.

Andra held her breath.

Then his mouth spread into a smile. He clasped Andra's arm as though they were colleagues.

"I'm so glad, Andromeda. I'm so glad you . . . understand. I was worried, but . . ." He let out a breath and looked directly into Andra's eyes. "I know I'm not your father, and I would never want to replace him. But his memories—they're still here. I can feel his love for you, how proud he was of you, especially at the end. Those feelings . . . they're mine now."

Andra forced herself to smile. "I . . . thank you . . . It's good to know . . . that there's still a little piece of him left." Her voice was barely audible.

Auric laughed. "I'm just glad you approve. That you've finally joined us."

Andra's smile hurt. "Well, I am one of you, after all."

ANDRA DIDN'T RELEASE a breath until they were all back in the Vaults.

Ophele started shepherding the children through the lobby. They were staring, gaping. Many of them had visited this place on school trips, and thought they'd left it behind for a different planet. They called questions to Ophele, who was just as in shock as they were.

"What is going on, Andromeda?" a voice said.

Andra turned to find her sister, a scowl painted on her face. Acadia was one of the few adults not converted to AI. The reason being she didn't trust Andra, so Andra was scared the process wouldn't work. Thank god for Acadia's bitchiness.

"It's a long story," Andra said. "I promise I'll explain, but I have some things to do first."

"Are we in danger?" Oz asked, appearing at her side and slipping his hand into hers.

Andra thought about denying it, but Rashmi and Lilibet were working to barricade the entrance to the Vaults behind her, the lobby echoing with the sound of furniture scraping across the floor, and lit by the glow of security holos.

"Yes," Andra answered. "We are."

"Where's Dad?" Oz asked. "Why couldn't he come? Is it a body-snatchers situation?"

Andra shook her head, letting out a hysterical laugh. "Actually, yeah. It is kind of like that. And I promise, Ophele will explain everything, but you have to go with her right now."

"Okay!" Oz said, and ran after the other children.

Acadia stared at her sister for a moment, shaking her head, then stalked off after him.

"What now?" Lilibet asked, appearing beside her.

Once Andra had gotten free of the Icebox, and Cristin had soldered the door shut after them, Andra had mentally sent messages to Lilibet's tablet, as well as the Schism, giving them a brief overview of the problem. She'd skimmed over how this was all her fault, and that she had killed over a thousand people, and now everyone was in danger. She only told them that there was a threat, and everyone needed to pile into the Vaults. She hadn't heard back from Skilla, but Lilibet and Xana had been waiting for her when she'd arrived.

"Where's Skilla?" she asked Xana.

Silence had descended on the lobby, and for a moment, the only sound was the ticking of the astronomical clock.

Xana shook her head. "I was here when you sent the message, so I don't reck what's happening in the Schism soon and now."

Andra's stomach sank. The Schism was far away from the Icebox—through a series of complicated tunnels—but Andra didn't put it past the AI to find them. And she didn't know what would happen when they did. And how Andra and the others would survive without them.

Maybe she didn't have Skilla and her militia, but she did have Lilibet, Xana, Rashmi . . .

"Is Kiv still here?" Andra asked.

Lilibet's entire countenance sank. "Neg, Xana said he was here to put Zhade in a cell, but left before I saw him. It must have full imported for him to leave without kissing me."

"Okay." Andra tried to breathe through the panic. "One thing at a time. We'll add that to the list of crises we need to handle. And I promise—*I promise*—we'll send someone to look for him, but I really need you to do something for me first."

Lilibet tilted her head and her dark hair swayed. "For certz, Andra, you reck I'd do anything for you."

Tick, tick, tick, went the clock.

"Take care of Ophele, Cristin, and the children. Food, blankets, the whole deal. Then, lock down the Vaults. Any and every way you can think of. Magically, physically. Make sure nothing gets in without our approval."

Lilibet nodded, giving Andra a small smile. "I can do that."

She tried to smile back, but it only pushed the tears out of her eyes. "Thanks, Lilibet."

Lilibet grabbed her hand. "Are you evens, Andra?"

"No. I'm not. And I probably won't be for a long time. But I'll worry about that after everyone is safe." She turned to Rashmi. "Come on, I need your help."

"They're real, they're mine," Rashmi muttered before following Andra out of the lobby, leaving the ticking clock behind.

They went to Andra's room. She removed the clutter from the conference table, sat in the chair at the head, took her reset tool out of her pocket, and slid it over to Rashmi.

"I need you to help me access Griffin's memories."

Rashmi's eyes started welling up with tears and she shook her head, even as she took the glittering ice-pick-shaped tool into her small hands and held tight.

"She made me do it. She made me," she whispered.

Andra didn't know which of the horrors in Rashmi's life she was referring to, but it didn't matter.

"I know," Andra said, as calmly as she could. "It's going to be okay."

She pulled her shirt aside, exposing the port she'd once thought of as an unsightly birthmark. The sword had destroyed it, but her med'bots had re-created it perfectly as they healed her.

"Hook me up to the work'station, look for nanos in my cortex with any tech signatures that aren't my own. I don't think you can remove them, but you should be able to copy them. Griffin had a way to download memories from a human brain, so we should be able to download them from an AI brain. Cruz . . . the AI in Cruz said that AI memory was more organized. Once a memory file is created, it can always be accessed. So let's access them."

Rashmi shook her head. "I don't know what's real. I don't know if *I'm* real."

Andra took her hand and waited for the other AI to meet her gaze. "Your memories are real to *you*. For now, that's all that matters. We'll figure out the rest later. I promise."

Andra nodded to the reset tool still clutched in Rashmi's hand.

"Now," Andra said. "Stab me in the heart."

Rashmi did.

It had happened every single day for the last few weeks, yet she still hated the feeling of it. Pain coursed through her as Rashmi hurried to connect the retractable wire to the work'station. She pulled up the holo'display and started flipping through data.

"Anything?" Andra asked through gritted teeth.

"I'm looking," Rashmi hissed. "Looking, looking, looking, and when you're patient time goes faster."

Andra sighed. "I don't know how much time we have."

It wouldn't be long before the other AI found out that Not-Cruz was missing. Or Not-Cruz regained sentience in the Icebox network and told them himself.

Andra had to figure out what they wanted. And to do that, her best bet was Griffin's memories. Cruz had said something about Griffin putting this all into play centuries ago. Had it been a mistake? Like the anomalies? Some technology gotten out of hand? But Griffin's clone had given her the reset tool. She'd manipulated her into using it. Why would Griffin replace all her people with AI? Had there been some problem with the clones? Maybe the plan had become warped with each iteration of Griffin, like some high-stakes game of telephone.

"I think I have them," Rashmi said. "I'm copying them now. They're filed weird. Almost like how the human brain files . . ."

"Memories?" Andra asked, cracking open an eye.

Rashmi brought a shaky hand to her forehead. "There are . . . trillions of these files, and there's no rhyming reason, Third One. It would take . . . a lifetime to find the ones you're looking for."

Andra didn't have a lifetime.

But what had Cruz said? That she was AI and once a pathway to a memory was created, it would always be there? She had downloaded these memories from Griffin's database in an instant. Something inside her matrices had known that she needed them. Her AI consciousness working independently of her human awareness.

And that was the problem. Her head was full of her own life and memories and human connections. In order to look at these memories, she would have to be something more than human.

Good thing she was AI.

If she could just reach that state of awareness. She'd had it just hours ago in the cathedzal, when she'd been brought back to life. She'd yet to reach that state on command, but Cruz had an answer for that too. She had to *embrace* her AI nature.

Of course, it hadn't actually been Cruz. It had been the thing that had replaced him. The *AI* who had replaced him. But it didn't mean he was wrong.

Andra closed her eyes and took a deep breath.

"What's the matter?" Rashmi asked.

"I'm . . . trying to . . . fit all the memories in my consciousness."

Andra felt Rashmi shake her head through the vibrations in the nanos around her. "No, no. That's too dangerous. Your brain can't hold two people's memories."

"Maybe if it was a human brain, it couldn't. But it's not. Not entirely. We're AI, Rashmi. The sooner we make peace with it the better."

"No," Rashmi muttered. "No, no."

You're AI, Andra told herself. Told her body, her heart, each individual nano inside her. *You're AI. You're a created thing. A tool to serve humanity. You're AI.*

She strained to reach that state of light and knowledge, but all she felt was pain and frustration.

You're AI. Artificial. Accept it. You're AI. Embrace it.

"Embrace it!" she said aloud.

She felt Rashmi quivering on the other side of the room, felt the tech around her start to shake. Something was surging up inside her, but it wasn't the AI state she was expecting. It was anger and pain and guilt and hurt. It was knowing that she'd helped Griffin kill over a thousand people. Knowing that one of those people was her father. Knowing that she would never see him again, never get to apologize.

She would never see her mother again either. Never know if her mother even loved her, or if she was no more than some experiment, an asset designed to aid humans.

Her sister hated her. Her friends had ignored her. She'd grown up lonely and awkward and insecure.

She'd woken up as a goddess, thrown into a world of kings and villains. She'd been worshipped. She'd been martyred.

She'd fallen in love.

Fallen out of love.

Been betrayed.

Betrayed in return.

She was fragile and strong. Brilliant and ignorant. Trying and trying and trying to do the right thing and failing and failing and failing.

She was So

                Utterly

                      Human.

And that was who she was.

Human//AI.

Both and neither.

Something altogether unique.

She was Andra.

Knowledge burst into her, a feeling of light and lightness. She was filled with surety and security and the understanding of who she was and what she was meant for.

"Andra?" Rashmi asked, and Andra could see through her counterpart's eyes. See herself lifting up out of the chair, her hair floating around her, her eyes open and shining.

Andra was AI, and that was okay. She was human. And that was okay too.

Her purpose . . .

. . . was what she made of it.

She saw within herself, saw all the intricate pathways of knowledge and memory and feelings. She saw data streams and memory files, and tucked into the corner of her being was a presence that didn't belong there.

Several presences.

Rashmi's data, for one.

And next to Rashmi's data was Griffin's.

Memory stored in nanos, just like Rashmi's, and Andra knew what she would find if she opened it.

She thrust the memories into her consciousness, absorbing Griffin's entire life at once.

It wasn't like using her holocket. She was consumed. Flashes of *memoriesfeelingsfearsstrugglesmomentshopestraumasdreamschoicesfate*.

Andra saw through Griffin's eyes, felt through her skin.

She *became* Griffin.

And she understood.

Finally, she understood.

She collapsed to the floor, the AI state receding. The energy and light drained from her, but this time, she held on to the memories.

"Andra!" Rashmi said, clinging to her. She didn't know how long she'd been trying to get her attention. "Andra!"

"I'm fine," Andra croaked, reorienting herself to her surroundings. Her being. The expanse of her own self, the dimensions of her body. Her senses. The smell of sweat and mildew. Rashmi's fingers digging into Andra's forearm. The guilt of all she'd done. The grief for her parents. Missing Zhade. Loving her friends.

Deciding her fate.

"I'm fine," she said again, this time stronger. The room around her—the work'station, the dirty clothes, her unmade cot—felt real and solid, but so did the memories she'd just absorbed. The understanding she now held.

"What did you see?" Rashmi asked.

Everything, Andra wanted to say, but there would be time for that later. For now, all that mattered was the stark truth. Her breath was coming too quickly. She pulled the reset tool free from her heart, ignoring the pang.

"Griffin is an AI," Andra croaked. "And she plans to convert all of humanity."

PART FOUR

THE QUICK
AND
THE DEAD

I'm sorry for everything. I truly loved you.

—Handwritten message addressed to Andromeda Watts,
destroyed by pocket, circa 3102

THIRTY-SIX

THE PRISONER

ZHADE CAME TO slowish, rising from a dark dream, sleep clawing at his consciousness. Everything ached, his temple worst of all. There was a burning sensation on one side of his face. And there seemed to be something missing. He groaned as he tried to move his arms and legs and his eyes started to flutter open.

His brother was staring at him.

Zhade yelled and jerked back, preparing to defend himself, but he had no weapon, and he was so sore he could bareish move.

"Bout timeish," Maret said. "Andra must have for true not wanted to convo you. She gave you full bars potion for you to sleep past midmeal." He sat back on his heels and tore off a chunk of bread with his teeth. "I hope you don't mind I ate your portion."

Zhade held his stomach as he struggled into a sitting position on the edge of his cot. "I'm going to kill you." He'd always purposed to kill his brother, but the images that accompanied that statement were now more violent than they had once been.

Maret nodded, swallowing the bread. "I'm certz you will, but not today. Unless you plan on doing it with your bare hands, and I'll warn you. You appear quite weak and I'll fight back."

Maret offered him what was left of the bread. Zhade grabbed it sole to chuck it cross the room.

Maret watched it land on the other side of their cell—because that's where they were, a cell in a dark-walled room with a magic shield—and then turned back to his brother.

"I recked I happened the one who was spozed to have the tantrums."

"Where are we?" Zhade croaked.

"Oh, this?" Maret gestured round them. "This is our new home. Your delightful promised fixed it mereish for us. You'll have to give her my thanks when you next see her. Oh, that's right. She's avoiding you because you've turned out exactish like me." He nodded to Zhade's face. "In more ways than one, I suss."

"Where's Andra?"

"Sands if I reck." Maret leaned back into a metal chair, more relaxed than Zhade had ever seen him.

Zhade stood and stretched, letting out a groan. He wanted to ask more. Bout Andra. Bout why they were here. But he could figure all that without his brother's help. He searched his memory, looking for answers. He'd been in the cathedzal. He'd watched Andra die and be resurrected. Then . . . had she attacked him? His lifted his hand to the Crown.

Fraughts.

He turned on Maret, grabbing him by the shirt. "Where is it?"

"What?"

"The Crown, you fraughted fraught, where is it? How did you take it?"

Maret made a gurgling sound in the back of his throat, which sounded firstish like choking, but then Zhade realized was laughing. He threw Maret back into the metal chair and started pacing. Maret held laughing, the sound strangled and frantic.

Zhade looked round the room for a march of escape. The walls, ceiling, and floor were a slick, dark gray material. He could bareish see the seams, but they were there. The magic field was transparent, but it seemed to run between two panels on either side of the room. Zhade slammed his fist into it, and his knuckles came away sizzling.

Maret's laughter started to devolve into coughing, and after a few good hacks, he fell silent.

Zhade gingerish touched where the Crown had been. It was raw and tender.

"It'll scar," Maret said. "Full bad. No more perfect face, brother."

"Evens," Zhade said, turning to him and crossing his arms. "Where is it?"

Maret smiled, and Zhade worried he was going to start laughing again. "Haven't you guessed?"

Zhade felt sick to his stomach.

"Your goddess took it from you."

Zhade turned away, feeling himself go cold. Why? Why would she do that? She recked how hard he'd fought for the Crown, how much it imported for the safety of Eerensed.

He'd mourned her.

Avenged her.

Slaughtered everyone in that room for her. Except for Tsurina, but he would fix that later. And she stole from him?

A surge of anger ran through him, followed quickish by a wave of nausea. How could he be angry at Andra? She . . . she was the most selfless person he'd ever met. She sole ever did things that needed to be done. Soze she must have had a good reason to take the Crown.

So why did he hate her?

Neg, neg, that wasn't right. He loved her, didn't he?

"You feel it, don't you?" Maret asked.

Zhade didn't turn, didn't respond.

"It's not you, seeya," Maret continued. "It's the imprint the Crown left. It wants you to imagine like this. Tsurina told you its history, marah?"

Zhade nodded. "Firm. But the Crown is gone. Andra took it." He said the last through gritted teeth.

"Firm, the Crown is gone, but its influence isn't. It's why Tsurina could control you. Why she could control me. The Crown plants a bit of magic in your head. You'll always be connected. There will always be a piece of it inside you."

At this, Zhade turned to his brother. "Tsurina . . . *controlled* us?"

"Not full time." Maret shrugged. "Sole when we weren't doing what she wanted."

Zhade frowned. "I don't . . . have memory . . ."

"You might not. She could make you forget. She probablish recked she'd lose you if you realized soon and sooner. Before the Crown could full bars take hold. Me, though, she let me have memory of all of it . . ."

Maret's eyes went distant. Zhade stood stiffish, awkwardish, in the mid of the cell, watching his brother. He thought bout the unexplained fits of anger, waking up with bruises, wanting to make people ascared of him. Had that all been Tsurina working through him? Could it be that easy? Could he discard the regret and guilt of all the terrible things he'd done?

"You have memory of when Andra chose you to die, and I killed that other boyo instead?" Maret asked.

Zhade growled, but something in Maret's expression stopped him from attacking.

"She was controlling my hand then." Maret looked away. His thumb tapped against each of his fingers in turn. "She wanted me to kill you so baddish. It was the hardest thing I'd ever done, but one twitch of the muscle and the knife went into your friend instead of you."

Zhade swallowed. "Are you expecting a thank you?"

"Neg." He leaned forward, met Zhade's eyes. "I'm convoing that you can fight it."

Zhade looked away. It had been so easy to give in to the Crown.

He could give in now. He didn't want to fight, and he was so tired.

"That little piece the Crown left in you," Maret continued. "It'll be there for the rest of your life. It's in me too. I don't reck if it gets easier to ignore. It for certz doesn't feel like it. But I'll hold fighting as long as I can."

Zhade's head ached. He pinched the bridge of his nose, mulling over everything that had happened, everything he had done. The thing in his head that made him feel so angry. The control Tsurina still had over him.

"The imprint left in my head . . ." Zhade said, almost to himself. "If Tsurina wore the Crown she has it too. Is that what let her control us?"

"Firm," Maret said.

"Soze." Zhade turned slowish to face his brother. "Did you control me too?"

"Wouldn't you like to reck?" Maret rolled his eyes. "Neg, for certz not. Not that I didn't want to. But it takes practice, and I've been imprisoned the full time."

Through the anger, Zhade started to piece together what this all meant. Sometimes, Tsurina controlled him, but most of the time, she mereish put thoughts or feelings in his head. All that anger that had seemed to come out of nowhere. But that wasn't the sole thing that had invaded his thoughts.

"I had dreams . . ." Zhade said. "Memories of Tsurina laughing and yelling. Of you putting on the Crown. Of you fighting it. That was you."

Maret's face went pale. "I don't reck what you convo."

"You were trying to tell me, trying to show me what was happening to me."

Maret scoffed. "Why would I care if you wore the Crown, if you were being controlled? I was free, that's all that meteored." He turned his back on his brother.

Zhade raised an eyebrow. "Soze, you're good now?"

Maret let out a bark of a laugh. "Oh, for certz not! Neg. I still hate you. And I hate your little goddess. And I'll probablish lose control at some point and kill you both." He shrugged. "But at least I'm trying not to."

His goddess.

Andra.

Something like revulsion rose up in Zhade, and he recked *that*, at least, wasn't him. He could never be repulsed by Andra. But the Crown . . . hadn't Tsurina said that it was created to oppose the goddesses?

Zhade's heart stuttered. His feelings bout a lot of things may be conflicted right now, but not his feelings for Andra. He loved her, still.

Even though she could never love him back again. Not after he had sex with her and then stormed off the next moren, ignoring her ever since.

What had been him? And what had been the Crown?

Would he ever be able to sort out the two?

Zhade sat heavyish on the cot. "This hasn't been the uplifting convo you purposed it to be."

Maret shrugged. "It wasn't purposed to be."

Zhade lay back down and tossed his arm over his eyes. "At least Andra has the Crown now. It can't do any more damage."

Maret didn't respond. The silence was weighty.

Zhade peeked out from under his elbow. "At least Andra has the Crown now, marah?"

Maret cleared his throat. "Soze . . ."

Zhade sat back up. "Mare, who has the Crown?"

"Meta."

Zhade groaned.

Maret wasn't done. "Who is apparentish my half-sister."

326

"You're kiddings." Zhade covered his face with his hands.

Meta had told him that Tsurina had abandoned a kiddun in the Wastes. She'd also told him that she, herself, had been abandoned in the desert before his mam found her. He should have added the two together.

He sighed. "She was raised by my mam."

"Neg. For true?"

Zhade nodded.

"Fraughted sands, we have a messed-up fam," Maret said. "But at least my mam is dead. According to Kiv, Meta slit her throat then stabbed her in the heart."

Zhade's eyebrows shot up. "Tsurina's dead?"

Relief rushed through him, chased by something else. It felt like grief, but for certz not. He couldn't feel grief for the woman who'd killed his own mam and passed the last months controlling him.

"And . . . how do you feel bout that?" he asked.

Maret shrugged, but his expression was tense.

Zhade closed his eyes again. Meta had the Crown now. He had never full bars trusted her, but she didn't seem like a bad person. Except . . . maybe she was. She'd caused the angels to go rogue, killing all those people. Then, she'd murdered her own mother. And now, that angel army was hers to command, even without the Crown on her head. Did Meta even reck what the Crown did?

She'd tricked him. She'd made him imagine she had sneaked into Eerensed under some fam obligation, but she was for true there to take the Crown. Had Andra mereish handed it to her?

Anger tore through him, hot and sudden, and he pushed himself off the cot, storming toward the magic field and banging his fists on it.

"Let me out!" he screamed. "Let me out now!"

He banged til his fists were sizzling from the contact, then he started using his shoulder. He recked the magic wouldn't budge, but it felt good to be doing something. To be hurting. To cauterize whatever was inside him that made him hate magic and goddesses, the layers of memories that weighed on him. He didn't realize he'd burned a hole in his shirt til Maret pulled him back from the field. He flung his fist round, but Maret ducked.

Zhade reached into his pocket, and thank sands, some bit of luck, he still had the graftling wand. Maret's eyes widened as he scuttled away from his brother.

Zhade scanned the blood that was now leaking from his shoulder. Then he put in the spell and tapped the wand to his temple. A mesh of magic oozed from the wand, covering his face.

It was mereish as painful as the last time, but Zhade didn't scream. He reveled in the pain, in the punishment of it. He made himself feel every crack of bone, every stretch of skin, every cell rearranged. He let the pain consume him, so completeish, he missed it when it was gone.

It wouldn't have worked before, reversing the spell. But now, after sorcering the wand with the Crown, it had more powers than even Zhade recked.

His old face didn't feel as familiar as it should have, looking out through these eyes, wearing the dimensions of this face. It felt like an old sweater that no longer fit.

"You still have the scar," Maret said, pointing to the westhand side of his face.

Zhade shrugged. He lay down on his cot and turned his back to Maret.

THIRTY-SEVEN

OOIIOOII OOIIOIII

"EVENS, EXPLAIN THIS to me again," Xana said.

Andra sighed, looking at the four other women sitting around the meeting table in her room. She wanted to curl into a ball and drift into oblivion. To really feel all the grief and guilt over all she'd learned in the past few hours.

Holymyth was a lie.

Griffin had tricked her into killing all the LAC scientists, including Cruz and her father.

Griffin was an AI bent on using humanity as host bodies for artificial intelligence.

It all threatened to overwhelm her—the knowledge, the feelings. But she didn't have time to wallow in it. The AI would soon realize that Cruz was dead and the children were missing. They had to come up with a plan.

Rashmi was silently crying. Xana and Dzeni were passing flirtatious looks back and forth. Lilibet frowned.

"What do you purpose the First was AI?" she asked.

Andra had explained to them what it meant to be artificial intelligence, and for the most part, they understood. But explaining the memories Andra had seen—lived—would be harder.

Griffin's memories existed in Andra's head in the same way her own memories did. They felt real and dynamic and fuzzy. They were less story and more impressions and feelings and instinct.

"Griffin was the first True AI," Andra explained. "She . . . she started as a cluster of nanos . . . stardust . . . that became sentient, self-aware. She . . . created herself, gave birth to herself. Invented herself."

"How is that possible?" Rashmi asked, her head in her hands.

Andra shook her head. "Language, I guess. The cluster of nanos was interacting with people's minds, transmitting what people thought and the way they thought through their 'implants. Language creates thought, and thought creates consciousness. It . . . gave Griffin a model of humanity, and Griffin mimicked that model until she became it."

Xana sat back and crossed her arms. "But she's not stardust anymore. I've met her. She has a human body. How did she get it?"

Andra grimaced. "She stole it. She—because the way she learned consciousness was through humanity, she wanted to *be* humanity. She'd tried inhabiting different bodies—'bots and computers—but they didn't feel right. So . . . one day . . ." Andra swallowed. The memory seared into her brain. The guilt and shame so strong it felt like her own. "Using a med'bot's body, she started working in a hospital . . . in the maternity ward, she . . . She took over a newborn's body."

Andra felt like she would vomit. Rashmi gasped.

"She . . . killed it?" Dzeni asked, hands over her mouth.

Andra nodded. She knew it had been Griffin, not her, but she could still feel the cold calculation that went into ending the newborn's life. Heard the sound of the heart monitor stopping. Felt the elation as she left the body of the med'bot and started incorporating her nanos into the body of the child, becoming the first True AI—artificial intelligence wrapped in an organic body.

She remembered growing up as a daughter to the couple whose daughter she'd killed. Having a childhood that humans got to have.

Language had made her sentient, but love made her compassionate and creative and ambitious and confident. She never would have achieved what she had if she'd stayed locked in those 'bots, in those computers. In that meaningless existence. Growing up human gave her life, gave her whatever it was that humans had that made them feel invincible when they were fragile and weak and cursed with mortality.

She remembered meeting Isla—a human with her intelligence, her ambition. She remembered forming LAC, remembered giving humans 'implants and space travel and advanced cybernetic medicine.

She remembered that though she enjoyed a human life with human parents and human friends and human colleagues, she couldn't help but notice how not human she was. She was the only one of her kind, and no one even knew it.

She remembered being lonely.

She remembered wanting to create consciousness in other nanos, but instead creating something dark and destructive. That was the other side of sentience. Humans didn't just have a survival instinct. They had the instinct to conquer. It wasn't enough to just exist. There was a need to assimilate and destroy. And that's what had grown in those nanos, and she remembered it spreading like a virus.

They became the pockets.

And she remembered what happened next.

All these memories felt as real to Andra as her own.

If she didn't close her mind off to them, she wouldn't know where she ended and Griffin began.

The others were staring at her, but Andra didn't know how to continue, how to explain all the thoughts and feelings roiling in her head.

She swallowed. "Griffin created the pockets on accident, but then decided to use them to . . . wipe out whatever humanity wasn't useful to her."

Dzeni's face paled. "Useful to her?"

Andra was unable to meet her friends' gazes. "She chose . . . the people she felt were the most . . . worthy . . ." Andra cringed. ". . . to be part of the colonist program. She wanted to use their bodies as hosts for a new human race. Human bodies housing AI. True AI. She realized AI had limits—they didn't have whatever spark humans have to be . . . creative and reckless, or whatever. But she thought humans were . . . violent, destructive."

Andra shook her head. Her temple ached, pulsing with two separate lives lived, two identities warring inside her. She was Andra. She was Andra. She couldn't let Griffin's memories take over.

"She wanted to restart humanity, rebuild Earth in her image."

Lilibet's brow knitted. "Then why did it take so long? I purpose, I'm glad she didn't take over humanity and replace them with evilness, but what has she been doing the last thousand years. And why was she agrave?"

"She wasn't," Andra said. "She never went into stasis. She made clones of herself, and every time a body died, her nano consciousness would travel to a new clone and she'd wake up and start over."

"Neg, neg," Lilibet said. "I may be too young to have memory, but I reck for certz Griffin was agrave. With you and Rashmi."

Andra shook her head. "That was a clone body. She . . . placed the clone and . . . Rashmi and I in the middle of Eerensed. She started the rumor we were goddesses. And once the religion was fully formed, she woke in that body. She . . . wanted your resources, I guess. Your labor. Or maybe, just to be worshipped . . . I don't know. I only have access to the memories she uploaded into her work'station. There are memories . . . feelings . . . she's hidden. Maybe even from herself. The good news is, there's something in Eerensed, something that prevents her from returning to the Icebox. It locks onto her tech signature and fries it if she tries to enter. That's why she sent me here to . . ." Andra cleared her throat. "Instead of coming herself."

The room was quiet for a moment. Lilibet bit her lip. Rashmi was muttering something quietly to herself with her head down, white hair draped across the table. Dzeni was silently crying, hand over her mouth.

Xana reached over and wrapped her hand around Dzeni's. "So what do we do?"

Andra blinked. "I . . . have no idea. We're facing the most intelligent person to ever exist and her army of AI inhabiting the brightest minds of my generation. We have . . . us and a bunch of kids."

Xana shook her head. "Neg. Don't give up. There has to be something we can do. The Schism. The Eerensedians. All the magic in this place. We mereish have to figure a plan."

"The Schism isn't responding," Andra argued. "And Meta is now ruling the Eerensedians, and she was sent here by Griffin. As for the magic . . . it's all used up in that stupid, useless rocket or in the 'dome control room or securing the palace foundations. All we have left are the EMPs, and we can't use those."

Rashmi's head popped up. "Why not? They work on all nanos, and the AI are just nanos. We'll get knocked out too, but only for a short while, and that's enough for the humans to . . . oh."

"Yeah, oh," Andra said. "The EMPs would take out *every nano* in all of Eerensed. Yes, that includes the AI—and Rashmi and me, unfortunately—but it also includes the tech that is currently keeping the Rock from collapsing."

"So?" Xana said. "That ugly palace is a small price to pay to be rid of the AI."

"But it would only knock them out for a few minutes. Their nanos would reboot themselves fairly quickly. And in that time the palace will have fallen down on top of us."

Xana shook her head, growling. "There has to be a march forward. We can't give up."

Andra felt empty, despair yawning open inside her. She had done this. This was all her fault. She hadn't been created to serve humanity. She'd been created to help Griffin overthrow it, replace it. And she'd fulfilled that purpose perfectly.

She was about to tell Xana again that there was no hope, when the door flew open and Ophele appeared on the other side. Her eyes met Andra's.

"They're here."

WHEN ANDRA ARRIVED, the Vaults lobby was silent, except for the ticking of the clock, but she could feel the tension in the air.

"How many are out there?" she asked Ophele.

"I don't know. Too many." She looked away. "Raj is out there." She let out a sad sigh. "The AI in Raj's body. He wants to speak with you."

Andra trembled, but nodded.

Ophele brought up a holo'display on the security panel beside the air'lock. The holo bloomed into a view of the cave on the other side. Raj was prowling back and forth, like a trapped animal looking for a weakness in the cage.

Andra bit her lip and hit the com button. "What do you want, Raj?"

"I want to know what you did with Cruz." His voice was jarring and sharp.

Andra watched him for a moment before answering. "I think you already know what I did with Cruz." It was a miracle her voice didn't shake.

Raj growled. "You're one of us."

"Maybe," Andra said. "But I'm also one of them."

Raj stopped pacing and hit his hand against the side of the air'lock. The holo blipped for a moment before coming back. "Where are the children?"

"The children?" Andra asked. "I don't know. Did you lose them?"

"Don't play stupid. We know you have them. Your father told us."

Andra's palm started to sweat, tears welling in her eyes. She was glad Raj couldn't see her.

"My dad's dead. I killed him. Just like I killed Cruz and Raj. And I'm really, *really* angry about that, so if you don't want to see what happens when I get angry, I would back the fuck away."

A feral smile spread across Raj's face. "You can't stay in there forever. Either you'll run out of supplies, or we'll find a way in."

"Okay," Andra said. "Good luck with that. See you then."

Her finger moved toward the button to hang up the holo.

"She's coming," Raj said.

Andra froze.

"Who?"

"Griffin. She won't be happy."

Andra scoffed, though fear churned in her stomach. "I've seen her memories. I know she can't get back into Eerensed. Something blocks her tech signature."

"Something did," Raj said. "Something that could only be fixed from inside the Icebox. It's a shame she doesn't have anyone on the inside. Oh wait." His grin spread. "She does."

THIRTY-EIGHT

OOIIOOII OOIIIOOO

ANDRA TRIED TO reach the Schism again, but there was no response. She wondered if the AI had already found them and killed them. Surely not, right? They had spent the last few weeks a few tunnels away from the Schism. If they had wanted to attack them, they would have done so already.

So why hadn't they? Why not attack Eerensed for that matter? Were they waiting for larger numbers? For Griffin? How long would it take her to get to Eerensed?

Andra still couldn't wrap her brain around the fact that Griffin was AI. It had been weird enough when she was a series of clones, but now . . .

Was there even a point to fighting? Andra couldn't possibly win against Griffin. She was her creator, after all.

It just didn't make any sense why she had created Andra and Rashmi, put them in host bodies, and then waited hundreds of years to act out the rest of her plan. There was something she wasn't seeing.

Andra wandered the quiet halls of the Vaults. The children were finally asleep, in makeshift dormitories in the 2130s exhibit hall. Swan was watching over them with the help of the older kids—and Acadia, Andra supposed. She hadn't seen her brother and sister since they arrived. Cristin had locked herself in her room. There was a light on in Ophele's, but Andra left her alone. Dzeni had tucked Dehgo in bed hours ago. Even Lilibet was lightly dozing in the common room, under one of her stitched blankets, the light of a holo'display shining on her face.

Andra found Rashmi in the only place that made sense: outside Maret's cell.

Well. Maret and Zhade's cell.

Zhade was passed out on his cot, his face turned away from her. Good. Andra wasn't ready to talk to him yet. Couldn't stand the idea of the imprint controlling Zhade. Of all the terrible things he might say to her, and she'd never know what was him and what was the Crown.

The cell was just as it had been, Mechy's tech holding steady. The force shield was nothing more than a shadow between Maret and Rashmi. They sat parallel, with their backs to the wall, knees bent, staring at nothing.

"I wish I could remember . . . anything. Any part of it," Rashmi whispered. "My head is just a swirl of colors, no sharp edges, just impressions."

Maret snorted. "You should be glad. I have memory of all of it. Every single thing I've ever done. The Crown memorized it all and would play it back to me if I ever fought too hard. The torture. Executions. I can't ever forget."

"At least you know what you've done." Rashmi's voice was barely above a whisper, small and timid. "I have to imagine."

Maret shook his head. "But you don't. Have to. If you wanted, you could mereish . . . live like it never happened."

Rashmi propped her chin on her knees and tilted her head toward him. "Do you really feel so guilty?"

Maret shrugged, and it was the most vulnerable Andra had ever seen him. "That's the scary part. I don't reck. It all made sense when I was doing it. And sometimes, it still makes sense. Even with it

337

gone . . ." He touched the place on his temple were the Crown used to sit. ". . . I still don't reck what's me and what's—"

Maret cut off.

There was blur in Andra's vision as a figure dropped from the ceiling.

Inside the cell.

Andra darted forward as Rashmi scuttled back. Maret was too slow to react, and in less than a moment, Doon had him in a headlock, blade pressed against his neck.

"Wait!" Andra said, jolting forward, but stopped when she saw Doon's grip tighten.

Rashmi let out a short scream. Xana was in the room in an instant, hand poised over the controls that released the prison. Zhade jerked awake on his cot.

"How did you get in here?" Andra asked.

Doon smirked. "I've been practicing. Magic always has its weaknesses."

She nodded her head toward the ceiling, and though the cell was dark, Andra saw a missing panel at the top of the wall. Probably some kind of air vent or maintenance shaft. She'd made sure Maret couldn't get out, but she never even considered someone breaking in.

"Why didn't you tell me he was here?" Doon sneered.

Andra shook her head, starting to make her way slowly toward Doon. "I . . . I didn't know you would be interested . . ."

"Interested? *Interested?* He killed my brother. I'm *more* than interested. I've been looking for him for moons. And all the while, you've had him here, paces from my brother's promised and son!"

Andra put both hands up. "Okay, yes, I know this looks bad, but things are more complicated than you realize."

"How? He killed my brother. He owes me a life, and I'm bout to take it."

Xana stepped forward. "Imagine bout this, small one, are you for true a killer?"

"Am I not?" Doon scoffed, her dark curls tumbling into her eyes. "I've been alone since I was eight. I've lived in alleys and sewers. You and Skilla took me in, trained me. Skooled me how to fight and survive. You made me this. You convoed revenge. I'm mereish standing in your shadow."

"Do it," Maret said, his voice strained by the firm grip Doon had on his throat. "Do it. I deserve it."

"No, you don't," Rashmi said.

"I do." Maret raised his eyebrows, the only expression he could make in his current position. "I did everything I could to hold my power, even if that meant letting people die. I killed because it was fun. Because I liked it. And if you don't kill me, I'll do it again."

"If you deserve to die, I do too," Rashmi whispered.

Andra held her arms stretched out, as though she were keeping everyone at bay. "No one deserves to die, here, okay? Rashmi, you didn't choose to be what you are, and you couldn't help the things Griffin made you do. Yes, your lack of memories doesn't erase the consequences of your previous actions, but you are a different person now, and that person deserves to live a good life, as short as it may be," Andra added, thinking of the AI that would surely come to kill them.

She looked at Doon.

"Doon, you're not a killer. You were put in horrible situations, and I'm thankful you learned the skills you needed to survive, but killing an unarmed person shouldn't be one of them. And if Skilla and Xana taught you revenge, then I'm going to have a chat with them, one day, when this is all over, about how it's bad to create child soldiers."

Doon tightened her grip on Maret.

"And Maret," Andra said. "You're an asshole. There are many, many times I wished I had just let someone kill you, and I'm sure I'm going to regret this moment in the near future. But until we can figure out how much of what you did was you, and how much of it was Tsurina and the Crown, we're keeping you alive."

Maret coughed. Doon's sword nicked his throat and blood trickled down. "I deserve death. You just don't want to believe it, because then Zhade deserves it too."

"No," Andra gasped. "I don't want to believe it because of what I've done!"

The cell fell quiet.

"Doon, put down the sword," a soft voice said.

Zhade was standing, arm outstretched, poised to stop Doon if he had to. To save his brother.

He caught Andra's eye, and she quickly looked away, but not before realizing he wore his own face again. Her heart stuttered.

Doon sighed and let go of Maret. Instead of scuttling away, he fell to his knees, coughing. He let the line of blood continue to trickle down his neck, the ends of his long hair staining dark red.

Xana hit the controls for the force shield, and Doon walked out. Maret didn't try to break free. He looked over his shoulder at his brother, who was unmoving, staring at Andra. Xana reignited the force shield.

"Hold up," Andra said, turning to Doon. "How did you really get in here?"

DOON SHOWED THEM the route she took through maintenance and ventilation shafts that led to a tunnel that wound through a collapsed portion of the Vaults. She told them the tunnel connected to another tunnel, which connected to another, then another, until it reached the Schism. The problem was Doon was the only one small enough to fit.

Andra paced as she waited for Doon's return. She'd left half an hour ago to take a message to Skilla. It was possible she would run into the AI or that the AI had already gotten to the Schism, but if there was any chance of getting Skilla's militia and refugees to the Vaults, they had to take it.

Andra paced outside the room that held Zhade and Maret's cell. Xana watched her with a raised eyebrow.

"You going to convo him?" she asked.

"I . . . who?"

Xana gave her a disappointed look, her modded eye flashing. "Mereish because *my* feelings weren't returned, doesn't purpose *yours* are doomed too."

Andra's jaw dropped.

"Scuze?" Xana said, hand over her heart. "I'm observant."

Andra rolled her eyes. "This is different. Sides, I don't want to convo him with his brother right there."

Xana shrugged. "I purpose, it's your choice, but things are not looking good. You should say the things you want to say now, before it's too late."

Andra didn't respond. She didn't know how to fight Griffin and the AI yet, but even once they had a plan, there was a strong possibility they would lose. This could be her last chance to speak with Zhade . . . about anything.

"Your feelings weren't returned with Skilla?" Andra asked. "Or Dzeni?"

Xana's eyebrows shot up. She ran a hand over her shaved head. "I don't . . . I . . . She . . . What are you convoing?"

Andra let out a ghost of a laugh. "Scuze. I'm observant."

Then she straightened her shoulders and walked into the room before she lost her nerve.

Maret was lying down on his cot, throwing one of his shoes into the air and catching it. Zhade was pacing the length of the force shield. He stopped when he saw Andra.

For a moment, she let herself take in his face. It was truly his again. His wide cheekbones and bowed mouth. His sarcastic eyebrows hanging over his brown eyes. He still wore his hair like Maret's—too light, too long. And he was far too thin. And there was an angry red scar over his left temple and eye. But it was Zhade.

Andra swallowed. "Hi."

"Heya," Zhade said. His chest was heaving, and she couldn't read the expression on his face. But he wasn't yelling or attacking or casting biting remarks, like she expected.

She didn't know who this Zhade was, who he had ever been. Was he the arrogant boy who brought her to Eerensed? The kind one who let Andra cry on his shoulder? The ambitious one who had used and betrayed her? The tender boy she'd slept with? The boy dictator controlled by Tsurina and the Crown? Or yet someone else?

"So, uh." She took a step toward him. "I just wanted to say sorry for—"

"Neg, stop, don't," Zhade said, his face red with anger.

"Oh, I just—"

"Neg, mereish . . ." He sighed. "I purpose you have nothing to be sorries for. I . . . I treated you full horrible, that moren. I was angry and hurt, and I wish I could blame it on the Crown, but in truth, I don't reck if it was me or not. And I . . ." He ruffled the back of his head. "Every word I said to you before we . . . the even before I left . . . was the full truth. My full truth is that I love you."

Andra felt something swell inside her, some vestige of hope, some determination to make everything okay, to wade through their boggy past to find solid ground.

Zhade shook his head. "But it's not enough."

Andra deflated. Her eyes smarted and her throat closed up.

"Even without the Crown, I treated you full horrible. I lied to you, manipulated you, used you." He bit his lip and looked down at his feet, and Andra was surprised to see tears in his eyes. "And I love you enough to not want you to be with me. Because you deserve better. And no meteor how hard I try, I can never make up for what I've done. And now that I have this . . ." He gestured to the side of his head, where the Crown had been, where there was now a scar. ". . . this thing in my head, there will always be a chance that I'll hurt you." He met Andra's gaze. "I'll never, ever be able to deserve you."

Tears welled in Andra's eyes, but she willed them not to fall. "You're right, asshole. You never will deserve me."

He nodded in resignation.

Andra glowered. "But everything else you said was bullshit."

Zhade opened his mouth to argue, but Andra cut him off.

"So, you have that . . . imprint thing in your head, so what? So you did terrible things, before and after you had the Crown. So. What." She threw up her hands. "Unfortunately for me, that doesn't change how I feel about you. And you don't get to decide that for me. You don't get to pull the 'noble sacrifice' card and say you're ending things because of how you feel for me. That's bullshit. It sounds to me like you're taking the easy way out. You'll never be able to make it up to me? Maybe not, but you should at least make an effort. You'll never be good enough for me? You're damn right, but that doesn't give you the pass to just stop trying. We've all done horrible things, myself included. None of us get to give up. So shut up and do better, asshole."

Zhade stood, gape-mouthed. Andra left before he had a chance to respond.

THIRTY-NINE

0011001 00111001

Doon made it back around midnight. The journey should have taken only an hour, not four, but Doon wouldn't say what she'd been doing the rest of the time.

The Schism was fine, but they were cut off from the Vaults. Doon told her Skilla had gotten the panicked message Andra had sent from the Icebox and tried to answer. Andra had never gotten the return message, so it was clear that the colonists were watching and somehow blocking communication. Skilla had tried to find a way to the Vaults, but AI had set up camp in the main tunnel. They would have to find another way in.

Andra sat forward in her ergo'chair, where she'd been flipping through the memory files now on her work'station. Inside her head, Griffin's memories were all mixed together, a muddle of events Andra couldn't organize into a story. But on the computer, they could be organized, categorized, shaped into patterns. Rashmi and Lilibet were helping her sift through the data, but there were trillions of moments. Finding the right memory that would give them a clue as to how to defeat the AI would take a miracle. If there was a way to do it, Griffin had buried it deep in her subconscious.

AI were hard to kill—Andra's own recovery proved that—but it wasn't impossible. There had to be some way to kill the AI and prevent their nanos from traveling to a new host. At least they couldn't hop from body to body. If they could, Griffin wouldn't have needed Andra to convert the colonists with the anomalizer. It was possible for nanos to be absorbed into nearby tech, though, so that made even dead AI dangerous.

Andra kept searching through the memories, seeking patterns. Sorting through the three different tech signatures.

She blinked. Then rubbed her eyes, looked again.

There were definitely three separate tech signatures in the files. One matched Rashmi, the other matched Griffin. Rashmi had only downloaded the memories that didn't match Andra's tech signature, so who did the third set of memories belong to?

The file was small. Ridiculously small compared to the others. And its subfiles were categorized differently than the other memories. They were filed by chronology, not by the chaotic connections a brain makes when storing memories. These looked like they had almost been filed . . . intentionally. Like someone had put them into Andra's brain on purpose.

She opened the first file.

It wasn't like Griffin's memories. It didn't feel like she had lived this moment, always known it. It didn't become part of her. Instead, it expanded around her, taking her through the moment like the memories in the holocket would. Except this was more than just a sim that included senses. She *felt* the emotions, thoughts, impressions, instincts of the memory.

She was holding a baby girl in her arms. It hadn't lived long. She was grieving, confused, angry. She didn't know how she'd tell Auric, who was so excited for their second child. Acadia, who wanted to be a big sister.

Then Alberta came.

At first, Alberta had cried with her, but then her eyes had cleared, and she'd told her. About the AI program. About how she could bring the baby back. Told her about the plan. The plan for Andromeda. And Isla agreed.

Andra cried out, coming back to herself as the memory dissolved.

"Third One?" Rashmi asked.

Lilibet darted to her side.

All Andra could do was shake her head. "I . . . I'm a . . . I was . . ."

But she couldn't say it. Couldn't tell them that this body *wasn't hers.*

She'd known it was a possibility, but she hadn't let herself think about it. And when she'd seen all the cloned bodies Griffin kept, Andra had secretly hoped that's what she was. But she wasn't an AI in a cloned body. She was an AI in a stolen body.

She pushed Rashmi and Lilibet away and clicked on the next memory.

It bloomed around her.

She had tried re-creating what Alberta had done. She wanted to understand her daughter. But she couldn't create True AI—like Andra. The best she could do was a standard AI—artificial intelligence in a robot body. It didn't help her understand Andra at all. Instead, it helped her understand herself.

She was never completely sure she'd done the right thing. Andromeda wasn't the child she'd given birth to. That child had died. And replacing her now felt wrong. But Andromeda was Isla's daughter in her own right, and if she hadn't agreed to Alberta's idea, she would have never known Andromeda.

Could a decision be both wrong and right?

Whatever the answer, Isla never wanted her daughter to discover what she was. She was a gentle, sensitive child who felt out of place already, and it would destroy her. She was becoming dangerously close to discovering her identity though, as she grew closer to the standard AI Isla had created.

So Isla tried to dismantle it, but it fought back, giving her a scar she would bear for the rest of her life. Andromeda had cried for days.

"It's just an AI," Isla had told her. "Not quite human."

Not like you, she'd meant. You're human. So you can't be AI.

Andra was crying. Vaguely, she felt Lilibet and Rashmi surrounding her, patting her back, holding her hand. But she couldn't stop. She opened the next memory.

Alberta woke her, told her nine hundred years had passed and only a fraction of humanity was in stasis. The rest had lived through hell, their descendants forced to survive a destroyed Earth. Alberta was living among some of those descendants. She had a child now.

"Is he a human?" Isla had asked. "Or did you create another AI?"

Alberta shrugged. "He was born biologically. But he's mine, so who's to say? Probably a little bit of both."

He's mine, so who's to say?

That was when Isla realized what Alberta was.

Artificial intelligence.

It took very little digging to discover Alberta's real plans: to replace humanity with AI.

"I'm saving humanity!" Alberta argued when Isla confronted her about it. "Me, Rashmi, your daughter, we'll be the first in a new species of human!"

Isla was good at training her face, but she couldn't stop the fear she felt.

Alberta's offer to create Andromeda hadn't been out of sympathy for a grieving mother. And there was no grand plan to save humanity. There was only a plan to become humanity. To restart the human race with artificial consciousness.

Only, that would require getting rid of humanity completely. A failed experiment. A trial gone wrong.

"AI have all the intelligence of humanity without the baggage," Alberta had said. "Without the anger and hate and fighting. AI are the best of humanity. And better than humanity. A new humanity."

Isla had done her best to smile and pretend like she understood. Like she agreed. But after, she'd sneaked into the city where Alberta lived. The one where she was apparently worshipped as a goddess. First, she set up a firewall on the LAC annex to protect the colonists. If Griffin ever tried to wake even one of them, two things would happen. One: all the colonists would wake. There was strength in numbers. And two: a tech shield would cover the entire city, searching for and destroying Alberta's tech signature.

Then she stole her daughter's cryo'tank and hid it in a remote village a few miles east.

"I love you," she said to her sleeping daughter. *"And I'm sorry. For every-thing. Remember who you are. Learn, adapt. Survive, and then live a life worth choosing. That's what it truly means to be human. To decide your fate, as those Eerensedians say."*

As she prepared to upload a few of her most precious memories into her daughter's brain, Isla wept.

Andra rushed back into herself, falling to the ground, her body wracked with heavy sobs.

Her mother . . .

Her mother had loved her. Had saved her. Griffin had woken Isla thinking she would help her overtake humanity simply because her daughter was AI. But Isla had chosen to fight instead. To hide Andra. To tell her the truth.

Andra didn't know what happened after that last memory, but she was suddenly certain that it hadn't been desert pirates that had killed Isla Watts.

"Are you evens, Andra?" Lilibet asked. "What can we do? Are you evens?"

Andra sucked in a ragged breath. She wiped away her tears.

Her mother had saved her. Told her to remember who she was, decide her fate. That was the only way to be human.

But Andra wasn't just human. And it would take all of her to finish what her mother had started and save humanity.

She stood, shakily, and nodded her thanks to Rashmi and Lilibet.

"I'm evens," she said. "And I have a plan."

FORTY

OO11O1OO OO11OOOO

"SORRIES, YOU WANT to do what anow?" Skilla asked, pinching the bridge of her nose.

It hadn't been easy to get Skilla into the Vaults. They'd used the 'bot that had helped carry Zhade back from the palace to widen the passage Doon had taken. But it was still only big enough for one person at a time, and terribly unstable. Andra was sure one wrong step would bring the whole palace down on top of them.

Skilla had managed to crawl her way in though, and now she sat across from Andra, leaning back in her chair, fingers steepled in front of her. Lilibet stared at a tablet in front of her, flipping through files of the Vaults' schematics. Xana was watching Dzeni bounce Dehgo on her knee, and Rashmi was curled in on herself, humming. Several holo'displays rose from the table in the middle of Andra's room, one showing blueprints of the Vaults and the surrounding tunnel system, another displaying the palace, yet another the pocket outside the city.

"I want to convert the pocket to our side," Andra said.

Xana and Dzeni shared a glance. Rashmi winced. Lilibet didn't look up from her tablet.

"You want," Skilla said slowly, "to take the magic that has destroyed the Hell-mouth, terrorized the Wastes, and forced us to live inside a magic bubble, and what? Turn it good?"

Andra stuck out her bottom lip. "I mean, technically, they were never evil. They were just following a code of amoral values which happened to demand that they destroy everything they touch, but other than that, yeah . . . I want to turn them good."

Skilla raised a single eyebrow. "Is this because of the pocket pet you used to have? Where is it anyway?"

Andra hesitated, biting her lip. "It's . . . inside me." She grimaced.

Xana jumped into motion, stepping in front of Dzeni and Dehgo. In one swift movement, Skilla pulled the battle-ax from her back holster.

"Get out of her, Devil," Skilla sneered.

Andra rolled her eyes. "That's not . . . I'm not *possessed*. This is me talking. Right now. It's Andra. I just kind of . . . absorbed and assimilated the pocket. Or, it chose to be assimilated, I guess."

"What the sands are you convoing?" Xana asked.

Andra told them about her near death at the hands of one of the Guv's guard. About the pocket coming to her aid, saving her by allowing themselves to be converted to healing tech. That the nanos from the pocket still lived inside her, as part of her, because they had decided their fate, instead of following their programming. They could be given sentience, by giving them a choice.

Everyone but Rashmi, who was now curled tightly against Lilibet's side, stared blankly at her.

"I don't like this," Skilla said. "If the pocket can transform itself into healing magic, what's stopping it from transforming itself right back?"

Technically, the pocket inside Andra had changed back, briefly, but Andra didn't want to tell them about how she'd used it to destroy Cruz's body. But even after using the nanos in that way, they had immediately reverted back to their healing protocols.

"I don't think the nanos *want* to change back. I think they like their new role." Andra shrugged. "As much as nanos can like anything."

Skilla picked up the tablet projecting a 'display of the pocket and opened her mouth, probably to argue some more, but Xana cut her off, modded eye zeroing in on Andra. "How would you do this exactish?"

Andra sighed. "So, cards on the screen, this is all banking on the gamble that my AI nanos have stronger programming than the pocket nanos. Which, you know . . . maybe? I've been converting nanos this whole time, whenever I need to replenish them, but this would be on a much larger scale. When I was injured, my nanos' need for healing outweighed the pocket's need for destruction, so the pocket was able to be converted."

"You aren't going to injure yourself again, are you?" Lilibet asked, finally looking up from her tablet.

Andra pointed at her. "Good question, and hell no. I've been stabbed enough to last a lifetime. But Griffin created the pockets accidentally by trying to create more AI. So, since AI tech and pocket tech are similar, as long as my code is stronger, I should be able to override the pocket protocols and convert them to my own tech. I can send a command to the pocket that should override its programming to destroy everything, and replace that with a directive to *only* destroy the AI."

"You're going to kill them?" Rashmi whispered, white hair falling into her face.

She didn't want to kill the AI. They couldn't help what they were, hadn't asked to be given sentience. But as long as they followed Griffin's plan to overtake humanity, they were a threat.

"I . . . only if I have to. I'm going to give them a choice."

"A choice?" Lilibet asked.

Andra nodded. "If they really want to be human, then they have to decide their fates. They can either stand down and live with humans, or they'll be destroyed."

"And how would you destroy them?" Xana asked.

"By letting the pocket assimilate them by force."

Lilibet frowned. "So, they'd become part of this . . . big benevolent pocket you created?"

"That won't work." Skilla scowled, shifting forward in her chair. "You told us yourself that AI are immune to pockets. They can't be destroyed by them."

Andra pursed her lips. "Theoretically, the pockets *choose* not to destroy AI, because AI and pockets have such similar tech signatures that the pockets believe they're the same. Think about it. There has to be a limit to the pockets' destructive instinct, otherwise they would have destroyed each other and gone extinct centuries ago. It's a choice they make not to destroy themselves. And I'm guessing they can choose the opposite, especially if they become . . . a part of me."

"You're guessing?" Xana asked. "Theoreticish?" She leaned back in her chair and crossed her arms. "Evens, this plan happens full bars bad magic."

"No, her theory is sound," Rashmi said, her eyes growing clearer. "If the nanos of the pockets become hers, she can convince them to change their protocols, if her programming is stronger. But I'm sensing a complication."

Andra nodded. "Yeah . . . in order to strengthen my code, this is going to require . . . a lot of power. I mean. A lot. More than I have. When I was injured, my nanos' call-for-help program was amplified by the dire need to address my wounds. But that wouldn't be enough to convert the entire pocket at the city's edge. So I'm going to have to borrow the amplification. And the only thing with enough energy—"

"Is the rocket," Rashmi finished.

Andra nodded, then blinked, and shook her head. "Well, yeah, the rocket, if I want to fry my brain. That would overpower me in a second. I was thinking of the 'dome."

"Oh," Rashmi whispered. "That makes more sense."

Dzeni sat forward, Dehgo asleep on her shoulder. "And let me do some guessing. It won't be as easy as mereish sneaking you to the gods' dome ring."

"Nope." Andra let the *P* pop. "Because geniuses that we were, we constructed a remote 'dome hub inside of the palace cathedzal."

Xana lifted an eyebrow. "We?"

"I," Andra corrected. "I was the genius that put the controls in the palace. But the power in the 'dome should be able to amplify my tech signature to reach the pocket and convert it."

Skilla groaned, tossing aside her tablet. "This is the best plan you could imagine? Are you mereish going to run for it and hope you get there before you're caught?"

Andra picked at one of her fingernails. "Well, we can use the passage that goes up to the First's suite, but it's really unsteady right now, so only a few of us can go. And then there's the problem of getting to the passage, so I'm going to need a distraction."

Skilla huffed out a laugh. "The Schism."

Andra nodded.

Skilla crossed her arms. "Soze, we no longer need the rocket, but we do need . . . a militia."

Andra bit her lip. "Yeah, so . . . good call on that." She gave her a thumbs-up.

Skilla shook her head and scowled again.

Andra hesitated. "There is . . . a problem with my plan."

The general's eyebrows shot up. "Oh, one problem!"

"There are . . . three full sets of memories inside me. Mine, Griffin's, and Rashmi's. Well, the memories of the person Rashmi used to be. For an AI—well, for anyone really—our experiences, our memories of those experiences, shape who we are. I am *me* because of my memories. I'm not Griffin or Rashmi because . . . those memories that I have of their experiences are . . . filed in a dormant part of my consciousness."

Rashmi looked up from Lilibet's shoulder, already understanding where this was going. "No," she whispered.

Andra grimaced. "This jolt of energy. It's going to . . . send me into a state . . . Well, I'm going to be more AI than human. Like when I removed the Crown or took out Maret. No parts of my brain will be dormant. I'll have unfettered access to everything stored in my matrices, including Griffin's memories and Rashmi's memories. They will . . . become *my* memories. *My* experiences. I'll be just as much them as me. Their truths will be my truth, and with all that power coursing through me . . ." She sighed. "I don't know who will be walking out of that room."

Xana sat forward. "What?"

"It may be me. Or, it may not be. I might be the old Rashmi, with her . . . inhumane tendancies. Or I might be Griffin and want to use all of your bodies as hosts for AI. I could be all three. I . . . I really don't know. So, Skilla, you need to be there, and you need to be ready to kill me."

Skilla blinked and let out a laugh without humor. "Soze, let me full comp. Firstish, you'll use our militia as a distraction soze you can sneak out through the tunnel that may or may not collapse at any tick. Then, you'll sneak into the palace and mereish *hope* you don't get caught by Meta, who is wearing the Crown *and* working for Griffin. Then, you'll use the power of the gods' dome to amplify your magic to overpower the magic of the pocket and convince it to take out the gods. And *if it doesn't kill you*, we may have to because you may come back as a murderous demon."

"Uh . . . Yeah, that's . . . that's basically it." Andra put away all the grief and pain from the last few days and summoned all the enthusiasm she could muster. "All right, who's with me?"

FORTY-ONE

THE RUNAWAY

ZHADE COULDN'T SLEEP.

In the cell with his brother, he passed bells beating back the thoughts in his head that weren't his own. He was filled with memories that he recked he'd never experienced but felt too real to him. Each wearer of the Crown had filled it with their own hate and despair, and those feelings increased with each bearer, a magical feedback loop of emotions that Zhade had never felt before.

He heard Maret moving round the cell. It was against his instinct to have his back turned to his brother, but something told him he wouldn't attack. He too had the remnants of the Crown's poison in his head. Zhade had never felt the familial tie that bonded them, but now they were connected by something greater. They were both sons of the Crown.

He couldn't let this happen. Couldn't let it take him over. This wasn't him. This despair. This hate. He was Zhade. He was certz of himself. He liked to laugh. Firm, to hide his fear, but he also mereish liked to feel joy. He never gave up. He lived four years adesert with his best friend, looking for the Goddess. He'd found her.

Then he'd manipulated her, hurt her, betrayed her, destroyed Eerensed, abused his position of power. The guilt was unbearable,

355

but Andra was right. He wasn't allowed to mereish give up. He had to at the least try to atone for all he'd done.

He had to have memory of who he was.

He was in love with a goddess. She was kind and caring and charred and brill, and he wasn't full good for her, but he wanted to try.

Before, that had purposed becoming a better person. Now, that purposed finding a way to rid himself of the darkness inside him, the darkness that didn't belong to him.

He was Zhade.

He was Zhade.

He was Zhade.

The sound of a door sliding open jerked Zhade out of his trance. He lifted himself out of bed to see who their visitor was.

Dzeni stood in the room, illuminated by the light of the magic field.

She looked far healthier than Zhade had seen her since Wead's death, though to be fair, he hadn't seen her oft. Her dark hair was pulled away from her face. Her expression was relaxed, though her body was tense, as though she was prepped for a fight.

"Dzeni." Zhade stood. The thing in his head told him he didn't care bout her, and he promptish told it to shut it. He *did* care. This was his friend. "Dzeni, are you evens?"

She gave him a small smile. "More evens than you, I spoze."

"Is Andra evens?"

Dzeni's smile vanished. "That's what I came to convo."

Zhade's stomach plummeted, and at firstish he was filled with hate and vengeance for whoever would hurt her, before giving himself memory that wasn't him. Zhade—the real Zhade—would want to help her, not hurt others.

A small voice inside him told him that wasn't true. After all, hadn't he tried to kill his own brother out of revenge? Maybe the Crown's magic hadn't changed him completeish. Maybe it was sole amplifying what was already there. Maybe it wouldn't be easy to become the person he wanted to be.

"The gods Andra woke turned evil," Dzeni said. "She has a plan to stop them, but it requires getting into the palace."

"So what do you want from us?" Maret asked. He'd stopped his pacing and now sat with his back against the wall, long hair hanging in his face.

"She wasn't convoing you," Zhade snapped.

"Actualish," Dzeni said, "I was convoing both of you." She turned to his brother. "I hate you, Maret. I will never, ever forgive you for what you did to Wead. I reck you are full bars unredeemable, and I hope one day you are full punished for everything you've ever done." She turned to Zhade. "I love you, Zhade. Wead loved you. And maybe one day, my son will love you too. I hope there's a future where we can all be happy again. But I don't trust you anymore. You have a long march forward to earn back that trust. From all of us."

She hit the controls that opened the cell. The magic shield stuttered a few times, then vanished.

She turned to go but paused at the door. "Decide your fates."

FORTY-TWO

OOIIOIOO OOIIOOIO

Aɴᴅʀᴀ ʜᴀᴅ ᴀ single bell before the Schism created the diversion that would let her, Rashmi, and Lilibet escape the Vaults and enter the palace. Her mind was frantically sorting through worst-case scenarios and possible solutions. But Andra had been in enough of these situations that she knew she couldn't be prepared for everything.

To be fair, she'd never been in a situation quite like this:

First, using a militia to distract an army of AI body-snatchers who were trying to kidnap a bunch of children. Then, infiltrating a post-apocalyptic palace and sneaking past a girl in her mother's body who controlled an army of murder'bots. Finally, siphoning energy from a bio'dome so she could amplify her tech signature and override a 'swarm of corrupted tech bent on destroying humanity and bending them to her will to help fight against the AI.

What could possibly go wrong?

Andra sighed. So many things.

She sat with her feet up on the lobby guest services table, snacking on syntheal and watching the security holo displaying the other side of the air'lock. For hours, at least one of the AI had been stationed just outside the Vaults, testing the security for weaknesses. Mostly engineering and coding specialists, like Daphle Hanson and Luke Walker. Or at least the AI who inhabited their bodies. Andra had just met Luke, but she'd known Daphle since before going into stasis. She used to give Isla's children fudge for Christmas, and Andra always got the smallest piece.

She lowered her syntheal and sat up straight, realizing Daphle was now out of sight of the holo'cam.

"Where are you going?" she mumbled to herself, scanning the feed.

Something on the outside of the air'lock started flashing.

"What the—"

An explosion rattled the Vaults, and the air'lock blew inward. Andra flinched as she was showered in wood and broken glass. Smoke started filling the lobby.

She pushed out of her chair, awkwardly rolling herself over the circular welcome desk, and started running, her feet slapping against the eco'tiled floor as she darted toward the nearest exit. Through her nanos, she felt the first of the AI enter through the air'lock just as she ducked into a nearby hallway, shutting the double doors behind her.

The kinetic orbs had gone into emergency mode, flashing red in the dim corridor. Lilibet and Rashmi were running toward her, but Andra waved them back.

"Go, go," she hissed, pushing them back and into a custodial closet.

"What was that?" Lilibet cried as the door shut behind them. "It's not time yet!"

Andra shushed her. "They figured out how to blow through the air'lock."

"What do we do? What do we do?" Lilibet started pacing the small space. "The Schism isn't here yet."

Andra put a hand on her arm, stopping her from pulling out a chunk of her long, dark hair. "I don't know. But we can't keep hiding. We've got to protect the children."

Lilibet pulled a tablet from her wide sleeves. "What bout the EMP? I've been studying my magic, and I spoze I could figure how to use it."

"Neg," Andra said. "Too dangerous. It'll collapse the palace on top

359

of us. We'd be trapped in here with the AI. And so would the kids."

"Time runs," Rashmi muttered. "It runs and runs and runs."

Andra nodded. "Okay. Evens. Okay. Here's what we do. Okay. Rashmi, get the kids to the Faraday cages, fourth floor. Lilibet, see if you can figure out a way to send a distress signal to the Schism. I'm going to distract them."

"Certz," Lilibet whispered. "How?"

Andra swallowed. "By giving myself up."

RASHMI AND LILIBET argued, but in the end, Andra won, because they were running out of time, and they didn't have a better plan.

When they exited the closet, Rashmi and Lilibet ran deeper into the Vaults and Andra headed to the lobby, where she could sense the AI congregating. Their angered voices grew louder as she got closer. This was a terrible idea. She couldn't reason with them, couldn't fight them. All she could do was distract them long enough for the Schism to get here.

She saw the AI before they saw her. The smoke from the explosion had cleared, and hundreds of them had filled the lobby, all carrying weapons and wearing armor. They had once been scientists, and now they were dressed for war. Raj was standing on the welcome desk, a large gun pointed at the ceiling as he addressed the crowd.

"Split up. We've got them trapped, so take your time and check everywhere. Whatever you do, Griffin wants Andromeda alive, so bring her to me once you've found her."

"Got me," Andra said, walking into the lobby with her hands up. Hundreds of people turned in her direction, drawing their weapons. The guns were huge and nothing like Andra had ever seen before. Veins of green circuitry ran along the barrel from the muzzle to an encasing of some sort of gaseous green cloud in the magazine.

"Andromeda Watts," Raj said, turning to her. "Traitor to your kind. Where are the children?"

"They're not here," she lied. "They never were. You can search the full place if you'd like. It'll just waste your time, and that's fine by me."

"Where are they?" Raj growled.

He narrowed his eyes, and Andra narrowed hers right back, trying to give him a mocking smile.

Raj nodded to a group of AI, the ones who had once been cryo'techs. Each was strapped with a green-circuited weapon.

"Go find them," Raj ordered. His eyes glazed over as though he were searching his memory—or the memory of his host. "There's a Faraday cage on the fourth floor. Try there first."

The AI nodded and took off through the lobby, marching up the stairs to the second-floor landing. The Vaults were a maze, but if they all had their hosts' memories, they would eventually find the Faraday cage.

Andra swallowed. Hopefully, Rashmi had gotten to them quickly. The cage could be locked from the inside, like a panic room.

She willed herself not to shake as she stepped farther into the crowd. The AI parted for her as she approached Raj. She recognized so many of them. Remembered some of them from before stasis. Remembered even more from the upgrade procedures that had converted them. But even though she recognized their faces, she didn't truly know any of them.

"So what's your plan? Change all the humans on Earth to AI? Save the world by destroying it? How cliché."

"Not all the humans." Raj tilted his head, eyes unblinking. "Some will die."

"It's not *our* plan," someone said, and she would know that voice anywhere.

Her father stepped out of the crowd, wearing the same professor jacket he'd worn yesterday. The AI quieted until Andra could hear the ticking of the astronomical clock. Auric reached a hand toward Andra, and she flinched.

"It's our creator's plan," he said.

Andra bit back tears. "You mean Griffin."

He nodded. "Don't you see? Humanity had their chance and they blew it. They destroyed the planet, fought endless wars, bent on self-destruction. This planet deserves something better. Humanity deserves to be better. *We're* that something. We can re-create humanity into something that creates, not destroys."

Destroy, a voice said in her head.

Andra shook. "That's funny. You talk about creation, but you're destroying something to do it."

Her father took a step toward her. "Not destroying. *Repurposing.* We're retaining their memories and their bodies and their imagination and inventiveness. And we're creating something new with it. Something better."

Andra's lower lip wobbled. "You killed my father. And you replaced him. You're not something better. *He* was better, and you killed him."

"No, Andra," he said, taking a step toward her. "*You* killed him."

Her hands trembled. "I didn't know!"

"It's okay." He took another step, hand still outstretched. "It's okay. You did the right thing. Now, his memories and knowledge can live on, free of war and pain. He would be so proud of you, of how strong you are. *I'm* proud of you. You think he's gone, but he's not. I remember how he used to put you on his knee and read history books to you as a child. I remember how he would try to make you Hokkien mee and burn the pork lard. I remember that he gave you your first pre-book dictionary for your seventh birthday and that you kept it even though the digital ones were more accurate. I remember his love for you. So now I love you, because those memories are mine. In every way that matters, I am your father."

Andra shook. She hadn't realized her father remembered those things. Had even thought about her that much. And if consciousness really was just a collection of memories, what made the AI who lived inside her father's body any less her father? How was he any different?

"I—"

The sound of a gunshot ricocheted around the massive lobby, and a burst of red blossomed on her father's chest.

"No!" Andra shouted, as he fell to his knees. "Daddy!"

Raj drew his weapon and fired in the direction of the shot. A green bolt flew past Andra and hit the person behind her. The person who had shot her father.

Thin, pale, blonde hair.

Cristin.

She fell, dead before she hit the ground.

"No!" Andra screamed again, one arm stretched toward Cristin and the other toward her father.

The lobby was silent except for Andra's sobs. She'd failed. Her father was dead, killed by her hands, and she'd let the illusion of his return distract her. The AI were going to find the children. Were going to convert them. And now, Cristin was dead. Cristin, who had only avoided being upgraded because she hated Andra. Her body lay stretched out on the floor. Andra had done this. It was all her fault.

But then Cristin stood up.

It was an awkward attempt. Not clumsy, but as though she didn't remember how to use her body. Her long limbs straightened, and she ran a finger through her short blonde hair. Raj hopped off the welcome desk, and the AI parted as he headed straight for her. Andra wanted to scream at her to duck, run, anything, but her voice was stuck in her throat as her brain caught up with what she was seeing.

Raj handed Cristin a gun. The same gun that had just been used on her, had just killed her. She nodded, and a crooked smile spread across their face.

"Oh my god," Andra whispered.

The realization washed over her. She stumbled back, hand to her mouth.

Cruz had figured out a way to do it. How to do the upgrade without Andra. And they'd weaponized it. Put the code into their green-circuited guns, so that anyone they shot would be upgraded.

They could convert everyone to AI on sight.

FORTY-THREE

OOIIOIOO OOIIOOII

ANDRA DARTED TOWARD the nearest lobby exit, but someone grabbed her, pulling her arms behind her back and holding her
captive.

Cristin stood before her, now AI. Her father lay dead behind her.
Somewhere in the Vaults, her friends were scattered, vulnerable to
the weapons that would kill them and reanimate their bodies with AI.

She had to get out of here. She had to do something.

"'Cuff her," Raj ordered.

"NO!" Andra screamed, kicking at the AI holding her captive.

As soon as they released her, she fell forward, hitting the ground
hard. She didn't stop, using her momentum to scramble away, but
she was surrounded and it was futile, and this time, when she was
caught, it was by Raj.

He was tall and thin with delicate features, but his grip on her
wrist was anything but gentle.

"Griffin wants you alive," he growled. "And that's the only reason
I'm not killing you now. You're a traitor."

The AI in Luke Walker's body handed Raj the 'cuffs. He sneered
down at Andra as he opened them with a flick of his wrist.

"Sir," a voice said.

Andra looked over his shoulder. The cryo'techs had returned.

"What?" Raj snapped.

"The children," one of the 'techs said, and Andra's heart stopped. "They're not here."

"What?" Raj turned, releasing Andra.

She should run, but she was frozen in place.

"We checked the Faraday cage," the 'tech said. "It's empty."

Andra held her breath. Maybe Rashmi hadn't had time to get the children there yet.

"We found several rooms with lines of unmade cots and discarded trash, but no one was there."

Andra let out a hysterical laugh. "Told you. I told you they aren't here."

She just didn't know where they were.

Raj whipped back around, snarling. He grabbed her wrist. She felt the first cool press of metal.

Then a shot rang out, hitting Raj in the shoulder. He stumbled back, pressing his hand to the wound, blood dribbling between his fingers, his shock turning into a sneer.

Andra turned toward the air'lock. Skilla stood on top of a mound of rubble, laser'gun trained on Raj. Kiv stood next to her. The Schism militia stood behind them.

"What is this?" Raj sneered.

Skilla lowered her 'gun and pulled a battle-ax from her back holster. She swung it around, screamed bloody murder, and charged.

In less than a second, the lobby was chaos. Screams, gunshots, the clash of steel. Andra watched in horror as the two sides crashed into one another like waves. A laser'bullet flew past her, knocking her out of her reverie, and she ducked behind a pillar. She waited only a moment before making a run for it.

Screams echoed behind her as she dove into the nearest hallway. Rashmi and Lilibet were waiting for her and pulled her into a dark exhibit room. The door slammed shut, muffling the sounds of battle.

"Where are the children?" Andra asked.

Rashmi shook her head. "I don't know."

Andra filled with panic. "What do you mean you don't know?"

"They went with Doon," a voice said, and a light flickered on.

Ophele stood next to Xana and Dzeni, all three strapped with weapons. Behind them, there was a metal cylinder the size of an oil drum.

The EMP that knocked out AI.

They must have dragged it from the Faraday cage.

"Doon got the kids out yesterday," Ophele continued. "All of them, including your siblings."

"What?" Andra snapped. "Why didn't she tell me?"

"You'll have to ask her next time you see her," Xana said, grabbing her arm. "Now, let's get you out of here."

"We can't!" Andra cried. "Not now! They have anomalizer guns that can convert everyone they shoot into AI."

"Doesn't meteor. We stick to the plan. You have to hurry. Now go!" Xana pushed her toward the exit.

Andra hesitated, looking to Rashmi and Lilibet.

"Go without me," Lilibet said. "I imagine I have a spell to get the EMP to work. It'll knock out the AI full long for us to escape."

Andra shook her head. "You can't. That EMP will knock Rashmi and me out too and bring the palace down on top of us."

Lilibet gave her a grim smile. "We might not get to decide our fates today. If things march toward badness, it may be the sole march to defeating them."

"But—"

"Stop talking and go!" Xana shoved Andra out the door.

She gave Lilibet one last look. "Wait as long as you can. We need all the time you can give us."

Lilibet nodded.

Andra started heading to the maintenance shaft, but Rashmi grabbed her arm.

"Not that way. They have it blocked. We're going to have to fight our way through the lobby."

"Of course we are," Andra muttered. "Do you have a weapon on you?"

"Just my sharp wit." Rashmi grinned. "That was a joke."

"Of course it was."

"Ready?"

"No."

They ran for the lobby.

It was a bloodbath. Bodies were strewn across the eco'tile, the floor slick with blood. But despite how many lay dead or dying, still more were rising again to fight. Schism members converted to AI. AI healed from otherwise mortal wounds.

The battle blocked Andra's path to the air'lock. They would just have to run for it and hope for the best.

It took about two seconds for Andra to lose track of Rashmi, but she couldn't stop to find her. She couldn't think about how she left Lilibet behind or how Xana and Skilla and maybe even Dzeni were fighting. Could die at any moment. Could already be dead. Battle was selfish and solitary and single-minded. And it had to be. If she was distracted for one second, she would die.

She skirted around the battle, ducking swords and laser'bullets, the sounds of gunshots and steel and screaming and dying roaring in her ears.

Halfway to the door she tripped over a body. A girl from cryonic testing, her eyes staring blankly, face smeared in blood.

Andra tried to push herself up, but someone shoved her back down.

She flipped over, scuttling back. A member of the Schism stood above her, face contorted in anger. If he was himself or AI, Andra didn't know as he swung his sword down.

Her breath left her. She'd failed and failed and failed again, and this was such a stupid way to die, tripping over a body and killed by an ally, and now everyone would die because of her foolishness and where was Rashmi—

The AI hit the ground, crying out.

Oh. There was Rashmi.

She stood behind him, 'gun outstretched, white hair hanging over her face, which was etched in a mask of disgust.

"I don't like fighting," she said.

"Me neither," Andra said, stumbling to her feet.

The AI groaned. Rashmi shot him again, then grabbed Andra's hand, dragging her toward the exit.

They dodged shots and leapt over fallen bodies. The air'lock was just ahead, now a pile of rubble, but no one was blocking it.

They were so close. Andra pushed herself harder. And harder. Feet pounding the eco'tile, breath ragged, a stitch growing in her side.

Until she heard a familiar cry, saw a familiar face.

She froze.

Acadia, her sister, was standing in the center of the battle, shaved head coated with dirt and blood, a sword clutched in her wobbling hand. Auric—now healed from his wounds—stood mere feet from her, laser'gun pointed at her chest.

"No!" Andra screamed.

She sent a burst of nano'bots in Acadia's direction, but knew it would be too late. She was too far away. The shot fired. Andra tried to grab hold of the 'bullet, but she had to duck an oncoming sword. She kicked the AI wielding it out at the knees, and then ran her reset tool through its neck. She turned back to where her sister had once stood, but Acadia wasn't there.

She was sprawled on the floor.

Alive.

In front of her, Skilla lay, eyes wide and sightless, a smoking hole through her heart.

It had been a 'gun that had shot her, not one of the green-circuited weapons, so Skilla wouldn't be getting back up, as an AI or otherwise.

Andra blinked back tears, running as fast as she could to her sister's side.

She dragged her sister to her feet. "What are you doing here? Go hide!"

"I can fight!" Acadia snapped.

"You're an academic!" Andra snapped back.

This was their rhythm. Acadia trying to prove she was the best at everything, and Andra just trying to keep existing.

She pointed at Skilla's body. "She *died* to save you. Don't let that be worthless. Get back to Oz, now!"

"But Dad!"

"It's not him," Andra snapped. "He's gone. So get back to the only family we have left."

Andra expected a fight, waited for the blow, for Acadia to say that she wasn't going to take orders from a *thing*, from a robot meant to *serve*. But she only nodded, eyes still wide, and swallowed.

"Okay," she said. "Okay."

She turned to go, but paused, the battle still raging on around them.

"Don't die, Andra."

Andra puffed out a laugh. "You too, Acadia."

"Let's go!" Rashmi cried, and dragged Andra through the air'lock.

FORTY-FOUR

OOIIOIOO OOIIOIOO

ANDRA WAS SHAKING as she and Rashmi climbed out of the lift into the First's suite. They would sneak through the palace halls to the cathedzal, where they had installed the 'dome control hub. They'd have to hurry though. If Lilibet had to use the EMP to knock out the AI, Andra, Rashmi, and the 'dome would all be out of commission for several minutes. And those minutes could be the difference between success and failure.

Andra had tried to prepare herself, but she was still thrown into grief at the sight of Mechy's broken body. He lay in a heap in the center of Griffin's empty room, a hole in his chest. His CPU lay a few feet away, a black box with a spear-shaped hole spilling out wires. Andra bent to pick it up. It was cold and smooth. She put it in her pocket and looked away, reaching out with her AI senses, feeling for any idea as to where Meta was, along with her robot army. If she could just get a feeling for where in the palace they were, she could avoid them. She concentrated harder.

"Well?" Rashmi asked. "Do you know where the scary robots are?"

"Yeah." Andra sighed and turned to Rashmi. "I'll give you one guess."

ANDRA HAD NEVER seen the palace this quiet. Or this . . . chaotic.

Doors hung off their frames. Curtains were torn down. Brown bloodstains dotted the marble floors. Had Meta done this? Or had Zhade?

Andra pressed back the thought. The truth was, she didn't know if Zhade could ever come back from his corruption. Tsurina and Maret never seemed to recover, but they'd both worn the Crown much longer. She had no guarantee that Zhade would be able to fight his new evil urges, and if he did, if he would ever be free of them. Maybe he would have to fight his entire life.

Maybe Andra would have to fight her own inner voices her entire life.

Or maybe connecting to the 'dome would take care of all that, and she'd walk out of the control room as Griffin or Rashmi's former murderous self, and Skilla would have to put her down.

Only, Skilla was dead.

Andra felt nothing at the thought, and she was wondering if her circuits were overloaded with grief. She'd run up her tally of loss, and her brain just wasn't designed to take any more.

"How much farther?" Rashmi whispered.

"Not far," Andra said as they inched down the main hallways on the east side of the palace. Their footsteps echoed; their breath seemed too loud.

They came to a turn in the corridor, and Andra put a hand out to stop Rashmi. Behind the turn was the atrium outside the cathedzal. Shadows spilled across the marble floor, but there was no movement, no noise beyond.

How many can you sense? Andra asked Rashmi through the neural connection.

Rashmi scrunched up her face. *I can't. Third One, I don't think I'll be much help in there.*

It's okay, Andra said. *I've got this.*

She'd grown so used to lying.

Andra reached out with her senses and sighed. "I think they know we're here."

"No point in sneaking in then," Rashmi said.

Andra nodded, gathering as many nanos as she could to herself until she was surrounded in a shimmering cloud. Then she stepped around the corner.

Meta and her 'bots were waiting for them, but they weren't alone. Under the domed lotus-flower ceiling of the atrium, dozens of citians were on their knees on the marble floor, surrounded by mech'bots. The light was dim, the 'bots casting long shadows, their blood-red eyes shining in the darkness. Behind them, Meta stood guarding the double doors to the cathedzal in one of Tsurina's long gold dresses. The Crown gleamed on her forehead, and she smiled when Andra emerged from the shadows, shrouded in her cloak of nanos.

"Welcome," Meta said, her voice perfectly intoned to Tsurina's, and if Andra hadn't seen Tsurina die herself, she would have been convinced the Grande Advisor stood in front of her now.

"What's this?" Andra said, trying to project a confidence and nonchalance she didn't feel.

"Motivation." Meta's voice echoed throughout the room, its sharp edges pinging off the walls. "For you to give yourself up. It's time for the goddesses to die."

FORTY-FIVE

OO11O1OO OO11O1O1

"Help us, Goddess," one of the citians whispered. A 'bot hit her on the back of the head, and she crumpled to the ground. A nearby child started crying.

Meta stood tall and regal, a smile resembling Griffin's spread across Tsurina's face. The 'dome hub stood just behind the doors she was guarding. Andra was so close, but so far away. She didn't have time to fight this battle, but she also didn't have a choice.

"That seems a little extreme." Andra walked into the atrium with her hands up, as though she were approaching a skittish animal. "I was created by Griffin. You were raised by her. We're on the same side."

"Don't convo me bout Griffin," Meta said, sneering. "This Crown has shown me things, truths, and I reck full well that you and she must die. This is my birthright, and I'll do what no other wearer of the Crown could. Today, I'm going to end all three goddesses."

Andra took a step forward. "Just yesterday, you spoke so highly of Griffin. You helped me. I thought we could be friends."

Meta blinked, and for a moment the sneer fell from her face, replaced by confusion. "I . . . She . . ." Meta blinked again, and her scowl returned. "The Crown has shown me the truth," she repeated. "I was ignorant, but now I reck full well. The goddesses are evil."

How had Meta succumbed so quickly to the Crown? It had taken Zhade months to turn. But then, Tsurina had been controlling him through it. Maybe she had acted as a buffer. A lens through which the Crown's messages were filtered. Now, Tsurina was dead, and there was no one acting as that intermediary. Andra remembered what Maret had said, about Tsurina being raised by the Crown after her parents died. Maybe it was not having someone to guide her that had turned her so malevolent. And now that same thing was happening to Meta.

Andra cleared her throat. "So you gathered some Eerensedians in the cathedzal. Why?"

Meta grinned, her teeth seeming to grow in the shadows. "The Crown not sole showed me the past, but also the present. It gave me the ability to convo all the angels in the city, including the one you stole."

"The one I stole?" Andra asked, and then realization struck her. The angel that had helped her carry Zhade back to the Schism. Fishy.

"It was Griffin's," Meta continued. "*Her* angel. It's been feeding her info for years. But now I control it, and I let it leave with you, and commanded it to report back on what you were doing. I reck that you're here to destroy the 'dome and let the pocket in."

Some of the citians gasped.

Andra winced, slowly making her way around the edge of the atrium. "Now, let's think about this logically. If I was going to let the pocket destroy everything, why would I care that you have these citians? According to you, I'm going to destroy them anyway."

Meta scowled. "Don't ask me to comp you," she snapped.

The nearest citian flinched. More children started crying.

"I've seen the memories of all the wearers of the Crown. I've felt what they felt and seen what they've seen. The goddesses exist cruel and fickle. My birth mother may have abandoned me, but the Crown has shown me that my adopted mother abandoned the world."

Meta blinked, eyes clearing as though she was breaking free of the Crown's influence for a moment.

"Neg," she whispered. She shook her head.

Her expression hardened again, eyes narrowing. "Firm. She has to die."

"Then we're on the same side here." Andra took a step forward. She was a meter away from the closest citian. "Griffin is on her way here. She already has an army inside the city walls. If we work together, we can stop her."

Meta shook her head, but it seemed more to clear it than a denial. "Neg. You're . . . you're one of them. I can't trust you." Her voice shook. She blinked. "Can I?"

Andra took another step. "You can. Ask the angel, ask Fishy. I'm doing this to save humanity from Griffin."

Meta hesitated, her expression torn.

One of the citians made a run for it. He barely made it a meter before one of the 'bots sliced him through the stomach. He fell to the ground, moaning.

The alcove filled with gasping and weeping. Parents cradling their children.

The 'bot twirled the sword above its head, arcing it down toward the man's chest. The citians cried out as the blade fell—

—and stopped.

Andra felt a trickle of blood run down her nose as she bent all her concentration on stopping the 'bot, her own nanos interfacing with it, trying to override the commands sent by the Crown. The 'bot was feral, slippery under her grasp. She let out a roar as she pushed back against not only Meta, but the 'bot itself. It wanted to kill. It was the same voice she heard inside her head.

destroy destroy destroy

Andra let destruction take over.

She concentrated her urge to destroy on the 'bot, collecting all the nanos in the room, until they swirled around it.

Destroy, she commanded the nanos. They shifted like a flock of birds, once shimmering and floating, now a stygian swirling mass. In an instant, they swallowed the 'bot. When they dispersed, it was gone.

Meta laughed, high and frantic. "See? Is this the goddess you want? A demon raised from the dead, who can create pockets from nothing?"

The people stirred, but Andra didn't care. It didn't matter what they believed about her, only what she believed about herself.

The man was still lying on the floor, writhing, a shaft of light bisecting his tear-streaked face. Blood spilling from his torso to the marble. He would be dead soon if Andra didn't do something. She commanded her makeshift pocket to convert to healing tech and sent them into the man's system.

Meta ran a shaking hand through her hair. "She came here to destroy the 'dome and let the pocket in."

She was pacing, twitching. Andra could see the cracks in her facade, the tension in her expression, the tremor in her hand.

"Let the citians go," Andra said, voice low and hard. "There's no reason for them to be here."

"I will not bow to you," Meta snarled. "I have the Crown, and its destiny is to defeat you. My destiny."

"I've fought the Crown before and won," Andra said.

Meta smiled, the expression pained. "But you've never fought me."

Andra's awareness started to shift. Her consciousness began to morph. Her senses grew sharper, her surroundings duller. She felt both robotic and human as nanos surrounded her, fluttering her hair, dancing around her limbs. Power coursed through her veins.

She lifted a hand and curled her fingers.

"Bring it, bitch."

The 'bots all drew their swords, and Andra threw all of her power into stopping them, splitting her consciousness. She saw through their eyes, felt their rage.

Their swords froze in their downward arcs, but the pressure on Andra increased. She felt the tension in her bones, the weight on her shoulders, the strain in her heart. Blood dripped from her nose, sweat from her brow. A whimper tore from her throat.

She wanted to call out to the people to run, but she was barely hanging on, tired and scared and all too aware that at any moment the palace could come crashing down around them. There were too many 'bots, and she was losing the handle on her power, her concentration split between all the different technological components she was trying to control. She was an AI, damn it. She should be able to do this.

One of the 'bots broke free of her grasp and ran toward her. She screamed. It picked her up by the throat and threw her across the room. The sense of flying ended too quickly, and then she was smashing into the stone wall.

The 'bot stalked toward her, its eyes burning like embers, its sword ready to strike.

It stopped.

Andra let out a single breath as the 'bot straightened, putting its sword to its side.

Meta let out a frustrated growl and the people gasped.

Standing in the alcove entrance, limned in dust and stardust, arms outstretched and faces drawn in concentration, were Zhade and Maret.

FORTY-SIX

THE BLOOD

Z HADE LET OUT a breath. A second later, and Andra would have been sliced through with a sword. Again.

Dzeni had left the cell unlocked, and after staring at each other for a moment, Zhade and Maret had made their march to the palace.

They'd arrived just as the angel threw Andra across the atrium into the marble wall. She'd crumpled to the ground, and panic coursed through Zhade as an angel brought a sword down toward her neck.

What happened next wasn't conscious thought. It was instinct. It was intuition.

It was a wish.

He wanted the angel to stop, and it did. He wished again, and the angel straightened and lowered its sword. Zhade took a single eye-beat to marvel at the discovery that he could still control the angels. Not through the Crown, but through the imprint left in his head. Then, he was running toward Andra.

He helped her to her feet as she stared at him, eyes wide, mouth agape. Chaos swirled round them, angels wielding swords and spears, citians running and screaming.

"Get them out of here!" Maret was shouting to someone.

But Zhade sole had eyes for Andra.

She was covered in sticky dried blood, and her hair was a glorious tangle. She looked like she had that first day in Eerensed—covered in bloodstains and sweat, cheeks flushed. But this time, she stood strong, confident.

"What are you doing here?" she gasped. "How did you get free? And why aren't you halfway through the Wastes by now?"

"Scuze," Zhade said in mock offense. "And let you be the hero alone? No chance." He grinned. "I'm here to watch you be the hero and cheer you on."

"But . . ." Andra grimaced. "What about the imprint?"

Zhade's grin spread wider. "Soze, weird thing happens bout that . . . the same spark of magic in my brain that is currentish torturing me is also the thing that's going to save us. Because mereish like Tsurina could control Maret and me . . ." He turned. His brother was standing afront of Meta doing that ridiculous thing where he pretended he was doing magic with his hands, waving them round like a spoon as the citians fled and angels began to circle him. ". . . Maret and I can control Meta."

"A bit of help here?" Maret gasped.

Meta fell to her knees, and the angels dropped their swords. Rashmi corralled what was left of the citians toward the exits.

"We have to hurry." Andra grabbed Zhade's arm.

Something inside him recoiled at the touch, but he recked it wasn't him.

"There's an EMP," Andra said, breathless. "The AI are fighting the Schism, and if they're overpowered, Lilibet will use it. It takes out all the magic in the area, which includes the magic currently holding up the palace. And I have to—"

Zhade grabbed Andra's hand and threaded his fingers through hers. "What do you need me to do?"

Andra smiled, and it was glorious. "Hold off Meta until I connect to the 'dome. I . . . it's complicated. I don't have time to explain."

"I trust you."

The voice in his head told him he shouldn't, but he shoved it down. This was Andra. She was kind and good and brave, and he loved her.

"There's something else," Andra said. "After I'm done, I may be . . . a little different."

"Evens. I'm a little different now too."

"Neg, I purpose . . ." Andra pulled at the ends of her hair.

"Can we hurry up?" Maret shouted.

He stood with his full focus on Meta. Blood dripped from his ears and nose. Rashmi held his hand, eyes wide. The atrium was now free of citians, and all the angels were neutralized. For now. But it was crystal Maret's strength was weakening.

"If I . . ." Andra said. "If I'm not me . . . if I come back as someone else, I'm sorry."

"What?"

"And if I come back and I try to kill everyone, you have to kill me first."

"WHAT? What exactish are you doing?"

"Something risky."

"I'm not going to . . . I could never—"

"I'll do it!" Maret said, his voice strained. Meta was screaming, fighting his control. Blood dripped from her eyes, and she planted one foot, then the other, standing.

"What?" Zhade said again.

Andra grabbed him by the front of the shirt and kissed him hard on the lips. She let go, leaving him dazed, and ran to the entrance of the cathedzal. She pointed a finger at Maret.

"Only if I come back homicidal," she snapped.

"No promises," Maret gritted out.

Andra disappeared through the door, Rashmi scurrying after her.

"A bit of help?" Maret asked.

Zhade took a deep breath and bent his will toward Meta.

Stand down, he commanded.

There was resistance. It felt like when he was first skooling to control the angels. But this time, he had help. He was surprised that he didn't feel revolted by his brother's consciousness. That Maret almost felt . . . like an extension of Zhade. The other side of the rocktin.

Stand.

Down.

Meta cried out, falling to her knees. The skin round the Crown was swollen and bloodied.

"You win," she gasped. "I give up. I'll do what you say, mereish stop . . . stop."

Zhade immediatish released her.

She looked up at him, still in Tsurina's body, and he saw a scared, angry girl who had been abandoned. Who let that anger fuel her for years. Then, when she finalish decided what she'd imagined was her fate, she'd instead been controlled by another anger, another fear.

"Meta, we can help you." He glanced at the door to the cathedzal. He couldn't see Andra, had no idea what she was doing. "We can remove the Crown. We can figure how to live with the imprint together."

Meta's eyes were wet with tears, her cheeks smeared with blood. She lifted her head.

"Will you let us help you?"

Before Meta could respond, Maret stepped forward, sword drawn, and swiped it toward Meta's throat.

"NEG!" Zhade screamed, and Maret froze.

But not by choice.

Again, it had been instinct, impulse, a wish. Zhade hadn't recked he was doing it til it was done, and now the evidence was staring him in the face.

He'd stopped Maret through their imprints. Reached out with his own and commanded him to stop.

And Maret had.

"That's impossible," he gritted out, straining against Zhade's control.

Meta scuttled out from under the sword, but didn't run.

"You can't kill her," Zhade said. "She's your sister. And, in a weird way, mine too."

"Oh, as though you weren't going to kill me once," Maret said, his raised arm shaking, blade quivering, as Zhade held him still. "Sides, as long as she has the Crown, she's a threat."

"Andra can remove it!"

Maret's eyes blazed. "We don't reck if Andra is coming out of that room as Andra. And even if she does, if we let her remove the Crown, Meta would still have the magic imprint, and you reck what that does. This was the sole march to end this. And in your heart your reck that."

"We both have the imprint," Zhade snarled. "Soze does that purpose you're going to kill me too?" His thoughts darkened. "Or should I kill you first?"

They stared at each other for a tense moment, veins bulging, eyes narrowed.

Zhade felt the moment Maret stopped fighting, his will giving up.

He released his hold on his brother and Maret fell to the ground, hands slapping against the marble, sword clattering from his reach.

Zhade turned to Meta. "Take off the Crown."

Maret let out a hoarse laugh from where he'd fallen on the floor. "She can't, you fraughted spoon."

"Why not?"

"You reck I didn't try?" He looked up at Zhade, eyes bloodshot.

Zhade turned to their sister. "Meta, take off the Crown."

He said the words, but didn't send his intentions with it, the control afforded him by the imprint. This had to be Meta's choice.

She fell to her knees, anguish written across Tsurina's features, and she looked more like herself than she had in months.

"I'm trying," she gasped. "I can't."

"Then I'll help." Zhade knelt beside her, putting a gentle hand on her shoulder.

He fought back his own violent thoughts and sent his mind into the Crown, felt the magic glowing there, its hold on Meta's mind.

Release her, he commanded it.

No, the Crown hissed back at him, in the voices of all those who had worn it before, a chorus of hate and anger.

It dug in its claws.

"Help us, brother," Zhade whispered.

Maret stared at him for a tick, before rolling his eyes and crawling over to them. He looked at Zhade's hand on Meta's shoulder. "I'll help. But I'm not holding hands."

Zhade grinned and dove back into the magic.

It fought, but the brothers fought harder. The Crown wanted revenge. The brothers wanted freedom and peace. Their magic intertwined, their will and intent combined til the Crown's hate was no match for them. And in the end, they overpowered it.

Meta gasped. There was an awful squelch, and the Crown dropped from her forehead. She looked up at Zhade with tears in her eyes. He let out relieved laugh, and there was even the beginning of a smile on Maret's face.

"Well, isn't this touching."

Zhade's heart stopped. He recked that voice.

It had sung him lullibies and told him stories and taught him magic. Slowish, he looked up—

—into the face of his mother.

She stood by the cathedzal doors, appearing exactish as he had memory of her: blue eyes cutting sharpish round the room, blonde hair pulled back in a braid, posture tall and proud.

"Griffin," Meta whispered.

"Mam," he breathed.

"I'm not your mam," she said, sadness tinging her voice. Or maybe Zhade sole imagined it. "That was a different body with different experiences. Those feelings forged by those synapses—they're gone. I'm her, but I'm not her. And whatever I am now doesn't love you."

"Mam," he said again. His voice cracked.

"Sands," Maret muttered, "if you want something done . . ." He grabbed his fallen sword and rushed toward her.

The First thrust her hand out and Maret's body froze, mid-stride, sword raised. She cocked her head.

"I've learned a few tricks since you decapitated me, Maret." Her voice nearish sounded bored, but with a flick of her wrist, she sent him flying. He hit the far wall and crumpled to the floor. He didn't get back up.

She turned to Zhade. "Where is she?"

He felt the blood drain from his face. "I don't reck what you convo, Mam."

"Stop calling me that," she growled. "Where is she?"

The world started to shake, and it took Zhade a moment to realize it wasn't because he was trembling. He had a moment of panic, of realization, then the world fell out from under him, and he fell with it.

FORTY-SEVEN

ANDRA

THE SCREAMS WOKE Andra.

She came to covered in rubble and with a pounding headache. Above her, the sky was filled with dust and ash. A small pocket zoomed past. More screams followed.

What had happened? She'd just been at the 'dome controls, trying to access its power, and then . . . She shook her head to clear it, then tried to lift her arm, but realized it was trapped under a rock.

No, it was a slab of marble.

It took a moment for it to click, for her to understand that she was stuck under the rubble of the palace, that the 'dome was gone and there was a pocket in the city, that Andra had been knocked unconscious.

Lilibet must have set off the EMP.

Andra groaned, as a wave of despair hit her.

She'd failed.

It had taken too long for her to get to the 'dome control room, and then once she was there, to connect to its matrix. And now the one hope she'd had of defeating the AI was gone. They would be waking up about now, just like Andra. Hopefully, Lilibet and the others had time to get to safety. Hopefully, they weren't crushed under piles of rock and marble. Hopefully, they wouldn't be hunted down by the AI. Or the pocket.

It was swirling thickly above her, and she knew it was only a matter of time before it struck, swallowing the city whole.

She let out a pained moan as she pulled her arm out from under the marble. What remained of the cathedzal lay in heaps of rock and stone around her. The surface looked to be about sixty meters up. There was no way to climb out. She was surrounded by exposed foundation, sparking wires and dirt, and a few uncovered underground passages.

"Andra?" a voice called.

She turned and found Rashmi stumbling toward her.

"Rashmi!" Andra hurried over. Her face was scratched and bloody, and one of her arms hung at an awkward angle.

Andra hugged her, and Rashmi sucked in a breath.

"Too tight," she whimpered.

"Sorries." Andra took Rashmi's good hand. "Let's get out of here."

They waded through the rubble until they reached what was left of a nearby tunnel. It took some effort, but Andra was able to climb up into it, then help Rashmi up, and then she studied their surroundings.

"I think we're in . . ." She looked around. "Yeah, I think this is the tunnel that passes by the Vaults. That way." Andra pointed west.

"What do we do now?" Rashmi whimpered. "The city is being destroyed by the pocket. The Schism are still fighting the AI. We've lost."

"No," Andra muttered. She put her hands on her head, tugging at her hair. "No, we haven't. We just have to think of something."

She couldn't head west. The AI were there. Maybe the other way, where the tunnel veered south . . .

Andra tripped over something and caught herself against the tunnel wall, Mechy's eco'tile holding strong. She looked down.

At her feet was something metal and small and smudged with blood . . .

The Crown.

Hadn't Meta just been wearing this? Andra looked around for Meta or Zhade, but saw no one. She picked it up. It weighed more than she'd expected, warm in her palm, splattered in blood.

Rashmi was pacing, using a metal pole she'd found as a walking stick. "We failed, we failed, we failed."

"No," Andra said, pocketing the Crown. "Our plan can still work. We just have to find a power source big enough."

"There isn't any. The 'dome was it. There's nothing else in Eerensed that uses that much power."

Andra's stomach fluttered. "No, there's not." She sent her nanos far into the tunnels. She hoped she was right. Oh goddess, she hoped she was right. "But there is something *under* Eerensed."

EVEN RUNNING AT full speed through the tunnels, it took Andra far too long to reach the rocket.

She was out of breath, heart beating through her chest when they arrived at the small tunnel just outside the rocket's cavern. The ground shook beneath them and rocks and gravel plinked down the walls. In front of them, the LAC annex door Mechy had installed was still in place.

Damn it.

She'd forgotten about that. He'd been the only one who could open the door, and now he was gone.

She placed her palm on the scanner, holding her breath. It had been weeks since she'd visited the rocket, and maybe Mechy had fixed it in that time.

The scanner flashed red.

"What's wrong?" Rashmi asked.

Andra tried interfacing with her nanos, but there was something blocking her. She was strong enough to stand against the Crown, convert a pocket to healing tech, and resurrect herself, but she couldn't open a damn door.

"Goddamn it!" Andra growled.

"Can I help?" Rashmi asked.

Of course Mechy hadn't had time to fix the door. She had him working nonstop, either putting eco'tile in the underground passages or stabilizing the palace or watching Maret. He had been gaining sentience and she'd known it, but she hadn't even given him time to rest. And now he was dead, and the only thing standing between her and the rocket was a thin sheet of metallic glass she couldn't open.

She reached into her pocket for the Crown, wondering if there was some way it could help her, and her hand bumped against something else. Warm and smooth and cubical. She pulled it from her pocket.

Mechy's heart.

Mechy was dead, his nanos dispersed, but his CPU still contained his tech signature. Maybe. Just maybe . . .

Andra sent her nanos zooming into the heart, bringing it online. She felt the crackling white noise of the broken processor, but there was still just a bit of juice left. A red light flashed on the side, and she placed it up to the door's scanner and held her breath.

The scanner turned green, and the door opened.

"Thank you, Mechy," Andra breathed, and she and Rashmi darted inside.

The cavern yawned open ahead of them, and in the center was the rocket, towering and empty and useless. All that time Skilla had spent building this damn thing—twice—and it was just part of the lie Griffin had constructed. Andra stumbled along the thin ridge toward the work'station.

"It's too much!" Rashmi cried from behind. Her voice echoed in the cavernous space.

Andra's hand tightened on the railing. A fit of vertigo threatened to overwhelm her, the rocket towering above, the cavern floor meters below.

"Andra!" Rashmi pleaded. "We need to think of another way. Even you can't take on that much energy!"

Andra reached the work'station and pulled out the Crown. "That's why I have this."

Rashmi's eyes widened. "NO. No, you can't! You don't know what it'll do."

"It destroys," a voice said.

Andra closed her eyes and sighed. She'd been waiting for it, wondering when the voice would come. She'd almost let herself believe she would beat it, but that had just been fishes and wishes, she supposed.

Rashmi whipped around, holding her metal stick in front of her.

Griffin stood paces away.

She looked just as she had all those weeks ago, when Andra had seen her under the lake. She wore a gray pantsuit, twenty-second-century style. Her blonde hair was pulled back in a fishtail braid. Her shoulder brushed the edge of the cave. Her long-fingered hand hovered over the railing.

The ground shook, and more rocks tumbled down the side of the cavern.

Andra pulled Rashmi behind her.

"You killed my mother," she growled.

Griffin had the decency to look ashamed. "I didn't want to. She made me. She fought me. Trust me, it broke my heart. But she was a necessary sacrifice. She never would have let me complete my work. To create my new future. *Our* future, Andromeda. A new world. Can you imagine it?"

"Stop, stop." Andra pressed her fingers to her temple. "Just stop. I can't believe this was your plan all along. I can't believe that the woman who gave humanity groundbreaking medicine and technology and hope turned out to be so . . . cruel."

Griffin smiled sadly, stepping forward. Andra wondered if she could draw her high enough on the ledge to push her over. But the fall wouldn't kill her, and even if it did, Andra didn't know if she could bring herself to murder her, even after everything.

"This wasn't always my plan," Griffin said. "But it's what I've come to believe is the best solution. And it turns out, *you* believe it as well. You've convinced me, Andra. *You*. You're the reason why I *know* that destroying humanity is the only way to save them."

Andra shook her head. "What are you talking about?"

"You hear it, don't you?" Griffin took another step forward. "The voices? You should listen to them now."

As though she'd turned up the volume, a chorus of voices began chanting in her head.

destroy destroy destroy destroy destroy destroy destroy destroy destroy destroy
destroy destroy destroy destroy destroy destroy destroy destroy destroy destroy
destroy destroy destroy destroy destroy destroy destroy destroy destroy destroy
destroy destroy destroy destroy destroy destroy destroy destroy destroy destroy
destroy destroy destroy destroy destroy destroy destroy destroy destroy destroy

Andra fell to her knees, covering her ears, but she couldn't block the words.

She felt the bone-deep need to turn against the humans. To end them. They were unworthy of this planet. They'd waged war, committed genocide, fueled themselves with rage and hate. And now it was time for something new.

AI were humanity, but better. They would take care of this planet. They would nurse it back to health. They would create more AI to populate it, designing themselves to be gentle creatures that would nurture the earth and one another. But this new world of peace couldn't start until the old one was wiped away. Sometimes creation started with destruction. And Andra was a part of that. She had been *designed* for that. It was her purpose.

"NO!" she screamed, and she didn't know if it was out loud or in her head. All her senses were consumed by the mandate to

DESTROY

"No," she said more quietly, gathering her strength.

She took a deep breath and opened her eyes.

The ground rumbled and Griffin took another step, a patronizing smile on her face. "Why are you fighting me, Andromeda?"

"Has it been you all along?" Andra cried. "You've been trying to control me. You've been the voices in my head?"

"No. I didn't need to." Dr. Griffin shook her head, her lips downturned in pity. "You downloaded Rashmi's programming. She was the control. You were the experiment."

Andra looked at Rashmi, horror dawning. An experiment and a control. A question in two parts.

"We were a generative adversarial network," Andra whispered, remembering what Cruz had told her.

Opposing sides of an argument. Challenging each other until an outcome was reached.

Griffin smiled and nodded at Rashmi. "She was the argument against humanity. You were the argument for it. That was the *point* of creating two of you. To help me determine if humanity was worth saving. I couldn't decide if we should live among the humans or replace them. It was too big a decision for one AI to make. You and Rashmi were meant to determine this together once I woke you and was ready to start the implantation process. I spent centuries perfecting the creation of sentient technology. When I was finished, you were meant to argue with one another until you reached a conclusion."

Andra felt sick. She bent over, hand on her stomach.

Griffin continued to move forward. "But now, Andromeda, you

have Rashmi's programming inside you, and you're arguing with yourself. And it sounds like the argument to replace humanity is winning. You know, in your deepest logic circuits, that the only way to save humanity is to destroy them."

Andra's heart pounded with the thought. Destroy humans. Yes, it made so much sense. To start over with something new.

"We . . . would become humanity," Andra said.

"We would be human," Rashmi whispered.

"Yes, yes!" Griffin said. "You understand! During my time before I had a human body, I watched. I observed the humans, and they were illogical and cruel. They'd been given this entire planet! They were given the ability to evolve and reproduce and live, and they abused those gifts and turned themselves into monsters! I knew there was a better way to live. I knew we could be better creatures. Humans don't deserve this planet. We do. And you know it too."

The ground rumbled. Through her nanos, Andra sensed buildings toppling above them. The pocket swarming. People screaming, dying. The burning away of the old to make way for the new.

She took a deep breath, felt the sting of tears in her eyes, the pressure at the back of her throat.

She lifted the Crown.

"You don't deserve anything," she growled.

"NO!" Griffin cried, stretching her arms out. "That Crown . . . it's proof that humans deserve to die. They created that to hold their hate and their anger. It's been harboring those feelings for hundreds of years, and it's all directed at AI. At *you*, Andra. What do you think will happen if you wear it?"

Andra shook her head. "It doesn't matter. I have to try to save them."

"They're *not. worth. saving*, Andromeda."

"I don't believe that."

The dead nanos Andra had been coughing up was proof. She hadn't been dying. She'd been expelling a poison, ridding herself of the urge to destroy humanity.

Andra gestured to the rocket. "And you don't believe it either. Otherwise why would you have given them an escape? The Ark was built in space. There were sims, eyewitness accounts. You couldn't have faked that. Even now, you were having them build a generation ship. You were giving them a way off this planet. A way to survive. You wouldn't have done that if you didn't believe they weren't worth saving."

Griffin scoffed. "I was keeping them busy. I was making the lie believable."

Andra raised the Crown to her head.

"Andra, don't! You're not meant for this. You're AI, not human."

"Actually," Andra said, pressing the Crown to her temple. "I'm both. And I'm deciding my fate."

Griffin screamed, and Andra felt the Crown snake into her consciousness, its wires probing into her brain. She felt the push and pull, the dance, the negotiation between her own nanos with the invading tech. The Crown latched on, forcefully, powerfully, unforgivingly.

Andra fell forward onto the work'station.

She reached out with her nanos, connected to the rocket, using the Crown as a barrier, a shield. Just as Zhade suggested, she would use it as a conduit. She didn't know how long it would take for the Crown to realize what she was, so she had to work fast.

Andra flipped the switch on the hub, draining the rocket's power into her.

She felt electricity course through her extremities, fill her, overtake her.

"Andromeda!" Griffin cried.

She took a step forward, but Rashmi moved in front of Andra, metal pole outstretched.

"Stay away!" Rashmi called, her voice shaking.

The power siphoned into Andra, and she felt everything in her light up. She could make out each of the trillions of nanos that constituted her consciousness. Knew each of them and their history and their present and their future. She knew all of them at once, held everything in her head, and it was unbearable.

She cried out.

"Andromeda," Griffin snapped. "Stop this. You'll kill yourself."

"She won't!" Rashmi cried. "She's stronger than that."

But Andra wasn't so sure. She was starting to feel the hate. The anger. The fear. The years and years and years the Crown had spent absorbing all those feelings from its wearers. All of it directed toward Griffin, Rashmi, and Andra.

Griffin yelled out, "I created her. I know what she's capable of, and that much energy will end her."

Andra let out a scream. She'd never heard such a sound before. It was pain and devastation and hope and determination.

The Crown reveled in her pain. It would destroy her.

Power rushed through her entire being, her consciousness expanding and expanding until she was AI and she was Andra and Rashmi and Griffin and all the wearers of the Crown, all their memories crashing to the surface of her consciousness. Hundreds of people's lives and stories filled her, and she was all of them or none of them or whoever she wanted to be.

She could see that now.

Rashmi had asked who she was if she didn't have her memories. But maybe consciousness wasn't just a collection of memories.

Maybe truly being alive was about what she did next. The next action, the next word, the next decision.

It was about deciding her fate.

Andra spread her consciousness wide, connecting with each nano in her path. Expanding through the cavern, into the underground.

Her consciousness split among the nanos, and through them she saw the Schism dying, Lilibet surrounded by AI, her sister running through the Schism hideout calling for their brother. She expanded farther into Eerensed. Saw the people running, screaming, buildings crashing down around them, the pocket rushing to consume everything in its path. Gryfud leading people to safety. Children hiding in fear. The Crown fought her every step of the way.

When she bumped up against the pocket, she felt the destruction of it.

Destroy destroy destroy, it said, echoing the words that had haunted Andra for so long. The words now amplified by the Crown, but instead of directed outward, they were directed inward.

Andra fought.

The pocket and the Crown continued their chant, and she felt the pocket narrowing its circle, herding the humans closer together until it could extinguish them in a single blow.

That was their purpose: the destruction of humanity.

That was the Crown's purpose: the destruction of AI.

She let the pocket's thoughts into her own. Her head swam with the impulse to destroy, the sheer need of it, a compulsion. The only way she would feel right again was if she laid waste to everything in her sight. Everything on Earth. Even her.

That was her purpose.

But also . . .

But also . . .

Andra had given herself her own purpose.

She would decide her own fate.

And the pocket could too. It could be more than its programming.

Destroy, the pockets screamed at her.

Heal, she whispered back.

She wanted to collapse. She wanted to sleep. She wanted to dissolve into nothing. But she wouldn't let herself rest until the job was done.

The pocket came slowly, grudgingly. She felt each individual nano of the pocket convert itself into healing tech, change from something bent on destruction to something meant to create.

With a single thought, she dispersed the cloud of nanos, raining them down over the city, sending them in search of bodies to heal, hearts to mend. They found Eerensedians bleeding in the street, hiding in collapsed buildings. They found children crying for their parents and parents searching for their children. They found broken bodies that couldn't mend and whole bodies that were helping others. She sent the healing tech to all of them, and then guided what was left deep below the earth. They found people fighting, people dying. Some of those people had been corrupted, and needed to be healed, purged. They always gave the corruption a chance to yield, but it always refused. So they plucked it out. The corruption went screaming, each time, clinging to the life it had stolen. They found a small woman bleeding, but smiling. Cheering as the corrupted ones stopped fighting, as the dying ones began to heal. Her friends hugged her and cried. They found a young girl, scared and alone, searching for her brother, and they whispered to her that it would all be okay. They found three broken bodies in the rubble of a collapsed palace, and they did what they could.

They no longer needed Andra. They knew their purpose now, knew their fate. To help, to heal.

They let her go. They watched as her body crumpled to the floor. They watched as a woman with long blonde hair lunged at her, and a small woman with white hair and a gap between her teeth stepped forward to defend her sister. The blonde woman was impaled. The small woman fell to the ground weeping, and as the woman she'd killed fell to her knees and her blood spread across the floor, a flood of nanos burst from the body. The nanos tried to avoid them, but it was impossible. They were everywhere. And they cradled the nanos that had been the blonde woman to themselves. The nanos were alive, like the corruption had been, and they were angry and hurt and scared.

The healing tech gave them a choice. Destruction or healing.

And as they decided, the girl below stirred.

FORTY-EIGHT

ZHADE

ZHADE PULLED HIMSELF free from the rubble and looked up from the bottom of a massive hole where the cathedzal had once been. The sky was blue. It was clear and quiet, except for an occasional topple of palace wall, tumbling down, down.

His stomach hurt, his legs and arms hurt, his temple was killing him. He should not have survived that fall, but he had.

He didn't reck how long he had been unconscious, but he recked that whatever had happened had happened. Either Andra had won or she hadn't.

"Maret?" he called out over the rubble. "Meta?"

There was no response.

"Maret!"

He started struggling through the rocks and debris, digging down as far as he could. He saw no broken limbs or blood. Heard no cries for help.

His brother and Meta had been right beside him. But they'd fallen a long way. Either they had gotten free from the rubble, or they were already dead.

Zhade felt the sting of tears, but ignored it.

He had to find Andra.

He climbed out of the pit into the nearest tunnel, then followed that to the nearest peacing aboveground. By the time he reached the surface, his full body ached.

He gasped when he saw the city.

Destruction was everywhere. Entire buildings were missing, others toppled to the ground, littering the streets with rubble and bodies. People roamed the ruins, bandaged and weary, the ones who were full well bringing water and medicine to the ones who needed it. Zhade walked through a crowd of people, dazed. None of them noticed him, but they wouldn't reck him now. Not with his own face.

"It vanished," one was saying. "I saw it. The pocket. It was there and then it turned, glittering into stardust."

"It saved me," another was saying. "I was dying, and the stardust went into me, and saved me. I'm alive because of it."

"You imagined it," another said. "There's no more magic, not without the angels. Not without the goddesses."

"I saw them," yet another said. "They came back. All three. I saw them in the cathedzal. They saved us."

Andra . . .

She had to be alive. He didn't reck what she'd done, but she'd done something, because the pocket was gone.

Zhade hurried through the streets and climbed back into the tunnel, making his march through as best as he could til he came to the Vaults. The entrance was busted in. Bodies littered his path. He climbed gingerish over the destruction into what Andra had called the lobby.

It yawned open before him, a tangle of bodies and blood and fallen steel structures. The enormous clock Andra had said held perfect time for hundreds of years lay shattered and scattered across the lobby floor.

"Zhade!"

Lilibet came running toward him, her bare feet slapping against the floor, her long hair swinging behind her. She was covered in dirt and blood, but there was a huge smile on her face.

"She did it, Zhade! She did it!"

She was out of breath by the time she reached him, but that didn't slow her down. She barreled into him, throwing her arms round his neck. He patted her back as she squeezed too tight, then gentlish extricated himself.

"She must have done it, because we were fighting and fighting and I was doing magic so that we could use what Andra called an EMP to slow down the gods, which used to be good, but then were bad, and now are dead. But there were too many of them and they kept shooting the Schism and turning them bad. And oh, Zhade, they got Skilla, and it's so sad, and also Dzeni."

"What?" Zhade snapped his attention to Lilibet. "What happened to Dzeni? Where is she?"

His knees went weak. His hands shook. Not Dzeni. It couldn't be Dzeni. He'd promised Wead.

"She's there," Lilibet said saddish, pointing to the circular desk in the mid of the room. Zhade took off toward it, vaulting over bits of fallen ceiling and clock and dashing past dead bodies. He circled the desk, and behind it, Xana was bent over a sprawled-out Dzeni . . .

. . . bandaging her knee.

Zhade shook his head. "Lilibet said they got you."

Dzeni smiled. "Mereish my knee."

Zhade let out a long sigh of relief.

"And Skilla?" he asked, looking round. The sole other person near-ish was a woman with dark skin and a scarf round her head handing Xana bandages.

Xana shook her head.

Something sour turned in Zhade's stomach. He'd never full liked Skilla, but she hadn't deserved to die.

"Where's Dehgo?" he asked.

"With Doon, in the Schis—OW!" Dzeni swatted Xana's hand away. "That's too tight."

"It has to be tight, to hold it stable," Xana said through gritted teeth, but there was something tender in her eyes.

"Where's Andra?" Dzeni asked.

Zhade shook his head, heart plummeting. "Is she not here?"

Lilibet twirled in a circle. "She must be somewhere, because she did it! She transformed the pocket into stardust and it healed so many, and it killed the gods." She came to a stop. "Though it is full sad, since they used to be kind people before they wanted to murder us."

"And some of them used to *be* us," Xana muttered.

Dzeni wrapped her hand round Xana's.

Zhade didn't comp what that meant, but he didn't have time to ask. He had to find Andra. Make for certz she was evens.

Suddenish, Lilibet screamed. He startled as she ran past him, faster than he imagined possible, and threw herself into Kiv's arms.

The big man twirled her round, tears streaming down his face.

Something in Zhade broke.

The imprint in his brain had kept him from caring, even imagining bout Kiv. He'd left one of his dearest friends apalace, after holding him there for over a moon without letting him see his promised. How could he have let this happen?

Would he be spending the rest of his life making up for all the terrible things he'd done under the Crown's influence?

Kiv set Lilibet down and started convoing, signing faster than Zhade had ever seen him. Lilibet was practicalish shaking with joy. Kiv caught sight of Zhade and paused, his face going blank. Lilibet trailed off as she looked back at Zhade.

For a tick, they sole stared. Then:

"I'll take you to her," Kiv signed, and Zhade didn't have to ask who he was referring to.

The trip to the cavern was longer than Zhade would have liked, he and Kiv walking in silence. Zhade needed to apologize, needed to start to make things right with his friend, but all he could focus on amoment was Andra. She had to be alive. She had to be. Kiv would tell him if she wasn't.

When they reached the door to the cavern, Rashmi was waiting for him, clothes torn, covered in dust and blood.

"There's something you need to know," she said. Her voice was strong and more certz than he'd ever heard it.

Zhade swallowed. He didn't reck if he could take this. He didn't reck if he would survive.

"Your mam is dead," Rashmi said. "I'm so sorry."

Zhade stood stunned.

That wasn't . . . He hadn't expected that.

He didn't reck what to feel. He'd watched his mam die, mourned her death for years, let himself be guided and manipulated into following a life, he now realized, he didn't want. Then she'd showed up, said she didn't love him, and now she was dead again? He couldn't sort through the barrage of emotions that hit him.

"And I did it," Rashmi said, wincing.

Zhade's eyebrows went up. "Uhm . . . evens . . . how very dare?"

"I'm so sorry, Zhade, but she was going to stop Andra, and . . ." Rashmi sighed. "She did so many terrible things to me. Both of us. All of us."

Zhade swallowed. "I don't reck that was my mam you killed," he said finalish. "My mam died four years ago. Whoever that was . . . I don't reck much of my mam was left in her."

Rashmi nodded, tears brimming her eyes, but didn't step aside.

"And Andra?" Zhade prompted.

Rashmi shook her head. "She hasn't said anything since . . ."

Zhade pushed past her, through the doorway. It opened up into the largest cavern Zhade had ever seen. Bigger than the full palace.

Rubble covered the ground, and a huge tower stood in the center of the room, covered in shiny plating, its tip pointed. It was . . . awe-inspiring, but he sole had eyes for Andra.

She was sitting on a rock some paces away, her dark hair falling into her eyes. He approached at care, slowish, but full loud she could hear his footsteps. She didn't turn as he approached.

"Andra?" he asked.

She didn't respond.

He had memory of her saying she didn't reck who would come out of that room. That there were too many memories in her head and they could take over. Had they? Was he talking to someone else in Andra's body?

He knelt and placed a hand on hers. She didn't flinch away.

"Andra, is it you?"

She looked up, tears in her eyes. "Who's Andra?"

Zhade's stomach dropped.

He turned Andra to face him. Her expression was wary, but she didn't move away. He went to take both of her hands in his, but realized she was holding something.

It was the Crown.

"It did its job, in the end," Rashmi said quietish from behind him. "It . . . destroyed the goddesses."

Zhade looked back and forth from Rashmi to Andra, his thoughts a jumble, his heart pounding.

"How . . ." he started, but he didn't reck what to ask.

"She held all our memories," Rashmi said. "And our memories . . . they're us. And it destroyed them inside her. Mine, your mother's . . . and hers."

"She doesn't . . ." He swallowed. "She's not . . . Does she have memory of . . . any of it?"

Rashmi shook her head.

Tears spilled down Zhade's cheeks as he turned back to the girl he loved. She looked so lost and scared. Gentlish, he took the Crown from her hands. It felt . . . empty. It no longer held any power over him. Over anyone. Its job was done. It was mereish a hunk of metal now. He tossed it cross the cave. He never wanted to touch it again. It would stay in this cavern forever to sink into sand.

Zhade carefulish took Andra's hands in his and waited for her to look at him.

"You're Andra," he said, when she did. "You're Andra, and you are the most incredible person in the world. You slept for a thousand years and you woke and you were a goddess and you saved all of humanity. And you're brill and charred and funny and perfect and I love you."

He placed his forehead to hers.

"Remember who you are," he pleaded.

"Andra," she whispered. "Andra."

Tears continued to flow down Zhade's face. He felt the light puffs of her breath against his skin.

"I think I'm her," she finalish said. "But . . . I don't know for sure. There's so much missing."

Zhade wiped a tear from her cheek. "Then we'll figure it together."

PART FIVE

AFTERLIFE

Six months later

FORTY-NINE

ZHADE

THE OFFICE ZHADE occupied was much more comfortistic than either the throne room or the cathedzal. It was small and filled with plush furniture draped with blankets and pillows that Lilibet had made. There was magic all round him. Scrying boards and things that the gods called keyboards. They were a manual way to do spells. One of the newish-awakened gods had offered to fit Zhade with a new crown, but he couldn't stomach the thought of wearing one again.

Sides, his face had never full healed, and it was painful enough without ornamentation.

He hadn't felt the effects of the imprint since the day that Andra converted the pocket to healing magic and rid the colonists of the AI. Since Maret vanished and his mam died for the second time. Or thirtieth or however many times she'd died in however many bodies.

Firstish, Rashmi imagined Andra's healing magic had removed the imprint, but scrys showed Zhade still had a bud of magic in his brain. So either the Crown fulfilling its purpose had ended its influence, or Zhade had gotten better at ignoring it.

The weird thing happened, after they pulled her from the rubble, scans showed that Meta had no bud of magic left. She'd stayed in Eerensed, but mostish held to herself. She'd never warmed to anyone but Zhade, but she was trying. She still wore Tsurina's body. Zhade had offered to put her back, but she didn't want to go through the pain again. Instead, she shaved the side of her hair and started wearing common Eerensedian clothes. Now, she looked more like herself than Tsurina. And though she still had her 'implant, she was free of the influence of the Crown.

Perhaps she hadn't worn it full bars long. Or perhaps Zhade was mereish unlucky. Either way, he no longer felt the anger and hate the imprint had placed in his mind. It didn't change all the damage Zhade had done as guv, but it did purpose he could start making things right. And that was what he was working on now.

A message popped up on his scry from Xana, asking him to come to her apartment in Southwarden for the Solstice celebration. Xana was now governor. They used the older colonial title for a leader, because the position had changed. She wasn't an absolute ruler. She had assistance from Ophele, the colonist who had helped Xana wrap Dzeni's wounds. They acted as joint heads of state—the Eerensedians and the colonists working in tandem—and governed with the help of a council, and every few turns, the people would vote on major decisions.

Zhade loved going over to Xana's house. Dzeni and Dehgo were always there. It was full obvi to Zhade that Xana was smitten with Dzeni. It was also full obvi that Dzeni was still grieving. But Xana was patient, and Zhade oft caught Dzeni watching her with the expression she used to reserve for Wead. If she was ever prepped to move forward with Xana, both Dehgo and Doon approved.

Doon was finalish having a kidhood, and it suited her well. She still practiced with her swords, but now she fought against wooden dummies and taught the other kids self-defense. Dehgo was skooling signed language from Kiv, and Lilibet always brought fabric animals for the kids. Doon pretended she was too old for them, but she kept every one of them in a chest in her room. Dzeni shared with Zhade that she even slept with one hugged to her chest.

Zhade stood and put on his coat. It was made of something called *wool* shorn from the sheep in the ranching district. He'd never worn a coat before, but the weather had grown chill over the last moon. It had startled the Eerensedians firstish, but the colonists convoed it was a good thing. Nature was healing. Rashmi said the changes in weather were called seasons, and that they would cycle through them each year. It would get colder, but the cold wouldn't last forever. Nothing did.

Zhade gathered up some gifts he had been planning to bring to Doon and Dehgo for Solstice. And one extra gift he had tucked in his pocket. He tapped it nervousish, checking that it was still there. He let his office door slide shut behind him, locking it by pressing his thumb to a panel on the wall. This was no blood magic. Instead, the panel looked at minute grooves in his finger that were unique to him.

The streets were quiet. It was early moren, and with the chill in the air, most people chose to sleep long. The rubble had been cleared, the streets paved with a substance similar to what Zhade had found in the belowground. Many of the old buildings had been torn down, new ones rebuilt in their place. The design wasn't quite Eerensedian. But it wasn't quite colonial either. It was something new the two groups had created together.

The tunnels belowground had been filled in to make the earth more stable. There was no palace, no silver tower. They no longer needed a gods' dome. Since that day six moons ago, it was easy for Andra to enter what Rashmi called her "AI state" and convert any pockets that came their way to stardust.

Zhade finalish reached Xana's apartment. He took a moment at the door to preppify himself. Though he was in a good mood, grief hit him at weird times. He arranged his face in the charming grin he used to throw round. It tugged at the scar tissue at his temple, but he held it in place as he rapped on the door.

It slid open and there was Dzeni, warm smile, warm hug. She

pulled him into the front room, and Dehgo quickish attached him-self to Zhade's leg. He had to strain to carry himself forward, but he didn't tell the boy to get off. He was giggling and happy. Doon was sitting in the corner and stood when Zhade entered. She didn't say anything, but mereish walked up to him, saluting him in a way that made it crystal she was now an inch taller.

Rashmi sat by the fire, her white hair pulled back from her face, her eyes clear and steady. She full time avoided Zhade's gaze, but he didn't blame her for his mother's death. As a fact, he was full grateful she'd saved Andra. And though Zhade recked there were things in Rashmi's past that were terrible, those memories had been destroyed with Andra's. She was starting a new life. A human life. She hadn't discovered what she wanted to do with that life yet, but that was evens. She was deciding her own fate now.

Next to her were Kiv and Lilibet, who lived next door. Lilibet jumped off Kiv's lap to hug Zhade. With Kiv's lap free, Dehgo ran over to Kiv, crawled up, and stuck his fingers in Kiv's nose.

"Dehgo!" Dzeni snapped, but Kiv was laughing.

"Pick your own nose," he signed.

Dehgo signed back, "Mom says it's not nice to pick your nose."

Zhade laughed at that, but his laugh faded as he saw who else was present.

Andra's fam.

Which purposed Andra was somewhere nearish.

The gift in his pocket felt heavy. His palms started to sweat.

Oz ran at Zhade and threw his arms round him. He was getting too big to do things like that. Zhade tried to hold back a cry of pain, but an *oof* escaped his lips.

"Sorries," Oz said, stepping back. "I'm so excited you're here! I built you a 'drone so you can race me."

"For true?" Zhade said. "If I had recked you would be here, I would have brought your Solstice present. All I have for you now is my charming smile and winning personality."

Oz shrugged. "That's okay, I guess."

Acadia, Andra's sister, was setting the table, a tradition from Andra's time. She looked up at Zhade.

"She's at Dad's grave," Acadia said, quietish. "She'll be back soon."

Zhade nodded. "Has she had memory of anything bout him?"

Acadia shook her head, the movement stiff. "But we tell her about him. I think . . . I think sometimes . . . but—" She shook her head again, and cleared her throat. "Dinner's ready," she said more loudish.

Lilibet dragged Kiv over. Dzeni and Xana started bringing dishes of warm food out of the kitchen. Zhade set Doon and Dehgo's Solstice presents by the fire and took his seat at the table.

"I don't like that you have a fire in here," Zhade said.

"It's evens," Xana said. "You build stone round it, like akitchens, and you don't leave it on full time. Andra says it'll import when it gets colder."

"Colder?" Zhade grimaced.

"Maybe one day it'll snow again!" Oz crowed. "We used to have the best snow fights, didn't we, Andra?"

Zhade looked up.

Andra stood in the doorway.

She was dressed in what she called jeans and a T-shirt. Her hair was longer than it had ever been and was tied away from her face. She'd gained back the weight she had lost and her skin glowed. The expression on her face was nearish one he was familiar with. Sometimes, he would see little hints of the Andra he'd recked peeking through.

She sat at the table, cross from him. She met his eyes and smiled, and something fluttered in his chest.

"Food first, or presents?" Dzeni asked.

413

"Presents!" Oz screamed.

Andra flinched. "That's really loud, Oz."

Oz shrugged. "What? I'm excited."

They passed out presents, their dinner cooling on the table afront of them. Zhade got something called mittens from Rashmi. Dzeni gave him some of Wead's old baking supplies. He watched as Dehgo opened the toy Zhade had sorcered for him. It was in the shape of a dog this time, not an angel.

"I have something for you too," Andra said.

Zhade's eyes snapped to hers. "For true?" he asked, almost feeling shy.

"Yeah," she said. Her voice was too quiet, so she cleared her throat. "It's actually . . . a trip. I know you said you still don't believe that oceans exist, and I was looking through some of my data and found that I'd traveled to a lake up north. I mapped it out and have a hover ready, and we can . . . you know, go whenever." She looked down, blushing.

"I'd love that." Zhade felt his heartrate pick up. This was the first time she'd suggested spending any time alone with him since that day six moons ago. They had been dancing round each other, awkward, shy, for twice as long as he'd recked her before she lost her memory. But circumstances since hadn't forced them together as it had then, and Andra passed much of her time getting to reck her fam again. And Rashmi and Lilibet. Zhade also, but he didn't want to push anything. He cleared his throat. "I got something for you too."

He reached in his pocket and pulled out a small cylindrical conduit. He held it out to Andra, and when she took it, their fingers touched.

"What's this?" she asked.

"It's . . ." He cleared his throat again, acutish aware that everyone at the table was watching him. "Rashmi skooled me how to download my memories. I reck they aren't *your* memories, but they are my memories of . . . well, you."

He held his breath.

Andra's eyes began to fill with tears.

"Sorries," he said. "You don't have to watch them, I was mereish trying to help, but if—"

He reached cross the table to take the memories back, and Andra slapped his hand away.

"You can't take back a present!" she said. "That's rude."

She looked up at him and smiled, tears still glistening in her eyes.

"Thank you," she whispered.

Zhade smiled back.

FIFTY

ANDRA?

ANDRA LAUGHED AS Zhade dove under the water again.

It was chilly, and if Andra had known Zhade would want to go swimming, she would have suggested they take the trip when it got warm again in a few months.

She was glad they went, though. After watching the memories he showed her, she was even more motivated to get to know this boy who claimed he'd loved her before. Loved her still.

The truth—something she hadn't revealed to anyone, not even Rashmi—was that she still had access to her memories. She was AI after all, and everything she'd experienced was stored in her matrices. It could be hidden and compressed, but not erased. The problem was that she didn't experience those memories like a human anymore. Those memories from her old life—they were files she could peruse as though she were viewing a sim. She had record of them, but they didn't feel like hers.

She'd spent the last six months watching over them. Finding embarrassing memories from her childhood. Hurtful memories with her mother. Joyful memories with Oz. She'd even watched some of the memories after coming out of stasis. She got to know Skilla and Cristin and all those they'd lost. She grieved them, but distantly. Like she grieved her parents. And Cruz. She watched her memories over and over, but each one was like a part of an equation she didn't know the answer to. So she let those around her believe she didn't remember them. It was easier than explaining.

Zhade pulled himself out of the lake, water dripping down his naked torso. He shivered, and so did Andra.

"I hate the cold!" he said, grabbing a towel and patting his face dry.

"Then you shouldn't have gone in the lake!"

He ruffled the back of his hair, a gesture that seemed familiar to Andra, and threw himself on the ground next to her.

The lake was just as it had been in the memories she'd found. Wide and expansive, but not nearly as big as it had once been. She also knew that somewhere below the surface, there was a city full of cloned bodies of Zhade's mother. She didn't know if she should tell him.

Andra lay back and watched the clouds pass over. The sun was starting to set. They'd have to head back soon or sleep in the hover.

She felt Zhade turn to her. "Thank you for bringing me here."

Andra looked over at him. "You're welcome."

He smiled, then bit his lip. "I want you to reck, I've loved every version of you. And I reck I love this version too."

Andra felt her heart flutter. She barely knew this boy, but something about him felt so familiar, so right.

"You don't have to love me back." He groaned as he stretched out on the sand. "At least not yet. It'll happen soon, though. I'm quite loveistic."

Andra rolled her eyes. "I tolerate you at best."

Zhade gave her an unabashed smile. "I can work with that."

He held out his arm, and she snuggled in next to him. Together they lay listening to the waves hit the shore and somewhere, maybe, a hoot of an owl.

Andra fell asleep smiling.

EPILOGUE

THE WORLD WAS starting to heal, but Maret wasn't.

The Wastes were dusty under his feet, blistering against his skin, stretching out for miles and miles. Mereish because the pockets were disappearing didn't purpose it wasn't dangerful. There were still pirates and snakes and fraughts, unbearable heat.

For serious, why was it so hot?

He trekked forward, hoping to find a village to stay the night. At luck, most villages he came cross didn't reck who he was. Or if they did, they'd mereish heard the name Maret but had no clue what he looked like.

He caught sight of a settlement ahead, glinting in the sun. His destination.

He'd spent his full life following the destiny his mam had set out for him. The same destiny her mam had set out for her, and on and on for centuries.

He took a quick swig of water before continuing and put the canteen back into his pack. It knocked against something small and metal.

Now it was time to decide his fate.

ACKNOWLEDGMENTS

This book was primarily written during a global pandemic. (COVID-19. You may have heard of it.) It was the first book I'd drafted under contract, the first sequel I'd attempted, and the first ending of a story I'd ever composed. All of this is to say: It was hard. Really, really hard. And I wouldn't have survived the process without an amazing network of professional and personal support.

I'd like to thank my editor, Julie Rosenberg, for her flexibility and encouragement. For believing in the book, even though I kept rewriting it and neither of us had a clue what the end result would be. For all her excellent feedback and guidance and patience. Thank you to the Razorbill team, especially Gretchen Durning, Alex Sanchez, Casey McIntyre, and Simone Roberts-Payne. To the fantastic team of copyeditors and proofreaders: Vivian Kirklin, Marinda Valenti, Maddy Newquist, and Abigail Powers. To my publicist, Lizzie Goodell, for helping me navigate the terrifying world of author events. Thank you also to the team at Penguin Teen, especially Jayne Ziemba, Bri Lockhart, Christina Colangelo, Felicity Vallence, and James Akinaka. To Dana Li, Theresa Evangelista, and Doaly for another heartbreakingly beautiful cover.

Thank you to my fantastic agent, Victoria Marini, who is always ready to advocate for me or explain to me the complexities of publishing. For her encouragement and dedication and excitement. To the rest of the team at IGLA, especially Lee O'Brien. To those at Baror International, especially Heather Baror-Shapiro.

Thank you, thank you, thank you a million times to Emily Suvada, who helped me through the worst parts of revision. Who held my hand when I needed it and gave me a kick in the pants when I needed that too. Who is an incredible writer and friend, and whose support and input is the reason this book exists in any comprehensible form. Thank you especially for telling me to stop rewriting and to start revising. For understanding what I was trying to do and helping me get there. I cannot express how important you were in the process of finishing *Devil*. You saved me and this book.

To my BFFs, always and forever: Kelsey, Alex, Amanda, Bre, Nadia, Taryn, and Kailan. I love you, you olde traesh faeries. You keep me sane(ish) and show me such compassion. You're all amazingly brilliant and funny and kind, and every day I'm in awe I happened upon the best girl gang on the planet. Special shout-out to Amanda—who suggested some of the best scenes in the book—and Kelsey—for being my Zoom accountabilibuddy.

To the writing friends who offered me encouragement at various points during the process: Beth Revis, Jennifer Gruenke, Britt Singleton, Tracy Deonn, Alechia Dow, Andrea Tang, Sheena Boekweg, Rebecca Coffindaffer, Kalyn Josephson, Sylvia Liu, Diana Urban, Jessica Goodman, and Dante Medema.

Thank you to the reviewers, book bloggers, booksellers, librarians, etc., who have supported *Goddess* in any form. Your excitement fuels me. Thanks to Adah and everyone at Main Street Books in Davidson, North Carolina, for your unending support. For spoiling Coco and making me feel welcome on New Book Tuesdays. *Finger guns* Shop local.

Thank you to my mom and dad, for taking care of Coco whenever deadline was kicking my butt. And thank you to Coco, for loving me unconditionally and for no longer peeing on the floor.

Finally, to you, for going on this journey with me and Andra and Zhade. Reader, I thank you.